Aimee Danroth was born and raised in Northern Alberta and currently resides in Central Alberta. She has a son, and anytime that is spent away from him, she uses that as an opportunity to write fiction.

For my best friends; Delaney, Rylan, and Keesha.

Aimee Danroth

THE BASILISKS

Brittney

Fifteen months earlier

The slush from the crosswalk crunching under my feet is just reminding me how thankful I am that it's March and the snow has melted. I can't wrap my head around why I'm still in New York and not California bathing in the sun all year round. The sidewalk cleared for a chance for me to run to the driest part. Even with the foot traffic, puddles still existed. My six-inch heels are my biggest regret of the day.

God, my biggest regret of the day is wearing heels in the spring when I am on a mission to find the closest bar and have a one-night stand. In the middle of the day.

Neon lights caught the corner of my eye from across the street. The sign says *Willie's*, awful name for a bar, but what the hell. Traffic has come to a complete stop; like any New Yorker, I take any chance I can to get to where I am going. I run across the street, only paying slight attention to the vehicles around me.

I swung the door open and the smell of hot wings came wafting towards me. With the sun being at the highest point and bright as hell, it's taking a few moments for my eyes to adjust to the dark pub. Jerseys in frames are hanging on the walls, all the tables are packed. The only open spot I can see is at the bar.

I pulled out the chair that is taller than I am, struggling to pull myself up. I grabbed onto the bar and hopped onto my seat. The bartender is looking at me with her eyebrows pulled in. "ID?"

I rolled my eyes, digging in my handbag, and passed it to her. I'm 5'2", and I look like I'm twelve. Even with me wearing a full face of makeup. "Martini, please."

She passed it back to me, mixing my martini in a shaker. It feels so good to be the one that is getting served and not serving people. I don't know how much longer I can handle working with drunk college kids. I have been regretting my degree sense the moment I enrolled. I should have picked something other than Art History, maybe something with a job opportunity. The bartender placed my martini in fount of me, I picked it up and sniffed the drink. My face instantly scrunched up; I have never had one before but I serve at least ten every single shift. I put the glass to my lips and tipped it back.

"I don't mean to sound like a douchebag, but you have to be the most beautiful women I have ever laid eyes on."

I'm forcing myself not to smile or look flattered. I placed my cup on the marble bar listening to the ding. I know that voice, he is in a few of my classes in school. I have been trying to get the nerve to talk to him, but I always chicken out and walk the other way once the rest of his group is around him. It's impossible to get a moment alone with him.

I turn in my seat, looking up at him. He is leaning against the bar, with his eyes focused on me.

Brittney your plan for a one-night stand is done. He is so much more than that.

I put my hand on the bottom of my disgusting martini glass with the stem between my middle finger and index finger. I want to match his confidence, but I am scared I won't be able to form a normal person's sentence. "Well, if it isn't Spencer Cohen."

Spencer leaned into the bar staring at me, trying to place where I know him from. "Do we know each other?"

I wasn't expecting him to remember me, or for him to even know I exist. We have had one class a semester together for three years, but despite what he said about me being beautiful, there is nothing special about me. Put me in a room with my best friend Lizzy and all eyes are on her and her sky-high legs.

My eyes have made their way down to the floor, my stomach is tying itself in knots. It stings that he has no idea who I am, but why would he? "Not exactly."

I spun around in my chair, facing forward, trying to hide my crumpling face from him. I picked up my martini, right when Spencer snatched it from my hands. "You are not drinking that shit."

My mouth dropped open as he pulled the cocktail glass from my hands, walking behind the bar and dumping it in the sink. He picked up an alcohol bottle, pouring it into a mixer. The girls behind the bar are protesting against him and demanding him to leave the bar. My eyes travel up him in his suit, he is the sexiest man I ever saw. No actor or Abercrombie model would stand a chance next to him. Spencer looked up at me, laughing at the girls; when he realizes I'm staring at him, he winks at me.

He walked back to the empty seat next to me sliding the drink over to me. "It took me a second, but we have history together."

The orange peel in the drink is a dead giveaway that he just made me an Old Fashioned. Butterflies are forming in my stomach, I never thought I would be this close to him. I feel like a sixteen-year-old girl who's meeting her famous crush.

"Your charm isn't going to work on me so just move along." Why the hell did I just say that?

Spencer opened his mouth, putting the tip of his tongue on his teeth. "Ouch."

I slammed back the drink and placed it back on the bar, already feeling the alcohol in my system. I have no fat on my body so alcohol hits me hard, plus I've never drunk this strong shit before. I raised my cup to the bartender, asking for another one. Spencer is still sitting next to me. Either he is stunned from getting shut down for the first time in his life, or he is working up a game plan.

The bartender placed another drink in front of me and I took a big sip. I can still feel Spencer's body in the seat next to me. "Why are you still here?"

The bartender froze, bursting out in laughter. I hate being such a bitch to him, but I know his ways. He isn't nearly as bad as a few of his friends. Hell, he's a saint compared to two of them. I just can't sleep with him, I know he is too good for me. I would rather have him hate me than me sleep with him and have my feelings get even more out of control.

Spencer shook his head. "Damn, you're a fucking bitch."

I don't know why I'm going this to myself. I chugged the rest of my drink, pulling my card out of my purse and fighting back the lump in my throat and the sob that wanted to leave my lips. He is a heartbreak waiting to happen and I will never go through that again. I am just a kid, but the pain was too much.

"I'm sorry, Spencer."

Without saying a word, Spencer stood up from his chair and walked away. Before I even thought about it, I reached out for his hand and tugged on it for him to stay. Maybe another heartbreak is worth it. Maybe he will be worth it.

"April, another round." Spencer grabbed my hand with his other hand and sat down. "What the hell is your name?"

"Cameron." The name left my lips and I regretted it. When I meet someone at a bar, I always tell them my middle name to avoid the awkward social media search.

We spent the next four hours laughing, eating, and enjoying each other's company. I had an image in my mind of what he was really like and he went way above all of it. He is perfect.

Spencer's phone rang for the tenth time; after ignoring it for so long, he finally looked down. "I'm going to kill my roommates. They want me to pick them up food."

"I better get going anyways." I reached in my purse, quickly budgeting the next month; I had overspent.

Spencer is looking at me slowly, forming a smile on his face. "You're coming with me." He grabbed my hand and I jumped down from the seat. I look up behind me and he is trying not to smile and start telling me every short joke that I have already heard a million times. He stood up and put his arm over my shoulder. "Oh, this is going to be fun." He stopped, rotating his body, but not taking his arm off me. "April, tab it."

Spencer parked his car on the street in front of his house in the quiet neighborhood. My heart has been beating out of my chest for almost six hours. I'm honestly surprised he hasn't heard it, and if he has, he does a good job at playing it cool. Unlike me. Every single time he talks, I sink further into my seat. Hearing his deep voice is enough to make my thighs weak.

I turned my body, grabbing the door handle to open it; before I got the chance, Spencer flung it open with a smile. He reached out his hand to take mine, butterflies forming in my stomach with his touch. He bent in the car behind me, slamming the door shut. I grabbed one of the plastic bags from his hand in an attempt to make his juggle easier. Looking around the house, it was barely spring but I can tell the yard is taken care of, flowerbeds have fresh soil in them. The white picket fence is confusing me. If the rumors are true about Spencer and his suit-wearing buddies, then I am shocked.

Spencer held open the door for me; walking in behind me, he silently gave me his elbow to help me take off my heels. With a smile and quiet laugh, he watched me lose six inches from my height.

Spencer sighed, looking down at me. "You needy fucking bastards. I'm here, you pulled me away from something important."

Spencer took a sharp left into the house outside of the entryway. I stepped out, watching Josh and Adam run upstairs. I feel overly creepy how I know everyone's names. I really hope they are clueless and don't drop the bomb of my real name. That would be too much embarrassment for one day.

I can lie about that forever, right?

When they both look up at me, they instantly start to smile. Adam walked backwards into the kitchen, not taking his eyes off me. He came back around with a cup half full of amber liquid.

Spencer is shaking his head in disappointment. "Jesus, Adam, I'm not trying to get her drunk here."

I walked up to Adam and took the glass, taking a sip. Acid would burn less. I pulled the cup from my mouth with my eyes closed tight. "It burns."

I opened my eyes, taking another sip with all three of them laughing. Thankfully, I have this weekend off. I was sober after all the food we inhaled. I never clued into why *Willie's* and *White Rock* have the same menu, I knew everything without having to look at the menu.

Spencer nodded his head, walking towards the narrow staircase leading upstairs. "Jesus Spencer. I'm not going to sleep with you."

He stopped in his tracks, cranking his head around and looking down at me. "Did I ask you to? No, I don't think I did."

Note to self: He has no sense of humor.

Bummer.

He was perfect.

Spencer ran up the stairs, taking two at a time. My short legs can't take more than one at a time. I got upstairs to a long hallway, the light is on in the first door on the left. Walking in, he isn't here. I'm standing in the room awkwardly, holding my right elbow with my left arm looking around. His life is all over the walls. His friends are plastered on the walls, I recognize all but two from school.

I don't know how it was humanly possible for a friend group to have so many attractive people, but here they are all seven of them, looking fine as hell. Spencer's bed is made with a red and black blanket. His room is the cleanest I've ever seen. All of his clothes are put away, his garbage can is empty. His textbooks are stacked on the desk.

"I'm a bit of a clean freak." I heard Spencer's voice behind me and I turned around fast, wondering how he read my mind.

He is standing in front of me in a tight black t-shirt, showing off every single detail of his muscles. The sleeves are tight, fighting to fit around his biceps. Tattoos are covering his arms. Images are popping up in my head and all are very inappropriate. He looked back at me and saw me staring, a smile appearing on his face.

My mouth is open. I put my hand up to my eyes and shut it. How embarrassing. "I'm sorry."

"I need help with history, are you any good? I can't fail."

I nodded my head and walked towards the desk, looking for the textbook. The next hour was spent with me breaking things down, watching him take notes, repeating important dates back to me. I don't think he is failing at all; I think he is just trying to make me stay.

I pulled out my phone and texted Lizzy.

I think I may have met someone, tell you later

Not even thirty seconds later, she responded back.

Who is it?

I tossed my phone on the pillow next to Spencer, not wanting to reply. I can't waste a second of my time with him.

His body is calling out to me, every time he flips a page making his arms flex, his tattoos, his amber eyes, his brown hair. I can't handle this anymore; when I get home, I am going to regret not making a move. I sat on my knees, moving his textbook to the side getting closer to him. Spencer is looking at me with sparkling eyes, I can't help but think I have been driving him insane too. I'm only a few inches from his face, I can't back down now, I need to do this.

I tilted my head when he grabbed the hair on the back of my head, pulling me in the rest of the way for a kiss. My heart is racing; never in my life I thought I would be in Spencer Cohen's bedroom kissing him. He moved his hand from my hair, placing it on my back.

Without separating our lips, I crawled onto his lap, putting my arms around his neck. I opened my mouth and he slid his tongue in my mouth like he has been starving for me. He pulled me against his chest, holding me tight. The bulge under his zipper is saying he wants me as much as I want him.

I pulled away and put my face in his neck. "I was out of line; you just have no idea how long I've had a crush on you." I know I needed to do something, but I feel completely embarrassed.

Spencer grabbed the loose hair from my face, tucking it behind my ear. "If it meant you kissing me like that, you should have told me ages ago."

I pulled my head away from him, he is worth any heartbreak that will happen. He moved his arm just enough from me to see a tattoo of a snake on his wrist.

The rumors are true. I grabbed his arm, examining the snake slithering up his arm. "Basilisk."

Spencer tipped his head back against the headboard with his eyes shut tight. Fear, anger, hatred, regret, sadness—all crossed over his face. He started to stand up, making me fall on my back against the mattress. "I can give you a ride home, but you would probably prefer to find your own way home."

I haven't been around Spencer to read him, but I can tell he is upset. Everything in me wants me to make him happy and help fight away the sadness.

It wasn't until he started to walk out his bedroom door, I came to the realization he had kicked me out. "Fuck!" I yelled, hitting my hands on the mattress beside me.

I just officially met him and I am insane to be upset about him kicking me out, but I am upset. I'm not moving from this spot. He has to go to bed sometime.

Who am I kidding, I'm not *that* crazy.

I grabbed my handbag, stuffing my phone in it and walking out of the room; I have no idea where I am, so getting out of here is going to be impossible. I can feel another sob wanting to be let free. I fall too hard for people. Damn, I think I loved him after the first time I saw him. Kissing him just made the fairy tale a possibility. Down the hallway is a wider staircase; hopefully, if I take that way, I won't get lost.

I followed the stairs and saw Josh sitting on the couch with a fire going and textbooks opened. "What's the address here so I can call a cab?" I am trying to not let my voice come off as shaky, they are all going to think I am a psycho bitch.

"I'll just call one for you." Josh pulled out his phone, looking down, not turning around as he spoke.

I'm definitely kicked out. Spencer walked into the kitchen from the stairs leading downstairs. I grabbed the strap on my shoulder. "Don't worry, I'm going to wait outside."

The truth is, I don't even know if I have enough money for a cab and if I do, it's going to be cut into my food bill for the next week. I swung open the door and rain is falling hard against the sidewalk. I grunted. "Fuck." I turned around, knowing no one was going to acknowledge me, I still never heard Josh talking on the phone. "Don't bother, I can't afford one anyways."

I slammed the door behind me and a tear ran down my face. This sucks. I thought I actually had a chance with him; if I would have kept my mouth shut, we would have been fine. I pulled out my phone and put in my address, dreading the walk in the pouring rain. I took off my heels and started walking.

This is worse than the walk of shame.

"Cameron, wait," Spencer called out behind me.

I turned around, my teeth chattering. "I already knew." My voice is low. I don't even know if he can hear me. "I didn't know what group, but we've gone to school together for three years, you guys aren't secretive about it. Earlier today you had a gun, I could tell by the way you held your arms."

"You knew?" Spencer picked me up, not waiting for me to argue.

I dug my face into his chest, scared to pull my face away from him.

He opened the door and let out a laugh. "She fucking knew."

"That's why you don't act like a dick," Adam's voice echoes into the living room.

Spencer put me on his bed, the blankets under my ass are soaking wet. He tossed me a towel and I stood up, wiping the makeup from my face. The towel is black from my eyeliner and mascara. I stood up from the bed, looking in the mirror. "Your blanket's wet, I can put it in the dryer. I'll call my friend to come and get me."

I'm looking at Spencer in the reflection in the mirror, he put his arm on the doorframe resting his face in his arm. "I knew who you were today. We've had one class together every single damn semester and I never knew your name. I've pointed you out to all my friends, hoping someone knew who you were, but they didn't. When William and Liam never knew you, I got unbelievably happy that you never slept with either of them."

I turned around to face him. "Do you have a shirt or something?"

"You're staying?"

I nodded.

He's walking over to his closet and ripping a shirt off the hanger and tossing it to me. He shut his bedroom door, facing it with his hands on it and leaning into it. I took off my jacket, dropped my pants to the ground, and took off my shirt. I looked up from the floor, standing exposed in my black lacy bra and panties with Spencer gazing at my body. I don't feel uncomfortable, it feels right to be standing in front of him so exposed.

He walked over to me, picked me up, and I wrapped my legs around his middle, kissing him; this time felt different; it feels like we were both taking our time, but eager for the same thing. He opened his mouth and I slid my tongue in, tasting every part of his mouth. He put me on the bed and started kissing my neck, making his way down to my chest and stomach.

Spencer moved his head up, looking me in the eyes. "As much as I want to do this, as much as I have been wanting you. This doesn't need to happen."

"Just don't leave me after." I reached behind my back and unclipped my bra.

"I'm already addicted to you."

I tossed my bra across the room as he slid my panties down my legs. He ran his fingers over my pink skin and my body tensed. He put his head between my legs and started kissing, licking, and doing tricks with his tongue. I grabbed the blanket with fists, letting out moans. I sat up, pulling on his hair to look at me. I kissed him with more determination I thought was possible, reaching out I pulled down his sweatpants; he is fully erect, waiting for me.

Spencer pulled away, walking to his dresser, opening the drawer, ripping open a condom wrapper, and came rushing back to me, leaning over me and kissing me once more. I spread out my knees, telling him I'm ready. He put his palms on the mattress, trying not to hurt me.

He is being gentle, enjoying every second. Tracing his muscles, I grabbed onto his arm, moaning. He is leaning down, kissing me, moaning into my mouth, a smile on his face. I never want this to end. He is working harder to please me. A moan escapes between his lips, I'm terrified that he is almost done.

I dig my fingernails into his back, letting out a loud moan. My legs are growing weak. Sweat is dripping from him, landing on my torso, allowing him to move against me easier.

I kissed his lips, raising my mouth to his ear just in time for me to let out another moan. "Spencer."

His body jolted. "Cameron, Oh. My. God."

He kissed me again, falling onto the bed next to me and pulling me into his chest. Both of us are out of breath. "I'm not letting you make another guy ever feel like that, okay?"

I laughed. "You just met me."

"I don't care."

Spencer pulled me into his chest and a heavy breath left his mouth. I pulled away and put my hand on his chest. "What's wrong?"

"You know about me, about all of us. I can't protect you now."

"I'll be fine."

"It's not just you but everyone you care about."

My heart sank. Theo, Max, Lizzy, my parents, their parents. "I won't tell them about you. You won't meet them. You probably haven't even seen them."

"I can't ask you to do that though you just met me." He nudged his elbow against my arm.

"When they ask, I'll just call you Prince Charming."

Brittney

Seven months earlier

The sun is pouring into Lizzy's bedroom. I grunted, pulling the pillow over my head; she needs some damn blinds. Her birthday is next week and I'm buying her the darkest blackout curtains on the market. I could just sleep in my bed, but after eight months of me sleeping next to Spencer in his bed, I hate sleeping alone. She isn't beside me, it's afternoon, and she is getting ready for work. I toss my legs over the bed, dragging my feet to the bathroom to get ready for the day beside her, even though it's 3 pm.

Spencer kept me up all night, I never got home till seven this morning. He got called away by Martin and I needed to be there when he got home, I needed to know he was alive. Him texting me isn't enough, I need to see him.

"The zombie is awake," Theo muttered.

"When the hell are we going to meet this guy?" Max asked, turning around in the couch.

I poured myself a coffee with too much coffee creamer, just the way I like it. "If you knew who it was, you'd shit yourselves. I'm not telling you, not yet. It's kind of fun keeping it a secret."

I stood next to Lizzy, playfully gabbing her while she got ready, waiting for my turn to use the mirror. She keeps glancing at me hoping I will tell her where I have been going; there's no doubt in my mind she would love him and his friends. I want to tell her, she wouldn't care about him being a Basilisk. Max and Theo would just be pissed that they wouldn't be able to kick his ass.

Lizzy stepped out of the way and sat on the toilet seat cover, watching me start my makeup. "Spill it, Brittney."

"Lizzy, he's perfect. I didn't know it was possible to love someone this much. I want you to know everything but not yet, okay? It will get too real."

She sighed, passing me my mascara. "I just don't get it, I have never seen you this happy before. We all need to know who he is. I want to know you're safe."

I giggled. I'm either in danger with him or safer than I ever been. "I am, he wouldn't let anyone touch me."

She must have been satisfied because she stood up and walked out of the bathroom, leaving me alone.

Digging through Lizzy's shoes, I come across a pair of flats; I need to see Spencer. It's only been a few hours and I already miss him. I pulled up his contact—*Prince Charming.*

"I was just going to call you." I can hear the smile on his face.

"One day I'm going to be Mrs. Cohen, you know that, right?"

He paused, not saying a word; I can hear a bag shuffling around along with cars driving by. "Meet me, Cameron. I bought us tickets to the Statue of Liberty six months ago. Can you be there by five?"

"I'll be there. Spence, I love you. I can't hide you anymore."

"I love you, you'll see what I have planned soon."

I hang up the phone, sitting on Lizzy's bed and putting on the shoes. A smile is on my face that I never want to leave. I have found my soulmate at twenty-two, I wish everyone was this lucky.

Damn it, I need to tell him my real name.

Today, when I see him.

I walk out of the bedroom, putting my hands in the air and swinging myself in a circle. "My fairy godmother called, Prince Charming is waiting for me."

I walk up behind the couch, wrapping my arms around Theo and squeezing him. He puts his hand on my arm and leans his head into mine. I let go, doing the same to Max, running over to Lizzy and squeezing her. I walk to my couch and put on my fluffy purple jacket before running to the door.

Opening the door, I turn around. "I love you, guys."

I hear them say it back. I shut it and run towards the elevator, jumping up and down and waiting for the number to land on the fourth floor; today is the day I'm no longer lying to him about my damn name. The elevator dings and I jump in, making the women in the elevator uncomfortable about my happiness.

The subway is only a few blocks away, I'm getting closer to him and my stomach is fluttering. A black station wagon turns around and slams against the curb. My heart drops as I watch a man looking to be in his late forties-early fifties run as fast as he can into a house in front of me. Gunshots are echoing through the house.

I need to go now.

I turn around and start running in the direction I came from, three more shots are firing but closer to me. I put my hand up to my chest and fall to my knees, pulling my hand away; blood is dripping down the sidewalk.

Screaming, pain shooting through my body in every direction, my vision is going black.

The room is bright, making it hard for me to open my eyes. The haunting smells of urine, bleach, and vomit are lingering. Beeping is filling the quiet room; the air is cold. I can feel wires attached to my body. I slowly open my eyes and look around. Glass walls are surrounding me, a man in a black bulletproof vest is standing at my doorway with his arms crossed. An IV is in my wrist, my chest is so sore it is hard to breathe without screaming out in pain.

I never met Spencer, he is probably worried about me.

I grab my IV and rip it out of my wrist, trying to stand up. I let out a groan and the man at the door turns around, looking at me wide-eyed, calling a doctor into my room.

I slam my head back into the bed, closing my eyes; the beeping is speeding up, keeping up with my heart rate.

A set of cold hands is grabbing my wrist. "Brittney, I need to put your IV back in."

I open my eyes, glaring at a nurse standing at my bedside, she isn't much older than me. She is probably fresh out of school. "No. Everyone is worried sick about me, I need to go home."

The doctor cleared his throat, bringing my attention to him. "You coded half a dozen times, each time was harder and harder to bring you back. The person who shot you called an ambulance, but by the time we got there, he was gone."

The nurse grabs my arm and I growl at her. "Don't fucking touch me," I said through my teeth. She looked at me, dropped my arm, and walked out of the room, storming back to the desk.

Two men and a woman walked in, all wearing bulletproof vests. "We need to talk to her." The woman came beside my bed and the white letters on the vest read FBI.

The doctor slammed the files on the desk next to the bed. "She is in a lot of pain. Go easy on the questions."

The doctor walked out, sliding the glass door. All three of them are standing around my bed looking at me. The man to my left is holding a file, he looks Spanish with his darker skin, brown eyes, and dark hair. I'm trying to swallow a lump in my throat, but I can't get it to go away. The heart rate monitor is speeding up again, amplifying my stress. I grab the monitor wires and pull them off my chest in one hard yank. If this is about Spencer, lying to the feds is going to be hard with that thing on me.

The monitor made a flat noise like I've heard on doctor shows. The woman next to me turned around and hit her hand on the power button, making the annoying noise stop before a code goes over the intercom.

I like her. She's looking at me with pain in her grey eyes, her blonde hair is pulled up in a ponytail.

The man who was standing outside my door when I woke up has a buzz cut, script tattoos on his forearm.

The man holding the files opened his mouth to talk. "I'm Assistant Director Rodriguez." He gestured his arm to the other man. "That's Associate Executive Assistant Director Nelson. And that is Agent Lee. We know all about you and your Basilisk boyfriend."

I stifled a laugh. "You're nuts."

"It's useless to lie to us." He tossed down the file and it landed on my chest.

With pain shooting through, I grabbed it and opened it. Pictures of me and Spencer are falling out of it. There are pictures from the first day we officially met, me standing in the rain after our first and only fight. One fell out and onto my lap, tears are filling my eyes. He's giving me a piggyback ride down the busy sidewalk, both of us smiling and laughing. I held the picture to my chest and tears are falling down my face. I can't bring myself to look at anymore.

My chest is moving so dramatically that pain is shooting through me. Between every few cries, I let out a deep breath, trying to catch my breath. They can't be on his trail, I need him. I love him.

They all pulled up a seat around my bed, waiting for me to calm down. I looked down at the picture of me on his back, wiping my face. "I need to talk to him. I need to see him."

The woman took the file from me but leaving me the picture on my lap. "We can't allow that. Everyone thinks you're dead. Spencer thinks you broke his heart."

Lizzy, Max, Theo.

My parents, I'm their only child.

Spencer. I would never hurt him.

"WHY!" I screamed.

Agent Rodriguez took a deep breath. "You will get back to them, but we need you."

"What the fuck is going on?"

Agent Nelson is leaning against the wall, crossing his arms. "You are going to be going through FBI training and helping us nail Martin. When the time is right, you will be back home explaining this to everyone, but for now we need you focused. A Basilisk is the one who shot you; given your involvement already, you will help us move this case along."

If it is possible for my heart to stop beating and me still be alive, I'm going through it right now. My friends can't handle me being 'dead', they will do something stupid. I can't live every day knowing that I broke Spencer's heart.

"Give me my phone!"

The woman grabbed my blankets. "I'm sorry we can't do that. The officers we are working with have it. We only need you for this one mission; after that, you will have a choice to stay on as an FBI agent or quit. As soon as you're healed, we are taking you in for your training, you will be living with another agent here in New York."

"I can't do that."

Agent Rodriguez leaned back in his chair, crossing his arms. "If you want to save your boyfriend, you will."

More tears are falling down my cheeks, I need Spencer to hold me and tell me everything is going to be okay. I need Max and Theo beside me giving me ideas on how to get out of this. I need Lizzy to encourage me to make the right decision.

Lizzy would tell me to do what I needed to do for the man I love, she would remind me that fairy tales always work out. My Prince Charming will come back to me. Even if that means I have to put him through hell.

My parents are going to be crushed, they will probably end up divorced.

Lizzy and Theo's parents are going to blame them.

Max's parents would take care of everything for my parents, making them not lift a finger for the next year.

I will one day wear a princess dress next to Spencer at our wedding.

I close my eyes, inhaling a deep breath. "Yes, but I'm not doing this for you. I'm doing it for him."

Charlie

Today is the first day of college and I am already going to be late for class. Picking out my look and trying every outfit on is more challenging than it seems. Last weekend, I went out and bought a new wardrobe. I am hoping a new look will be the perfect way to create a new life. My roommate left forty-five minutes ago, so I know I'm cutting it close.

I glance down at my phone, and the number lights up. "8:55, fuck! The class starts in 20 minutes."

I put on a pair of light blue skinny jeans, a black long-sleeved shirt that was just tight enough to show off my curves, and long silver and pink necklace that hung halfway down my torso—putting the matching bracelet on while scanning my jewelry box for a ring.

Racing down the dorm staircase, I saw a coffee cart with no line. I got my coffee, I quickly poured in my cream, and put sugar in it. Looking down at my phone again, it is now 9:05. The class starts in 10 minutes, I still have to walk across the campus. No choice left but to run. God, I hate running.

I was making good time. My coffee stayed in the cup where it belonged. Until I felt a body crash into me. I fell to the ground, hot coffee soaked my shirt, textbooks scattered around me. "My coffee! My shirt!"

"I am so sorry! I never saw you there." I looked up and saw his wide green eyes looking at me. "Well, now we are late for the same biology class. You are soaked, take my jacket."

I snatched his jacket from him and put it on. "We better get going. What a wonderful way to start the semester."

"According to my friends, the first week is useless anyways. Freshmen are the only people who show up. The entire week is an intro. The majority of sophomores and seniors don't show up till next Monday."

Sneaking into the class, the teacher looked up and glared at us. The only seats that were left were side by side in the front of the classroom.

Class ended, and he was right. That was pointless. I took off his jacket and handed it back to him.

"I never even introduced myself, my name's Dillon." He flashed me a smile.

"I'm Charlotte. Thanks for loaning me your jacket."

"Let me walk you back to your dorm so you can change. I'm starving! Let's get breakfast. I'm skipping the rest of the day; I should have just listened to everyone and not come to school yet."

Walking back to the dorm, Dillon told me about how he is a born and raised New Yorker. He has an older sister and an older brother. His roommate is one of their best friends. He is their cousin, but they are closer than normal families.

I walked up the dorm room stairs, taking two at a time. My shirt is weighing me down from the coffee. I fumbled around with my keys; as soon as I heard the click from the lock, I walked in the room, tossed my textbooks on my bed, and yanked my shirt over my head. I reached for the nearest tank top and dug around in the bags for my windbreaker. I locked the door behind me and raced back down the stairs.

Dillon is standing there waiting for me with two new coffees in his hands. He held up the cups as he spoke, "I didn't know how you liked it. It's just black with room."

I stopped and finally looked at him. He was at least six inches taller than me, bringing his height over six feet. Light green eyes, large muscular frame. I can see a tattoo hiding underneath his sleeve; from what I can see, it looks to be a part of a snake. He is wearing a black suit, with a dark blue tie. He is attractive in a sexy kind of way.

I smiled. "That's perfect. Thank you."

We arrived at the restaurant, the waitress grabbed two menus and led us to a table by the window. We have a view of a busy morning in the city, watching people rush by the window and hearing car horns is oddly relaxing.

Dillon is stirring his orange juice with a paper straw. His voice pulled me away from my gaze of the city. "You have been so quiet all morning. I was talking too much for you to speak," Dillon said, laughing once.

"I'm pretty simple. There isn't much to me." I hated opening myself up to people. If I'm sure of one thing, I never wanted anyone here to know my unfortunate life story. "What's your favorite thing on the menu here?"

Right as Dillon was about to answer, the waitress came. "I'll have eggs Benedict, medium eggs, with shredded hash browns and a waffle."

Laughing as he's ordering, I never heard someone order so much food in such a casual way.

"Waffles for me." The server barely remembered I was sitting across the table from him.

Looking around, I realized the girls were in awe of Dillon. I leaned into the table and whispered. "Don't look now, but every girl in here has their eyes on you."

Dillon never even looked up from the table. "You wouldn't even believe how often that happens." He looked up at me, and I rolled my eyes. "They aren't my type."

"What's your type?"

"Well, for one, men."

Laugher is erupting from my body. Those poor girls are about to be let down.

We were laughing the entire meal. As time went on, I slowly started letting my guard down. I feel like I can really trust him. We are both in open studies with the same classes every single day. We made plans for study dates at his place after school every day for the next month. He is already making this transition across the country so much easier. I never knew what it was like to connect with another person so quickly. The bill came, and Dillon made sure I knew I was not paying for my breakfast.

"We already skipped our second class. Are you going back after lunch?" He raised his head right from the debit machine when I shook my head no. "Liam and William are home, and they sent me a text, they are asking if I want to go see a movie, do you want to come? It's not until two."

I glance down at my phone. It's only 11 am. "I need to go back to the dorm until then and finish unpacking the rest of my things."

"I will help you."

"You really don't need to do that."

I tried to get him to not come with me to my dorm, but he insisted. He is too stubborn for me and I'm not ready to fight him on it. The walk back to the college is a lot shorter than I expected, and I'm a bit disappointed. I've been in the city for three days and haven't done anything I was planning to do.

I unlocked my door, and Dillon ran to a bed and lay down. I laughed and pointed. "That's my bed." I watched him running across the room.

Dillon landed on my bed, he pulled out his phone and called someone. "I need four tickets. May 10th works. Dillon Taylor. Thank you."

I am standing in the doorway, staring at him. "What was that?"

He shrugged as he tossed his phone on the bed. "I booked us tickets so we can go see the Statue of Liberty. You normally have to book six months in advance, I couldn't get in any earlier than May."

I'm trying to keep my happiness in check. I was never able to make plans eight months ahead of time, I never knew where I was going to be living, or what school I would be attending. All I wanted to do was jump around the room in joy, New York is the best decision I ever made.

I walked to the end of my bed, collecting my clothes with a smile that stretched across my face. "Why open studies? I would think a guy like you would have a plan set in stone."

Dillon is starting to open the bags that I toss onto the bed. "I have a plan. But my parents want me to join the family business. They had a plan set out for me and my siblings before we were even born. I just need to get a degree or some schooling to make them happy. Education is a huge thing in my family. Downfalls of being a Taylor."

He stood up, examining my clothing. I stole his place on my bed. "Okay, if that wasn't the case, what would you take." I sat against the wall, hugging my pillow.

"Fashion design and styling. We need to go shopping; these clothes don't work for your body type!" A sigh left his mouth and even though he hated what I had, he was still able to make me an outfit. "What are you leaning towards after open studies?"

I buried my face into my pillow. "I don't know. I had a plan, but after finally being in New York, my entire mindset changed." I pushed myself off the bed and sat up. He picked out a white blouse, black skinny jeans, brown knee boots. I felt a phone vibrating on my bed. "Liam is phoning you."

"Go change, I won't look."

He turned around, looking out the window. "Hey. So late lunch then a movie? Yeah, I might have to talk Charlotte into it though. I will try. *Willie's* 2:30. Got it."

Dillon spoke, still staring out of the window, afraid to turn around. "That was my brother, him and William just want to eat first and then go to the movie after that. Are you okay with that?" He paused. "We just ate."

I laughed. "I can guarantee, I probably eat more than anyone you know. You can turn around now." I started crunching numbers in my head. "I really can't afford to spend that much money."

I lay down on the bed and watched Dillon run out of the room. I cover my face with my pillow. Somehow I already managed to scare off another person. I let out a loud sigh, pressing the pillow onto my face harder. I am terrified to let anyone in, abandonment issues are my one and only weak spot.

I'm cursed.

My dorm room door flew open and I heard Dillon start talking. "You will learn quickly that I have an uncontrollable caffeine addiction." The bed creaked, knowing he sat back down. "Why don't you have any photos of your family?"

I pressed hard on the pillow, pushing it to my face again, trying to come up with a question to distract him. "Business, you said your family has a family business. What are you expected to do when you graduate?"

Dillon must have understood not to push me because he went with it. "We own a pub; that's where we are going. My sister manages it. We also own a shooting range and, believe it or not, a strip club. I would rather not be enrolled in college. I am just doing it to make everyone else happy. I was raised with a business-oriented family, so they want me to take something over for them."

I sighed and sat up. "I might have to bail on you tonight. I have an interview next week, but there's no guarantee I'll get it." I took my coffee from his hands and took a sip. "You can't just live your life to everyone else's expectations."

"You won't be paying. We get everything for free."

Dillon let out a sigh and stared across the room, something in him changed. He went from being happy to putting a wall up. "If that is your mindset, you are going to be good for us to have around."

"Who's us?"

"There are seven guys in our group."

"If they all look like you, I am in trouble."

Dillon laughed. "You are in trouble, believe me."

The building has a large red neon sign spelling out *Willie's*. Trailing behind Dillon in the pub, it is a sports bar. The smell of hot wings and citrus from the garnishes of cocktails lingering in the air. Televisions hung all around the building. A dance floor is in the middle, signed jerseys hung on the wall in frames. I know nothing about sports, but I see a few teams from basketball, baseball, and hockey that I recognize. Dillon leads me up a small staircase to the back wall. The wall has large round tables with neon lights shining down, coloring the tabletops.

I was feeling good about the day until I saw him, I let out a small gasp. I can't take my eyes off him. He is wearing a charcoal grey suit, which makes his grey eyes stand out. His suit ends at his wrists and I can see a tattoo sticking out from his forearm; what I can see looks to be matching with Dillon's tattoo. His jaw becomes tense when he looks up at me, I can see how confident he is.

Dillon sat down, patting the seat next to him, gesturing for me to sit down. I could tell the instant he looked at me because he was laughing. The sound of Dillon's laughter knocked me back into reality.

"Charlotte, sit your ass down and stop staring at my brother."

"You fucking dick," I growled back at him.

Liam spoke, and the sound of his voice made goosebumps on my arms. This man is absolutely perfect. "I need a beer. Who's in?"

I replied in a weary tone, "I'm only nineteen."

Dillon is smiling at me. "Hey! Me too!"

The server came back and took our drink orders. Ordering a pint of house beer.

William finally arrived by the time we were all two drinks in. "Are we even going to make it to the movies, or are we just day-drinking?"

Glancing up at him, he is tall, muscular like the other two. His face is thin, with a five o'clock shadow. There is no doubt about it he is eye candy.

I replied without even thinking, "Day drinking." I laughed, causing everyone else at the table to laugh. "I take it you're William?" William nodded his head and shook my hand. "I'm Charlotte; but just call me Charlie."

"We should share appetizers," Dillon speaking into his pint glass.

All of us nodded in agreement.

I glance up from the table and see William looking at me. "So Liam, William, you are seniors? What are you studying?"

William broke his gaze. "Major in science."

Liam looked up at me with a smile. "Major in English. What are you taking?"

I sat up straight, taking a sip of my beer. "I am on open studies right now—actually, I have every class with your brother this semester."

Liam leaned into the table, taking full interest in what I was saying. "What direction are you heading into then?"

I shook my head. "I really don't know. Everything is so up in the air."

Liam sat back in his seat. "New York is overwhelming."

The food came around, and we kept drinking. I can feel time passing us by. "I need to get back to my dorm soon."

I can feel my mood change, I'm getting happier. My body is starting to feel lighter and my mind is becoming clearer. I really don't want to leave, but I have to. When I drink, I talk too much. I really don't want to start telling the truth.

I sighed. "I need to go after this beer. I am underage, last thing I need to happen is get arrested. Especially when you have no family to bail you out." After realizing what I let slip out of my mouth, I put my hand to my face, covering my mouth.

I rolled my eyes, there it was, word vomit.

Dillon looked at me. I wasn't looking at him but I'm sure his expression said *what the fuck are you talking about?* "Is that why you moved here from LA?"

Taking a sip and setting the beer glass on the table hard enough for it to make a clinging noise. Not taking my eyes off the light brown liquid, I took a deep breath before I spoke, "It's easier when you have no one holding you back. I applied for schools in September. The family I had before I aged out of the system let me stay with them. My social worker helped me get my loans for school. As soon as I got everything figured out, I got the hell out of that city."

"Dude, she's perfect," William said with a smirk.

Both Liam and Dillon spoke in unison, "Dude, shut the fuck up."

"Why don't we buy a case of beer and head back to the condo. Go watch a movie since everyone bailed." William is getting out of the booth.

I started twirling my blonde hair around my finger. "I really do need to go home."

William looked at me with disappointment in his voice. "We have a couch."

Dillon laughed once. "Hell, I'm gay; you're safe with me."

Liam looked at me, concerned. "Guys, I don't think that's what she's worried about."

William sat back down and reached across the table and put his hand on mine. Liam spoke in a quiet, yet protective voice. "If there is anyone you are safe with, it's the three of us. We would never do anything to hurt a woman." He moved his lips to the side of his mouth. "On purpose."

Liam opened the condo door and the first thing I see is a couch and chairs. Walking in and looking around, there is enough seating for the seven of them, so this is probably where they hang out the most. A big TV is hanging on the wall and a door is wide open, I am assuming it is a bedroom. These guys are not the cleanest, but it's tolerable.

I went down the hallway and walked right into the bathroom. Looking at myself in the mirror and for the first time in my life, I can see a light of happiness in my eyes. Lighting up my phone to see the time, the numbers light up and read 5:06. I quickly fix my makeup and reapply half of my face. It's only 5 pm and I have a buzz on; for once, it's a good thing.

I open the bathroom door and see three bedrooms, two look like they had someone who slept in them. The other one looks vacant. "What the fuck! You guys have a 4th bedroom? Why am I cuddling with Dillon?"

I can hear the guys' laughter get clearer as I get closer to the living room.

Liam stood in the kitchen, twisting his beer bottle open. "William and I are both having a girl over tonight. We figured you wouldn't want to have the room right next to ours when we are getting laid."

I jumped on the couch next to Dillon. I was watching the guide as Dillon flipped through, even though I knew nothing would be on. Liam came over to me and passed me a beer. He is slow to move his fingers out of the way and when we touched, my entire hand got numb and butterflies formed in my stomach. He sank into the couch beside me, feeling something hit my elbow; looking down, it's his phone opened to create a contact. Not second-guessing it, I put my number in.

My mind just went blank. Why the hell did I give him my number when he has a girl coming over?

Charlotte, you're smarter than this.

Dillon is looking at me the entire time. When I finally realize he is paying full attention to me, he flashed me a smile and shook his head. "Charlie, are you going to class tomorrow?"

I took a deep breath. "I'm still drinking so, no. I'm probably going to read head ahead though."

"Let's do that together then; do we need to get your books? We can go for a walk if you would like?"

"Fuck it, let's all go! I want to do something anyways." William looked at Liam and nudged his arm with his elbow. "We might find some hot freshman on the way."

Liam looked at me and winked.

Dillon spoke with a protective tone in his voice. "Liam, can I talk to you for a second?"

The boys went on the balcony to talk. William started to talk to me and it caught me off guard. "I'm sorry, what did you say?"

William repeated his words, not taking his eyes off his phone. "You are still able to get your money back on your dorm. We have an extra bedroom here. If you can handle the girls coming in and out, you can take it."

Completely taken back by what he said.

He continued, "You are going to be over all the time anyways. May as well save some money." The patio door opened and I watch Liam come inside from the corner of my eye. "Do you two agree with me? She's going to be over every day so why not just bring her things with us when we get her textbooks?"

"Wait, you mean today? Go get my things right now?" I opened my mouth in shock.

Dillon came over and wrapped his arms around my shoulders. "Why not? With the money you are saving on the dorm, you don't need to have that interview next week."

I shrugged. "What the hell, why not. I'm in!"

I don't even know them, but moving in suddenly was unfortunately not the craziest thing I have done.

Moments later, my phone buzzes. My phone is generally quiet, so it made me jump.

the girl I'm attracted to is my new roommate

I shoved my phone back into my purse, feeling disappointed in myself for having a crush on Liam.

Forty-five minutes, that was all it took to bring my things from my dorm to the condo. I am so embarrassed that I had no belongings. We brought everything into the spare bedroom, I set the boxes down and my trigger for smoking began. When I was sixteen, I started smoking, moving houses was my biggest trigger. I thought I had gotten over it when I quit, but it happened on Friday when I moved into the dorms, and it is happening right now. It took everything in my power to quit a year ago; of course, this is the most I have drunk since then, so I have been trying to kick the craving to the side since *Willie's*. I know the guys smoke and seeing them doing it and looking at the packs along the condo is making it so much harder to resist the craving.

I tried to stop myself, but my arm is already reaching into Dillon's pocket for the pack. He is looking down at me, smiling while shaking his head. I got the pack out of his pocket and he grabbed my arm, pulling me down the hallway, through the living room, and onto the patio.

Dillon slid the patio door open. "So, my brother?"

I looked at him, wary what to say. "I would never make a move on my friend's brother, you don't have to worry about that, and besides, we live together now, this would get messy."

Liam shouted from the living room, "Martin's calling!"

Dillon stood up. "Stay out here!"

Sitting on the balcony, hearing a car squeal up, then the front door slam, then moments later the car squealed away again.

My phone buzzed. *Stay here, we won't be long. There's a pack of smokes above the fridge, the beer is in the fridge, and we have lots of food. Remember it's your home too.*

I didn't know what was happening, all I know is what just happened isn't normal behavior, so I texted back, *Stay safe*

I set my phone back on my lap when another text came through. *we will be home in less than an hour.*

With that, I saved Liam's number into my phone.

I am another beer in, in my new bedroom hanging up my clothes that Dillon was so turned off by. Lucky for me, there are already hangers in the closet, sheets, pillow, and a comforter. I made my bed, put my shampoo, make-up, towel, and brush that was in my bag and set them on the nightstand.

The front door opened and the guys are chattering very loud amongst themselves. By the sounds of it, their moods have improved a lot. "Charlie! There is a party! Let's go!" Liam shouted.

Dillon rushed into my room. "Change your top."

I pointed at my closet. "My clothes all suck, remember?"

"No, I found something earlier—here it is!" Dillon's holding a black halter top. "Do you have pink or red lipstick?"

"Both."

"Put one on and let's go." Dillon walked out of the bedroom.

I took off my shirt, put my lipstick on, eavesdropping on the guys down the hall. All of them are unaware I can hear them. "She's just changing. I'm taking her shopping soon, she sucks at shopping."

"Be nice," Liam whispered in a harsh tone.

I walked out of the bedroom and I saw them all standing. "Is this how it's going to be every night, the three of you lined up, waiting for me?"

William tossed me a beer for the walk. "When you take forever, yup!" He swung open the door for us to all walk out.

I looked up at Dillon. "Can you please text me the address of the condo, so then I can make it back in case something happens."

I can hear the party from a block away; as we get closer, I'm watching the crowds of people swarming into the house. The front yard is packed with smokers, red plastic cups are scattered everywhere. I feel bad for the people on the cleanup crew. We walk into the house and we all go our separate ways. I finally spot the girls the guys are hooking up with and they are absolutely gorgeous, even though they have extremely short dresses and a lot of cleavage showing. Something tells me that those girls are one of Liam's and William's regular encounters.

Dillon was not even there for ten minutes before he was waving at me gesturing, he had found a guy for the night. This is my chance to meet people, so I have to do what I am good at and float around the party, talking to different people. I start to dance with girls I have just met. I walk away towards the keg and I can see the party getting out of control.

The group of people on the lawn extended out on the street. I am surprised it took so long for the cops to get called. But they showed up. I ran to where I last saw William, Dillon, and Liam. I can't find them. This was not the first time I was running from the law, so I know what to do, only difference is I can't remember what way I came. This house is a maze and no one knows the best way to get out to the street without getting arrested.

I can see a window facing a fence on the side of the house. I need to take my chance with it and hope I get lucky. I open it and climb out, I can hear people on the street and the doors of the police cars opening and closing. I jump up on the fence, pulling myself up, wishing I was taller. I pushed myself off the top of the fence and landed on the ground. I ran across the street that I recognized us walking down to get here. I crouched down beside a car parked by the sidewalk, putting the address in. My breathing is turning into panting. A bright light caught my attention and I rolled my eyes, more people from the party ended up on this street and there are police cruisers with spotlights.

This college must have some wild parties for this much police attention.

I pushed myself up of the ground, looking at the map. There is a back alley behind me so I begin to run down as fast as I can. The GPS is telling me the condo is in the building to the right. I stopped at the fence and pouted, before I stuffed my phone back in my pocket. Once again, I have to jump up and pull myself over. I landed on the ground and ran around to the front, opened the door, and ran up the stairs.

I walked into the room, panting and looking at the floor, trying to catch my breath. "Can I have a fucking beer please?"

I look up from the floor and see all three guys sitting beside their dates. I grab an unopened beer from William's hand, twisting the lid off. "Fucking. Brutal. I jumped fences. How did everyone make it here so fast?" I slam back my beer and watch Dillon grab William another beer.

Dillion's date spoke, looking confused, "We all got a heads up."

"Charlie, no one could find you!" Dillion said, staring at me.

"Mingling." I took another sip, collapsing to the floor. I notice William, Liam, and Dillon are all exchanging looks.

Dillon walked into his room. "I need to phone Adam."

The girl next to Liam started complaining. "Baby, I am bored." Liam cringed when she spoke, and I laughed into my bottle.

I stood up from the floor. "You guys go do your thing, I am going to have a smoke and finish my beer on the balcony."

"Thanks for your permission, whoever you are," Liam's date snarled at me.

"Calm the fuck down." Opening the patio door, I climbed outside.

Having the ability to be myself, not a fear of being ashamed of who I am, or the shitty things I have done in life has a huge weight off my shoulders. I can't imagine being anywhere else at this very moment. As crazy as I feel, I love feeling this way. I know everything is going to come to an end and shatter around me like always.

My train of thought broke with my phone buzzing; it's Dillon: *feel better by tomorrow. Parents are having a back to school dinner and we are forcing you to come. We are going shopping for clothes in the afternoon. Oh, my parents drink a lot so round two. Don't need me tonight.*

My phone has never gone off as much as it has tonight, it's nice to be needed for once. I put my smoke out in the ashtray and go to the bathroom. I am trying to get ready for bed, but I can't stop listening to the argument through the doors.

"Will you shut the fuck up for once, Stephanie!" Liam started opening his door so I ran into my room.

I took off my clothes and put my pajamas on. I crawled into bed and I heard a soft knock on the door. "Can I come in?"

"Of course, Liam, what's going on over there?"

"She's in a mood. Do you mind if I stay in here? I can't even kick her out, the police are still out there."

"G-rated only. Shut the door behind you! There's way too much sex going on in here."

I heard Liam laugh as he crawled into bed next to me. I rolled over to my side, I could feel him put his hand on my hips and my thighs started tingling. I had to resist the urge of my body creaming to not climb over him.

Charlie

The sun lights up my room, forcing me to get out of bed. I can feel Liam's hand on my waist, I slowly move it, trying not to wake him. I quickly did my morning routine. I walked into the kitchen and I saw the mess. I knew the condo was a bit messy, but I never noticed the tornado that erupted. These guys really needed a woman in the house. I tried to ignore my hangover while I cleaned and searched for Advil.

"Uh, you're still here?" Stephanie looked at me with her hand on her hip, still pissed about last night.

"Clearly." I rolled my eyes.

"I don't know why you're here. None of the guys would sink to your level."

"You bitch. Just leave." My voice was starting to rise and I pointed at the door.

Getting in spats isn't anything new for me; because of that, I was suspended and moved from homes more times than I can count. I missed what she said next, but I started to lunge myself in her direction. Before I was close to her, Dillon came out of his room and wrapped his arms around me.

"Good morning, you crazy bitch," he said, resting his head on my shoulder and kissing my cheek. "Stephanie, get the fuck out. I can't deal with you right now, don't come back."

Liam walked down the hall around the corner. He is shirtless. I want to run up to him and jump him. I have to hold back every part of my body that wants him. He yawned and stretched, then rested his body against the wall with his arms crossed, causing his biceps to flex. "What the fuck is going on?"

Stephanie held her nose in the air. "Liam! They both kicked me out."

"You better leave then." Liam walked towards the kitchen, muttering, "I need Advil."

I jumped with the sound of the door slamming. "It's on the counter. Dillon, when are you planning on dragging me shopping today?"

Dillon sat on the couch with his arms over the back. "Go shower and get ready, we'll go after he leaves." Nodding toward his bedroom door. "And after we eat. I need to relax a bit." I nodded my head while biting into a croissant.

Dillon is eyeing up Liam. "If Steph was in your room, where did you sleep?"

Liam looked at me and winked while pointing at me.

I quickly stepped into their conversation; my voice is more defensive than I meant it to be. "Nothing happened! I'm going to go shower."

We had a blast shopping. I wanted a girly look with a bit of an edgy side. Dillon, picked out a lot of pink, lace, and ruffles. He added two fake leather jackets, one black, and one brown. Having an uncertified fashion stylist as my best friend was something I needed. I always loved fashion, but I never cared enough.

According to him, I have a pear-shaped body: thin shoulders, broad hips, and thick thighs. My wardrobe is filled with outfits to make me look slimmer. I tried to buy casual clothes, but Dillon refused. He made sure all of my clothes were dresses and fancy ones. I don't understand why, but I never argued. He even tested to see what color of undertones I had.

Whatever that is.

We got back home and he scanned my jewelry box, he looked impressed. I explained to him that every few months, I would buy myself something from a jewelry store. It became the one thing that was constant in my life; something to look forward to.

I promised him so many times that I was going to pay him back, I started to annoy myself. I calculated the total from the receipts and I almost cried when I realized he had spent over $1,000 on all my new clothes. I can't get over how much disposal money a college student has. I'm tempted to ask him how he had it, but I stopped myself. I'm almost too scared to hear the reason if he tells me the truth.

There's a knock at my door. "Come in."

William pushed the door open. "Dress to impress tonight. All of our parents are going to be there." I cupped my hands to my face. "Martin is scoping you out to see if you're worth it."

"Worth what?" I said with my hands still on my face. I took a deep breath as I moved them.

"Family business." He put his hand on the doorframe. "I like you, so I hope it works out."

Wonderful. Just fucking wonderful. Parents intimidate me. No pressure.

I pulled out my phone and texted Dillon. *You ready to study?*

Within minutes, Dillon is in my room lying on his stomach on my bed with a huge bowl piled high with purple grapes.

Time flew by and we only had an hour and a half until we had to leave. I have knots in my stomach that I can't get rid of. I know something is going to happen, I just had no idea what. Studying is hard, I can't concentrate. My hand is cramping and for the last few pages, everything I read just vanished from my mind as soon as I flipped the page.

Dillon is able to spot me getting distracted. I'm not trying to show my nerves, but I couldn't stop fidgeting. A pink dress with an oversized bow on the shoulder is tossed onto my bed. I close my textbook and start to get ready, ignoring every bad feeling that is rising.

It feels like time is dragging on, the knots in my stomach are becoming more intense. The only thing I want right now is a strong drink. We pull up to their parents' house, I'm taken aback by what they live in. I'm sure what I was expecting, but this isn't it. Their home has a metal fence surrounding the property. A speaker at the house to greet ourselves with a guard watching the cameras. The house stands four floors tall, made with stone walls. The driveway is up a hill that lead us to a four-door garage.

"This. Is. Amazing."

Dillon opened my door for me to climb out of the backseat of the Mustang. "That dress looks amazing on you!" Dillon looked at me with pride. "They will love you!"

I replied, taking a deep breath, "I don't know why I'm so nervous."

The door swung open with Dillon and Liam's mom standing there. She is one of the most beautiful women I ever saw. Long brown hair, every strand is perfectly placed on her head. She is wearing a long red dress, showing off her sun-kissed skin. "Boys, I'm so happy to see you!"

When I walked in the house, I saw a staircase that wrapped around itself, leading up to the next floor. Paintings hanging all over the walls. Their mother popped her head around Liam and saw me standing there next to Dillon with his arm wrapped around my shoulder.

"Charlie, come! Help me bring the food out! The boys need to talk to their father first."

I smiled and walked behind her. "Mrs. Taylor, your house is breathtaking."

She leads me through a hallway that wraps around the house; through the open doors in front of us is the largest kitchen I've ever been in. Our heels click on the tile, echoing through the wide-open room. Every surface is shiny and white. All of the cupboards have glass to see in, lights are hanging from the roof shining down on the island. The sink has its own island in the middle of the kitchen. There isn't just one, but two separate stove tops plus a wall oven.

"Thank you, dear, but please call me Kinsley! We are feeding 30 people tonight. I gave the cooks the rest of the day off, so it will just be family tonight. I have most of the table set up; I just need help carrying this turkey. Here, grab that side of the tray and we'll walk."

Kinsley walks backward, running into a set of doors that flew open. The room has a long table that a royal family would sit at. It looks like it is aged, definitely passed down through generations. Chandeliers hang down close to the table. Every few feet, there is a window with a curtain blocking the sunshine from pouring into the room.

"Come with me!" Kinsley said, eying another door.

Kinsley leads me down a staircase. I can feel the temperature suddenly drop. The walls are made from cedar, just like a sauna would be. We open the cedar door, and the room has wines lined up on shelves from roof to floor.

"What is your favorite?" Kinsley turns around; she is proud of her collection.

"Sparkling sangria!" I can't take my eyes away from the hundreds of bottles stored away.

"Take this one. It's my favorite. Let's head up and see if they have completed their talk."

As we are getting farther up the staircase, I can hear voices. Kinsley opens the door, the voices stop, and everyone turns to look at me. The room is full of men. We are the only females here, that I can see. Everyone is wearing a suit. I feel on edge, standing in front of so many dressed up people.

This is not a back to school dinner.

Liam approaches with a smile on his face. "My dad wants to speak to you."

I am getting led into a door straight ahead with Dillon and William close behind. Something is wrong. Very wrong. I can't ignore the knots in my stomach any longer.

"Please sit down, Charlotte!" Their dad's voice filled the room. This family was cursed with good genetics. Their dad looked just like Dillon and Liam, but older. He has tattoos covering his body and he is double the boys' size in muscle. "Do you have any idea what our family business is?"

"Dillon told me there were multiple businesses." I sat down and shifted in the chair, uncomfortable.

I glanced up at Dillon and he smiled. "All three of them rushed out of the condo so fast last night, and by the looks of this house, I know it's more than just a few local businesses."

Mr. Taylor looked at me and smiled. "I had a few people investigate your life. They work fast, I got everything only an hour ago." My eyes shot towards the boys. I immediately got more uncomfortable. "It's not a bad thing. We are just very protective of our family. We did notice you have a juvie record. Would you like to explain that to us?"

I could tell from his tone that it was not a question. "I was thirteen." I slowly started, picking my words very carefully. "There were a few kids on my block who were tormenting my foster siblings. They had a harsh life with their family, and somehow those kids found out very personal information on them."

I stopped and looked at Dillon, he walked over to me and sat in the chair next to me with his hand on my leg. "I brought a baseball bat out on the street, and I beat the one kid who started it all. I got three years in juvie for defending my foster siblings. I know now I needed to stop and make better choices." I was going to continue, but he put his hand up for me to stop.

"You're right. We don't have this money from local businesses. We run parts of this city. The boys have informed me about you. We don't allow girls unless they have been born in this family. Even then, we rarely let them in. Unfortunately, you are not blood-related."

"I have never seen any of them connect so fast with someone who isn't blood or working for me. Last night when the cops showed up, that wasn't an accident. I taught my men never to go to a party that would get so out of control, so they left right after they arrived—you were tested. You managed to get away in a foreign area. We want you to be one of us."

"What is 'us' exactly?"

"We are the Basilisk Mafia. I know you don't have a family. Everything you could have is at the tip of your fingers. We already got this made up for you." When he placed it in my hand, I saw a black ankle bracelet with a snake charm.

"If you accept, we have to do a ritual, just to make it clear if you can't stop running with us. If we get double-crossed, we will kill you in cold blood. But if you do agree, you will achieve a lot in life. More than you could ever imagine. We would never leave you." He paused. "If you decline, you already know too much. We don't like having people around that know too much."

I looked over at Dillon; he was staring at me with big round eyes waiting for an answer. If I say no, they will kill me.

"I feel like I don't have a choice here. So, yes."

William walked up to me, wrapping his arms around me. "I was not ready to shoot you."

Dillon picked me up and carried me like we were on a honeymoon. I went with it and wrapped my arms around his neck. The table is seated—two open seats side by side in the middle. One is next to a girl with fire-red hair. She looks to be in her mid-twenties. The other empty seat is set next to a man with matching hair. They must be siblings. Dillon pulls out the chair for me to sit in beside the girl. Kinsley has already put the wine I picked out in front of my seat.

Mr. Taylor started speaking, "We have a new member amongst us!" He let out a huge sigh. "It has been pointed out I need to wait to do the baptism after dinner, so I don't destroy her hair and makeup."

Dillon nudged me while whispering, "You're welcome."

"Eat and drink. I'm fucking starving."

"Open your wine." Dillon nudged me again.

I looked around the table and I was the only one with an entire bottle in front of me. I was not going to argue.

The girl next to me tapped my shoulder. "My name's Violet."

"Your name's Violet? Ironic considering you have the reddest hair I have ever seen." I looked at her and I was amazed she's a member. She's tall, but her arms were the size of toothpicks.

"Believe me. I never let my dad live it down."

Trying to eat but I have completely lost my appetite. The more wine I drink, the more the knots in my stomach settle. I give Violet two glasses of wine, even though I just want to pick the bottle up and chug it. This has to be a joke. None of this can be real. Noticing a few sympathetic looks from older men at the table. Each time someone looks at me, it feels like my heart is getting ripped out of my chest. I pour my last glass; now that I know this isn't a sick joke, I know that I am fucked.

"Martin, let's do this!" A man called from the table.

Mr. Taylor stood up from his seat. "Charlie, come up!"

I stood up from my chair and all the alcohol hit me at once. I walked beside the table, running my hand over the back of the chairs and trying not to stumble over; I feel everyone's eyes on me as I'm walking past them. Getting closer and I see a huge wooden bowl with detailed snakes carved on the outside. I stand behind the table beside Martin and my eyes are drawn to a knife with a giant snake as the handle. I can feel my heart speed up against my ribcage.

"This baptism is a symbol of a new start and a new family! We have a few codes. They are directed towards males, but they are still valid for you. Code one, we do not attack each other unless we have a valid reason and proof. Code two, Do not make moves on another man's significant other, unless you have good intentions." He paused and shrugged his shoulders.

"Number three, respect. It doesn't matter who you are dealing with, you will always be on your best behavior and be a gentleman." He sighed and looked at me. "I wasn't kidding when I said girls don't join us."

I forced a smile and managed to let out a small laugh.

"Code four, you will always wear a suit and look your best when you leave home. Unless you need to dress down, not to cause attention to yourself. Code five, you will protect all of the Basilisk members with your life."

The last code intimidates me. Protecting people and putting my life on the line for people I don't know is terrifying, I don't know if I have it in me.

"Now, you must prick your finger on this knife." He held it up from the table. He held my arm up past my head. "Everyone who isn't blood-related has had this knife connect them with blood for a hundred years."

The knife pricked my finger. Within a second, I felt a fist full of my hair in his hand. It caught me off guard, so I tried to get away from him and fight him off.

I failed. My head went into the water. Once I realized what was happening, my body relaxed, I let it happen. I'm trying to count the seconds, but I can't breathe. My fight instincts are trying to kick in, Martin is too strong for me to try to fight. I tapped the side of the bowl, trying to gasp for air. Martin pulled on my hair, and I am finally out of the water. Standing with my hands against the table, catching my breath.

"Your training starts tomorrow."

Kinsley walked straight towards me with a towel. I scrubbed my face and wrapped my hair up. She shouted out behind her, "Dillon, why did you let this poor girl wear this much makeup if you knew this was happening!"

Violet walked towards me; arms open for a hug until she burst out in laughter. "Girl, follow me."

She led me back to the table and pulled out makeup wipes from her bag. "This is hilarious!" Between laughing, she tried to keep talking. "You did well." When she was done wiping under my eyes to get the rest of the smudged eyeliner, she handed me my wine from the table.

I got home and I jumped into the shower. I was attempting to get the knots out of my hair. Finally, after struggling for what seemed to be forever, I'm able to run my wet brush through my hair. Thoughts are running through my mind about earlier. I never wanted to be a member of a Mafia. That wasn't my plan. I want to run away and hide, but I know they would find me. I want to live, I want to have a life. I wasn't given a choice. I can't think of the person that I'm going to turn into. I have to do everything to keep myself together. I don't want to lose the only good side of me that I have left.

I walked out in the living room with a towel wrapped around my body and a towel wrapped around my hair. "Does someone have a speaker with an AUX cord I can borrow? Just need like 10 minutes alone."

"Yeah, I'll bring it in." Dillon stood up from the couch, walking right into his room.

He opens my bedroom door, watching me apply a gel mask to my skin. "Here you go! Don't stay here too long."

I looked at him and smiled. I opened my phone to my music app and scrolled through my country playlist. One of the best foster homes I was in, the dad used to be a farmer until his wife got to relocate to LA. From the first day I was in that house, country music calmed me down; it ended up being my happy place. I need that, I need to feel like my life is okay, even if it is only for three minutes.

I flipped through the songs until I found one. I turned the music up to drown out my voice and lay on my bed, and I sang my heart out. When the song was over, I washed my face and got dressed. I stood in front of the mirror trying to remind myself of who I am. I took a deep breath and walked out to the kitchen to grab a cigarette in an attempt to relax.

"Why is everyone staring at me?" I reached for the pack on the table.

"That was incredible." Violet is looking at me in awe.

"Yeah, you weren't supposed to hear that. I'm going outside. Anyone wanna come?"

Liam stood up and followed me outside. He pulled a pack from his pocket. I was watching him from the corner of my eye. "You should quit that, you know, I heard it will kill you."

Liam laughed, shaking his head. "I'm happy you aren't set on anything in school. Mixing it with this life is brutal."

"Wait, I thought college was mandatory!"

"No. You get paid more for every year you go. With us, Martin pays us eight percent more a year we attend. The majority of us opted into it. Either way, you are already set for life. I'm not saying quit."

I'm looking at the smoke exhaling my mouth. "I don't know how you guys keep yourself together. I am panicking."

"We have all lost ourselves at one point or another. Our dads all sucked us in when we turned sixteen. Our group is so close because we need each other."

"Dillon said there are seven guys, is Violet not one of them?"

"No. She has her own group of people with her brother; she's our cousin, we aren't every close. We are all more dependent on each other. We are the hitmen, she's the getaway driver. She doesn't understand our daily struggles."

My heart sank. "I'm doing the work with you guys, aren't I?"

Liam hesitated. "We will know for sure over the next few days, but yes."

I raised my smoke to my mouth; I can see my hand trembling in fear. "I can't do this."

Liam put his arm around my shoulder and pulled me into him. "Yes, you can. You have the most loyal group behind you."

Charlie

William woke me up at sunrise with a protein shake and a bottle of Advil. I searched through my closet, I found spandex shorts and yoga pants to wear over the top, to be safe with changing fall weather. I slipped on a tank top and tossed a sweater on. We rode a subway across Manhattan.

Once we got off, we walked a New York block. A tall building blocked the rising sunlight from shining in our faces. William led me behind the building, through a door, and up a staircase. I looked up, I can see the roof, it has to be at least fifteen floors up.

We got into the room, the walls are covered in mirrors from top to bottom. Punching bags hung from the ceiling. Every exercise machine that I can think of was to my left, free weights in front of me.

William walked straight ahead and picked up two red pads. "You're a firecracker. Show me what you got."

I walked up to him and started punching the pads. He is moving his hands and I am able to hit the pads each time. One pad went in front of his stomach and I kicked it, causing him to fall back slightly.

"That's incredible."

William spent time showing me how to watch my opponent, how to study their next move. "You are going to be challenging men who are taller than you, bigger than you, and a hell of a lot smarter than you. Be ready to attack. You are shorter than all of us. Always assume you will be fighting men my size. It will need to become second nature to you."

William started explaining it while showing me the motions. "Step with your dominant leg. Raise your fist over to the jaw and punch downwards. When they are in shock from getting hit, punch them again either in the face or the stomach, whatever you need to do to win. Make sure never to be standing there, always be moving. Backing up, punching, or kicking, just never stand there. Try it again but do what I said."

William picked up the pads again, moving his hands slowly. I have his words replaying in my head. I'm able to hit the pads without missing a beat. He did it again but faster, and again but even faster. We kept doing it repeatedly. I was faster than he was. I moved my arms to punch and I hit him directly on the cheekbone. I threw my hands up, covering my mouth.

"Charlie! You weren't supposed to hit me!" He dropped the pads.

"William, I am so sorry."

"You're going to pay for that." He touched his face. And laughed. "You are the easiest person to train. We can head back now, but now since you punched me, I am making you run back home."

I hung my arms to my side, tipping my head back and sighing. I did not want to run, but I'm happy all those fights I got in actually paid off.

The run is the hardest thing I could have ever forced myself to do. I am out of breath and panting. I can hear my heart beat in my ears. William is keeping me focused. I was never one to give up, so I forced myself. My body is screaming at me, but I kept going.

The instant my feet hit the hardwood floor of the condo, I fell on my knees, fighting the urge to throw up on the floor. Taking deep breaths, I'm able to fight the nausea off.

"Christ, William. What did you do to her?" Dillon fell back on the couch with his mug full of coffee.

"The run back from the gym then this happened." He shrugged his shoulders and headed toward the kitchen.

Three guys are sitting on the couch; they all burst out in laugher when William came in their view. "You got beat up by a girl."

"This is priceless."

"I love her already."

"I am so sorry." I used the wall to get myself off the floor.

I looked up and one of the guys on the couch is looking at me. "William, you broke the love of my life."

Dillon laughed. "Shut up, Spencer."

I went for a drink of water, holding my side and trying to catch my breath. "Tell me it gets easier, please. I need a shower and a nap."

I looked at the couch and the three guys are staring at me. One is batting his eyes at me, I figured that is Spencer. He has light brown hair, he is wearing a purple shirt under his suit, bringing out his amber eyes. Next to him was a brunette with hazel eyes, smaller than the rest but he looks so much meaner. I looked next to him and our eyes met. He has blue eyes, blonde choppy hair, defined cheekbones. I can see a tattoo sticking up from his suit's collar onto his neck. I broke our gaze, looked down at the floor, and smiled.

I heard a voice talking to me. "I'm Josh, this dumbass is Spencer."

Trying not to look at the guy next to him, but I can't help myself. He is taking my breath away. Neither of us are able to focus on anything else, but each other.

I saw Josh from the corner of my eye look at both of us and start smiling. "That's Adam."

Violet came out of Dillon's room with her arms stretching above her head, yawning. "Like hell you are napping, you still have training to do. Get in the shower and we are taking you driving."

The driving lesson began by Violet explaining that this was the lot that was bought by previous bosses who set it up as a driving course. I looked around and saw the entire lot had lines painted in the cement to mimic a road. She told me the cars are always simple, never anything to draw attention to ourselves. Green, white, grey, dark blue, and brown are the only colors that are driven to allow us to get away. Station wagons and SUVs are the best choices for blending in.

"For the love of God, do not squeal your tires ever!" The emphasis in her voice is making me wonder how many times they were almost caught.

"Get away fast but make sure to have taken a lot of turns so you do not end up getting followed. Drive legally, stop when needed, never forget to signal, stop at yellow lights, be sure to study the cars around you. If someone is following you that you don't recognize, speed up and lose them. Look casual, be happy, have a conversation with your passenger. If you need to get out and run, try to get in an area where you can hide to get yourself more time. One last thing, when you are traveling at high speeds, turn hard."

I got in the driver's side and did my seatbelt up. I looked in my rear-view mirror. "Who is that?"

"It's Dillon. Let's do this."

As she was talking, I started scanning the road in front and behind. My eyes are glued to the side mirror. I signaled and got into the lane. I stopped for stop signs. I looked in my rear-view mirror and saw two cars following me. I sped up and took a sudden left turn. Down that road, I took a right turn. I never saw the cars behind me, so I slowed down.

Out of nowhere, I can see Dillon coming down the road traveling right in our direction. Without thinking, I turned right again, pulled a U-turn in the next intersection, and sped up as fast as I could. More cars are on the practice street. I swerved around them. Dillon is coming at me full speed, I cranked my steering wheel taking a hard left turn. I looked around a few times, following the rules of the road. I heard a recording of sirens playing.

"Now we have to ditch the vehicle. All of our cars have the traceable numbers scratched off. There's no way we can be traced back to them."

I turned into a small alley with props set up. I remembered what Violet had said, *make sure to park where you can hide.* I slammed on my brakes and we got out. Violet quickly grabbed the insurance papers out of the glove box and unhooked the license plate rope from the back-windshield wiper.

She looked at me. "Never forget to grab these." She held them up. "I wish we had found you years ago."

Multiple members piled out of the cars and walked towards us. I noticed the man Dillon had sat next to at the dinner, Violet's brother. "Can she fight?"

William shook his head laughing as Violet started talking. "That's my brother, Sammy."

Josh looked at Sammy. "His eye, she did that."

Sammy looked at me. "How do you feel?"

I'm not about to lie. "So overwhelmed."

Liam got out of a car and pulled me to the side. "I'm going to take you out on a date tonight. 9 pm. Be ready."

My alarm is sounding from my phone. I woke up and dragged my ass to Dillon's room, falling on his bed. "Do you know what your brother has planned for tonight? So, I can dress accordingly."

He stopped what he was doing and fell onto his bed. "You're going out with my brother?" I nodded my head, confused. "Dress casual. He is trying to convince you, so he will just be planning to spend time with you. I can't believe you actually said yes."

"Is it okay? I can cancel and spend time with you."

Dillon started laughing. "Go get ready."

I spent too much time on my hair and makeup, I'm not trying to impress Liam, but code number four kept running through my mind. *You must always wear a suit and look your best.* I really hope he wasn't going to mistake me being dressed up as me being interested in him.

I stood up, right as there was a small knock on my door. Liam is standing in front of me; his cologne is making my mind flustered. I stood in the doorway awkwardly, holding my arm. The way he dressed, his tattoos sticking out from his sleeves, his confidence mixed with his cologne made me so much more attracted to him.

The sight of him made me take back my last thoughts. I am interested in him.

Liam wrapped his arm around my waist and led me out to the cab. He makes me feel extremely nervous. He makes me want to let the wall down that I built. As much as I hated to admit it, I want to let him in my heart.

That scares me.

My excitement took over me when the cab door opened, flashing lights light up the darkness. I know exactly where we are. Times Square. I don't know how he knew, but being here is a dream come true. I stood there with a big smile on my face, I put my hands up to my hair, and I spun in a circle. Without thinking, I give Liam a huge hug.

We walked along the street until we came across a bench; we sat there talking and laughing, I never want to leave. Times Square is more than I could ever imagine it being. Being here doesn't feel real. It feels like I am going to wake up in my bed and the flashing lights, the crowed of people, will all disappear. Being here is so surreal. The night is passing by faster than I had hoped.

"We better get going." Liam looked down on me and must have seen my disappointed frown. "On second thought, we can walk further then catch a cab. Can I ask you something?"

"Of course!"

"Why are you still holding yourself back from me?"

"I'm not."

Liam stopped and looked at me. "You have been standing so far from me all night. You haven't made eye contact since we got here."

I thought about it, and he was right. I inhaled a big breath of air. "I really don't know if I can get involved with someone like you. The fear of losing you. What happens when we have to do a job separately, and we don't have a chance to say goodbye, and something happens?"

"I don't know."

"See. Losing someone you are in love with is different than losing family."

"Look, Charlie, we all go to a funeral once a month, if not more. We are used to death; it's just something that happens along the way. It stops affecting you. Chances have to be made. If I lost you, I would be destroyed, but what if I don't lose you?"

Looking up at Liam, the lights are lighting up his face, showing off his muscular jawline and lighting up his wrist with a tattoo that matches my anklet. I know I've been staring at him for too long, he intertwines his fingers with mine. Every muscle in my body relaxes.

I grab his arm that is holding my hand. "We better get home."

He lifts my hand to his lips and kisses it. "I had a wonderful time tonight."

Charlie

Martin called me first thing in the morning. Today is the day I'm going to be taught how to shoot. The shooting range is called 'Targets'. I thought that title a bit cliché, but I'm not prepared to tell him that. I walked in and the girl at the front counter is having a conversation with him. The front entrance is huge, signs are posted everywhere about gun safety. There are guns in a glass case locked away with price tags on them.

"Sorry I kept you waiting, Martin." I smiled at the girl who gave me the sign-in sheet.

"No, it's fine. We better get started."

We walked through the big steel doors. It's quiet, probably the best time to do shooting lessons, first thing in the morning.

Martin started loading his gun. "Everything you think you know about shooting a gun, push it out of your mind." He passed me the loaded gun. "Stand here. Focus on the target. Shoot, I want to see your aim."

I shot the gun and I hit the target on the bottom corner. "You shot him in the hip. Watch me."

Martin stood there, shooting his gun. I counted five shots. He lowered his gun and I stepped forward to look.

"How did you do that?" I asked in amazement. All five shots went into the chest area highlighted on the target.

"Aim with your dominant eye. See the two notches on the top? Line those up. Focus your dominant eye by closing your other eye. Find where you want to aim. Concentrate."

I did everything Martin told me and I shot too far up. "Do it again. You have it. Breathe. Aim. Shoot."

I took a deep breathe, I aimed, and I shot. "Holy shit."

"Holy shit. You did it." He pressed the button and the target came forward. "Keep doing it."

I kept doing it and hitting the target perfectly. We went through a few practices runs and everyone was successful.

"There are a lot of times we need to shoot when running away, or someone pops up. Do what I taught you but a lot faster."

I had my gun pointed to the side and I saw the target raised from the side of my eye. I turned and shot exactly where I needed to. "I don't understand how I did that."

"Where did you learn to shoot?"

"One of my foster dads used to be a farmer and used to hunt a lot. He made it a weekly thing for his sons to go with him for target practice. He started bringing me once he learnt he could trust me. I started to go with him a few times a week. He figured out it helped with my anger. I had to listen to the same gun safety rules for an hour each time. I thought I would have lost all of it by now."

"You are an amazing addition to this family. I have a call coming in. Good job today, kid."

"Dillon, you ready to go? The funeral starts in 20 minutes." I rest my head on the door. "Who is he, anyway?"

William tossed me a bottle of water. "We don't even know. We go to funerals too often. We are all so numb to death."

"That's so sad."

William picked up my jacket from the couch. "It makes our life easier, harder to do hits when we know there's a value to life."

I grabbed my jacket and put it on. "You are making my point even clearer. None of you are the monsters you make yourselves out to be."

Dillon walked out of his bedroom. "Don't tell anyone else that."

Liam walked up to us, ready to leave. "Rachel, if you don't leave now, we are leaving you here alone."

She came out of his room in a short skirt, tight tank top, and heels in one hand. Classy. I tried not to stare at him and ask what he was doing. I want to scream at him and tell him that I have feelings for him.

William escorted us out the door and down the stairs to the car. Liam sat in the front seat, boasting about Rachel.

Dillion whispered, "Are you okay?"

"Yeah, why?" I'm trying to hide all of my insecurities.

"I'm not an idiot. He might be, but I'm not."

"I'm fine, I promise you. Everything is fine."

We arrived at the cemetery. It is packed. We don't know who we were burying, so we stood off in the distance for support rather than up at the grave. I looked around everyone who is standing at a distance, it's another day for them. Someone dying is not something you should become immune to. William and Liam spotted the rest of the group in the sea of people and walked over to them. Dillon wrapped his arm around me; he can sense that I'm bothered by all the unaffected people.

The family at the grave is a mess. Exactly what you would expect. We watched them say their goodbyes, the daughter singing, and eventually, they were able to pull themselves away from the grave. Dillon handed me a smoke and we stood in silence.

I am not prepared to do this to families. Nothing will ever prepare me.

We all sat on the couch and started eating our fast food. I'm too unsettled, I can't do anything but pick at my fries.

We all heard a knock. "That's for me!" Liam stood up and charged toward the door. The sound of a girl giggling is echoing throughout the condo.

I can't sit in the living room around people, I had to stay clear of my room, I would hear every noise. I brought my food into Dillon's room. I sat on his bed, lost in my thoughts.

Dillon is outside the door. "I have to go to work. I'll see you in a bit."

I managed to finish my food and gathered it all in the paper bag. I can feel my eyes burning, but I forced the tears back.

William is sitting on the couch, watching me leave Dillon's room. "Charlie, do you mind grabbing me a smoke too?"

I tossed him one and he lit it. "You don't go on the patio?"

"Not always, I'm just too lazy. Sit. Liam's a dick. Any guy who has a chance with you needs to go for it, not this."

"I don't even know why it's bothering me, I can't be with another Basilisk." I sat down next to William, he put his arm over my shoulder and brought me in to cuddle.

Liam said goodbye to the girl and walked around the couch. He saw my eyes; it was apparent that I was upset. He is acting oblivious. "What's going on here?"

William spoke between inhales, "Do you care?"

"Not really, no."

I pushed myself off the couch and walked into my room. I opened my textbooks on my bed and started studying. I hate myself. If he wants to sleep with random girls, I can't stop him. We have had one 'date'.

I have been waiting to take a shower but I keep hearing the pipes whining from the water rushing through them. After I heard them shut down for the third time, I know it's finally my chance.

I ran to the bathroom, turning on the shower; I took off my clothes, testing the water. I am so relieved that I don't live in dorms. I would be missing out on this type of freedom, not to mention my own bedroom. Even though my best friend put me in a life-or-death situation. I am pissed at him for that.

I got out of the shower, wrapped myself in the towel, and opened my bedroom door. Liam is sitting on my bed. "What are you doing in here?" I attempted to make my voice as cold as I can.

"You need to tell me how you feel."

"I need to get dressed."

"Tell me how you feel."

I raised my voice. "You know how I feel." I lowered my voice, pushing out every word. "You know exactly how I feel."

"Then let's go on another date."

"No."

"Then why get so worked up when I bring home a girl?" His voice is rising more with each word. "Do you just want it to be you on the mattress?"

"It's our jobs. It's our life."

"That's nothing but excuses. Tell me!" Liam raised his voice.

I'm staring at him. He grabbed my hair and kissed me. I dropped my towel to the ground and took off his shirt. "You could have just asked. I'll be right back."

He ran into his room. I could hear a few things falling out of the closet. "Fuck!" His door shut and I heard a knock on William's door. Their voices were muffled so I can't make out what they said.

As soon I saw him, I started kissing him again. Everything about him drives me crazy. He is stubborn, the sexiest guy I have ever seen. I let out a small moan.

He put his arm around my back and lay me down on the bed. My entire body is relaxed into his. I can't stop thinking, what if this is the only time I'm ever going to be this close to him? My heart is beating faster with every second.

The butterflies in my stomach are making it extremely hard to concentrate. I wrap my arms around him, listening to every noise he makes. We both let out a loud moan. I kissed his lips, and his body shook.

He looked me in the eyes and ran his fingers over my face. We are frozen. I can feel him drifting away from me. "I better go to my room."

There it is. I closed my eyes and turned my head. "Yeah." He never stays with a girl after. They always leave as soon as they are done. I bit my lip. "I guess you better." I rolled on my stomach and buried my face in my pillow.

The bed squeaked as he stood up. "I don't have to go."

I took a deep breath. I could feel him standing over me. "No, it's what you do after a one-night stand, right?"

"That's what you think this was?"

Before I had time to respond, the bedroom door slammed behind him. I instantly felt guilty.

Charlie

William and I jogged to Central Park, the trees are changing colors from the seasons changing. Families are playing on the fields of grass. The path is flooded with runners. Laughter fills the park's air. I can't stop looking around at my surroundings. Everything I know about this place is from movies. I had no idea how it feels to be so close to nature in such a large city.

I had to catch my breath before I spoke. "This was one of the things I was looking forward to the most when I got to New York. This is my first time being here."

"That's just depressing." William playfully shoved me. "I'm surprised you can even run after the other day. I didn't think you would be able to move."

"I push myself way too hard all the time. I can't just stop."

"Then why did you stop with Liam after the other night?"

"Why does everyone bring him up to me?"

"Because neither of you are being fair to each other."

"He's the one who still brings girls home, William. I am the one who gets hurt over and over again. I don't want to talk about this."

William looked at me, ignoring my bitchy tone, and we kept running. The air is blowing past us. Before I moved here, I had a feeling that this was going to be my favorite place in the city, I had no idea how right I was.

William grunted. "Shit. Martin is calling me." I stood there, admiring the park and catching my breath. "We both have to go. You are my driver. We have to run home."

We ran home as fast as we could. When we got there, William got inside and grabbed our guns. I jumped into the driver's seat of the SUV that was dropped off. This is my first job and my fear is starting to hit me. Nothing in this moment is going to make me feel better. I'm trying to keep calm, but it's almost impossible. I watch William punch the address into the GPS. I started driving and at each intersection we passed, I know my life is changing faster then I'm going to admit. I grabbed a cigarette from my smoke pack, my hands trembling. I felt William put his hand on my thigh. He is trying to ensure me that everything is okay.

Nothing about this is okay.

I pulled up in front of the house, it's a nice-looking area. Yards are kept up, hopscotch is drawn on the sidewalks. My heart sank. Whoever has the hit on them, he is a family man.

My heart is racing. I turned on the radio at a low volume. I could hardly hear it. Gunshots fired, so I started counting. "One…two…three…" My body is tensing up. "Four…five…" I can't breathe.

William opened the door and jumped in. I signaled and got out as fast as I could while still following the rules of the road. I kept my eyes peeled in front of me and William is scanning behind us.

"Black SUV," William panted. I turned left. "Still there." I went straight and swayed through traffic. "I still see them." I drove past a few more cars and turned right hard down a back alley. "Gone." I did a few more turns to be safe. "They are coming at us from ahead."

William reached in and grabbed the insurance and registration. I raced out of the SUV and grabbed the license plate from the back-window wiper, he reached his arm out to me and grabbed the license plate from my hands. We looked ahead of us and ran as fast as we could.

I screamed to William, "Meet me back at home!"

We went our separate ways, but the car is following me. I touched my pants, I let out an annoyed sigh and remembered William took my gun when he grabbed the insurance. I'm getting fired at. I found a walking path that a car would not fit in, and I ran as fast as my legs would take me.

I know where I am, Central Park is not far, and the car is nowhere in sight. I stayed on the back roads and jumped fences to stay out of their line of sight. I am running out of breath. I found a parked vehicle and sat down beside it. I heard the engine getting close, I stayed hidden behind the car.

My plan now is to stay behind them so I can get home without being followed. The vehicle drove past so I stayed in the blind spots. I saw them turn right again, but I needed to go straight. I ran around people, trying to make it look like it was just a jog. The condo is just down the road, I picked up my pace and before I knew it, I ran up the stairs. I opened the door and fell to the ground, trying to breathe. My entire body is shaking.

I put my head between my legs. And I heard a girl speaking. "That was a bit of a dramatic entrance."

Liam put his hand on my shoulder and looked up at her. "Get out." The door shut behind her, and he looked at William. "What happened?"

William put his hands on my other shoulder. "I didn't notice that I had your gun until I got home. I've been worried."

William explained everything to Liam, Adam, Spencer, and Josh.

I finally was able to catch my breath, I looked at Liam. "You didn't need to kick her out."

I think I put too much emotion into my eyes. "Yes, I did, no more girls. I'm done." He pulled his eyes away from mine. "William, how long have you been home for?"

"Almost an hour. I was starting to think she wouldn't come back."

"I'm going to shower. Can we all go out for food later?" I grabbed onto Liam's arm, pulling myself off the floor.

I rinsed my hair with shampoo, thinking. I wonder if Liam meant he was done with girls, I guess I will have to wait and see. I don't even know why I am still chasing him. He is going to be the death of me. I am more annoyed that the instant a girl walked out the door, he tries to tell me he's done with one-night stands. I wrapped my hair in a towel and grabbed a second towel and wrapped my body up.

I ran into my bedroom and found a simple sweater and jeans, dried my hair, and tossed it into a bun.

I walked out into the living room. The instant William saw me, he wrapped his arms around me. "Never scare me like that again." He is still hugging me but is talking to five of us. "We passed that restaurant today by the park. It is Italian. How does that sound?"

I looked at how they were all both dressed. I forgot about the uniforms. "Shit, I forgot I need to be looking good at all times. I need to fix this." I moved my hands up and down. "Time me. I'll only be like ten minutes."

I bolted back in the room, put on a dress. I took my hair out of the bun and scrunched it up with my hands, letting it fall. I sat down at my vanity trying to do my makeup the best I can, as fast as I can. I opened my door and walked back to the guys.

William stopped his watch. "Nine minutes and thirty-three seconds."

I opened the door. "I didn't mean it literally."

Pulling out my cigarette pack, I handed both Liam and William a smoke. Walking is not easy to do, my muscles are burning. Glancing behind my shoulder, the three other guys are way back behind us, talking secretly.

The restaurant is only a few minutes away from the condo. I opened the door as I looked around, and I saw every girl staring. "It's official, I can't go anywhere with any of you without drawing any kind of attention."

The guys were smiling, taking it all in. I felt an arm over my shoulder and looked up. Liam whispered in my ear, "I told you no more girls. I don't want anyone looking at me as much as you don't want it."

I remembered the girl who had left the condo less than an hour ago and my body tensed when he touched me.

We followed the hostess to the table I never even got a chance to sit before Dillon phoned me.

"Hey, Dilly."

"Where are you?"

"I don't know what the restaurant is, but it's not far from home."

"Go home. You're my driver."

I hung up the phone and sighed. "Sorry, guys. I must drive. Again. Do you mind just ordering me anything and bringing it home? I'm starving."

I jogged home, ignoring my muscles shaking, I've had enough running today. My body wants to give out, but I won't let it. The sidewalks are busier now than they were five minutes ago. I'm trying to not act like a busy New Yorker, but when I have somewhere to be in little time, I can't help it. The closer I am getting to the parking lot, I can see Dillon standing against the car smoking.

I opened the door. "Let's do this. Let's hope this goes better than earlier."

Dillon punched in the GPS. "What happened?"

By the time I was done explaining, we were there. "Be safe, Dilly. I love you."

I watched Dillon get out from the corner of my eye, I fought the urge I had to look around. I can't handle seeing another hopscotch drawn on the sidewalk.

Hearing guns firing, I'm counting the shots in my head. I only got to one, Dillon is running out of the building, getting chased. I opened my door, stepping out of the car; I pointed my gun—Dillion saw me and moved over. I fired my weapon and the bullet went right through his chest. Splattering Dillon with blood. We got in the car as fast as we could and drove away.

"I think we are good. I don't see anyone." Dillon is dabbing the blood off his sleeve with a napkin.

"Are you okay?" I asked, concerned.

"I'm fine. I just want to go home."

We walked in and Dillon started stripping his clothes in the doorway. "I'm showering."

Liam watched his brother walk to the bathroom, still covered in blood. "What happened?"

I sat down, lighting a smoke. When I held the lighter, I noticed my hand was shaking. I just killed someone. I can feel my chest tightening. I have been showing too much weakness, I need to ignore what happened.

"It's not his. He was chased out of the building. I ended up firing the shot. It was close range and Dillon was just in a bad spot. How was the rest of dinner?"

William looked at me with a serious look. "As soon as you left us, the piranhas attacked. I just wanted one dinner with friends."

Liam looked at him. "Women are a bunch of animals."

I started laughing. "Oh, it must suck to be attractive."

Liam puffed on his cigarette. "It also sucks when I'm trying to make a point."

I looked at him and smiled. He winked back at me. "You really meant that then?"

Dillon came out of the shower with a towel wrapped around him. "Oh, he meant it or I will kick his ass myself."

Charlie

BANG! "Someone help us!"

I shot out of bed and ran into the living room. Liam is standing with blood pouring out of his side. I ran to the bathroom and grabbed the first aid kit. Adam has blood-stained hands from supporting his body. William lay down a towel on the couch and put Liam on top. William stood over him while he cried in pain.

"What happened?" My mind is racing. I'm trying to keep focused but it's not enough.

The door flew open again and Josh has Dillon under his arm. I ran to the bathroom and grabbed another towel from under the sink. Adam rushed over to Dillon, searching for the bullet in his side. Dillon is screaming from the pain.

The room is spinning. I'm trying so hard not to cry. "Charlie! Come here." William called out for me while not taking his eyes from the bullet hole in Liam. "I need you to hold your flashlight over my hand. I can't see what I am doing."

I held the flashlight and Liam is frantically looking for my hand. His eyes met with mine and all I see is pain.

"Damn it! I can't get it." William yelled as he sat back on his knees.

"William, I know I haven't done this before, but maybe you should step back." He nodded his head. I looked at Josh. "Can you hold the light for me?" I stood over Liam. There is so much blood. "I need a towel to wipe his skin!" I don't know who gave me a damp hand towel, but one appeared in my hand. I wiped his side; my voice is shaking. "Liam, what did you do?"

I held the flat tool that William was using and looked at it. "Is there another one like this that's sanitized?"

Josh turned around, looked on the table, and handed me the matching piece. Trying to concentrate, but Dillon's screaming is scaring me. Wiping the wound again, Josh moved the light closer, I can see the bullet. Managing to get the flat tool underneath it, I stuck the second tool on top and gently pulled it out of his side. With every move I make, Liam is holding onto the back of the couch with his life, screaming.

"It's out!" I turned to look at Dillon.

Josh took over for me. "Brace yourself, Liam." He dumped alcohol over the bullet hole and Liam's face crumbled.

I fell in front of Liam with my hands on his face. Horror taking over me. He grabbed my hands and held on to me.

"I need to check on your brother." Forcing my hands from Liam's grasp, running over to Dillon.

Falling in front of Dillon and cradling his head with my hands, I kissed his hair. "Don't scare me like that."

Everyone is sitting around the room silent. I went to the fridge and passed out a cigarette to everyone.

William is in shock. "What happened?"

"We were all at Martin's. Fuck, it's bad." Adam is slouching against the couch.

Dillon yelped out in pain. "He called us, so we went over. He ended up telling us that we are the drug cartel. We were not going to allow that. We ended up challenging him, well, we tried to. We told him if he gets into the drug game, he is going to lose everyone from the Basilisks. We made it clear it's going to kill us."

Liam sighed in pain; after hearing them both cry out, I rushed over to the kitchen and got them both Advil and a glass of water. "We tried to be civil with him, but he didn't like us trying to tell him that it was a bad idea. Our jobs start in two months."

Josh put his elbows to his knees, making a fist with his hands. "This is going to start a war."

Adam looked at me and looked at Liam. "Your girl looks like she's about to puke."

I stood up against the wall and slid down it. I heard Liam. "She's not my girl—not yet anyways."

"You could have fooled me."

I am so new to this I didn't want to ask a dumb question, but I have to. "Why is he changing what we deal with, why now?" It wasn't a dumb question because no one had an answer to it.

Dillon turned his head and looked at me. "I don't know." His breath is cut off and he grabbed his side.

I jumped off the floor. "Do you want me to get you in bed so you can rest? I can stay in there with you."

"Just help me up. I can keep William on call if you can handle Liam." I nodded. He stood up and yelped in pain again.

Without thinking, I was supporting his body up with my arm. I walked him into his bedroom and found pajama bottoms and took off his jeans. "You can't sleep in these." My eyes are burning with tears, Dillon can see right through me.

"Charlie. I'm okay—we're both okay." He pulled me in and kissed my head. "I love you."

I covered him up with his blanket. "I love you." I left the room with tears starting to escape.

William pulled me down on his lap. "Thank you for taking over for me. You did a hell of a job."

I wrapped my arms around William's arm, holding on to him. Everything is changing so fast. I don't know how the four of them are acting so casual.

Josh looked at me and smiled. "We are so lucky to have you."

Adam stood up to leave. "Seriously man, what's holding you back. I've never seen you look at someone like that before."

"Her." Liam pointed. I stood up walking towards him. "I'm sleeping with you tonight, right?"

"Are you sure that's a good idea? It might be better if you sleep alone, considering." I put my body under his arm to help him up off the couch.

"See," Liam muttered under his breath in Adam's direction. "Adam, call your brother. He is going to need to know what is happening."

Every step we take to his bedroom, pain shot through Liam's body, his face would tense, and he would grab onto my shoulder tighter and tighter.

"Where are your pajamas? I don't want to be digging around in here."

"Top drawer in the dresser. You wouldn't find anything if you did look."

I unbuckled his dress pants and brought them down to his ankles. "Left foot. Right foot. Okay. Left foot, now right foot."

"Can I please stay in your bed tonight? Please?"

"We are staying in here tonight. I am skipping school tomorrow. I need to look after you guys. Does Martin normally shoot his children?"

"No. That's why we are so freaked out." Laying Liam in bed and covering him up. "I'm sorry."

"For what?"

"William told me what you said. I didn't think bringing so many girls home bothered you. I didn't think you had feelings for me."

"I'm going to kill him." I sighed. I pulled the covers over him and crawled into bed next to him. "I pretend like I don't. Chances of the hottest guy I have ever seen, having feelings for me is slim. Besides, I stand by what I said on our date, being in a relationship with someone we work with is going to be hell. What happened tonight is proof. I was panicking getting the bullet out of you. I was scared I was going to lose you."

Sitting on the bed next to him, I can feel every wall I have built in my life come crashing down. "Liam, I've been wanting to do this since you came in the door. I haven't been able to breathe proper since you got home." As soon as our lips touched, everything in my life fell into place. I felt a smile on his lips, but he kept kissing me. "I love your smile."

"I love you." The instant the words came out of Liam's mouth, his body tensed. I can see him raise his hands up to his face from the small amount of light coming through the windows. "Shit, I didn't say that, okay?"

"You need to relax; you're going to be in more pain." I put my fingers over his abs and kissed him. I can feel his body start to relax.

"I'm sorry. You better get some rest. We woke you up." He is trying to sound cheerful, but I know he is not okay.

"Do you need anything?"

"Sleep. I finally have my girl. I have everything I need."

I can feel Liam trying to get comfortable and after an hour, his breathing finally evens out. Him saying he loved me is still playing in my head like a broken record. I can see more light shining in the windows, I don't know what time it is or how long I have been lying here awake. I don't know how he fell so fast for me, but one thing is for sure, I don't love him back.

Charlie

"Charlie, wake up." Liam's voice broke with pain.

I sat up and put my hand on his arm. "What do you need?"

"Can you get me my phone? Also, a drink of water?"

I nodded, standing up out of bed. I must have only slept for an hour at the most, my head is killing me and my eyes are heavy. I ran out to the kitchen and I turned on the cold water, waiting. William was standing beside me, he put his head down. He didn't have to say a word, I already know him well enough to know that Dillon is in an intense amount of pain. Martin shooting them wasn't just a message to his sons, it was to all of us. The seven of them must push and test Martin a lot. I have a strong feeling that this is going to be a regular occurrence.

I got back in the bedroom and Liam is trying to sit up. "Adam is coming over with some pain meds for us. I've been shot before, but this is worse."

My phone started buzzing. "Martin."

"I am assuming you are going to cover for my boys?"

"I am taking their workload for today and tomorrow."

"Your ride will be there any minute, don't fuck up this hit."

I heard a honk outside. "My ride just arrived."

The line disconnected and I feel nervous knots rise in my stomach.

I grabbed Liam's hands. Reaching in to kiss him. "I have to go."

"Be safe."

I turn around and to my surprise, everyone is standing there. I heard the horn honk multiple times, so I ran out of the condo. I wish I knew what they were saying, but I had no time.

I'm sitting in the passenger seat and I can't breathe, the seatbelt is tight on my chest. It feels like my chest is closing in on me. I'm the only passenger in the car, so I knew I was making my first hit alone, with no backup. I know Martin told me on the phone, but this can't be real. I'm completely unsettled. What if I mess up? What I freeze? Ever since I got released from Juvie, I have been trying to make myself a better person. Last thing I needed was the tiny bit of the good in me to surface at the worst possible time.

Looking around, recognizing the hopscotch on the sidewalk. I turn to Violet with my mouth open. "I drove William here a few days ago. Violet, they followed us and chased me for an hour. Don't fuck around when you get us out of here."

"Comforting." She rolls her eyes. "You have multiple people today. They are all in one spot; it was supposed to be passed around. Since Martin went gun crazy, it's all on you." She watches me shift uncomfortably. "These are the guys."

"Six of them! Seriously?"

"If any get out, I will handle it. Got it?"

I nod while strapping a gun holster to my ankle and putting a silencer on the gun I am carrying. "This is ridiculous. I'll try not to be too long."

I jump out of the vehicle and run towards the house, I get to the front window and I look in. I can see all the men standing there scattered in the living room. I take a deep breath and run to the door. I thought the best approach would be to get the door opened and stand off to the side.

I let out a sigh of relief when the door was unlocked. As soon as I opened the door, someone came running out. I pointed my gun and the silencer covered up most of the noise of the gunfire. I got in the room and I started firing my weapon. Before I knew it, three more men were lying on the floor. I emptied my clip, and my heart sank.

I still have two more men to go.

As I reached down to my ankle, I poked my head out from the entryway and saw two of the men still standing raising their guns. I hid back behind the wall, finally losing my holstered gun. I was trying to count to see how many more shots they had in their clips but with two people, it was useless. Taking a deep breath, walking out of the entryway towards them, when a bullet was fired.

Pain radiating through my body. I can't stop. I can't look down. I need to focus. I saw them starting to reload. I stood tall and started firing on them. One man fell. I got closer so I was only a few feet away. Trying to shoot but my clip is empty.

I run up to him and hit him as hard as I can with my revolver. I know I have been in here too long. I need to finish this and go. I grab a gun from the last man that fell and fire on the last man standing. Before he falls, he fires his gun a few times more in the wrong direction.

My ears are ringing from all of the gunfire. I turn around to walk away; for a split second, I forget I was shot. Every single step starts to send pain through my body.

I open the door of the SUV and Violet slams it into drive. "Charlie, there were almost fifty shots."

"We need to go. Now." I look at my shoulder and blood is pouring out.

"I can't bring you up. I need to go get my brother for another job."

"It's fine. The condo is swarming with people. I don't see anyone following us. I think we're good."

I got out of the vehicle and I focused on getting inside. I pulled myself up the stairs. The faster I can get inside, the faster I can get this bullet out of me. I fell against a wall, I can't breathe, the pain was too much. Giving myself ten seconds. I started walking again and I reached out my arm that wasn't covered in blood, twisting the door handle. That was a stupid idea. The pain got worse throughout my body. I walked and kicked the door closed behind me.

I stood behind the couch, thankfully no one had left. "I need help." My hand was covered in blood. My clothes were stained.

"What the hell." Adam ran past me to grab the first aid kit.

Josh set up the couch, I walked over to my spot as carefully as I could. The pain was getting worse and worse. Liam and Dillon both have terror in their eyes. Josh grabbed the scissors and cut the sleeve of my shirt to get access.

William sat beside me. "What happened?"

I let out a cry, trying to get enough energy to answer his question. "When we got there, I recognized it. It was the same house I drove you to."

Josh started digging in my arm for the bullet. I meant to grab the back of the couch, but instead I grabbed Adam's hand. I started screaming. This pain was too much for me to handle. My body was trying to black out.

Josh looked at me. "Get ready." He poured the alcohol over my arm and I started to move forward.

Adam pinned me to the couch. "It's almost over."

I watched Josh start the stiches. "I really need a cigarette." William passed me one and I lit it. Trying to explain what happened. I can feel my body become weaker, every word that came out of my mouth was getting weaker and harder to say.

"No one does hits like that in their first year, let alone first few weeks. I don't think I've ever heard of anyone in our group going to something like that alone." Spencer is hovering over Josh, watching him do the stiches.

"How often do you guys get shot? I wasn't worried about it but after the last twelve hours, I'm kind of terrified."

"Not nearly this much. Normally, if we get shot, we die. But this could have been avoided. It was Martin's responsibility to send you in backup. He's trying to show his power and he's doing it in the worst way," Josh said as he finished my arm.

I stare off into the distance. "I just killed six people." My voice is low. "I need to go have a nap."

Lying in bed gave me no sort of distraction. I needed to be around everyone. Every breath I took shot agonizing pain through my shoulder. I shut my eyes tight and let out a scream as I forced myself off the bed. I slowly opened my eyes, Spencer was standing in front of me with his hand out to help me stand up. It was oddly comforting to have so much support. This was what Liam must have meant on the balcony my second night here.

I managed to get out to the living room, whimpering every time I moved. As soon as I sat down, Josh handed me a glass full of alcohol and a lit cigarette. I looked up at him with a broken smile, trying to fight back the tears that wanted to run down my face. William turned on *Family Guy*, just the distraction I needed.

We were all so caught up with the show, we never heard William's phone go off. "Sorry boys, we have a job to do. Adam, Josh, and Charlie."

Liam looks at me. "You can't go. Spencer, you go!"

Spencer is about to agree but I interrupt, "I really didn't want to piss Martin off already. I do need to go. I shot a gun earlier. If I need to, I'll do it again." I kiss Liam and stand up.

William exhaled his smoke. "So, here's the plan. Adam, you stay in the driver's seat. Charlie, you keep an eye out from your seat and if anyone comes in or leaves once we are in there, shoot them, no questions asked. Josh, come in with me and be my backup. Charlie, if you hear an excessive amount of gunshots, come in because we are probably dead."

A lump formed in my throat. I nodded my head and reached out for William's arm. He looked back at me and got out of the vehicle. I know he was kidding, at least I really hope he was. I can't lose them, every single time anyone gets called away, it was like I couldn't breathe, I could feel my heart rate pick up, the walls close in one me until they come back.

I glued my eyes to the entrance. "I thought New York would be like living in a movie; I was wrong about that."

Adam laughed. "If you ever need to get away from those three, call me. We are all a lot to take in."

"I will." I tossed up my phone with contacts opened.

"Charlie, doors opening. Stand guard."

I jumped out of my seat. With my gun over the hood. I watched a man with an exceptionally large frame come outside. I don't know how he didn't see us in the line of vehicles, he was standing with his gun by his legs with both hands on it, waiting for William and Josh. I can hear gunshots firing from the inside. I can't take my eyes off him. He started to turn so his back was facing us with his attention on the door. I shot my gun three times, getting him in the back. He hit the ground with blood pooling on the sidewalk. I jumped back in the vehicle with my hands shaking.

Adam looked at me from the review mirror. He could see the horror that crept onto my face, he never looked at me in an intimidated way. It was like he understood the pain I was going through.

He tossed me back my phone and I smiled. I know he doesn't feel the same way about me, but none of that mattered; I am with Liam, at least, I think I am.

I heard the doors opening to the building and I shot my head up, pulling away from my thoughts. I saw William and Josh run out and I felt calm.

As soon as William sits in the passenger's seat, I smack his arm. "If you ever tell me you'll probably be dead again, I will be the one to kill you."

Josh laughs. "William befriend a girl, I thought hell would freeze over first."

William leans back in his seat, offering cigarettes. "Clear."

Charlie

Violet took me to a dark street in Manhattan. I can't pay attention to the street numbers. I am trying to focus on my breathing while concentrating on the picture that Dillon gave me. As we started to approach the building, I could see it was abandoned. It had broken windows with wooden boards where the glass should be. My adrenaline was rushing.

I'm not ready for another job. I'm not ready to kill any more people. I joined the Basilisks a month ago and I have already taken eight lives. After every job, I want to go home and scream at Dillon for destroying my life. As much as I want to, I can't. I know he wouldn't bring me in to hurt me, I think he brought me in to save himself. When he is around me, he's different than when he's around the guys. When he is with me, he's free; when he's with them, they are all soldiers under Martin's command, it's heart-breaking.

I charged into the building. The layout was wide open with garbage cans covering the floor, paint cans scattered throughout the building. It looked like they were trying to clean the place up. I hid behind a garbage can that was large enough to keep me hidden. I peeked above and recognized the man from the picture. He was pacing back and forth, trying to speak over the group of men sitting in a circle, arguing. I removed my gun from the back of my pants and raised the one from my boot to have better access. Making sure no one can see me, getting closer to the men, hiding behind a part of the wall that extended into the room.

Peeking over, inhaling a deep breath, I focused as best as I could, starting to fire shots. Before they noticed, I shot off six of my bullets, hitting four men through the chest. The one man that I came here to kill started walking towards me, firing his gun in my direction. I counted to six while reloading, hoping that was all his clip could hold.

I consciously moved my head out and saw him walking towards me. I stood out in front of him with my gun pointed right at him and pulled the trigger. He fell to the ground; walking up to him again, I shot him in the head. I turned around and ran as fast as I could to the car. Violet had the gray SUV running, waiting to go. I jumped in, and we drove off.

The first few blocks passed us by. I was looking out at my mirror to make sure we were okay. We talked about the date I had a few weeks ago with Liam, and how easy it had been with him so far. I was trying to stay cheerful, but my eight kills had just transformed into thirteen.

"We are good! You fucking did it!" Violet passed me her unlocked phone. "Text Martin."

There were five guys. It's done.

We arrived back at the condo, and the look on William's, Dillon's, and Liam's faces was nothing but relief. I walked over to the fridge and grabbed two beers. Before I made my way back to the couch, half my first beer was already gone. I twisted the lid off the second one, putting it on the table in front of me. My hands were trembling, I lit a smoke, trying to ignore every awful thing I had done in the past few weeks. No one in the room said a word to me. I was sitting on the couch watching my cherry burn and watching the thick clouds of smoke leaving my mouth.

Other than the TV noise, Dillon is the first to talk. He is speaking sweetly to everyone, trying to convince us to watch a movie. I'm sure that's what he is saying, I'm just nodding. I am in my own world of self-swallowing. Liam pulls me against him so I am cuddled up to his chest.

I look up at Liam. "Follow me." Leading him to my bedroom.

I shut the door behind me. I started to walk into his chest for a hug. After minutes passed, I stepped away, looked into his eyes, traced his jawline with my fingertips, and kissed him. Without any hesitation, he wrapped his arm around my waist, pulling me into him. I put my arms around his waist, holding him.

He is holding me so tight I know that he has been in the same spot I am right now. He is resting his chin on my head and stroking his fingertips along my back. No one can do what we do and not have it affect them. I don't know why I was so worried about showing weakness.

Suddenly, a loud bang on the door echoed through the condo. My entire body tensed. Liam led me back into the living room, we all exchanged confused faces.

Liam kisses me on the head. "Go sit on the couch. I'll be right back."

We watch him look through the peephole. "It's just my dad." He opens the door. "Fuck, dad, you scared the hell out of us."

Martin storms past Liam standing in front of me, holding a folder. "We need to identify the four other guys you killed."

I nodded my head, taking the folder from him. I really didn't get a good look at them, this was probably going to be useless.

Martin sat down beside us. "Edwin has been watching these guys for weeks. I don't understand how he wasn't alone."

I'm still flipping through these photos, the file has over sixty pictures of men. I see one blonde with his hair pulled up. I give the picture to Martin and continue looking. "These are all of them right here." The image has the other three guys standing in line with weapons.

Martin takes the picture, looking at it. "The other three guys were on our hit list anyways. If anything, you just made our life easier." Martin shrugs while standing up to leave. "Normally, such a new person doesn't do such big hits alone. Just know it's not going unnoticed." The door shut behind him.

"You guys, I'm falling asleep, I'll see you in the morning," I say mid-yawn.

Liam grabbed my hand and pulled himself up off the couch. He led me to his bedroom. I casually shut the door behind me. I watched him take off his shirt. It was like a reflex, I walked right towards him, slamming my lips into his. Liam picked me up, and I wrapped my legs around his waist. He stuck the tips of his fingers into the back of my pants and I let out a small moan.

Liam set me down on the bed, kissing me while pulling my tank top over my head. I watched him go to his closet and pull out a box of condoms. He came back and kissed me, gently pushing me down onto my back. Reaching behind me, he unhooked my bra and took it off. He started kissing my neck, then down my body, then he started to pull my pants off slowly. He studied my body while unbuckling his jeans.

His body was on top of me, kissing me again. I slowly felt him go inside of me. Both of our breathing started to increase.

It felt like hours passed us by.

Our bodies became one. The butterflies I was feeling before slowly vanished. With every thrust, we got closer and closer to each other. As our breathing increased, we both got louder. Liam put his face into my shoulder and his body shook.

Liam lay next to me on his side, pulling me in closer and running his fingertips along my spine. I kissed his neck and looked up into his bright grey eyes. "You are the only girl I'll ever want."

Charlie

The next morning, I wake up and kiss Liam's cheek. I have a habit of waking up before everyone else. Every Sunday, I clean from top to bottom before they wake up. Every single time I close my eyes, all the shitty things I have done since I became a Basilisk appear in my mind. Trying to block them out had become mentally exhausting. Killing is not something I want to get used to. I need to do what I do best and sing the thoughts away. The first band that comes to my mind is Spice Girls. As I dance with my broom, Dillon walks out of the bedroom.

I'm in the middle of the lyrics when I see him standing there, staring at me, holding back laughter. He grabs an orange from the counter and sits on the couch so he won't be in the way.

"When you are done, we have an early morning meet up at the docks. We have a crate coming in. Martin will tell you this when he sees you, but you will just be watching how we handle them. You will be with us in the next few exchanges. To get the hang of things. Normally, it's civil but be armed. Sometimes things just happen."

Dillon and I got out of the van and met up with Martin at the docks. We started walking towards the water. Martin explained what Dillon had said earlier that morning. "Stand beside me. Pay attention."

When we get to the dockyard, five men are standing on the pier, unloading a large ship. "This is my brother, who did the pick-up."

I nodded my head to him as he continued to unload the create.

One of the buyers is starting to open the crates with a crowbar. He holds it up, inspecting the gun. "9mm. Like promised."

"There are five hundred guns in there. $500,000 for the entire crate. Do we have a deal?" Martin is the most intimidating person I ever met.

The men exchanged looks and nodded their heads. A man passed Martin a large envelope filled with money. Dillon's uncle jumped off the boat and followed us back to the vehicles. We got in our own separate cars and drove in opposite directions.

I look at Dillon with a shocked expression. "Half a million dollars just like that?"

Dillon nods. "We are going by his place tonight to pick up your pay for the five jobs you have done so far."

We walk into the condo. William and Liam are sitting on the couch playing *Black ops*. Liam pushes pause and looks up at me, smiling. "I woke up, you were out of bed, and it was too quiet in here for you to be cleaning. Dillon wasn't here, so I figured you went out. There's a Pumpkin Spice Latte here for the both of you." Liam's eyes have had a sparkle in them since we started dating. Last night must have been incredible for him because his entire face is lit up.

"We are going to dad's tonight. We have to get both of our paychecks." Dillon is eyeing down his coffee.

William looks up from his phone. "Wait, that's where you guys were? Martin must approve of you. He's only brought a handful of people to meet buyers. Let alone train them."

I shrug my shoulders. "Next weekend is Halloween! What are we doing?"

William and Liam are back to playing their game. "What we always do, get drunk, and get laid."

Hours passed with me studying. I'm ready for any test in any of my courses. I know it all inside and out. My phone has been receiving text messages for half an hour. I refused to break my concentration, so I ignored my messages.

after we go to dad's, we are going out for dinner.
get fucking dressed.
Why are you ignoring us?
CHARLOTTE
Answer. Your. Phone. Damn. It!

Surprisingly, most of them are from William. I get out of bed and stomp down the hallway. "You could have just fucking come and talked to me! You lazy fuckers! If you three came to my room to tell me to pull my head out of the books, I would be ready, and we would be gone." I roll my eyes and put my hand on my hip. I can see Adam, Spencer, and Josh from the corner of my eye staring at me and trying not to laugh.

"Go get dressed. We are going out tonight." Liam has amusement in his eyes.

"I'm never going to get used to having to look my best whenever I go somewhere," I mutter down the hall as I walk away.

I put my makeup on as fast as I could, I tossed all of it in my purse. Put on a black cocktail dress and leather jacket. Found my long pink necklace, slipped on my stilettos, and rushed back into the living room.

"You look beautiful." Liam kisses my forehead, knowing my lipstick isn't dry yet. "Let's go pick up your first check."

We pile into Martin's workroom. He is standing at his desk, calculating how much money he owes me. "This will do it!" He hands me the envelope and start to laugh at the look of shock on my face.

The envelope is bursting at the seams with cash. I feel guilty taking this. I would have to work three years to make this much when I was in high school. My stomach is sinking thinking how much everyone else makes in a month when they are in their fourth year of college. I can't keep this all to myself, I need to donate most of it. Maybe I can take some of the guilt off my shoulders.

Probably not, but it's worth a shot.

"Dad, you better give me the money. We are going out." Liam drops his hand from my waist, taking the envelope.

Martin looks at us and smiles. "I knew it wouldn't take long."

I look confused. "You just called him Dad, it's always Martin."

Dillon spoke from behind me, I almost forgot he is with us. "It's always Martin in front of people when it has to do with work. Just to remind everyone of power."

We opened the door and stepped inside *Willie's*, I immediately spotted our regular group of people and additional people who I remembered from the dinner. Tables are pulled together in the middle of the room on the small dance floor to make enough space for us.

As soon as we sit down, a girl comes up and places our drinks in front of us. I'm not sure if we come here too much or if they just take extra care of us because Martin owns the bar. I'm looking around *Willie's* and I am noticing the people around the bar are taking extra caution of not looking at our table.

I wonder how many people know we are gangsters. I mean, it's not hard to put together. This is New York. Organized crime isn't anything new to this city. Not to mention, I am dressed up, and every guy at this table is wearing a suit. I know we try to keep it on the down low. I just don't know how well that is working for us.

I leaned into Josh beside me. "You do know everyone here knows we are mobsters, right?"

Josh smiled and laughed once. "Everyone knows when they look at us. They just don't know what group we are in. The servers love it though, no one tries anything."

"Dillon told me they have a sister; does she know?"

Josh paused and leaned into my ear. "William, Dillon, Liam, and Kinsley have no idea she knows. She's known since we were kids. Just let them believe she's an idiot. Got it?"

Josh's voice became stern. I pulled my head away, looking at him and nodding. I haven't met her, but Josh is protective of her.

I'm on my fourth martini, my gums are numb. I feel great. I stand up and push out my chair, almost falling over. Liam swung out his arms and caught me from falling on the ground. I reached into his pocket and pulled out a smoke pack. I got back on my feet and Liam had his arm around my waist with a smile on his face. I opened the door to step outside, every smoker who is standing outside walked to the opposite side of the entrance, giving us space.

I light my smoke and within an instant, everyone is completely sober. A gunshot is echoing from the buildings. I fall to the ground with unbearable pain shooting through my arm. I can hear Liam talking to me. I can hear everyone who is outside start to panic and run away. My vision is fuzzy, I can't see straight. I can feel another Basilisk on the other side of me covering my arm with cloth. My vision clears along with my hearing.

I grabbed Liam, and a tear ran down my face. Looking down at my arm, I let out a sob. I was trying to calm down, but it was almost impossible. I looked over my injured arm and watched Adam wrap my arm up with his shirt.

"Why did this happen to me again?" I let out a loud cry.

In a calm hushed tone, Adam spoke, "Charlie, you made the hit last night. Did anyone see you?"

I inhaled a deep breath of air. "We have to go. Cops are going to be here any minute. Where is everyone?"

Liam grabbed my good arm to help me off the ground. "They tried to track him down. You're right. We need to go."

We rush back to the condo. We have to take the chance of walking, we can't risk being noticed by a cab driver. We are only a few blocks away. It will be longer to call someone. Every step I take, the pain radiates throughout my body, I am starting to cry out in pain. Without hesitating, Liam picks me up and carries me the rest of the way.

We swung open the condo's door, I can see William, Spencer, and Josh. "Thank god, you are all here." Liam got me on the couch and poured me a tall glass of whisky.

I looked down at my arm, blood pouring out. "Not again, I can't do this again." My voice was shaking. I was sobbing. I looked up at Adam. "To answer your question, last night, the area was clear. There was no one around that would have seen me."

Dillon was pacing back and forth. "We need to call Martin."

I'm listening to the chatter in the room while watching William sanitize the knives.

Before I know it, William is cutting off my jacket. He is starting to dig in my arm for the bullet. Each time he moves his hand, new tears run down my face. I'm moving too much, four sets of hands are on me, pinning me down, trying to stop me from moving. I can't stop myself from crying.

William spoke for the first time in a while, "It's out. It is not over yet though. Brace yourself."

Vodka is being poured over my open wound. I'm trying to hold in my screams, but I can't.

"Adam, I need you to do the stitches. You're better, and I can't keep hurting her." William's voice was shaking.

I turned to the guys. "Did anyone see anything? What the fuck happened?"

Spencer hung up the phone. "Violet was keeping an eye out yesterday. She thought she saw someone lurking in the shadows where Edwin was hiding. He has been there for weeks. She thought it was him."

Liam kissed my head. "Anyone driving would have thought that. Has anyone called him?"

Adam sat beside me. "Josh and I have called him multiple times. It's going right to voicemail. Martin is heading there now. Okay, Charlie. This won't hurt nearly as bad, but it won't feel great."

"Just get it over with, please. If it's anything like last time, it will feel like a relief." I could hear the shaking in my voice. He started, and I watched the needle go in and out. "My arm is numb. I can't feel it much." I took a breath. "I've been shot twice in one week. Does this mean I qualify for a tattoo now?"

Everyone let out a laugh.

Liam's phone started ringing. "Are you sure?" He exhaled a deep breath. "I'll tell the guys."

Liam tossed his phone on the coffee table. "It was Edwin that Violet saw in the window. He has pictures in his hideout of all of us. He's been watching us for a long time. He knew that we let Charlie in. He was at dinner. This was a message. He's not stopping until we are dead."

William flew up from the floor. "We need to find him." The fire in William's eyes started to glow. He was out for blood.

I stole a smoke out of Liam's hand and lit it. "First, we need to calm down. If we go to find him guns blazing, a lot of us are going to get killed. What do we do in this situation?"

"Martin is coming over so we can figure that out. Be ready for a long night, boys." Liam put his head in his hands.

"Tell me what the fuck is happening right now." Violet ran into the condo with her arms crossed.

I grabbed Liam's hand. "Stay here. I will catch her up."

I walked with Violet. I needed to take my makeup off my tear-stained face. I told her everything that had happened that night from when we stepped outside of the pub to the phone call we got from Martin.

"I just don't understand this. Edwin was raised as one of us. How are you controlling these men's emotions? How are you still okay?"

I can see Martin walk into the condo in the bathroom mirror. Everyone started talking over each other. I can barely hear myself think. I stormed into the living room. "For fuck sakes, guys! Shut up! Level your emotions out."

"We need to split up and find out where he's hiding. Liam, take Charlie and William, Noah is going to pick you three up. Dillon, you're riding with me. Spencer, Josh, and Adam, you're with Violet. We are sending the locations we will all be at to your phones. Take pictures of the people you see coming and going. Sleep in shifts. Be ready. Keep the communication open."

William is in the front seat. He has a pillow pressed up the window and covered by a blanket. Liam is sitting in the back seat with me. He is holding my hand, not taking his eyes off the window.

I spoke softly, "Why don't you get some sleep? I can watch. Noah knows who Edwin is. If he shows his face, we will wake you up." Without second-guessing himself, Liam fell fast asleep instantly.

I want to sleep, but everything in my body is telling me not to. I can feel the exhaustion taking over me. Sitting here looking out the window for someone who may or may not appear. I don't understand how someone could be raised as a Basilisk and still double-cross us. I feel my eyes get heavy, I start to doze off and my body jolts itself awake.

Hours passed of us sitting in silence. I forgot I wasn't in the car alone. Hearing Noah's voice for the first time in almost six hours made me jump. "Martin, he's fucking here."

By the time he hung up the phone, both Liam and William were awake. "This is the plan. Charlie, we need you to go out there. Act confused, emphasize your pain. Tell him you recognized him from pictures at your house and Martin's dinner. Make it clear you don't know where you are. You've been wandering around all night. Get him over here. They aren't far away."

I looked down at my arm and saw my stiches. I knew this was going to turn out bad. I jumped out of the vehicle and stumbled into him. "Edwin…" I trailed off and fell into his arms.

"Charlie? What's going on? What happened?"

"What, what time is it? I was shot. I don't know where I am. Help me." My voice was lowering the more I spoke.

My exhaustion and the bags under my eyes were making it so much more believable. He grabbed my arm hard, and fresh blood was on his hand. I let out a sob seeing my blood on his hands.

"Where did you come from?" His tone changed. He saw my stitches.

"*Willie's*. I need to find Dillon. Please. I—I remembered you from Martin's dinner."

I started bawling my eyes out. I don't know if it was from stress, or I got surprisingly good at acting. "Please, help me." I'm pleading for my life and my family's life.

I'm not acting anymore—the tears are real. I lost my legs, my body can't hold my weight up anymore. "I just want to go home."

"Let's go. We aren't far from your place." He pointed in the direction. "You live just two blocks that way."

Wrong. We drove almost an hour.

Edwin grabbed my arm and pulled me up. I shrieked, my arm was bleeding even more. "Let's go," he commanded in a stern voice.

As we walked, I scanned the bushes, waiting to see someone. No one was there. I looked at where the car was, and it was replaced with a black van. I had to start talking. As we were getting closer, his hand was squeezing my arm. Pain was radiating through my body.

"Can you please move your arm? It really hurts." My voice is weak.

His nails dug in my open wound, I fell on my knees crying out for help.

"Shut up!" Edwin growled. "Something is wrong." He looked straight ahead, pulling my arm with every ounce of force he had in his body to get me back on my feet.

I saw Martin from the corner of my eye. I know now was the time to escape his grasp. I took a deep breath and pulled my arm as hard as I could; he still had a tight grip on my arm. Thankfully, my right hand was my dominant hand, and it wasn't the one that was shot. Ignoring the pain, I formed a fist in my hand and pivoted my body. I punched him in the face. All of the anger I was feeling was forced out of me with one hit. I hit him hard enough for blood to gush out of his nose, and he let go of my arm.

The black van that was parked in front of us pulled up carefully, not making a noise. Josh opened the door as they drove up to us. Adam and Spencer got him in the van, and Josh shut the door as soon as he got dragged in.

I walked over to the car Noah was driving, and I got in without saying a word. The ride to Martin's was silent until I broke it. "Is there a napkin or something in here? I need to put pressure on my arm." I can start to feel pain as my adrenaline was starting to disappear.

"We need to get to Martin's now!" Liam's voice was demanding.

I soaked every fast food napkin that was in the car full of blood. I forced my words out, "I'm really light-headed."

The room is bright. I look around, there is an IV attached to my arm. "Liam." I waited. "Liam." I tried to sit up, but I have a headache. "Liam, where are you?"

"Charlie, I'm right here!" He runs into the room and holds my hand. "I've been so worried about you."

"How long was I out?"

"Eight hours."

"Where are we?"

"My parents." Every time I spoke, Liam squeezed my hand. "Dad has a doctor on call for times like this. I'm going to go get him, but I need to kiss you first." Every emotion Liam had felt in the last 12 hours was explained by the way his lips touched mine.

I don't know if what I'm feeling for him is real, or if it's just the hell we went through in the past few hours.

I looked him in his eyes. "I love you." He kissed my forehead and I watched him leave while running my fingers over my lips, forming a smile.

The doctor walked in, looking at my charts. "Hi, Charlie. You had an eventful night."

"That's a way to put it." I'm finally able to sit myself up.

"When your arm was grabbed, your stitches broke. On the way here, you lost to much blood in addition to earlier in the day, plus it was thinned out from the alcohol. Your body was going into shock. I brought in O negative blood and did a blood transfusion. Why don't you come out and get some food?"

I slowly got up out of bed and headed out of the room. When I got to the dining table, everyone was there. I sat down at the table. The doctor was talking to Kinsley. Liam never left my side. Once Dillon and William sat near me, I knew they weren't going anywhere.

I looked at the three of them and smiled. "I don't know where I would be without you guys."

As much as I wanted to eat the food in front of me, I couldn't. I don't know who had to deal with Edwin, but my heart ached knowing someone in this room killed one of our own. I shook off every bad thought in my mind and stood up. I needed to talk to Martin.

Martin smiled when he saw me approaching. "What happened? I'm sorry, I tried to do everything I could." I looked to the side and saw Spencer, Adam, and Josh keeping an eye on me from across the room.

"He was taken care of. You did everything right. When you feel better, we can get you your tattoo." He winked at me. "None of us could leave this room until you woke up."

Liam grabbed my hand and Dillon came out of the room holding my shoes. Every single part of my body hurts. I am exhausted. If this is what the life of a

Basilisk is, I am already tired of it. I am living in fear now, I am scared to get shot again. I'm scared my friends are going to get shot. I'm scared to die. If I lose any one of them, I am going to be dead inside. This is the worst possible way to live.

Brittney

A month and a half of physical therapy, five months of FBI training. I wasn't fully healed when my training began and it almost bit me in the ass, but I was dedicated to graduate and help put Martin away so I could be back with Spencer, if he will even take me back. I had been trying not to think about him because the reality was too much to handle. Why would he ever take back a girl who shattered his heart? What was I supposed to do, just show up at his doorstep and say, 'Hey, remember me? I was shot, I almost died six times, I didn't so will you marry me?'

My legs hurt, my brain hurts, everything fucking hurts. Thank god I wasn't alone and I had a lot of help with my training; I wouldn't have been able to do it if it wasn't for Agent Lee. She was compassionate in the hospital and she saved me in training.

I am bunking with her in her apartment, since I am only with the bureau temporarily. I can't get my own place, and I can't go home to my roommates who think I'm dead.

"Brittney, are you ready? Meeting is in half an hour!" Sam yelled out from her bedroom.

I put on my dress suit and walked out, leaning on her doorframe. "I hate this outfit."

"Just wait till you get to wear the vest." She winked at me, shoving me along the hallway out to the front door.

I am still in New York city and it is torture. I am only a few blocks from Spencer's and I can't stop thinking about showing up on his doorstep and feeling his lips touching mine one last time. The elevator takes us down to the underground parking lot and I hop into the passenger side of her Charger. She is only three years older than me and it is surprising how she has been in the bureau for two years, I never thought kids grew up wishing to be in the FBI, but her stories about growing up show she always knew she belonged here.

Hearing her talk about the job makes me wish this was something that I am excited about. The ride isn't as long as I thought it would be to the office, she put on music loud enough to drown out my thoughts. The tall buildings come into my line of sight. She opens the middle console and passes me my bag with my picture that was taken halfway through my training. Everything about my employment has been sped up, for obvious reasons.

Little do they know; this is going to turn into a fucking disaster. No one is going to listen to me after what they thought I did to Spencer.

She parked her car and opened her door, I took a deep breath. This is the start of me protecting him and he doesn't even know it.

The path up to the door is lined up with flowers, the yard is taken care of, fresh mowed grass is lingering in the air. We get to the door; Sam flashes her badge and I do the same, following her lead, pretending I know what the hell I'm doing. The building is full with agents and police officers. Pictures of fallen agents are on the walls with their names engraved on the plaques under them.

Sam grabbed the metal handle on a glass door, opening it. "Shit, they are already in Rodriguez's office. Follow me, Agent Hill."

I shook my head with shivers down my back, a FBI agent in love with a mobster, that was a disaster waiting to happen.

I walked in behind Sam, listening to the comments of everyone.

"Where is the girl?"

"I want to know what she sees in a soulless gangster."

Agent Nelson looked at me and slammed his fists on the table. "Enough."

I cleared my throat. "It's fine, I may as well get used to it now."

I'm fighting back the tears forming in my eyes, this is going to be so much harder than I ever thought. All the agents in the room turn their heads to look at me in amazement. Being the center of attention was Lizzy's job, not mine, I'm missing her more than ever right now.

"So, will you tell me what you see in him?"

Sam pulled out her chair, glaring at him. "Shut the fuck up, Jones. Would any of your exes do this for you?"

He darted his eyes to the table, shaking his head. No one has addressed Spencer as my ex before, my heart feels like it is wanting to jump out of my body.

It feels like I'm dying.

Rodriguez tossed another file on the table and everyone passed a piece of paper around. "We all knew they brought a girl into the Basilisks, but we all underestimated her. Charlotte Young is a lot more relentless than we could have imagined. We are keeping up with her track record; in a month and a half, she has thirteen kills."

My mouth dropped open, looking at the files, I recognize the guy from Spencer's wall that I never saw at school. He is standing with her with his arm around her shoulders, she has the same darkness in her eyes. I shake my head, not knowing if I'm allowed to speak. "She doesn't want to be with them, look at her. I can see it in her eyes, the same thing Spencer has. He's better at hiding it, but she isn't a killer."

Rodriguez met my eyes along with everyone else in the room. "What would you recommend?"

"Look how he's holding her, she's holding them together."

"He brought her in."

"Maybe to save the rest of them."

"Do you know him?" I shake my head. "That's Dillon Taylor."

"Martin's son."

Sam glanced up at me, smiling like a proud big sister.

Nelson leaned back in his seat, crossing his arms. "Rodriguez, she needs to be the one watching them. She knows them better than any of us."

I shook my head in protest. "I only know three, Spence, Josh, and Adam. Spence kept me away from everyone, like I kept him away from my friends. We were trying to protect me and them."

Jones is tapping his fingers on the desk. "You knew about him then?"

I nodded my head and they all exchanged a look Rodriguez slid a picture across the desk, I grabbed it and looked at it. The man in the picture is wearing a police uniform, every inch of his arms are covered in tattoos. He has blue eyes and blonde hair just like Adam does. Like Dillon, I recognize him from the bedroom walls. "Why are you showing me a picture of a police officer?"

"He's a Basilisk. He is doing a hell of a job hiding it. If there is an explosion, I can guarantee Erik Watson is the one with the grenade pin in his suit pocket. His captain called us in, we are going to be dealing with him in our own way; our plan is that if he is more loyal to the police department, he will help you get Martin. There's one other thing you should know."

He slid me another picture across the table and it was Spencer standing on the phone holding a ring box. Another picture is being slid to me with him standing outside of the Statue of Liberty looking down at the box—he was waiting for me.

He was going to propose to me.

I slam the picture on the desk with my hands next to it on the table, taking staggered breaths. No one is saying a word; the only noise in the room is me trying not to cry. I'm trying to hold myself together at work, but I'm failing miserably.

Sam grabbed my arm. "There's more. I'm sorry to show you this, Britt."

She placed six pictures on the table of Spencer making out with girls. I caught my breath and I wiped my face, standing up tall. "What do I need to do?"

Rodriguez walked me to the back office with dozens of boxes filled with files stacked high. All day, him, Nelson, Sam, and Jones have been knocking on my door all day trying to remind me to take breaks, but I can't. Nothing is going to pull me away from Spencer. Hell, I even miss Josh and Adam. The farther I get into the files, I am discovering more and more sadness in Spencer. I have covered him from being a sixteen-year-old Basilisk balancing high school and now college. I even have his grades, he has a 3.5 GPA in history; if anything, he should have been helping me the first night. I knew then what he was trying to do and it still brings me joy that he was trying to make me stay.

The more recent photos are of him, Adam, Josh, Liam, William, Dillon, and Charlie. There are photos of him with his roommates and Erik. Erik is never around all of them, I think that's because he is trying to protect his cover.

The more I look at Erik, the more I can see him and Lizzy together. Spencer has talked about him a lot, we discussed setting him up with Lizzy, but bringing her into the basilisks was too risky. I wouldn't put her in any danger. She has spent her entire life watching over me since we met in the grade two-three split. Even though I knew they would be perfect, it wasn't fair for me to put this burden on her.

April has her own file, I remember her from the night I met Spencer at *Willie's*, I still remember her laugh. I don't even need pictures to explain her, all I need to remember is the way Spencer talked about her; he loves her. Erik, Adam, and Josh all love her.

The pictures of Spencer and his one-night stands have been haunting me; ever since I looked at them this morning, they have been flashing in my mind. He needs to know I'm alive, I need to tell him I love him.

The door opened into the office and without looking up, I'm listening to a voice I don't recognize. "Agent Hills, you've been in here for thirteen hours. We are the last people in the office. Everyone went to Rango, it's the hotel's bar next door. You need alcohol and a lot of it."

I hung my head back over my seat, my ass is numb. I haven't had a sip of water, food, or even a bathroom break since I got here. I know everyone has been looking in through the blinds at the crazy Basilisk girl all day. Every time someone interrupted me, I screamed at them to go away, I didn't care if it was my boss or a coworker. They wanted me and now they have me.

I sighed. "You're right." I turned around in my office chair and I'm looking at a short redhead with pale skin. If I didn't know he was an FBI agent, I would mistake him to be no more than eighteen. "Agent?"

"Johnson."

The bar is rowdy with agents from the office. As soon as I walk in, faces I recognize from this morning start whispering. This is worse than high school. I walked up to the bar and ordered a whiskey on the rocks. Damn it, Spencer; his drinking habits wore off on me. I pulled out the seat and jumped on the barstool, telling the bartender to keep them coming. I placed my elbows on the bar, holding my head in my hands, and finally started to let the tears fall down my face.

I don't care that I am crying in front of my coworkers; no one knows the hell that I am going through and if they wanted me to explain it to them, I can't, I can't find the words fucked up enough to explain this.

I wiped my face, slamming the cup on the bar. Without hesitation, the bartender came up to me, pouring into my cup. It's 8 pm on a Friday, Spencer is probably at *Willie's*, only a few blocks away from me.

Nelson walked up to me, sliding a phone in front of me. "This is your work phone, all of our numbers are programed into it." He paused. "This is a burner phone. We have already discussed Lizzy, Theo, and Max with the chief in the jurisdiction we are working with. Erik Watson's number is programed. Your friends have gotten themselves into trouble. The address they are at is in your work phone's text messages."

I never looked up at him. I glanced at my phone; moving my eyes to my drink, I picked it up and chugged it back. They need me, I can't wallow in self-pity. I jumped off the chair, freezing; the four shots of whiskey I have taken in less than ten minutes all hit me at once. Taking a deep breath, I run out the door, finding the closest cab.

The address given to me is the one apartment with drug busts and murders on a regular occasion on the news. I'm across the street watching my three best friends walking into the apartment looking like train wrecks. Lizzy would never walk out of the house looking like this, she looks like she isn't more than ninety pounds. Max and Theo have both almost lost all their muscle mass.

My hands are shaking, I still manage to pull out my burner.

"Hello." Erik's deep voice answered.

"Officer Watson?"

"Yes?"

He is the closest I have gotten to Spencer and now he is the closet I will get to my family. "I need you to go to the South Western Apartments. There is a female in a black low-cut dress, with two males in jeans and t-shirt. You will know when you see them. I don't care if you have to wait all night, get them home safely."

"Who is this?"

I pulled the phone from my ear and flipped it before he was able to say anymore and before I fucked up everything. Staring at the phone, I dialed Spencer's number. I deleted the numbers after staring at the phone for what felt like an eternity.

The wind is picking up, my dress suit isn't enough to protect me from the October weather. I pull my eyes from my phone just in time to see my best friends walking out of the apartment. I stifle a laugh in amusement watching Theo put down Lizzy onto the ground, back on her feet from his shoulder. A cruiser pulled up in perfect time; Erik stepped out and got on his knees in front of Lizzy. Watching his face light up when he laid eyes on her gave me all the comfort I needed.

I tossed the phone into the garbage beside me and walked down the road, calling a cab on my work phone. I got into Sam's apartment with all of our coworkers playing a card game with an empty bottle of bourbon in front of them. For the first time all day, I have a smile on my face, my friends are going to be okay, they just don't know it yet.

Jones walked up beside me. "I'm sorry for my comments today."

"I'm going to head to bed."

Without listening to anything else, I set my alarm for six, stripped off my clothes, and fell onto my mattress. I shouldn't be sleeping alone, I should be with him. I let out an uncontrollable loud sob knowing that Spencer isn't alone right now. He is probably with a random girl trying to forget about Cameron.

Somewhere between catching my breath and trying to breathe, I fell asleep.

"Can I look now?" Spencer has his hands over my eyes leading me into a room.

"You are the most impatient person I have ever met," he said with a laugh.

"I'm not impatient, I just spent all day at school, then at work pretending I didn't know you."

"I have to be at your work, I need to make sure guys aren't hitting on my girl."

Spencer kissed my neck and my body became weak. I leaned back into him smelling his cologne, feeling his body against mine.

He pulled me in closer to his chest with his hands still covering my eyes. "I know you have been stressed out lately, I really wish you would just let me pay for your tuition." He uncovered my eyes and back out of the bathroom, shutting the door behind him.

Rose petals are covering the floor, a bath is drawn with bubbles almost overflowing the tub, candles are alight and a new bottle of perfume is sitting on the counter. I roll my eyes, spraying some in the air. Everyone always makes fun of me because of my 'Drunk Grandma' perfume. I strip off my clothes and climb into the bathtub. I sink into the water humming. This is what I need.

"Babe, I have your pajamas." Spencer opened the door and set a pair of purple silk top and bottoms on the sink.

"Those aren't mine."

"They are now. I also replaced the pillowcases with silk, so you can stop nagging me about anti-ageing."

"Why are you doing all of this?"

Spencer shut the door behind him, leaning up against the door with his head in his hands. He is quiet.

I sat up, reaching my hand out to him. After a few moments, he grabbed it. "Spence, I love you. I love everything about you. I don't love the Basilisk in you, but that one thing doesn't change anything. I just need you, and that includes your baggage."

Spencer is looking at me with wide eyes. I have told him I loved him so many times in my head, but never out loud. Fuck, it's only been a month.

"You love me?"

"Since the first time I saw you."

Spencer ran to the bathtub, putting his arm behind my back, pulling me out of the water, and kissing me. "I love you."

I flew out of bed, my heart racing and my face soaking wet from tears. That memory felt too real. I pulled out my phone and texted Rodriguez: *I can't do this, I'm returning my badge. Meet me in my office.*

I grabbed my dress suit and put it on, running a brush through my short hair and walking out the door to find Sam waiting for me on the couch. I know my eyes are red and puffy, I don't even need to look in the mirror to see that. Sam groaned and walked into my bedroom, grabbing a small makeup bag and shoving it into my purse and making sure I saw what she was doing.

After a short, but long ride to the office, I opened my door before the car even came to a full stop, I ran to the door, flashing my badge, and walked right into Rodriguez's office, slamming my badge on the table in front of him.

"I need to go to him."

He pushed my badge back to me and I shoved it back at him. After the fifth time, I lost count of this pointless cycle.

"Damn it! Just let me be with him!"

Nelson shut the door of the office and sat in the chair next to me. "Sit down, Hills."

Out of frustration, I sat down. "Watson is still at work. Put your makeup on and clean yourself up." He slammed my makeup bag on the table. "You'll thank me later."

"What's the point?" I mumbled under my breath.

"Get your vest on, we leave in twenty."

I slammed my hands on the table, grabbing my makeup and storming down the hall, following the signs to the bathroom. My hands are shaking, my plans to quit have been a complete failure. Being extra careful to make straight lines of eyeliner, applying my mascara, cover-up, and lipstick, you would have no idea I spent all night crying in my sleep. I stormed out of the bathroom with

Sam standing at her desk putting on her vest. I put mine over my arms, fighting with the Velcro to make it tight, putting the ammo in my gun and holstering it to my hip. Sam looked at me with a smile and nodded her head for me to follow Nelson, Rodriguez, and Jones out the door.

The entire ride I have been fidgeting with my fingers in the back of the black SUV. It may as well have 'Feds' written in glow in the dark paint along the side of it. No one has said a single word since I left the office in a storm. We arrive at the police precinct; I have walked by this brick building many times before, but today it feels different. Tall windows are only a foot apart from each other, the intersection beside us is humming from the cars driving by. Today, this decade-old building feels hopeful. Everyone is looking at us, citizens, police officers. I have to admit, I'm happy they wouldn't let me quit before I got to strut my vest and gun, it feels pretty badass.

"Chief Davis," Nelson greeted the police officer waiting inside of the building.

"Right this way. He is on his way back from patrol now. He has instructions to meet me in the office." Chief Davis pushed the button on the elevator.

We got on the second floor and all heads turned to us, some police officers sank in their chairs and others looked at us wide-eyed. Davis opened the door to the conference room with a long table and chairs gathered around.

Davis sat down. "We need to cut a deal with him today. Once we get one on board, the other will follow. Mrs. Taylor has already been our eyes and ears."

My mouth dropped. "Kinsley is the reason for all of this?"

"She saw what it was doing to Liam and she immediately came to us. I got your supervisors on board and then you were shot, used you as an advantage."

Before I was able to put my thoughts together, the door of the conference room opened and Erik walked in with a puzzled look on his face. "Sir, what the hell is going on here?" Erik scanned us and my body tightened; he looked at me and opened his mouth, shaking his head.

My heart sank when I knew he recognized me. "Erik, let me explain."

"You don't get to fucking speak to me."

I caught my breath, turning around, and put my hands up to my head forcing back tears. I need to hold it together. I spun back around with everyone's eyes on me. "You know what? You don't get to fucking speak to me like that. I fell in love with a Basilisk and it almost killed me."

"It did," Sam mumbled.

I pushed out a laugh. "I'm doing this for him, for all eight of you actually."

Erik has a look of confusion and shock on his face, he hasn't taken his eyes off me. "You called me this morning. What the fuck is going on, Davis?"

Davis folded his hands on the table. "Did you call him?"

Erik looked back at me with hatred in his eyes. "I wish I didn't, but yes."

Davis filled Erik in on everything, Kinsley calling him, my involvement, his double-crossing. Erik held his hands to his head and I walked over to the water cooler, filling up a Styrofoam cup. I gave it to him and he looked down at me with apologetic eyes. I walked away, looking out the window, it's not far how I'm in the same room with Erik and not Spencer. I can't be in walking distance of his best friend and not even know where my boyfriend is. I can hear them talking, but I don't care what they are saying. All of their voices are floating around the room.

The door opened again and a voice I had been dying to hear walked in. "Erik, what the hell, man. Emily is sleeping in my bed, it's 7 am."

I gasped, putting my shaking hand to my mouth, not fighting back tears anymore.

"You might want to kick her out, Spence." Spencer never said anything. "Adam, sorry to wake you up. Get the girl out of Spencer's room now."

"Dude! What the fuck."

Still looking out the window and holding back sobs. My eyes are watering over so much I can't see straight. I broke his heart; he is going to run the other direction, he is going to be colder to me than Erik was. I can't live with myself when he hates me, I would rather have him think I'm dead. I wiped my face, hoping my waterproof makeup is true to its name.

"Brittney," Rodriguez said, knowing Spencer doesn't know my real name.

Davis quickly brought Spencer up to speed, he dragged a seat up to the table. I glanced over my shoulder, seeing my ex-boyfriend sitting at the table, staring at Davis distracted. Looking at Spencer, I can feel my heart breaking. He is so much more than I remember him. Even this early in the morning, while being half asleep, he still pulls off a suit. No other word can be used to describe him other than perfection.

Taking a step back to run to him, I freeze. I want to kiss him, but he's no longer mine to kiss. Instead, I'm quietly bolting to the door, slowly opening it and running out as fast as I can without bringing extra attention to myself.

"What are you doing?" Erik stepped in front of me, causing me to crash into him.

"I can't do this, he's better off if he thinks I'm dead."

"Turn around."

I wiped my face again, hesitantly turning my body around to face the office. Spencer is standing in the room looking at me with no emotion on his face.

"Erik, he hates me." I close my eyes, my body trembling. Not only does he know I have been lying about my name, he knows I've been lying about being dead. I pull out my badge and put it on the table next to me along with my gun from my holster. I loosen the Velcro of my vest, taking it off. "I tried, but without him, none of this is worth it. I'm sorry."

Looking up at the roof and ignoring the scene I had made and the crowd watching, I led myself to the staircase, running down. I'm between the first and second floor standing against the wall trying to catch my breath. My eyes are clouded over, turning around, facing my back to it, sliding down, putting my head on my knees, and hugging my legs.

His face is stuck in my head, I want to go home but I have nowhere to go. I can't handle my friends looking at me the same way. I can't come back from the dead twice in one day.

The smell of Spencer's cologne is hovering over me. "Jesus, Brittney." He wrapped me up in his arms, holding me to his chest.

I sniffled my nose, pushing him away from me and trying to find the words I have been wanting to say, nothing feels right. "Don't."

Spencer looked down at the ground, letting me go; my eyes let the tears fall down my face in time to watch one fall down his. "I thought you didn't love me; if I knew the truth, I would have never been with any of them."

I blinked hard; out of everything he just heard, he is more worried about sleeping with a bunch of other girls. "Babe." I shook my head in disbelief at my own words. "I'm sorry, out of habit."

Spencer pulled his eyes from the ground, raising both hands up to my face and kissing me. The way our lips melted together, it felt like no time passed us by. I opened my mouth and he slid his tongue in my mouth, kissing me genially, forgiving me.

Spencer pulled away with his hands still on my face, looking me in the eyes. "Marry me, Brittney."

This is not the way I thought this conversation was going to go. Spencer is serious, I have never seen him more serious in my life. I lean in to give him a peck on the lips. "Yes."

He grabbed the back of my hair and pulled me in for a kiss, but this time fiercer, he wasn't afraid of losing me anymore.

He pulled away with a smile. "Go get your badge. Do what you need to do to arrest Martin."

"Spence, this isn't going to be easy."

"We can manage."

Lizzy

I'm in a room that I don't recognize, filled with people I don't recognize. My brother Theo is sitting next to our best friend Max. The table is covered in dust from the cocaine, my vodka coke is half full, sitting on the table in front of me and my mind is spinning with regret. I sigh and get myself off the couch.

I have no idea where the bathroom is, I walk down the hallway that we came through when we got here and I start to open doors. The first one is a closet, the second one is a bathroom. I stumble into the second door. Max and Theo are right behind me, not taking their eyes off me. Both of the boys push past me and Theo grabs my arm, pulling me in while shutting the door behind me. We all are standing in front of the mirror with shame rushing through us. My pupils are dilated, my makeup is smeared. My natural brown wavy hair is tangled in large knots.

I can't recognize myself. I can't recognize any of us. These versions gazing back at us in the mirror aren't who we are supposed to be. The last seven months have been hell for all of us. Normally, everyone deals with grief differently, but we all turned to drugs and drinking.

This is our rock bottom.

Max grabbed the bathroom counter, putting all of his weight into his hands. "Where the fuck are we?"

I grabbed onto Max's shoulder, I watched Theo in the mirror look at me disappointed. Max pushed himself from the counter, looking at our reflection and shaking his head. I stared back at them, Max and Theo are as tall as I am. They both have buzz cuts, drops of blood on all of our shirts from wiping our noses. We are all so skinny that it is unhealthy.

They both tried to deal with their loss by joining the gym and working out whenever they started to miss Brittney. I turned them into something they should have never been. They never blamed me, but I blame myself.

Theo rubbed the back of his neck with his hand. "Let's go, we will find what street we are on and get us back home. No more fucking drugs for any of us."

I nodded with tears burning my eyes. I opened my purse and pulled out my cigarette pack. Seven months ago, none of us smoked. Seven months ago, we were a group of four. Max looked down at me and saw me putting the blame on myself. He put his hands on my cheeks then bent down, giving me a kiss on my forehead.

"None of this is your fault." Max dropped his hands, placing his hand on the arch of my back turning me out of the bathroom.

Theo is the first to reach the apartment door; he opened it and we all walked out. We all got out of the apartment as fast as we could. This building is proof we have hit our all-time low. Holes are punched in the wall, the carpet looks like it wasn't changed since the sixties. The heater made a loud banging noise when it kicked in, causing all of us to jump.

Drunk people are passed out in the hallway with bottles in their hand soaking the stained carpet. The carpet is so wet that it is leaving our footprints behind us. The hallway is filled with noises of people screaming at each other behind closed doors. A door started to open. Theo picked me up and tossed me over his shoulder as he started to run down the stairs.

Theo has all the training to be a firefighter but he stopped when I sucked them into my grieving process. I shut my eyes tight and I felt him set me on the ground outside. The cold October breeze swept through New York. I light my smoke, passing the lighter to Max.

Max exhaled a thick cloud of smoke. "Our place is fifteen blocks away."

We are all mentally exhausted. Cop cars have lights on as they fly past us. My body is shaking, I raised my hands out in front my face and cried. I collapsed down to my knees and I felt their hands on my back. No one is talking, we all share the same regret. Between my sobs, I can hear a car door shut. I moved my hands away from my face, expecting us to be killed. I'm looking at navy blue pants and black leather shoes standing in front of me, I let out another sob when I notice he is a cop.

He bent down to my level and looked at me with compassion. I know we are going to be arrested. "Do you guys need a ride home?" He sighed and scanned all of our faces.

The officer has deep ocean-blue eyes and blonde hair. He puts Theo and Max to shame with his muscle mass. I suddenly feel even more embarrassed for tonight. Looking in his eyes, I feel calm, like all the bad things from tonight have vanished.

Max is grabbing my arm to help me off the ground. The cop opens the back door for us to pile in. I slide in, looking out the window. Completely fucking embarrassed. I can hear Theo giving him our address.

Last thing I expected tonight was to get driven home in the backseat of a cop car. I'm just thankful we were going home and not to jail. Max slid in next to me, looking straight ahead. The cop slammed his driver's door shut.

Theo shut his door and started laughing. "I know I said no more drugs, but we are still drinking, right?"

"Hell yeah, we are just making better choices." Max sounded relieved.

We have been driving a while; mixed with my exhaustion and coming down from my high, I have never been this tired in my life. Ringing over the speakers filled the car and I jumped.

"Adam, I have three people in the car with me that I'm driving home." I heard a sigh from the front seat.

"No brother, nothing like that. I am just wondering if you wanted to go for lunch at White Heart today. Spence keeps going on about this hot server that works there."

I had to fight back laughter. Max and Theo couldn't hold back. I saw the cop look to the backseat, confused.

"My sister works there," Theo managed to get his words out.

Adam laughed once over the phone. "If it's her, I feel bad; he's pretty persistent."

I know exactly who Spencer is. Every single time he comes in, he makes sure to sit in my section. He always come in wearing a suit, choppy brown hair with Amber eyes. He would flash me a million dollar smile that I know has won over so many girls in the past. He is confident and never let it bother him when I shut him down.

I smiled and shook my head. "Can you tell him I'm not interested?"

Laughter broke out in the front seat and over the phone.

Adam cleared his throat. "I like you. We are definitely coming in tonight."

Max is grinning from ear to ear. "She works at six."

I woke up in bed between Max and Theo; there are only three hours until I have to go to work and I'm ready to start a new day and start changing our habits. I'm ready to push the reset button. I am not addicted to drugs, but I'm worried about the guys. They have a harder time saying no. As much as they say they hate them, I'm wondering if they can stop. One thing is for certain, we hate the regret, but when the regret mixed with grief became too much to handle, it is an easy way to shut it out.

Never-ending fucking cycle.

I pushed and wiggled myself to get out of bed between the two of them. Even in my king-sized bed, they both lay on top of me and were crushing me. It's been like this since the third grade. Theo is two years older than me, Max and I are both twenty-four. Theo and Max were originally best friends to start with, they met in football when they were younger. Theo and I have been tied to the hip since I was born; it was pretty clear that we were always going to be best friends.

I walked out of the bedroom, twisting the knob on my bedroom door, making sure it never clicked when the door met the frame. I took a deep breath and looked around the apartment; pictures of Britney hanging on the walls. Pictures of the four of us scattered throughout our apartment.

It's like she's still here. I can feel a tear rush down my face. She would be so disappointed in all of us.

I reached out on the shelf, picking up her picture. Her light green eyes, blonde shoulder-length hair. I raised my hand to my mouth, trying to cover up my laughter. I can still hear her freaking out when she saw that I had framed this picture of her. She despised this haircut. I put the picture to my chest and sighed.

"Brittney, if you can hear me, I'm sorry. I'm so fucking sorry. We will smarten up, I promise."

The bedroom door quietly opened. "Lizzy, go get ready for work. I will drive you." Max paused. "I honestly believe we never ended up in jail because she was watching over us. We fucked up bad, we have been every single day since she was killed."

I got into the bathroom, reaching under the sink and grabbing my make-up bag; I hate working at a bar. Doing my makeup perfectly every night. Wearing clothes that show off my boobs and ass forty hours a week. I have a bachelor's degree in education, but I haven't been trying to get a job. I couldn't dare look at children with the life I have been living.

I shook every bad emotion out of my body and started layering on my makeup. Saturday night means tips. To get more tips means I have to look good and flirt. After a year and a half of experimenting, I found I made the most when I wore pink lipstick, blush, eyeshadow, eyeliner, and a lot of mascara. I put my oversized black glasses on and ran a brush through my hair.

I walked out of the bathroom and saw the guys sitting on the couch drinking coffee. I wandered over to my bedroom and slipped into my work uniform. The low-cut V and my push-up bra makes an uncomfortable welcome for eyes to linger. I slipped on my shorts and walked straight to the coffeemaker and poured myself a cup, instantly regretting already having my lipstick done. Both Max and Theo turned around and glanced at me over the couch, both rolling their eyes.

"We are hanging around tonight," Theo mumbled.

"You don't need to babysit me," I snapped.

They have both been getting in fights on a regular basis since I was in the ninth grade, when they realized guys started looking at me. There's protective and there's overprotective. They are both extremely overprotective.

I can't stand looking around and seeing Brittney in our apartment. I raise my coffee up to my mouth and take a long drink. She is everywhere, no wonder we haven't been able to heal. All four of us lived in this apartment together, now it is just the three of us. Her room is even as she left it. We are waiting for someone to come back that will never show. I take another sip and set down my cup, walking to the hallway closet and pulling out a bin. I walk to the living room wall, taking a shaky breath and starting to load up the bin with her pictures.

"What are you doing?" Max's voice is low and broken.

"We can't expect to make changes in our life when she is everywhere. I'm not taking them all down."

Max and Theo both shook their head and stood at opposite sides of the apartment , staring at the pictures. I can see the hesitation they have, but they both started taking a few down. Leaving the ones up with the best memories and that had the four of us in them.

Theo gently set our memories in the bin. "I swear, I am going to find who killed her and kill them."

Max and I exchange a worried look and I hang my head. I know Theo is telling the truth. We both know he is serious. Max filled the bin and I let out a sob as I put the lid on it. I picked up the bin, fighting back tears, put it back in the closet and shut the door.

Theo wrapped his arms around me and whispered, "We already know the group who did it, it's just figuring out who did it."

Max turned to the wall and punched it. "Enough Theo! You are going to get yourself killed. You are going to cause more pain to your sister and me. Fuck you."

Max stormed past us, grabbing his keys from the end table, walking out the front door and leaving it wide open for us to follow him. We are around each other all the time; we fight multiple times a week, but we are never mad at each other for longer than needed. We have never held grudges. We have said things to each other that we never should have, we never forget what was said, but we always forgive each other.

Theo hangs his head, disappointed. He knows he couldn't avenge Brittney and it kills him. He waved his hands for me to walk out the door, pulled out his keys, and locked the apartment. Max pushed the button on the elevator, he is tapping his hand on his jeans, full of regret. He looks up at Theo and punches his arm with a smile on his face.

We pull up to the White Heart and get out of the car. The entrance is flooded with smokers standing outside. I step out of the backseat, bending over to grab my purse when I hear whistling behind me. I opened my smoke pack and saw Max starting to walk around the car so he can launch himself towards the group of drunk guys outside the door. Thankfully, Theo pulls him back. I tossed the pack on the roof for my vultures to grab a cigarette.

Theo started laughing as he looked at the parking lot. "No fucking way."

I looked up and felt a smile on my face. The cop from last night jumped out of a car with two other guys and Spencer. I tried to remember him from last night, but the only thing I can remember are his eyes. He's walking in our direction in jeans, a half-zipped hoodie with his sleeves pulled up his arms; from what I can see he is covered in colorful tattoos. I never noticed that last night.

"Holy fucking shit." I meant to say that under my breath but it came out louder than I expected.

The sight of him instantly turned me on. My thighs are numb and I feel myself breathing harder. There is something else about him. I feel like I already know him, I feel like I am already comfortable around him. I can't explain it, this man is really familiar to me.

I've been staring too long because the blonde next to him nudges his arm and nods in my direction. I instantly turn around and put my back against the car.

I saw Max standing beside me from the corner of my eye. "Brittney definitely sent him." He started laughing.

My alarm on my phone went off, telling me that it was time to head in. I started walking in with Theo and Max close behind. I hated how they always think I needed bodyguards. They know it drives me crazy, I think that's why they do it.

The White Heart is packed. It was a month into school so all the college kids had enough time to start making friends and started to go out for drinks. I walked right towards the bar and asked for a shot of tequila. We aren't allowed to drink on the job, but everyone does it. As long as the owners don't find out, we are fine.

I slammed it back, letting the tequila slide down my throat. I hated the burn, but I needed something if I wanted to survive this Saturday night. I slammed down the shot glass on the bar. "Samantha, give me another half." She is hesitant, but she does it anyways. I put the shot glass to my mouth and drink it.

Walking to the back room to hang my purse and inspecting my makeup in the mirror, I touched up my lipstick, tied my apron behind my back, and slid my notepad and pen in.

"Lizzy! Section two!" my manager called from the office.

"Lizzy! Spencer found out what section you're in!" Walter, our bouncer came in the back room with a smile.

I can't figure out how he is a bouncer. He is only 5'8", the same height as me and not much muscle. He must have a hard punch, or he's a dick and I haven't witnessed it yet.

I rolled my eyes and walked to section two. It was my regular section, it had the largest tables. It was in the center of the room so my brother appreciated it when he felt the need to treat me like a child.

I looked around the section and the only table that wasn't taken care of had Spencer sitting at it. I rolled my eyes, but then I felt a bit jittery when I remembered *he* was with him. The closer I got to the table, I noticed Spencer wasn't dressed up in his suit. I saw Max and Theo walk up to the table, I started to walk faster to stop them in case they said anything stupid.

"Thanks for last night." I shouldn't have overreacted. I knew Theo wasn't going to be stupid.

I got to the table and saw Spencer sitting at the end of the booth, I playfully shoved him. "What, you're not dressing up today?"

He turned his head towards me, batting his eyelashes. "You disappointed?"

"Fuck no, you look better casual. What are you guys drinking?"

In unison, they all said whiskey neat, they definitely hung out together way too much.

I walked up to the till, ringing in the drinks. I grabbed a tray and started tapping it with my fingernails, suddenly really nervous. I walked back to the till and punched in another drink for myself and hit the cash button, printing off the receipt. The four neat whiskeys were placed in front of me, followed by my shot of tequila. I really shouldn't have been having another one, but I feel a wave of emotion today. I try not to make up excuses but right now, after packing up her memories, I need another shot. Maybe another four by the time I'm off.

I set down the cups in front of them. The brunette sitting next to Spencer looked at the shot, confused.

"Shit, she's drinking on the job." He put his elbows on the table and rested in head in his hands. "I'm Josh." His smile was practiced, just like Spencer's. I started to wonder how much that really works for them.

The cop from last night looked at me, smiling; he raised his cup. I put the shot glass to my lips, preparing myself for the burn. I felt it slide down my throat. I pulled it away, squinting my eyes and shaking my head.

Spencer looked at me and the cop, confused. "How do you know each other?"

I shrugged. "He gave us a ride home last night." I twisted my head and looked at the cop. "I'm covering your first drink, just to say thanks."

Josh was about to open his mouth to talk but a bunch of college kids came in and sat in my section. I never even had to look up; the sound of their voices was enough for me to picture their gelled hair and preppy clothes. The group of guys who came in were from a frat, they have been causing me shit for the last year and a half. It isn't just when school is in, they are all from New York. Unfortunately, I get them all summer too. There have been multiple times they have been hit by either Max or Theo due to them putting their hands up my shorts. I suddenly felt relieved that they decided to babysit me.

"Not this shit again," I mumbled under my breath as I stepped away from their table.

I dropped my shot glass at the bar and gave myself a pep talk as I walked to the table.

"Hey." I learnt to stay a few feet away from the table. I could see that they had all drunk before arriving.

"You get hotter every time I come here!" He is slurring his words. I don't care enough to remember their names.

I knew what was going to happen before I even walked up to them. I had finished my third year of college before I applied here; I was hoping I would be done with the college boy bullshit.

I can see him trying to stumble out of the booth; I started to back away so I could either grab my manager or Walter. Somehow, he managed to move fast enough, his face is inches away from me with both hands planted on my ass. He put his mouth by my ear. I shut my eyes trying to ignore him, but his breathing down my neck is making me uncomfortable. My body jolted forward, two hands are holding each of my arms back. I feel like a tug-of-war rope. I can hear someone hit the floor and few of the group of frat boys started laughing. I opened my eyes, confused; everything happened so fast. Max and Theo dropped their hands from my arms and I saw the off-duty police officer shaking his hand off and walking back to the table.

Damn, I really need to learn his name.

The manager rushed out of her office and sighed. "Damn it, Watson! I can't even kick you out!"

"What the fuck just happened?" Max's face was blank as he watched Watson sit back in the booth like nothing happened.

I stormed up to the booth, shaking my head. "How did you not get kicked out? Why is a cop punching people?"

Watson looked up at me, smiling. "My parents are the owners. They would be disappointed you're drinking on the job."

My stomach sank. All of us knew they were going to find out eventually.

"Jesus Erik. Don't scare her." The blond next to him is shaking his head.

"Go get us all another drink and a shot for yourself." Erik squeezed my hand.

The one nice thing about working here is that we are extremely over-staffed. If something happens to one of us, we get to go home and it never turns into a fight. The owners make it very clear that no one is going to be at work if they are feeling overwhelmed. I have never met them, but that made me respect them. I leaned up against the wall and took a deep breath, I really need the tips, but I shouldn't have come in after packing up Brittney's pictures. I grabbed my purse from the hook, shoved my apron in it, and walked to the bar.

I rang in four more neat whiskeys and another shot. I quickly cashed out and dropped the money I owed into the office. I can feel the alcohol starting to hit me and I am loving it; knowing I made Brittney a promise not to turn to drugs, I can feel a boulder lift off my shoulders. For the first time in a long time, I felt a rush of happiness. I started smiling and I can't stop.

I set the cups on the table, still smiling. "I don't know how you guys drink this so casually."

Erik looked at my purse and frowned. "You're leaving?"

"Your parents have a rule where we don't have to stay if we don't feel up to it. What you saved me from happens more than I would like to admit."

"I'll pay so you can leave."

I shook my head and slammed my shot back. I turned away from the table to spare myself of the awful face I was going to make and dropped off my shot glass. I can feel my gums going numb, the tequila is hitting me faster than I thought it would have. I pulled out my smoke pack and turned around.

Erik is standing in front of me. I raised my head so I could look at him. He grabbed my hand and slipped a napkin in it. I looked down and saw his number.

I sighed. "I don't know if that's a good idea. I keep putting up red flags."

Erik smiled, looking at me amused. "Just call me, damn it." He walked away then stopped, turning back to me. "Actually, do you want a ride home? I know where you live." He is smiling at me, full of mischief.

Before I was able to respond, Max and Theo are standing beside us. Theo is playing the big brother act with his arms crossed, trying to look intimidating, but Erik is so taller and stronger.

Max pushed me forward, not knowing how much I had to drink; he put his arm out in front of me to catch me from falling. "Jesus Lizzy! You're at work!"

He laughed and looked at Erik. "You should have seen her when she saw you walk out of your car. It looked like she was about to rip your clothes off."

I put my head down in my hands, embarrassed. I walked through the three of them and stepped outside to finally have my smoke. I got outside and walked back to the car, shivering so I can grab a lighter. I was in such a rush to get out of the apartment, I never put on any extra layers to ward off the brisk air. I light my smoke, watching the clouds leaving my mouth, they are thicker mixed with the cold. Erik came outside and saw me shivering, he took off his sweater and held it out for me to grab. His arms are covered in tattoos, there isn't an inch of skin that isn't inked.

I took his sweater, held my smoke between my lips and pushed out a laugh. It is hanging off me down to my knees. He nodded towards his car; without hesitating, I followed him. If it was anyone else, I would have thought about it first. I feel way too comfortable around him.

I got in his car and Erik cranked the heat; to my surprise, he opened his console and pulled out a smoke. I glanced at him from the corner of my eye, hoping he was taking what Max said as a joke.

"I feel bad you just left your friends inside," I said.

Erik snatched the lighter from my hand. "They will be fine." He hesitated. "I'm sorry to ask this, but what was with this morning?"

I glanced around the car, looking anywhere but at him. We are still parked so I couldn't pretend to doze off. "Rock bottom." I shook my head and looked at Erik who was sitting there gazing at me. "We all hit rock bottom, it was a temporary fix that got out of hand."

Theo and Max drove out of the parking lot, staring at us as they slowly drove past. Max is laughing as he is driving past more slowly than necessary.

He sighed. "You don't even know how much I relate to that. My brother Adam, the one that was sitting next to me. We both went through a tough spot. I was sixteen, my best friend April pulled me out of it. When Adam was sixteen, I pulled him out of it."

I exhaled and let out all of the air that I was unaware my lungs were holding. "Now look at you."

"It's not that great, believe me."

"I have tomorrow off, do you want to come and have a few drinks with me? Max and Theo are heading home to wait and see if I make it back alive."

I unfolded the napkin and put his number into my phone. I looked at Erik from the corner of my eye, he was texting someone. His phone rang and looked at me, smiling.

"Now you have my number."

"Adam's coming out. He will pick me up later so I don't leave my car stranded."

I looked over and Adam was walking towards us. I unclipped my seatbelt and jumped in the backseat.

We got to the apartment with a fifth of whiskey; as I expected, the door was unlocked with Theo and Max sitting on the couch with their feet up on the end table. Adam drove Erik's car home; whenever he's ready to leave, his brother is on call. I tried to get him to stay, but he got called away by Josh. Max and Theo looked up and their eyes got wide.

Max walked up to Erik and took the bottle away, smiling. "I thought it was just a ride."

I'm trying so hard not to look at Erik, he drives me insane. The way he holds himself, his confidence that radiates off him, his muscles... I could go on forever.

I pointed to the couch for him to sit and I walked into the bedroom to finally get my work uniform off my body. I slipped on sweat pants and a tank top, probably the most unattractive thing. I know I am drinking and I have to limit myself, the only thing I can think about is him in my bed and I can't let that happen.

I stepped out of my room and shivered; my apartment is nothing nice, I live in Manhattan on a server's wage, I hated having people over. It's better than the place we ended up last night, but not by much.

"The walls look so bare." Theo reached out his hand for the cup from Max.

"We can put the pictures back up. I just thought it would help." I sat on the floor, leaning against the couch.

"No Lizzy. It just feels like we abandoned her. If we keep having a cop around, at least we will be safe from drugs."

"Shut up, Max."

"I take it someone died?" Erik is smart, but I think we made it pretty obvious.

I feel the guys watching me. "Yeah, Brittney. She was the fourth in our group."

I pushed myself off the floor and walked to the wall, grabbing a picture of us when we all had our first legal New Year's.

Erik took the picture from me and glanced at it, looking up at all of us. "What are your memories from this night?"

Theo, Max, and I started laughing. We talked about that night in great detail. We started to reminisce about Theo kissing her, thinking she was someone else and the face she made when she realized it was him. The three of us started laughing so hard tears were running down our faces.

The rest of the night was happy, we all felt a little bit of peace that we have been missing.

"I really hate to bail, but Courtney is blowing up my phone."

"I have to go too." Theo wrapped his arms around my neck, whispering, "We will be okay. No more stupid decisions."

Erik groaned when he looked down at his phone. "My brother's here."

I stood up and walked him to the front door. He put his hand on the door handle to leave, it feels like I lost control of my body, I need him. I got on my tippy toes and tugged on his shirt as soon as he looked down at me; I kissed him with everything I have. I can feel his body tense up, I started pulling away, I had made a mistake.

I pulled my lips away from his, right when he put his hands on my hips and with one sudden tug, he is pulling me into his body. I can feel the warmth of his tongue inside my mouth, I slid my tongue into his mouth and I can feel his arms holding me tighter. It feels like time is frozen, my nerves start screaming for him. I pull away with my eyes open, watching him.

He slowly opened his deep blue eyes, gazing at me. "Come back."

As soon as the words slipped out of his mouth, I slammed my lips against his. A rush of adrenaline passed through my body, Erik is holding me close though to his body, I could feel he wants me as much as I want him.

His phone started ringing, interrupting our moment. I pulled my lips away, resting my forehead against his cheek. I can feel him breathing deep. "Your brother is getting impatient, you better go."

"I'm going to kick his ass."

"You felt that too, right?" I pulled my face away from his, watching a smile spread across his face.

"I'm coming over tomorrow with breakfast. Text me what you want."

I nodded and stepped back from him. He grabbed the back of my head and planted another small kiss on my lips.

"Damn right I felt that. I'll be back in the morning."

I shut the door behind him, staring at the floor and leaning against the wall, smiling. I looked up from the floor and saw Max and Theo standing there with their mouths open. I forgot they were still in the apartment.

"He just violated my baby sister right in front of me." Theo stuck his hand in the air, pointing at the door.

I rolled my eyes and walked to the bedroom. "I'm going to bed, goodnight."

Max burst out in laughter. "I bet you are."

I heard Theo's hand hit Max then I heard some something get knocked over, but I didn't care. Tonight, I met Erik. I got undressed and jumped on my bed under the covers.

Maybe Brittney is right, maybe love at first sight is real. One thing is for certain, Erik is going to break my heart.

"Thank you for watching out for us, Britt."

Lizzy

For the first time in a long time, I fell asleep without lying in bed for hours. The sun was pouring through my thin curtains and my phone was ringing. I tried to ignore it, but it won't stop ringing.

"Hello." I can hear my raspy voice, I had to force out my words.

A laugh is erupting into my ear; realizing its Erik, I shot up into a sitting position and buried my face in my hand. "Good morning, sleepyhead. Can I still come over?"

"Yes! If you are still stopping, I want pancakes."

"I'll be there in an hour."

I got out of bed as fast as I could and dug in my closet for clothes. I have an hour to get ready, enough time for me to look the best I can. I am tossing clothes in the air, trying to find my jeans and the nicest shirt I can find. I only buy from thrift stores, so everything I own is worn down and obviously used. I don't know how he makes me so flustered; guys don't do this to me. No one has ever done this to me. I don't even know him and he makes me so unbelievably happy. I found my ripped skinny jeans at the bottom of my laundry pile that is never going to be hung up. I put my jeans on and saw a basic black short-sleeved t-shirt lying on the floor and a black lacy bra beside it. I bent over, picked them up, and put my bra on.

My heart is beating out of my chest, my stomach is twisting in knots from excitement.

I hope Erik is feeling the same thing that I am.

I am slipping the shirt over my head while walking out to the kitchen to start a pot of coffee. As much as I hate to admit it, I need to make everything perfect today. I get the coffee started and run to the bathroom, tossing my makeup on the counter.

By the time I was done with my makeup, there was a knock on the door. I shoved everything under the sink and ran to the door, taking a deep breath as I turned the doorknob. I saw him standing there, holding the bags up with a smile on his face.

God, he is the most beautiful guy I have ever seen.

I grabbed the bags from him and brought them to the couch, I can feel my heart pounding. I wasn't even trying but I can feel sexual tension, the kiss from last night is replaying in my mind. I can't think of anything else. I glanced up, watching him open his food and smiling; he sat down on the other side of the couch. That smile on his face is all the clarification I need. Erik is thinking the same thing I am.

I reached over to the table and picked up the remote, turning on the TV. I tossed it to him. I hate being the one to pick what we watch. With my luck, there is a *Friends* marathon on. He instantly turned it on without hesitating. I let out a small laugh; he looked at me and shrugged.

He keeps becoming more perfect. Scares the hell out of me.

The episode finished and we both set down the empty to-go containers.

"Shit, I made coffee; do you want some?"

"Thank god, I forgot to stop. I was in a rush to come here."

I turned my head towards Erik; he had accidentally slipped out the words; he closed his eyes and slowly opened them. I stood up and reached my hand down, pulling him up by his hand; as soon as I touched him, my entire body became electrified. I felt him grab my arm and pull me onto his lap. We made eye contact and I saw nothing but determination. I put my hand on his chest; he slowly raised his hand up my arm and put his hand in my hair.

I can feel my heart beating out of my chest, the way he's looking at me says that he feels the same way. I moved my face closer to him and kissed him. He let out a sigh and kissed me back. I opened my mouth and slid my tongue in his, he wrapped his arms around me, making me feel safer than I ever have. I am melting into him.

Seconds passed us by, but neither of us cared. To us, time was frozen, I felt his jeans rise and I let out a moan.

I froze and pulled away. As much as I wanted to bring him to bed, I had to try to resist it. He loosened up his arms with a smile spread across his face.

"How about we go get that coffee?" I started to lean in to give him another kiss but Erik leaned in faster to seal our lips.

I pushed my hands on his rock-hard abs to get myself off the couch. I need to take a leap of faith. I put my hand on his and he readjusted it so our fingers interlaced.

The day is flying by, we sat on the couch and cuddled, watching reruns; we started kissing when the commercials came on to pass them by.

A commercial came on; my head is laying on his chest, I felt his chest vibrate from his deep voice. "I need to know everything about you."

I instantly smiled and flopped over on my stomach, resting my arms on his legs and propping my torso up so I could see him. Erik is resting his back on the arm of the couch while running his fingers though my hair. "What do you want to know?" He started to smile and moved his lips to the side of his mouth, pondering what to ask. I let out a laugh. "Well, you already know where I work."

"I know I just met you, but I seriously hate you working there."

I shrugged. "I am barely getting by as it is, I make good tips. It's not worth what I deal with, but it's what I have to do."

We sat on the couch for hours while he ran his fingers through my hair, while answering my questions. He's twenty-six. Has a group of eight people, his brother is in love with their best friend's girlfriend and it kills Erik to see him in so much pain. He's been a cop for five years under his dad's command. Every time he spoke, I fell harder for him. I can see how much he cares about everyone, how gentle he is considering his intimidating appearance.

I can feel my heart pounding. My breathing started to get heavy, I felt a small laugh leave his lips. He started to stand so I pushed myself off him and sat on the couch cushion.

"You're killing me." Erik is bending down closer to me.

Before I could respond, he picked me up off the couch, I wrapped my legs around him and he started to kiss me. This kiss wasn't like our others, it was full of passion.

My messy room ran through my mind and I separated our mouths. "My room is a disaster."

Erik shot up his eyebrows. "We don't have to do anything. I just want to be with you. If that's what you want, I will not argue with you."

I nodded and slammed my mouth into his. He is able to hold me against him with my legs wrapped around his waist without any struggle. He moved his hands and set me on the floor without separating our lips. He reached down for my hand and slowly pulled away.

I started to turn around, dragging him behind me towards my bedroom. Every step I take, I start to hesitate. I have a history of falling too fast, I know I'm going to become addicted to him after this. I can already start to feel him breaking my heart. I felt him let go of my hand and touch my hips to stop in the tracks.

He moved his hands around my waist as he walked in front of me. "I'm going to regret saying this once I go home. This doesn't have to happen." He bent down and gave me another quick kiss. "Lizzy, I like you, I don't want us to move too fast."

I never had to have sex with him to fall too hard for him, I already did. He had already made his way into my heart in less than thirty-six hours. I ignored all the future pain and pushed him towards the bedroom. "I want this."

He put his arms around my body and started kissing me. I fought against his tight grasp and started to unbutton his jeans, Erik let me fully out of his grasp and pulled my shirt above my head, he unsnapped my bra, I took my arms out of the straps and took off his shirt. His chest was covered in tattoos. The exposed artwork made me so much more attracted to him. I looked down and my breath was cut off, his muscles were so defined.

I unsnapped my jeans, giving him one last push into the bedroom. I let my jeans and panties fall to the ground, I glanced up at him and he is focusing on my face. I placed my hand on his chest, giving him another kiss; as I pulled my mouth from his; I gently bit his bottom lip, I can feel him fighting through his loose zipper. Erik never broke his focus. I felt his hands on my bare back, pulling me into him. He picked me up and placed me on my bed.

He took off his jeans and boxers, I can't stop staring at him. He got on his knees on the bed, crawling towards me. I can feel Erik running his fingers over the inside of my legs, kissing me from my knee up.

I let out a moan, this was better than I ever thought possible and we haven't even started yet. He got closer to the sensitive part of my body and I grabbed onto the sheets that are covering my bed, preparing myself. He started kissing and a moan left my lips.

I opened my eyes and saw him sitting back up, smiling and shaking his head. The bed squeaked as he pushed himself off the mattress. I watched him walk over to his jeans, his back flexing with every step. I'm watching him rip open the condom package with his teeth; as soon as he got it on, he came rushing over to me.

I sat up to kiss Erik one more time, he put his hands on my cheeks kissing me back as he slowly lay me down. He made his way into me and I let out a moan.

"Holy fuck," Erik moaned.

He is trying to be gentle, but we are both too excited. He starts to speed up; the faster he is thrusting, the more I start moaning. Beads of sweat come rushing down his body; the more he sweats, the easier it is for him to move against me.

I let out a scream as he started to work harder. He grunted and put both of his forearms on the side of my face as I felt him quiver against me.

Erik moved off me and tossed the condom in the garbage next to my bed. He lay beside me and put his arm around me, pulling my face into his chest. I inhaled and the smell of his cologne mixed with my perfume became my favorite scent.

He kissed my hair without pulling away. "That was incredible. I have to do something, I want you to come with me."

"What do you have to do?"

"I just need to make a stop, but I don't want to leave you."

I felt him stand up, he grabbed my hands to pull me off the bed. "I need a smoke." I put my arm over his shoulders, hooking his neck and pulling him down for another kiss. "You may have gotten me hooked."

Erik let out a laugh as he tossed me my clothes. "That may have been my plan."

We both got dressed and walked out of the apartment hand in hand. I pulled out my cigarette pack from my purse as he threw his arm around my shoulder, kissing me on the head, I felt his lips touch my hair and I melted into him. His car is parked on the street; before I was able to reach for my door handle, he opened the passenger door for me.

Never once in my life did I ever think I was going to have a guy open a car door for me. I can feel my heart doing somersaults in my chest. He is absolutely perfect.

I light my smoke; as soon as Erik buckles up his seatbelt, he grabs my hand and kisses it.

"Where are you taking me?" I asked. Normally, I would have been nervous, but I feel so protected with him.

"Josh was blowing up my phone before that happened. They want us to go for a drink and I have a surprise for you."

"I hate surprises."

"I feel like you won't mind this one."

The drive isn't long, Manhattan is huge and the traffic is ridiculous. I don't even know why I own a car in this city. Erik is sitting in the driver's seat with a smile on his face that hasn't disappeared since we got in the car.

We got out of the car and parked in front of a bar called *Willie's*. Erik held the door open and I walked past him; he grabbed my hand and followed me in.

"Erik!" A girl with perfect brown hair came rushing up to him, giving him a huge hug. She is breathtaking. Her brown hair is placed perfectly on her head, she is only a few inches taller than me, her eyes are emerald green.

She put her hands on his arms and got a sparkle in her eye. The way she looks at him makes me feel jealous; I can feel myself becoming more stressed the longer she is standing close to him.

Why the hell am I feeling like this? I barely even know him.

Erik looked at me and kissed my hair; with his gesture, all of my jealousy washed away.

"Oh, you're jealous," he whispered. "You're fucking adorable." He kissed me and put his arm around my shoulders, looking at the girl.

"I'm April."

April is his best friend. I exhaled and put my head on his chest.

Erik started rubbing my arm. "Lizzy, I can't have you working at White Heart anymore. I am going to be knocking way too many people out."

April's eyes bounced back and forth between us and she started to smile. "Come work here. Don't put it past him, he will do it."

"I can't just come work here." Hesitation is thick in my voice.

"I'm the manager, I can have you come in tomorrow at three for training, if you want."

Erik backed away from me, turning me so he could look me in the eyes. "Please, my mom picked out the worst outfits for the servers and I would rather not have everyone in New York know what my girlfriend's ass looks like."

Erik's eyes went wide and full of worry. My breathing cut off. He never meant to say that, but I kind of liked it.

Okay, I loved hearing it. Even though it hasn't even been forty-eight hours.

The longer I went without talking, I could see Erik panicking even more. I tugged on his shirt and stood on the toes of my flats, kissing him.

I took a deep breath. "I would rather not have my boyfriend get shot when he's at work because he's distracted." I winked and Erik relaxed.

"I'm going to get us a drink." The further I got into the bar, the smell of hot wings and citrus garnishes filled the air.

Erik called out behind me, "Don't pay, tell them you are with the Taylors."

I got up to the bar and ordered an Old Fashioned neat whiskey. I felt a set of hands on my shoulders and I jumped. I swung my body around and saw Spencer standing there with a big smile on his face. I shook my head, glaring at him. This was the second day I have seen him where he was wearing regular clothes.

"No suit again, what's up with that?" I pushed out a laugh, facing the bar.

He rolled his eyes and raised his hand at the bartender. "Did you say yes to the job?"

"Did everyone know about that?"

"Just who's here. I'm warning you now if Liam, Dillon, or William come in, they are dicks to April. Ignore it."

April came up behind us, causing me to jump, again. "It's because they are related to me. You better not be hungover for tomorrow."

I raised my drink to my mouth, taking a small sip. "I won't be, I can't stay long."

Spencer laughed; he is staring at my drink with a smile slowly stretching across his face. "If the four of us aren't here, the other four will be. Erik would kick our asses if we didn't watch you."

Spencer nodded towards the table, I followed him with an unrealizable sense of joy. Everything finally is starting to feel like the pieces are lining up.

Charlie

We have been driving for hours. I don't know where the hell we are. All I know is if we are going this far out of the city, Martin has us dealing with some pretty serious shit. We are on a back road with trees surrounding us, I can hear train horns off in the distance, I know we are near rails. My mind has been racing this entire drive. Not only am I starting to panic about the buyers, but I'm also starting to think Liam is going to miss sleeping around. I don't know if he has it in him to be a one-woman guy.

I sighed. "Do you ever miss being single? If we never started dating, what would you be doing?"

Liam grabbed my hand, not taking his eyes off the road. "I don't miss being single, coming home to you is an incredible feeling. I can't stand to think of where we would be. I know Adam would have come and swept you off your feet."

Liam started to slow down his car when Adam's car came into our line of sight. "We are handling a lot today. I don't know why I was ordered to bring you."

I squeezed his hand. "What are we dealing with?"

"A drug cartel out of LA. They are buying over a million dollars' worth of semi-automatics."

We got out of the vehicle and walked over to the guys. Josh, Spencer, Noah, and Adam were unloading the crate from the train's car. We are walking up to the train, I am sticking my loaded gun in the back of my jeans. I am trying to keep my breathing light and calm, but my nerves are taking over.

Adam walked in front of us. "I am going to do the talking. You four stand behind me and Liam. Watch their body signals. Keep an eye out for anything that could go wrong. These guys are monsters."

A group of men are approaching us. I would rather be standing in the line of fire than standing here.

The man in the front is scanning all of us down. "We won't take much of your time."

A shorter man picked up a crowbar and opened the crate. He moved his arm just enough for a lion tattoo to show on his wrist. I remember seeing this tattoo on the news.

McKinnon's. Monsters was one way to put their family.

Adam and Liam shot each other an annoyed look. "So, are they good or not?" Adam asked him. I know he is scared, but his voice hid everything. Adam is made from stone.

"1.3 million?" The lead man is only standing inches away from Adam.

We are standing head to head with McKinnon's. To many alpha males are waiting for a fight. Finally, they pass envelopes to Liam. We all relax our bodies.

"Nice doing business with you." He signaled to his men to start loading up the crate.

We all grouped together, walking back to the vehicles. I can hear all of us exhale a deep breath of air at the same time.

"We need to stop dealing with them. They are wildcards. One of us could have moved slightly and we would all be dead," Josh said, annoyed.

I looked at the ground. "We can say we just came across the biggest drug cartel and survived. I have never seen them in person before, but the stories I heard are terrifying."

"Come on, babe. Let's get back to our day." Liam opened his driver's door.

I looked down at my ringing phone and flashed him the lit-up screen with Martin's name. "Maybe not."

I'm standing in front of my full length mirror examining my clothing and running through the plans for tonight. Thankfully, I had Violet's help getting ready, she picked out a long black dress with a jewel neckline and made me look six years older with the amount of makeup that is on my face. I relaxed my hand, opening my fist; three bullets are looking back at me with the names Dave, Ben, and Eli engraved on them. I grabbed my purse, shoving the bullets in. I set it back down and picked up a black shawl, carefully using it to cover up the scars from getting shot.

"This will definitely get you into that bar tonight. You look the part," Violet said with a smile.

We all decided it was best if I went alone. This is probably the easiest job I am ever going to have to do, but that isn't stopping me from being nervous. Luckily for me, over the past few weeks, I have been able to disguise my uneasy emotions and come off as my confident self. I caught a cab and headed to the Upper West Side. This was no doubt the longest and most expensive cab ride I have ever had. There was an underground club that only the rich attended. Somehow, these three men that had pissed off Martin are regular attendees.

The cab stopped and I got out. When I heard underground, I was imagining a sketchy club with a dark staircase leading downstairs. Outside are young and middle-aged people dressed in tuxedos and long elegant dresses. Normally, I am overdressed, but I feel so underdressed for this event. Compared to earlier in the day, this is nothing.

"Name." A large bouncer is at the door. I was about to open my mouth, but he cut me off. "Oh, never mind, young lady, please come in." I smiled in the most elegant way I could and added a small curtsey.

As soon as I walked into the room, I started scanning the people around me. A few people are looking at me, they know I don't belong here. It's not hard to pick people out in a crowd who don't live in the same universe you do. These are the classiest people I have ever seen in my life. In the back room, there is a table with three men and three women sitting at. Around the table is a red velvet rope. It isn't hard to notice a group of tattooed stocky men that are out of place, but they look so comfortable on their reserved table.

I reached into my handbag and grabbed the three bullets. I held my head up high as I walked over. I stood at the other side of the rope. "Hey, boys." I glanced down at my hand to make sure I had the night one. "Eli?" He looked at me and nodded. I tossed him the bullet. I glanced down again, tossing the other two. "Dave?" He looked at me with his mouth open and putting the tip of his tongue on his tooth. "Oh, don't worry, Ben, there's one for you here too! I'll see you three again very soon."

I started to back up, I turned around as fast as my heels would let me, dodging the crowd of people. I can hear them get up from the table and shouting for people to move out of the way. I'm managing to fight through the crowd and get out of the building before they can catch up to me. I ran around to the side of the building towards an alley, peeking my head around and watching them. All three of them are looking around; when they didn't see me, they all made a call, staring at their personalized bullets.

I walked down the alley. I stopped to take my heels off, a transit bus is coming in my direction. The bus stop is just across the street and I need to get out of this location. Thankfully, I made it to the stop with enough time to get my heels back on, protecting my feet from the cold sidewalk.

I opened the door and kicked off my heels. "Can someone please tell me why we live in a condo and not a house?"

Dillon spoke up, not taking his eyes from GTA, "I was just talking about this today. I saw a house a few blocks away."

"With what we do, we really shouldn't be living around so many people."

"We made it soundproof. But I agree. Let's go look at it tomorrow if we can."

"Where's my boyfriend?"

"They had to go meet with a seller."

"Another one!" I sighed. "We dealt with the McKinnon's today. $1.3 million in semi-automatics."

Dillon pushed pause and scoffed. "Why the hell did my father bring machine guns into America?"

I shrugged. "Liam told me today that if we weren't together, Adam would be trying to be with me."

Dillon laughed and started playing his game. "He is waiting for Liam to screw up."

Lizzy

Willie's is packed. It's a Monday at 3 pm and almost every table is taken. The smell of hot wings and citrus garnishes filled the air once again. I feel optimistic about starting my new job. My legs are freezing, I am still showing skin, but at least my shorts aren't playing peek-a-boo. April watched me come in with a smile on her face, waving above her head.

I ran up to the bar as fast as I could, putting my hands out to stop myself from hitting the bar at full force. "I'm so excited, I can't even start to begin to thank you."

She slid an apron over the bar, smiling. "The menu and computer system is the same as White Heart. My dad owns this place, we just had to put a transfer in with Erik's mom. Different companies but family friends."

"How is everything the same?"

"We appeal to older people, more respectable people. No one even notices; White Heart is all college kids."

I sighed and hung my shoulders in relief, this is going to be good.

April showed me the system and walked around the tables, telling me how they were numbered. Everything about serving is stressful, every night I lay in bed and my eyes shoot open because I forgot someone's damn ketchup. We walked around for a half hour, dodging groups of people storming by us. April told me it was always this busy, from open till close.

A girl with blonde hair walked in with three guys. She has long hair, curves. Her makeup is perfect. She is wearing a pink dress with ruffles. A guy walked in behind her, wrapping his arm around her. I notice they all are dressed up. The three guys all have brown hair with tattoos sticking out from under their sleeves. Guys who stood in front of them cleared their way and girls stopped to stare.

April grabbed my arm and pulled me out of their line of sight. "Lizzy, the guy who walked in next to Charlie is my brother Liam. The other two are my brother Dillon and cousin William. I'm going to give you drinks to drop off at their table. I can't go over there."

"Why not? They are your family."

"We hate each other. William is a little bit tolerable, but he's still a dick. Charlie is a sweetheart, but she's oblivious. When you ring them in, just use Taylor as the discount code and it will void the drinks."

I nodded my head, remembering what Spencer had told me last night. April is making the drinks behind the bar, I put my arms on the bar, putting my weight on my forearm. When they walked in, she put a barrier around her. She is generally affected that they came in.

"Erik told me yesterday that Adam is in love with their best friend's girlfriend; is that her?"

April nodded as she put the drinks in front of me. "The Watsons are like my brothers. The shit they have to listen about me is brutal. They stopped sticking up for me, I can't blame them. I just started acting out towards my family. When you drop these off, let's go out for a smoke."

I smiled and started nodding my head. I put the three neat whiskeys and a martini with extra olives on my tray and walked towards the back table. After watching what they guys were drinking last night it was easy to figure out that the whiskeys belonged to the guys and the martini was for Charlie. I got closer to the table and Charlie looked at me with a big smile, I'm not sure if it was directed at me or her drink. I set the drinks down in front of everyone and they all smiled at me. It's awkward that they have no idea who I am.

I held the tray to my chest and I exhaled the air from my lungs. I have no idea how all eight of them, plus April, are so attractive. I feel like I am going to be standing out, and not in a good way.

I have never felt so intimidated in my life.

Hours passed and I was still ringing the code in for them getting free drinks. I am surprised with how much money I have made; I would need to work two shifts at White Heart to make as much here. Theo and Max have been blowing my phone up with encouraging text messages and checking up on me to see how I am holding up and if I needed a bodyguard. After thirty messages of me reassuring them, they finally back off.

April wasn't kidding when she said the system was the same, the cash-out forms were even identical.

April made me an Old Fashioned and set it in front of me while I shoved the money I owed in an envelope. "Halloween is in a few days, I need all hands on deck. You up for it?"

I started to laugh. "Hell yeah."

"I know you and Erik barely know each other, but I swear, if you hurt him I will shoot you."

"I think he would be the one to hurt me. He is way too good for me and it's only a matter of time before he finds out."

I put my head down and took another sip. It killed me to say, but I know it's true. He has his life together, I am a disaster. He met me in the back of his police car, that says it all.

A set of hands touched my shoulders. I'm always expecting someone coming up behind me when I'm working, so I never jumped. "I know for a fact you are too good for me. You just don't know it yet." Erik's deep voice sent butterflies in my stomach. "I saw Charlie and Dillon walk out. Let's go meet Liam and William."

I swung around in my chair, jumping out of my seat, I wrapped my arms around him and kissed him. I miss him, and that feels crazy to me. What I already feel is crazy.

"Lizzy, bring these to them when you go over there, if you don't mind." April set the drinks down; before I could reach for them while balancing my drink, Erik reached his arms out and grabbed them.

I followed him to the back table in the corner; he scooted in the booth with me beside him. Liam and William's eyes are going back and forth between us, trying to figure out why I was sitting with them. Erik wrapped his arm over my shoulder and pulled me into his chest and I can see them both start to smile. I can tell from the way they smile it was just like Spencer used to reel girls in. Josh, Adam, and Erik were the opposite. Their smiles were genuine and not used to get girls in bed.

"I had no idea this was her." Liam leaned back in his suit while he crossed his arms against his chest.

"She's hot." I rolled my eyes. From the process of elimination, I know this is William.

"Shut the fuck up," Erik spoke between his teeth. He tightened his grasp around me, I don't even think he knew he was doing it.

I sat up and kissed his cheek, whispering in his ear, "It's kind of hot when you get protective."

Erik started to laugh and loosened up his grasp. "Theo somehow got my number and has been giving me the third degree."

I rolled my eyes. "He was going through my phone. I'm sorry."

Theo always played the big brother excessively; thankfully, Max was always around to balance it out. He isn't my brother but he loves to act like it. I have scared off a few girls playing his little sister role. If me and Brittney didn't like a girl, they were gone faster than they could blink. Having to play that role by myself has been hard.

I drank every last drop out of my cup until there was only an orange peel left. Erik has stuck to water because he is on the night shift. I hate dating a cop, I am going to be up all night worried about him. I pulled out my phone, knowing that Max has my car.

"Hey."

"You have my car, come get me."

Max grunted and hung up the phone. I stuffed it back in my purse.

I put my hand on Erik and gazed into his eyes. "You better be safe tonight."

"Being a cop isn't as dangerous as you think it is. I'll be fine."

Erik put his hands behind my head, tangling his fingers in my hair and gave me a kiss. I opened my mouth, welcoming his tongue, I bit his lip. Fighting against my urges, I pulled away, remembering the people around us.

I brought my cup to the bar and walked outside, pulling a smoke from my pack and waiting for Max to show up. The wind is brisk, I never timed this out at all. Someone put their hands on my hips and picked me up. I let out a scream and I heard laughter erupt from behind me.

I turned around and hit Josh. "You fucking terrified me."

He looked down at me, shaking his head. "That's some language for a girl."

Spencer reached down to my hand and pulled my smoke pack out of my grasp and lit one. I rolled my eyes and saw Max with Theo in the passenger pull up next to the curb.

"Who are those guys you're always with?" Josh asked before I was able to step away.

"The driver is my best friend and the passenger is my brother. We have been a package deal since I was eight."

I stepped into the car and Theo turned around to look at me. I saw the look in his eyes and I knew he was about to cause shit. "So, I started training again and one of the guys told me a Basilisk owns the bar."

I started laughing, that was insane. "No, whoever told you that is full of shit. The owner's daughter is the manager and she's a sweetheart. Erik's family is family friends with the owners."

Max shook his head. "I've seen the manager in here; there's no way she is related to a Basilisk. Plus Erik doesn't act like a gangster. I know what you are trying to do, Theo. Just stop. We can't do anything to bring her back."

Theo turned around in his seat after shrugging his shoulders and turned the music up in the car. In the past few days, I have noticed all of our moods have improved since we stopped cold turkey. I am not going to lie, I am waiting for one of us to slip. We won't because we now share each other's pain. Max was always the most level-headed out of all of us, even when we were eight years old. He is the least of my worries, but I am worried he will be the first one. As soon as one of us falls, we all will.

I made them stop at the closest fast food restaurant so I could dip into my $100 from my tips on a Sunday that I made in four hours. We got into the apartment and I quickly got changed into my sweat pants and a baggy shirt after I took off my makeup. I sat down, putting my feet up and drinking the largest fountain pop I have ever seen.

"Courtney is pissed." Max sighed.

I hate Courtney. I tossed a fry at Max. "Just break up with her. My god, man. She doesn't believe we aren't sleeping together."

Theo pushed out a laugh. "You guys are together all the time, same age, known each other your entire life. You really can't blame her."

Me and Max looked at each other with scrunched up noses, shaking our heads at each other.

Theo lit a smoke, sliding his pack in my direction. "I really like Erik. He is so good for you. I'm surprised you haven't scared him off."

I sighed. "I have crazy intense feelings for him, but I think he feels the same way."

Max laughed. "No shit; if he didn't, he wouldn't have gone through getting you a new job with no interview. I don't think you can scare him off."

"That's what terrifies me. He's so perfect, and I'm not."

Theo playfully shoved me against the arm of the couch. He tossed my phone at me when a text came through. *Have a good night, beautiful.*

I held my phone to my chest, smiling. This feeling is incredible. *Thank you for the unexpected visit after work. It made my day seeing you.*

Charlie

Today is the day that the house is finally finalized, so I have been packing like crazy. The entire condo is in boxes in less than six hours. I am so excited for the four of us to have more room. Two-story house, three bedrooms, two bathrooms. The outside of the house looks like a cottage, the inside is modern and up to date. Between working and school, it took us a few days to finally go look at it; as soon as the four of us saw it, we all fell in love with it.

I'm lying on my bed looking at the popcorn ceiling, finally taking five minutes to myself.

My phone started ringing. I let out a sigh, knowing it's work.

"Hey, Josh."

"How's the packing?"

"I'm exhausted."

"Drink some coffee! We are finally going after Dave, Eli, and Ben. By the looks of it, they let their guard down."

"When?"

"We will be there at 5 pm with Adam and Spencer to pick you up. See you then."

I hung up the phone and checked the time. It was only 2 pm. I headed out to the living room, and all the guys had their feet up. I rolled my eyes, I'm not shocked at all. "Adam is coming at five with Josh and Spencer. I'm making the hit tonight."

Dillon turned his head to wink at me then started laughing.

Liam looked at me and patted his lap for me to sit down. "Adam will be the driver. Spencer and Josh will be going in as your backup."

We sat in silence as we watched *Family Guy*. We are occasionally laughing. William, on the other hand, is laughing his ass off. "Fuckin' Stewie!"

Liam whispered in my ear, "Let's go talk in my bedroom." I nodded my head, and I held his hand, following behind him.

Liam sat on the bed, I covered up his hand with mine and sat beside him. "Do you want kids?"

I swallowed hard. I'm not even sure if I love Liam. "We live too much of a fucked up life for children to be around."

"Would it really be that bad?"

"Liam! Look at our lives. If that's what you are thinking of already, you need to slow down."

Liam stopped me before I could continue. "I'm not talking anytime soon. I sound crazy. We haven't even known each other for long enough. But when I picture my life in thirty years, I see you."

I leaned in to kiss him. "Let's go out to the living room." I need to get away from this conversation, fast.

I got in the car and the mood is surprisingly light. The guys are talking so much I can't even get a word in. They keep mentioning the names Erik and Lizzy, between all the back and forth, I'm not able to figure out who they are. Adam parked the car and they stopped talking.

I've been here before. I started putting my memories together. "Isn't this where Edwin was?"

Adam looked in his review mirror to look at me, holding up a pair of keys. He unbuckled his seatbelt turning around to face me "We got this off Edwin before we dealt with him. These people are the reason you were shot. He betrayed all of us for this group."

Josh turned around to face me in the backseat. "We keep to ourselves, so sometimes that can be a sign of weakness. Killing these guys is a message not to fuck with us."

Adam handed me the keys. "Use these at the front door."

"Who are they?" I'm scared to know the answer.

Spencer pulled a smoke out of his jacket. "McKinnon's."

I hit my head with the back of Adam's seat. "I seriously hate them. Who's coming in with me?" I sat back and screwed my silencer on my gun.

"That would be me." Josh unbuckled his seatbelt and jumped out of the car.

We ran across the street and I sighed. "It would have been nice to know who I was giving the bullets to before I got cocky."

Josh mimicked me, "I'll see you very soon, boys." He started laughing. I laughed and playfully pushed him.

I unlocked the door and we both stepped into the house. Josh quietly shut the door behind him. He turned the knob so it wouldn't click when he shut it. We are walking around the rooms on the main floor. I have a tight grip on my gun, ready for a fight.

Josh found the basement door and checked downstairs, there is nothing. I made my way up the stairs scanning the other bedrooms, and nothing.

Going back down the stairs, I heard the door open. I ran into the opening of the living room and the kitchen. I can see the entrance to the backyard from the corner of my eye. I glanced behind my shoulder and saw Josh standing there, waiting.

Two voices came into the doorway. The light flicked on, Eli and Ben are standing right there in front of us. This is it.

"I told you I would see you, boys, soon." My gun is raised before they could even get to theirs. I aimed, and I pulled the trigger.

Eli fell to the ground, blood spewing out. I moved my gun to Ben, and I pulled the trigger. He grabbed his chest and collapsed.

Josh ran past me, he's hovering over the bodies. "I hate to say this, Charlie, but you have on hell of an aim."

Josh reached out for my arm and pulled me outside, leaving the front door wide open. I am starting to think that the McKinnon family isn't a family like everyone thinks, but a group like us. We have seen way too many people around the same age that look nothing alike. It wouldn't be the first time false information was thrown around.

I opened the SUV's door and jumped in, mumbling, "I hate the McKinnon's."

I took off my hoodie, gloves, and hid my gun under my seat, and lit up a smoke. This is the first time my body isn't trembling. I don't know if it's because I am now numb to killing, or if it's because I know they are shitty enough people, and I don't care that they are dead.

"Adam, white car. Never mind. We're clear." Josh lit a smoke and relaxed in his seat.

Adam slowed the car down. I can tell by his tone that he is trying to stay calm, but his adrenaline is pushing through. "It's Dave. The street's clear, no one's around."

I pulled out my gun from under my seat. Unbuckled my seatbelt and jumped out of the vehicle, tossing my smoke on the ground. Before I was able to jump out and aim, his gun went off.

The bullet hit the side of my leg. I couldn't care less. I aimed and shot him in the head. A second gun was fired, getting him in the stomach. I looked beside me, and Spencer is lowering his gun, stepping outside to help me.

"How the fuck did you get shot three times, Charlie!" Spencer asked.

Spencer is supporting me with his body. I held on the handle above the door and pulled myself in. Spencer shut his door and Adam sped off, causing me to jolt to the back of my seat.

I pulled my sweatpants down to my knees looking at my leg. "I'm fine. It's a flesh wound. I'm going to need help getting up the stairs, though."

Adam shook his head. "I think you broke a record."

Josh looked back and smiled. "If this is your new habit, we are always coming prepared."

I threw my lighter at him. Spencer is putting pressure on my leg to stop the bleeding. I am trying to not be bothered by the pain. The muscle in my leg is making that impossible; even as a flesh wound, this is worse than the other two times I've been shot. Josh handed me a smoke and tossed my lighter back at me. I know I shouldn't be smoking with an open wound, but I need to keep my hands busy in an attempt at being distracted. Thankfully, Adam is one of the best drivers I have ever met, he got us back to the condo faster than I thought it would take.

Adam opened my door and wrapped his arms around me. He looked down at me and winked. For a split second, we looked each other in the eyes and it felt magical. He pulled away and I can see a sadness in his eyes.

I need to figure my shit out.

Spencer opened the door and ran to the bathroom, grabbing the first aid. I'm happy I know better and never packed that away yet.

"Babe, what happened?" Liam is taken aback. It's because I'm shot, but it also might have had to do with the fact I came into the condo in Adam's arms.

"I'm fine, I swear," I said, grabbing on the arm of the couch.

Dillon came with a bottle of vodka. "Just stop getting shot. I guess no Halloween party tomorrow!"

I forgot all about Halloween. "We don't have costumes! We have been so worried about trying to move!"

Liam sat down beside me, taking my hand. "I don't think any of us are feeling a college party. Let's just go to *Willie's* or something."

Dillon poured the vodka over my open wound and I cried out. He took the first aid kit and started doing my stitches. "Can you try to avoid people's guns now?"

Charlie

This morning is like any other, I woke up early before everyone else. But today felt different. I'm genuinely happy because I know none of us are going to get called away. One day where no one needs to worry about each other.

I got off the bed and yelped in pain. My leg is throbbing. I slowly walked to the door and used the wall down the hallway to get to the kitchen. Every step I take, I gasp. I managed to get to the kitchen and to pour a glass of whiskey, I'm ignoring the time on the clock. I needed a drink, I don't care how early it is. I sat on the couch and picked my leg up with my hands. I lit a smoke and grabbed my phone from the end table and went right into contacts.

"Do you realize how early it is!" Adam's voice is raspy, he is talking through his teeth.

"I'm sorry, I should have waited to phone you."

"Charlie! I'm sorry!"

"When you are awake, can you bring me a painkiller?" I can hear it in my voice that I am fighting back tears.

"I'm on my way."

I looked at my whiskey and thought it was probably a bad idea to mix alcohol with prescription painkillers, but I needed to numb the pain somehow. I tipped my head and drank the liquid in one shot.

I grabbed the leather from the couch, trying to ignore the burning in my throat. I turned the TV on and set it on a low volume. Last thing I wanted to do was wake more people up. I keep catching myself looking at the clock, waiting for Adam to show up. I don't know why, but he is always on my mind. Whenever I see him, my mood always improves. The more I keep thinking about Adam, Liam gets pushed to the back of my mind and I'm feeling guiltier and guiltier.

Hearing the front door open, I can feel a smile on my face.

"Are you the only one awake?" Adam passed me the pill and his bottle of water. "I sent Spence and Josh to go get everyone breakfast. If you aren't feeling up for it tonight, I don't think anyone will care."

"Oh, no. We are going, I'm not passing up a chance for us to wear matching costumes."

All of are taking advantage of having a day off with each other. We all turned our phones on silent to have a day where we get to enjoy each other's company like regular people. None of us are stressed out today, not having to worry about a phone call is taking so much weight off our shoulders. This is the first time I get to see everyone's real personalities and I love it. Josh and Spencer are constantly beating each other up. Adam is like the big brother who always has to break up the fights. William, Dillon, and Liam instigate them to start arguing. They would have been nightmares to raise.

I spoke sweetly to Spencer and convinced him that we needed Marvel costumes. He hates the idea of matching, but after an hour of sweet-talking, he pulls himself off the couch and goes to the store. Him and Dillon come back just in time for us to get ready and head to *Willie's*.

Walking is still a challenge for me, but I'm determined to have a good night. We got to our regular table and I collapsed in the booth. Our drinks are waiting for us when we arrived, I slammed back half of my martini, my pain meds wore off and the pain came rushing back.

William is looking around with the biggest smile on his face. "The girls tonight are on fire!"

Liam squeezed my arm in agreement.

We are all caught up in conversation and drinking when we were interrupted. "Do you guys want to dance?"

Everyone but myself, Liam, and Dillon stood up to follow; instead, Liam goes to the bar to get another drink. Dillon is looking at me concerned by the time I slam back my third martini after being here for an hour.

I looked around. "Liam's been gone for a while; I'm going to go find him." As soon as I got up, a man started walking over to Dillon. "Have fun."

I pushed myself to get up to the bar and order a drink. The bartender nodded when she saw me and started my drink. I looked back to the table. "Could I also get seven shots of tequila?"

"Go to the end of the bar!" she shouted over the crowed. I did what she said, and she followed with a tray and seven shot glasses. "You're one lucky girl."

Still looking around for Liam, my heart instantly started to ache. There is a girl hanging on to his every word dressed as Catwoman. He is standing two inches from her face. He pulls her face closer to his and starts making out with her. I let out a sob; that was the same way he kissed me. As much as I wanted to stop watching him, I can't. She jumps up on him, wrapping her legs around his waist. I force myself to turn around, letting a tear fall from my eyes. My hands are shaking. I pick up my drink and chug it back. I set the half-drunk martini at the bar and grab the tray to take it to the table.

I'm trying everything in my power to hide that I'm hurt. "I got these for us." I caught myself when I looked at Liam and the girl, I quickly pulled my eyes away and passed out the shots.

The guys have questioning looks in their eyes. They know something is wrong. I slammed back my shot and without saying a word, turned around and left. The music blaring from the speakers was drowning out their voices as I walked closer to the door. Dillon came up beside me and wrapped his arm around my shoulder, giving me a reassuring squeeze. I pulled out my phone and discreetly ordered a bottle of tequila and a pizza to arrive at the house the same time as we would.

As soon as I walked into the house, I stormed into the bathroom. My mind is racing. I'm not able to get my thoughts straight. I feel my heart beating out of my chest. This is everyone's worst nightmare. I stripped off my costume and put my hand under the water until it has reached the right temperature. I'm so mad that I can't cry. I want to scream, but I know that isn't going to make me feel better. I lathered up the shampoo in my hair and I let out a sob. I knew he wasn't a one-woman guy.

I turned the water off and heard Spencer. "Got room for four more?"

I opened the door and heard Josh ask Dillon, "Where is she?"

Dillon simply replied, "Shower."

I got into my room before everyone saw a towel wrapped around me. I quickly towel-dried my hair and got dressed.

I headed to the living room where Josh is standing in front of me and wrapping his arms around me. I looked over Josh's shoulder; Adam and William are standing behind him. Not saying a word but being there for me.

From the corner of my eye, I'm watching Spencer come out with shot glasses with Dillon following behind with the limes.

As horrible as I feel, it is nice to know I have five people in the room with me who are there when I need them.

The door opened and Liam came in. "Charlie, can I talk to you?"

I replied without turning around to look at him, "Oh, you came home alone, that's surprising."

"Just please come talk to me." I followed him down the hall. "I don't know what I was thinking. I'm sorry."

"Just forget it, it's our only day off. I'm not letting you destroy it for all of us."

I turned to walk away, but he grabbed my arm. I pulled my arm back to my body with force and he let go of me.

I shook my head at him, turning back around to the living room. "Sorry about that guys." I'm making my voice as cold as I can.

The night went on and we are still taking shots. I'm trying to have a good night, but I keep finding myself away from everyone, watching them have a good night. I hate this feeling, I hate wallowing in self-pity. Most of all, I hate feeling like I can be replaced.

My mouth has gone numb, the alcohol is making my head spin. "Dillon, I'm staying in your bed tonight. Then the guys can fight over my bed."

Dillon followed me to his bedroom and lay down with me. I'm doing a decent job of keeping my emotions intact. He wrapped his arms around me, and I fell apart. I'm sobbing, I couldn't even try to keep myself together. I know Dillon was feeling guilty, he was pushing so hard for Liam and I to get together. Every time I gasp for air, he pulls me closer into his chest.

My crying eventually slows down and I'm finally able to think. I need to go talk to Liam. I need to know why.

"I need to go do something." Dillon loosens his grip and lets me get out of bed.

I went to the living room and saw William, Spencer, Josh, and Adam sitting and talking. They all looked up at me. I needed to go see Liam. I put my head down to try and hide my face.

I knocked on Liam's door softly. "Fuck off!" He is angry.

"It's me." My voice is soft and broken.

He opened the door a crack and heard his bed squeak when he sat back down. I walked into the room and it slipped my mind on why I thought this is a good idea. I shut the door anyway, standing in the doorway in silence. He put his head in the palm of his hands.

My voice is angrier than I expected. "Why did you do it! Why would you do that to me!"

Liam stood up. "Because you were right; it is hard to date someone that does what I do!" He is screaming his words. "You've been shot three times. I was useless every single time."

"That's not a reason."

"I wanted to push you away from me as far as possible. I can't keep doing this, Charlie."

"Then that's it, I guess." I turned around, putting my hand on the door handle. "I'll pack my things tomorrow."

Liam put his hand on the top corner of the door, overpowering me and causing it to slam shut. "I'm an idiot."

"I'm not arguing that."

"I only want you." He wrapped his arms around me. "Can we work through this? Can you forgive me?"

I looked up at him and his eyes had tears. "If you ever do anything like this again, I won't be coming home."

Liam pulled me on the bed with him, covering both of us up. Every voice in my head is shouting at me to go back in Dillon's room and stay clear of Liam. I have to believe I'm making the right choice, but I know I'm wrong. I can't handle people leaving, I will put myself through hell to make sure no one leaves me. I can feel my heart ache inside my chest.

I know this isn't what love is supposed to feel like.

I inhaled a shaky breath, wiping my face with my free hand. Ignoring all of my demons, I let the alcohol put me to sleep.

Charlie

The next morning, we all look worse than what we feel. We slept in until the afternoon and even the extra sleep never helped our brutal hangover. Every breath all of us take, we have to fight the alcohol to stay down. None of us have said a word to each other, we sent out group text messages and decided we needed greasy food. We ordered by pointing at the menu; the waitress is holding in her laughter every single time she comes to the table. Liam has his arm around my shoulder and I can see the guys looking at us like they want to scream. The food came and the more we start to eat, I can see everyone feeling a lot better.

"Who's ready to get back to work?" Spencer muttered before he answered his phone. "Good thing we are all together. We have a buyer. You'll never guess who it is."

"Same guys as your last?" Dillon threw his fork on his empty plate.

"Charlie, you're in charge."

"Fuck." I slumped and crossed my arms across my chest. "Putting me in charge of this is a mistake. When do we head out?"

"I hope you are wrong. We need to leave now. At the docks."

I stood in front of the guys, glaring down the men approaching. Even from a distance, I can tell something is wrong. They walked up to me, nodding their heads at each other. "M1911?"

I nodded. "$400,000."

I'm watching them closely. There are no sudden movements. They handed me the money and left. Everything went smoothly. We walked away with no adrenaline rush.

I looked behind my back and whispered to Spencer, "That was almost too easy."

I'm the only one who thought so; we all are walking away, watching our backs. I'm standing behind everyone, waiting to pile into the vehicle. Someone wrapped their arm around my waist; I'm trying to fight them, but I can't. I started screaming.

William jumped out of the passenger side with fear on his face, he has no idea what to do to help me. One of the McKinnon's from the sale is dragging me backwards. Another body came up behind me, they are tying my hands up behind my back. Fear is taking over my body. A sack is covering my head, I can't see anything; the scratchy fabric is irritating my skin and making me fight back even harder. I can hear the guys screaming my name—guns are being fired. I know the guys have good aim, but they haven't hit one of us. The sound of a van door starts to open. My feet are lifted off the ground and I fall hard onto the floor of the van, smashing into the other side.

My body is shaking from fear. This is how I die.

I move enough and get the sack off my head so that I can see. "Why are you doing this!" I screamed. "You won't get away with this, I promise you." I'm growling through my teeth. "They will come for me."

"Naïve girl, that's what we want. Put the sack back on." The man beside me listened to the command.

The sack is on my head again and tears are soaking my face, they are using me to kill my family. I am trying to pay attention to where we are going. I know the Basilisks, I know my friends. *Protect everyone with your life.* I know that's exactly what they will do, but if it means either me or them to be killed, I will pick me over and over again. I know they won't give up, I know we will all survive this.

The van came to a halt and the door opened. Someone grabbed my jacket and pulled me out of the van. Before I fell and hit the ground, someone grabbed my arm. I'm getting pushed and dragged. "Tie her to the chair; don't make the call yet, show her what she is in for."

The set of hands that were on my arm push me down on a chair, they are holding their weight against me. I can feel ropes being tied around my feet; the ones on my hands are being untied and tied to the chair. I am trying to push myself away from the chair, but the person who is holding me down is a lot stronger than I ever will be. The sack is finally pulled off my head. I can see a tablet is on a table standing upright, pointing at me. I'm strapped in; I can't move, but that will never stop me from trying to break free.

Before I could even register where I am, a fist came into contact with my face, over and over again. I can see from the black screen my eyes are bruising, blood is coming out of my mouth. I never had to look at my dark reflection to know my nose is bleeding; I can feel blood dripping and the tickling is making me more irritated.

The black screen turned white with Martin, Liam, William, Dillon, and Adam looking at me with anger rising in their bodies. I spoke with as much confidence as I could, "They won't break me." As soon as the words left my mouth, someone punched me again.

I'm holding my head to the side, looking at the tablet. My mouth is bleeding more and my face is becoming more swollen. I tensed my body, raising my head. I'm pissed, I'm making it clear in my voice. "I'm stronger than this!" I spit blood out on the ground. "We didn't drive long. I'm in an abandoned building."

I'm trying to tell the McKinnon's that they can't break me. I'm also trying to tell the Basilisks that I won't give them up, no matter what they do to me. Dillon nodded his head at me, knowing exactly what I'm trying to do.

They hit me again, and I passed out.

My body jolted awake. I'm unaware how long I have been here for. My body is cold. I can't stop shivering, trying to keep warm. I can smell rotted trees in the air. By the look of this room, it has not been used for anything in over a decade, the perfect hideout. Something is different about this room, I never looked around before, but the smell. I have never smelt rotted trees before. My body flinches. I'm not in a chair anymore, I'm lying down on a hard board.

I can hear William from the tablet. I'm scared to look at him, I'm scared I will never see him again. "Charlie. Charlie." I tried to speak, but I'm too afraid. All that came out is a squeak. "Martin knows where you are. They need to wait for backup before they come."

I turned my head to look at him. His face went serious, murder lit up his eyes. I tried to reach for him but my hands are strapped down. "I love you, Charlie. I'll see you soon. My best friend does not give up, remember what you told me? You push yourself too hard, all time." I squeaked again, nodding.

I can't figure out why I feel so cold, I caught a glimpse of my torso. They have stripped me down to my underwear. I can see my discolored skin. Bruises have formed on my body where I don't even remember getting hit. I tried to put my thoughts together. My stomach is growling, I have hunger pains worse than I ever thought possible.

I have been lying here for hours, convincing myself that I will survive. William's words repeating in my mind like a broken record. Eventually, his voice faded and I'm terrified I will never see him again. Occasionally, I can hear chatter from McKinnon's outside of the room. Whatever they are eating, the smell is lingering into my room.

Starvation, one of the worst forms of torture.

Every time I move my neck, I can feel how tense it is. My body needs water, my muscles are tensing. I let out a scream from smelling the food. I am trying to fight out of my restraints, my muscles keep tensing, I move and get light-headed from dehydration.

I stop trying to fight and I'm staring at the tablet, I don't know what time it is, or what day it is but I can't peel my eyes away from the screen. I can't miss the chance to see someone.

"Is anyone there?" I'm not able to speak more than a whisper. "Please, I need to see someone."

Liam appeared on the screen. "Babe, we checked everywhere. We will catch them and we will end them. You'll be home soon. Don't give up." Liam's face grew intense.

The men walked in and put a cloth over my face, I can hear water sloshing around in a bucket. Water is getting poured over me. I can't breathe. I'm drowning. The towel is off my face, I gasp for air. My breathing is interrupted with a blow to my stomach. I let out a loud scream.

I glance at the tablet with a pleading expression for them to find me. Martin is standing there saying something. I can't hear him over more footsteps coming into the room, my hearing is focused on another bucket with water splashing around in it. The towel is on my face again, water is getting poured on me. With every breath, I can start to see my life flash before me.

I wake up and look around the room. I'm hoping this is just a bad dream, but deep down, I know it isn't. I don't know how long I have been here, the days are blending together. My vision is blurry. I can't taste anything but blood. I'm trying to remember to be strong, it's hard because they are wearing me down. This is what they want. The door opens, and I let out the loudest scream I can manage.

"I won't tell you anything. What do you want from me!" My eyes are locked on the tablet and I see Dillon and Adam slam their fists on the table. I'm trying to imprint their faces in my mind. I'm trying to remember their voices. Everything is fading and I'm not able to stop it. Terror creeped up onto their faces.

I know what is coming. I start moving my head, screaming, "No!" as loud as my lungs will let me.

I can't stop the unstoppable. The towel is on my face again, pouring water over my body, I'm panicking. Everything in the room is going black.

My body jolts awake; without opening my eyes, I feel a pair of hands gripping my shoulders, pulling me up from the table, and standing me up. "You haven't broken yet, but you will."

He tossed me into another man. I'm trying to fight him off, but my body isn't giving me the strength I need. I'm getting tired of trying to fight. Someone else came behind me and ripped my arms above my head. I looked up, opening my eyes; my wrists are being tied up. I felt someone's hands on my leg and I look down, they are tying my legs, the rope is connected to a metal piece attached to the floor. I tried to kick with my free leg, but I'm wearing myself out.

I can't do anything to fight back.

They grabbed my last free limb and I sobbed.

"Your crew will get brought down, and you are the first to go. We've been watching you." He punched me in my face, and I cried out for help.

"Just kill me already! I'm not telling you anything," I whimpered. "Just kill me. I'm not talking. Do your worst. You're wasting your time." I spit blood onto the ground. "Unlike you, I have a reason to fight. How long have you been wasting your time on me? Kill me, you coward!"

I started flailing when I noticed my back was to the tablet. I'm not going to see anyone again. Tears are running down my face. I can't stop crying. Everyone's face has vanished from my mind. My eyes are getting heavy and my head falls against my chest.

I slowly started to open my eyes to voices coming into the room. "She will break after this, boss."

"She better, we have a lot riding on the Basilisks' deaths."

Footsteps are getting closer and closer to me. I hear a whip crackle. My back feels like it's being ripped into a million tiny pieces. Blood is dripping down my legs.

I hear the crackle again. I can't stop screaming. My face is soaked in tears. My arms above my body tremble.

I woke up to pain. My entire body ached. I tried to open my eyes, but it's impossible. I can't see. My eyes have completely swollen shut.

I heard someone standing in front of me. "Have a sip. You need water." It was a woman's voice.

"No." My voice is shaking.

"You're tougher than you look." I can hear her pull up a chair, dragging it on the floor. "They are never coming, you know."

I try to scream my words, but I'm growing weaker with every minute that is passing. "If you've been watching us, you know we don't give up on each other."

I can hear someone breathing, I think they are standing in front of me. I look up where I think he is standing. I hold my head as high as I can, not showing fear. "Why are you torturing Mafias on the other side of the country?"

"Because of you, a lot of our men have been killed. This is what happens when you plan to deal in our territory."

"This country is big enough for the two of us."

Gunfire starts to echo in the building.

For the first time in days, a small smile appeared on my face. "They're here. I told you that you would be next."

"I'm in here." My voice is shallow and weak. No one can hear me. I hang my head in defeat.

"Help me." I managed to raise my voice a little bit, but it was still useless.

"You guys, I found her." The voice is low and full of fear.

"Josh?"

More people walked into the room. I heard gasps then I felt multiple hands on me, trying to get me down.

"Charlie, it's Liam. Dillon is going to catch you."

I'm crying out in pain from my back touching Liam's arms. I can hear everyone shuffling around. The deadbolt clicked from being unlocked and I know I am finally home.

I never thought I would feel the sense of home again. We never went up any stairs so I don't know where we are.

"The couch is right here. I'm going to set you down. Have some water." Liam held a straw to my lips, and I took a small sip.

I pulled away. "Where are we?" I'm weak, I have no more strength left in my body.

"The new house. We got all moved in."

"Wait, if you guys got us moved, how long was I gone for?"

The room is quiet. I can't see, but I'm able to pinpoint voices. "Five days. How did you not break after five days of torture?" Martin's voice is soft.

"Five days? I knew you guys were coming." I took a long pause. "Before you guys showed up, I was ready to die." I know everyone too well to know they exchange looks.

"Dr. Maxwell is on his way. He is bringing his nurse Annabelle to bathe you. She shows up in terrible situations."

"I really wish I could see you guys right now."

"Believe me, Charlie, we do too." Adam sounds heartbroken. I knew he was here, but knowing he's near is bringing me more comfort.

Liam squeezed my hand. "Maxwell is here."

I can tell from the direction of Maxwell's voice he is standing behind me. "We need a bed for the exam." Liam picked me up and carried me, but I screamed from him touching my back. "You are a lot worse off than I imagined. We have a portable ultrasound machine here. Hopefully, that will be enough."

Liam held my hand to the bedroom, guiding me in the foreign house. My legs stopped when they hit the mattress. I put my hands behind me; turning around, I sat on the bed and lay down. The weight of my body on my back is sending shocks though my back, the pain is radiating. I hear the door shut. Liam never said a word the entire walk or when he left the room.

"Charlie, this gel is going to be cold, but I need to take an ultrasound image. Annabelle, can you check her blood pressure?"

The gel is freezing. Being back in a bed is helping me stay calm. I'm finally home. The living room is filled with people who love me.

"You have internal bleeding. Your blood pressure is normal. We will keep an eye on you. Your abdominal area is bruised. Annabelle will take you into the bathroom and get you cleaned up."

Dr. Maxwell helped me into the bathroom and Annabelle undressed me. She helped guide my legs into the tub and started scrubbing me down. The warm water stung my body. I'm gasping, but at the same time, this was the first time in almost a week I have been safe. Water is over my head, and I can't stop screaming despite me being back home.

"I'm so sorry, Charlie! It's me, Annabelle. It's okay, you're home now."

Dillon is pounding on the door. "What's going on in there!"

Annabeth is helping me out of the tub. "She has a bit of PTSD. Everything's okay." She is drying me off with a towel; I was flinching whenever it touched my back and shoulders. "Those guys really care about you. When we first got to the call, all of them were in a panic. I've never seen a group of people who care so much about each other." I felt Annabelle slip my arms into my robe.

The bathroom door opened and I heard Liam call out, "We made you a smoothie."

I felt Liam's hands touch mine and he kissed my head, guiding me back to the couch.

I sucked back on the straw, it hurt so much. I wasn't about to say that and make everyone worry about me even more. "I'm okay. You guys can leave. Thank you for saving me and not letting me give up hope."

Dr. Maxwell told everyone I was unable to do any kind of work for three months and not to stress me out. Martin started a group discussion, all of us decided it was best that Liam, William, and Dillon also had the same time off as I do. I can tell from all their tones that it wasn't going to last. Martin needs all of them dealing with this war.

"Thank you, everyone." My body is trembling. "You guys saved my life."

Josh spoke, sounding concerned, "We are the reason you were taken. We were all there."

"This was not your fault. It just happened. We were watching our backs. I just let mine down too early."

Spencer spoke behind me, "Give me your hand." I raised it in the air and he kissed it. "I missed you."

As Josh and Adam left, I felt them both bend down and kiss the top of my head. The feeling of being home again and surrounded by the people I love is almost too much for me to handle. I never expected to see them again.

I listened to the front door open and close. "I really wish someone would say something. I'm under the impression that this doesn't happen much?"

Everyone is silent. William is the first to talk. It's nice that he is never afraid of being honest with me. "It doesn't happen, ever. I'm not going to lie. We all expected you to break after they first did waterboarding."

Dillon's voice is cupped by his hands, covering his mouth. "You just kept screaming at them. My dad even admitted he wouldn't be able to have lasted nearly as long as you did."

William's voice is getting closer and closer to me. "They kept cutting the connection down. Every time you reappeared, you looked worse and worse. It was always turned on when you screamed." He put his hands over mine. "They did a hell of a job of scaring us."

I squeezed William's hands. "What you told me got me through the longest. You were right, I don't give up and I do push myself way too hard."

Liam put his hand on my arm. "After you said that we would find you, they cut it for 36 hours. Whenever it shut off, we left one person behind. The rest of us went looking. We never stopped looking for you."

"We are going to drive each other nuts in these three months." I paused. I didn't know what way my head was facing, so I looked down. "I would have died before I said anything. I need to lie down in a bed. Everything hurts."

Brittney

Between keeping tabs on all eight Basilisks and my three best friends, I barely have enough time for me to eat or sleep. It's creepy how Spencer and Erik know I am lurking somewhere in the shadows, snapping pictures of them. It's the day after Halloween and Spencer blew up my phone with drunk text messages and apologies from him because he was dancing with another girl. Being engaged to him when he looks like that, and the entire world thinking he is single, is going to be extremely hard, but if he would have shot her down, it would have brought up way too many questions.

Outside of the restaurant, I'm sitting in the black SUV watching Dillon, Liam, Charlie, Spencer, Adam, and Josh. I am fully updated with Liam cheating on Charlie and her crawling into his bed last night. Everyone looks like they want to crawl over the table and kick Liam's ass. From what I can tell, no one has spoken a word; the amount of tequila they all ingested, I can only imagine how they feel.

My phone started to buzz. *I know you are going to follow us so be safe; it's a deal with the McKinnon's. I wish I could hold you.*

I love you, Spence.

They all piled into a vehicle parked behind me. Rolling my eyes at them—having more passengers then seatbelts.

I have been following them with at least four cars between us the entire drive. Liam is driving and he is trained to watch for followers. They turned off at the docks and I stopped before the yellow light, giving me a bit of time before I turn into the parking lot to give us more space. My heart is beating out of my chest, my nerves are shocked. The McKinnon's are a drug cartel and the worst people to have ever lived. The thought of my fiancé breathing the same air as them is anything but settling.

I parked in a stall, rolling down my window, reaching in my holster for my gun, and watching them. I'm not close enough to watch what is happening. I quickly leaned forward to my passenger console, grabbing the binoculars and trying to read their lips.

The man standing in front of Charlie said, "Sandwiches." Right now, I wish I had the lip-reading ability.

Envelopes bursting at the seams are being passed over to the Basilisks. I let out a small breath of air, knowing that it's done. I pulled the binoculars from my face, leaning my head against the headrest and feeling relief that he's safe. I opened my eyes just in time for the McKinnon's standing behind Charlie put a sack over her head.

"Fuck, fuck, fuck!"

I reached for my binoculars again, listening to the guys shouting; one of them fired a gun. I pulled out mine, cocking it and taking a deep breath, aiming for the vehicle's tire. I shot my gun then put the binoculars to my eyes, watching the tire deflate. I should have shot one of them, but I can't get us involved with two Mafias. I kicked the car into drive and followed the van closely.

Frantically, I grabbed my phone, calling Rodriguez. I heard him answer and I gave him no time to talk. "The McKinnon's just took Charlie. I shot the van's tire; they won't get far on the rim."

"Christ. Can you follow them?"

"I'm trying, sir, but they are on a mission. Even with three tires, they are impossible to keep up with."

That was an understatement. I am flying through traffic, swerving in and out. I slammed on my brakes, causing vehicles to almost rear-end me and honking their horns. The road branches off, I have no idea where they went.

"I lost them, sir."

"I'm calling Davis."

I swung around, driving over the cement block in the middle of the street, flicking on my sirens, and speeding back to the bureau. Never in my life have I known what panic is. I don't care what she has done, no one deserves to go through what they are going to do to her. My heart is beating faster than at the hospital when my coworkers showed up, I can only imagine how the monitor would be reacting right now. The only time I slowed down was when I was coming close to an intersection in New York; there are a lot of lights, I want to fly through them, but my instincts are telling me not to.

The drive only took me twenty minutes. Twenty minutes too long. I slammed the car into park in the parking lot and pulled out my phone to text Spencer. *I tried to follow them.*

Running inside, I flashed my badge and got in the elevator, trying to keep my emotions collected. This is probably the first for all of us working on a case trying to protect mobsters. I pulled out my phone with my heart sinking; Spencer hasn't replied to my text. I don't know what I'm expecting him to say, Charlie is one of his best friends. I don't even want to know what pain any of them are dealing with right now. The elevator finally opened and I ran into Rodriguez's office. All ten of the original people from my first day are sitting in the chairs waiting for me. Again.

I sat down and told them everything that happened.

"Martin is planning on drug smuggling," Nelson told all of us. "They must feel threatened. She is the newest and weakest link. If she breaks, our entire operation is blown up."

My phone rang, filling the stressed room. I looked down and Spencer's name lit up the screen. "Spence! I'm putting you on speaker."

"It's bad, they strapped her to a chair and knocked her out. She managed to scream at them. I think everything will be okay, we are her first family and she won't do anything to put us in danger."

"I hope you're right, Basilisk." Jones covered his face.

"Brittney, I need to see you." The pleading in his voice is breaking my heart.

"You will when she's home."

"Someone's coming. I love you." The line disconnected.

Hours passed of us looking at maps in the city for locations that would be close enough to the docks down the road I traveled. Me blowing out the tire was useless; it never made a dent in their dedication. We are using pins on locations that are color-coordinated. Yellow is a possible, red is too far of a distance, blue is places they have checked.

Erik walked into the room and immediately pulled me to his side. "Adam went into a building and they moved her. We got too close and spooked them. Brooks is out there right now."

I craned my head, looking up at him. "How many cops are living double lives?"

"Just us two."

Johnson is shaking his head. "I don't trust him."

"Neither do I."

I walked away from Erik and wrote down all the addresses that are a possibility. My hand is becoming numb from the writing. It is going to take days.

Erik took the paper from me, going over what I wrote. "The last address is blocks away from the others."

"If you guys are right about Brooks, check it," Sam said, I almost forgot she was in the room, she was never quiet for this long. "They have already had her for ten hours."

Erik is holding the paper I passed him in the air. "Thank you for everything."

He walked out, shutting the door. My eyes are so heavy from looking at maps all day I can't see straight. All of us are exhausted.

"We can't do anymore for them. We need to all go home. Agent Hills, if you hear anything, phone me." Rodriguez is rubbing his eyes out of frustration.

Brittney

The next four days passed us by slowly, waiting for a call that Charlie is home, but no one ever called us. The longer she is gone, the less likely of a chance she will make it out alive. The only good thing about her being gone for so long is that Charlie hasn't broken yet, meaning our operation is still a go. I don't understand why we need to wait to arrest Martin, we have more than enough evidence on him.

According to Kinsley, Martin is wanting to retire. If we wait any longer to make our move, he is going to flee the country. We can't have that happen. Yes, we can get the authorities in the other countries to make the arrest, but I want to see his face when we do it. I want to see his face when he knows he's been caught. Call it selfish, I don't care. I never felt hatred like I have towards that man.

Sleeping is almost impossible. I'm lying awake scared. Scared that Charlie will talk and everyone going down for it. I'm scared that we will fail. I'm scared that Lizzy will lose Erik and I'm scared that I will lose Spencer before we even set a wedding date, or before I get an engagement ring.

With a grunt, I kick my legs over the bed, forcing myself to get up. I am unbelievably happy that Nelson and Rodriguez gave us today and tomorrow off, unless we get called in. Even they have been useless at work, we all have been. I picked up my closest hoodie on the floor next to my bed, slipping it on over my head. Unplugging my phone from the charger, I put it in my hoodie pocket. I need a cup of coffee. Three hours of sleep in the last four nights is killing me.

I opened my door, rubbing my eyes with the knit fabric of my sleeves; I moved my hands just in time to see Jones standing in front of me, shirtless in his boxers. I covered my eyes and yelled at him, "What the fuck are you doing here! Where are your clothes!"

"Uhhh, shit."

"Oh my god! I'm sorry, Brittney!" Sam shrieked.

I cupped my hands over my eyes, looking at the ground and leading myself to the coffee pot. "Is this a stress release thing?"

Sam came running into the kitchen, wearing a white spaghetti strap and spandex shorts. "Please don't tell anyone, it's against every single rule."

I let out one laugh. "I'm sure my engagement is breaking more. Just tell him to put fucking clothes on, girl."

"Already dressed, Britt!" Jones came out of Sam's bedroom wearing sweats and a tight grey t-shirt.

He pissed me off on my first day so I never really looked at him before. I wasn't missing much; besides him being a douchebag, he is average-looking. Buzz cut, stubble for facial hair, tall. Compared to me, everyone's tall though. He isn't in the best shape, just enough to pass our physical. Without looks backing him up, I don't know how he has made it so far in the world acting the way he does. If I didn't have to see him every single day, and breathe the same air as much as I have to, I wouldn't put up with his shit. God, I hope that's just an act at the office. If I have to deal with him at home too, his shit is going to get old fast.

I pulled out three coffee cups from the cupboard, placing them on the counter. Sam is beside me filling the cups with Butter Pecan creamer. This is the farthest thing from my medium white chocolate mocha, in a large cup with extra whip cream, but it will have to do.

I picked up my cup, hugging it in my hands. "What's an affordable hotel around here? I need one night with Spencer."

"I bet you do." Sam winked at me. "Just stay here. I can go to Tim's and he can come over. A secret for a secret."

"I'm not kicking you out of your place."

"I'm not the only one that lives here. You haven't woken up next to him in eight months. You're really fucking grouchy, you need sex."

"Oh, fuck you." I stormed past her and walked into my room.

I slammed the door behind me and heard them both laughing. Damn it, she's right.

I don't know when I'm ever going to be able to be with him again and that kills me. I haven't shed one tear since he found out I'm alive. We never get to talk, but at least I belong to him and he belongs to me. I was planning on staying in bed today, but until I hear from him, I'm not going to be able to get a moment of peace. Taking a big drink of my coffee, I open my makeup bag, standing at my dresser and looking into the mirror. I'm going to go buy lingerie, something that will blow his mind.

Walking into the pink building, confusion hit me all at once. I should have bought something online.

A salesgirl is walking up to me with a customer service smile. "Can I help you with anything?"

I sighed. "I need something sexy."

She nodded and started walking to the back of the building. The closer I get, I can see mannequins wearing exactly what I'm looking for. Everything is black, I'm already white enough and I don't want to look like Casper the Friendly Ghost more than I already do. Red makes me look tanner, but it's the same color as the eyes on his Basilisk tattoo. Royal blue is his favorite color, but it's not my color.

"Do you have anything in light pink?" I asked.

She nodded, looking at my body and searching for the size she thought would fit. She grabbed a light pink one-piece with lace that would tie behind my neck with a low-cut V down to the waistline. Lace would be covering the parts of my body that would tease him not to see. I grabbed it from her hands, noticing it's crotchless; I nodded my head in agreement.

Spencer is going to love this.

I got home and fell onto my bed, regretting my decision to get a bikini wax. I want to pick up my phone to call Lizzy just to hear her laughing at me. Not having her around me every day is making it hard to keep staying dead. I know Max and Theo are having a hard time not having me around. I know my bedroom is set up the same as I left it. No one would touch the disgusting mess I left behind. I just hope one of the three grabbed my coffee cups I left in there.

Max is probably happy not to follow me around with a vacuum, picking up the crumbs I leave behind. Theo is probably happy that I'm not walking around with my perfume stinking up the place. Lizzy, she isn't okay. She is probably saying she is, but she isn't. Her motherly love lets her stay strong for everyone, but as soon as she's alone, she will crumble into a million tiny pieces. I hope one day she gets to be a mom, because that child is going to feel love in ways no one ever knew existed.

I want to say Theo and Max will be okay too. I know whatever they were on the other night wasn't the last time they will touch it. They will both think that numbing the pain will make me go away. I have been so caught up in

Spencer that I haven't even thought to think about my best friends, about my family. It's too painful to think about them, it's too real to know I fucked up everyone's life.

I put the pillow over my face and let the tears fall again for the first time in days. I can't wait until I get back home. Max and Theo won't question me showing up, Lizzy is going to hate me. As much as the four of us fight and forgive each other right after, this isn't going to be one of those times. I am going to have to work my ass off for her to forgive me.

My phone started to ring. I never even bothered to open my eyes to check; I just answered it. "Hello?"

"Babe, what's wrong?"

"I'm fine. What's happening? Is everything okay?"

"We just dropped Charlie off at home. I need to see you."

"I'll text you the address."

I hung up the phone, feeling more selfish than ever. I sent Spencer the text message of where to come and sent Sam one telling her that he's coming over. It isn't fair that Spencer gets to know I'm alive and gets to come to me for comfort when everyone else I love doesn't get that. I know I'm doing all of this for him, I don't regret any of it. I wouldn't redo it. I just wish my friends and my parents knew I was alive and okay. I wish they knew of the person I am today.

I wouldn't normally be this emotional; not sleeping is screwing with my mind.

Shit.

Spencer is coming over.

Either I have been stuck in my thoughts for a very long time, or Spencer drove way over the speed limit. Either way, I don't care. I can hear his deep muffled voice down the hall through my bedroom door. I shoot out of bed just in time for my door to open. There he is standing 6'3", gorgeous amber eyes looking down at me. He looks like hell, just like me. We both have visible bags under our eyes. We are both gazing at each other in disbelief that we are in the same room together, alone.

He ran up to me, bending over, sliding his arm under my ass, picking me up, and making me as tall as he is. He slammed his lips into mine and we both made a humming noise from our throats. This is only the fourth kiss we have shared in the last eight months and we are still so in sync with each other.

He set me back on the floor and I wrapped my arms around his waist. I let go as he started to take off his shirt. I took off my shirt along with my bra and slipped on a tank top. As much as I want to spend the night feeling every inch of his body, I want to wake up next to him tangled up in his arms even more.

"Brittney, you're not okay. What's wrong?" Spencer asked as he crawled into his side of the bed against the wall.

"I miss my friends." I choked the words out, trying not to cry again. I lay down beside him, getting as close as I can into his chest.

"I've been attaching myself to Lizzy, it's pissing her off. She will be my best friend, whether she likes it or not."

I pushed out a laugh and smiled, nuzzling my face into his chest. She was never interested in making friends after the four of us became attached at the hip. None of us were, we all had each other and we were all any of us ever needed. Of course, in school, Theo was two grades higher than Lizzy and Max, and I was one grade under those two. It made life harder for Theo and I but we managed.

I forgot to text my supervisors. I rolled over, grabbing my phone and creating a group chat for the three of us. *She's home. We can still complete the operation.*

Take tomorrow off still. We have been working nonstop.

I gave Spencer my phone; he's reading the text messages smiling. "You mean I get you all day tomorrow?"

"Only if Martin doesn't call you in."

"Fuck him."

I rolled my eyes and smacked his arm. "Seriously, you can't be pissing him off."

"He already agreed to give us tomorrow off. I'm buying us a house. You can live there until you come back from the dead and I'll move in with you when that happens. I can see you more often."

"You know, I'm messy, you are going to lose your mind."

"Only every five minutes." I laughed and he sighed. "I'm serious, I don't care how crazy I go, we lost so much time together."

I closed my eyes tight. "I'm sorry I broke your heart."

He is holding me closer to him, tightening his grip. "I can never go through that again, all of us love harder because we could die any second. I would have rather been dead then live through that hell again."

"I'm sorry."

"You are here now. I'm here. As far as I'm concerned, nothing else matters. You don't need to apologize when you are doing all of this for me."

I nodded my head and sank farther into the mattress. Being here with him was exactly why I was doing what I was doing. I closed my eyes, soaking up this moment and falling into a deep peaceful slumber.

Lizzy

Even after a nine hour sleep the past five nights, I am exhausted from working on Halloween, it's a nightmare. The past few days, I have been more exhausted than I ever have been in my entire life. I'm blaming all that on how crazy *Willie's* has been.

April slammed the door of her office and ran out of her office at full speed. "Have you spoken to Erik today or yesterday?"

I felt a lump form in my throat. I haven't spoken to him since he came in on Halloween, six days ago, to check up on me. I shook my head no, trying to fight back the tears.

"Goddamn it!" April screamed as she kicked the bar in front of her. "Call him and get him to stop by. No one is getting back to me."

"What's going on?"

"Just call him please."

I took off my apron and walked outside, going to his contact in my phone.

"Lizzy, I'm so happy to hear your voice."

I felt a shaky exhale leave my throat. "April is losing her shit."

The line disconnected and I saw him walking up to me in his police uniform. Without thinking, I ran up to him, wrapping my arms around him and squeezing as tight as I could with his bulletproof vest under his jacket.

I backed up to look him in the eyes. "April made a scene, I thought something happened to you. Why haven't you been answering my calls? Are we okay?" Tears started to escape my eyes, running down my face.

Erik wiped away my tears with his thumbs, pulling me in and kissing my head. "I'm okay, Lizzy. We are okay. There has been a lot of bad shit happening at work. I have been pulling twenty-hour days to help."

I sank into his chest; ever since we met, we have been spending every day together, falling asleep next to one another; if we weren't at work, we were together. I have fallen hopelessly in love with him, I need to tell him but I'm terrified. It's only been two weeks.

"Are you in danger?"

Erik stayed silent; he held me against him even tighter and I let out a sob. His arms are shaking, he isn't his normal confident self.

"Erik, I love you. You need to be safe."

He grabbed my shoulders, pushing me backwards and looking me in the eyes; he bent down and kissed me.

Erik pulled his lips from mine. "I love you, Lizzy. I'm going to end this shit right now."

"You need to talk to April before you go anywhere. I'm going to stay out here and try to fix my face. Come see me before you leave."

He backed away from me, still holding my hand; all I can see in his eyes is pain. I don't know what's going on; as much as I want to know, he won't tell me for my protection.

The front camera on my phone revealed me looking like a swamp monster. The fact Erik was able to tell me he loved me for the first time with eyeliner running down to my cheeks was incredible. I poked my head around to the side of the building and saw no one, so I walked down a few feet and wiped my eyes with my shirt. I sniffled a few times and heard Erik's shoes against the sidewalk; he wrapped his arms around my middle from behind, pulling me into him.

"I'm sorry I have been distant. I didn't think you would worry so much about me. As soon as we are done and I finally get to sleep, I will have an entire day cleared for us to watch *Friends* and cuddle."

I took a deep breath, absorbing him into me. I nodded and he spun me around, planting his lips on mine. Even when he gets less than three hours of sleep a night for almost a week, he is still beautiful.

I started to pull away and put my hands on his face. "You really need to go."

"As soon as we finish, I will text you. I love you. I love you. I love you."

Erik took one step away from me and ran back to his police cruiser. I can't shake the feeling, but it feels like he was preparing himself to say goodbye. I waited for him to drive away and I walked into *Willie's* to get back to work. I swung open the door and the smell I once enjoyed hit me all at once.

I started to gag, and I ran to the bathroom, pushing the door open. I hit the bathroom stall with my shoulder and I threw up.

What the hell is happening?

"Are you okay?" Of course, April would walk in.

"I'm fine." I leant up against the bathroom stall, wiping my mouth.

She swung the door open and kneeled down in front of me. "Jesus, Liz. Are you pregnant?"

Between fighting the urge to puke again, I started to laugh. The bathroom door opened again and the smell came wafting in, I turned to the toilet just in time for me to start puking, again. I can feel April hovering behind me, holding my hair. I leaned up against the stall and she grabbed me toilet paper. I tossed it in and flushed the toilet.

"Can you pass me my phone? I don't know where I dropped it."

"I found it outside the door."

I shook my head. "I really love you, I hope you know that." She started smiling. "Did Erik come and talk to you?"

Watching her nod, I opened my period tracker on my phone and I instantly felt all the color wash away from my face. It feels like I'm going to be sick again. I don't know how I didn't notice my period was two weeks late.

"Lizzy, what the hell is going on? I'm giving you a ride home."

I opened my mouth a few times trying to push the words out but nothing was coming out. I forced my mouth to work with my brain. "I don't think I can afford to miss work."

She snatched my phone out of my hands and I watched her eyes get wide. "Shit. You need to get a test."

April stood up and reached her hand out for mine. We both washed our hands in silence and walked out to the bar. I looked up at the clock and saw it was time for me to leave. I texted both Max and Theo and told them to pick me up at the closest store. I ran to the store with my legs shaking. Every emotion I ever felt is pouring through my body. If that test shows up as a little pink plus, this is going to destroy our relationship. We haven't been together long enough to even think about kids.

I ran through the automatic doors, reading the signs on top. I ran towards it and grabbed the pink and white box. I got to the till and saw my car pull up in front of the doors. I rounded up and left the cash before I stuffed the box in my purse.

Thankfully, they never asked what was wrong with me the entire ride. I sat in the back, biting my nails. Thinking of the worst possible conclusions.

He's going to ask me to get an abortion.

He's going to leave me.

He's going to leave us.

My parents.

Oh god, my parents.

They already want nothing to do with me or Theo because of how we have been acting out the last few months. The only family I have left is Max and Theo.

Max never even put the car in park, he is still slowing down to park; I opened the car door and jumped out and ran up the stairs as fast as I can. I dropped my apartment keys twice trying to unlock the door; a sob left my throat. Theo gently pulled me to the side while Max used his key to unlock the door. I pushed past them both and went right into the bathroom, ripping the box open.

Three minutes felt like it was never going to come. The seconds dragged by. My phone rang and I saw Erik's name light up with a picture of us.

"Are you okay?" I wiped my face to get the escaped tear.

"It's good. I need to see you, I can't wait until tomorrow. I just need you."

I moved my hand, bringing the test in my line of view, and the plus sign is staring up at me.

"Lizzy?"

I shook my head, wiping my face. "Yes, come over. I really need to see you."

"I'm going home to change and I'll head over."

I hung up the phone and grabbed the test, running to my bedroom. I sat on my bed, pulled the blankets over my shoulders, and sat there, staring at the pink plus sign.

The bed creaked under Max as he sat down beside me.

Theo gasped. "Jesus. What the hell are you going to do?" I shook my head, unable to speak. Theo grabbed my hands with one hand and used his other hand to turn my face to look at him. He used to look at me like this all the time when we were little. His dark green eyes are full of compassion and love. "Whatever you decide, we will be here."

I'm still looking at him, trying to find the words. "I need to call Mom and Dad."

Max put hand on my knee. "Fuck your parents. They don't get a word in this. We all know they are going to tell you to end your pregnancy and we all know that isn't happening."

I moved my head and looked at both of them; in this moment, I feel so loved. More tears fall from my eyes. "Brittney is supposed to be here for this, she's supposed to kick Erik's ass."

No one said a word. We all sat on the bed staring at the life-altering test.

Theo lit a smoke and hesitantly passed me one. I know it's bad, but I needed to process this until Erik gets here.

I lit it while watching the cherry burn. "What if he leaves. I can barely get by as it is, I can't pay for the medical bills let alone a crib, diapers, and baby clothes." I can hear my voice shaking while fighting through the tears.

The front door flew open and I let out a heavy breath. Erik is here. "Lizzy!" He called from the entrance.

"She's in here." Theo stood up from my bed.

Erik came in the room with his smile fading when he saw my upset expression, Max and Theo both put their hands on his shoulders as they walked by, causing Erik to panic.

"What the hell is going on?" I can see his chest moving fast from his short breaths. He made eye contact with me as he fell on his knees on the floor in front of my bed. "Lizzy."

"If you want to leave me, I understand." His eyes went wide. I tossed the pregnancy test closer to him. "You aren't trapped. You don't have to stay."

No emotion crossed Erik's face, he looked as overwhelmed, confused, and scared as I feel. We have been sitting in silence for five minutes, his gaze is still focused on the plus sign.

"What are you going to do?" Erik slowly made eye contact with me.

"I'm not making a decision without you. Spend the night so we can try and figure this out."

Before I was finished talking, Erik stripped down to his boxers. I stood up and took off my work clothes, replacing them with a tank top and pajama bottoms. I moved my face sideways to glance over my shoulder, he's lying on my bed with his arm under his head, supporting it up; the other is on top of the blankets, ready to cuddle me. We are facing the hardest, most confusing obstacle a new couple can face, and he isn't going anywhere.

I shuffled my feet to the bed; the closer I get to him, I can see the bags under his eyes from being overworked and sleep-deprived. I am such a shitty person to make him deal with this right now. At least it's only 6 pm.

It's only six at night and I'm going to bed. Being pregnant already sucks.

I crawled into bed and covered myself up, I moved closer to Erik and kissed him. I tried to pull away but he put his hands behind my head, pulling me in. I missed the taste of his lips, the smile he would get when he kisses me. It finally feels like I'm home.

"I'm sorry for dumping this on you. I know you had a few bad days."

"If you want to do this, I'm all in. I thought you were breaking up with me, I was trying to come up with an argument."

"Before I took the test, I was working myself up to all the bad reactions you would have."

"That's my baby in there. I'm not going anywhere."

Erik held me against his chest, making me feel safer than he ever has. I still had a million worries, but he is still here. I have support. I can almost, maybe do this.

I felt his breathing even out. He fell asleep.

I didn't think it was possible to fall in love so easily and so fast. I always thought movies were full of shit with love at first sight, but I was wrong. We are moving at hyper speed, but that's okay.

Just like what Brittney used to tell me, *everything happens for a reason, princess.*

Brittney

The next morning, the obnoxious siren alarm from my phone quickly awoke me. Moving one hand and feeling around the mattress, opening one eye and sighing. Spencer isn't here. Covering my hands with my face, I'm terrified that he is going to run from me scared that I'm going to hurt him again. I know he loves me, but I'm wondering if that is enough for him at this point. I can handle my own, and now I have a team to back me up; after what happened to Charlie, I hope he doesn't try to leave me in his own way of protecting me.

I got out of bed, flicking on the light and closing my eyes, preparing myself for the shock of the brightness. Walking over to the closet, I found my robe draped over the door. Shutting off the light and opening my bedroom door, I can smell bacon; I can hear the humming of the coffee machine. I walked down the hall and checked the kitchen and the living room, but he isn't here. Walking over to the patio and looking through the glass door, he is sitting on the chair in his suit pants and a purple shirt from the night before. My heart is fluttering at the sight of him.

I opened the door, stepping outside. I didn't think this through; the mats under my feet are frozen. "I thought you left."

He exhaled the smoke, turning his head to look at me, reaching his hand out for me. "Why the fuck would you think that?"

I shrugged. "Recent events."

"Me not being with you wouldn't make a difference at this point, Ms. FBI agent."

It never once occurred to me that Spencer would be proud of my new job title. The way he said it and the way his eyes are sparkling, he is proud of me. I turned around, pulling my fingers away from his and opening the door, stepping inside. The warm air is making my ice-cold feet numb. I don't understand how it is this cold outside and we don't have snow.

Standing in the kitchen, grabbing coffee cups, plates, and cutlery, and noticing Spencer made the bacon just the way I like it: crispy to the point of almost burning. Even after all this time away, he still remembers the smallest things about me. He is behind me, wrapping his arms around my shoulders and pulling me into his chest.

"You know, I don't care that you're a smoker, but I would like you to live as long as you can. Have you ever thought about quitting?" I tried to make it sound like I hated kissing a fucking ashtray, but in the nicest way possible.

"It's the only way I can manage my stress, my stress gets out of hand and my anger issues come out." He is looking down at me, I brushed his answer off. "How about I quit the second I'm no longer a Basilisk?"

I nodded my head with an open mouth smile. Neither of us know how long that is going to be, but it's going to be in the near future. I can deal with another six to twelve months of kissing an ashtray.

Everything about this morning has been perfect. We have been careful to pick shows and movies that won't be a trigger for me, nothing I used to watch with my friends or family and absolutely nothing about death. Neither of us wanted our first day in eight months together end up turning into him consoling me.

Spencer is sitting on the couch with his foot rest out. I am laying across the couch with my head in his lap, he has been running his fingers though my platinum blonde hair this entire time. Just like he used to. I haven't been looking at him this entire time and I still know what facial expressions he is using when he talks.

"Do you want kids?" I grabbed his thigh, giving him a squeeze.

"I never did until I met you. Now that I know we only have a bit longer until freedom, I want them even more."

"We need a house with extra bedrooms then."

He is squeezing my arm, I know he is smiling, tipping his head back and thinking how happy and lucky he is. "I need to get you your ring. I feel pathetic proposing to you in a stairwell and you still not having it."

"No! I don't want it until I'm back. Everyone at the office knows not to look at the Basilisk girl."

Spencer's body vibrated as he laughed. "They call you that?"

"I beat them to it."

I rolled onto my stomach, propping my body up with my arms and looking at his face. He has the same expression on his face as he did the day when I was soaking wet from the rain. I sat up, giving him a kiss and pulling my mouth away. "I'll be right back." He reached his arm up my robe, grabbing my ass.

As hard as it is to pull away from him, I somehow managed. Walking back to the bedroom with my numb legs, I got into the room, taking off my robe and shoving all my clothes in a hamper. I reached into my closet, grabbing the pink box from yesterday and placing the thin pink fabric on my body. As I predicted, the lace is just covering up my breasts, the thin tight fabric is hugging my sides. Not only do I feel beautiful in it, I know it's going to drive him insane. I open the door of the bedroom and walked down the hall to go find my fiancé. Spencer is sitting on the couch with the remote control in his hand, flipping through the guide. He isn't even doing anything, but he is the sexiest man alive.

He cranks his head in my direction and a smile is appearing on his face. "Holy. Fucking. Shit." He flew up from the couch, walking over to me.

I met him halfway with only one thing in mind. As soon as I put my hands on his hips, I remembered that I don't have any condoms and I'm assuming that he doesn't either. "After you slept with those girls, did you get tested?"

He cupped the back of my head with his palm, he's hating this conversation as much as I am. He is looking at me with a realization of my question. "I always used protection, but I got tested as soon as I knew you were alive, just in case." He sucked back air. "Have you…"

I shook my head no, immediately grabbing his hand and leading him to my bedroom. He is following me with no hesitation, all he wants is me. Spencer shut the door behind him; before he has the chance to pick me up, I unsnapped his dress pants, pulling his pants and his boxers down to his knees. I bent down and brought him into my mouth. My lips touched him and Spencer is moaning, he has a fist full of my hair, helping me bob my head back and forth.

He is letting out a long moan. "If you keep doing this, I'm going to finish a lot sooner then you want."

I pulled away, standing up. Spencer is kicking off his pants and taking off his shirt. I forgot how good he looks shirtless, his colorful tattoos making his muscles look more defined. He picked me off my feet and dropped me onto the bed, crawling on top of me. He is lowering himself towards my body to kiss me. I met him halfway, slamming my mouth into his, opening it and waiting for his tongue to meet mine. He is kissing me back with the same amount of urgency, if not more. His hands are touching my sensitive pink skin. I can feel a smile on his face, he's satisfied.

We are gazing into each other's eyes, the look in his eyes isn't domination but pure uncontainable love. This isn't us as a couple anymore, this is us as future husband and wife.

We both let out a moan at the same time as he pushes himself in me. I lock my ankles on his back as he is thrusting against me. My legs are growing weak, my body is tensing. I dig my nails into his back, rolling my eyes in the back of my head at the same time he pulls out.

Sweat is dripping from his hairline. He raised his hand, wiping his face crawling into bed beside me. "I stand corrected, you better not make a guy feel like *that*."

I smiled, remembering the first time we were together. "Only you, baby."

It took no convincing for Spencer to spend the night. The rest of the day and night we have been looking for houses, condos, townhouses, for us to buy. At this point and how much we miss each other, anything was going to do, even if it was only a temporary home. We are both using this as an excuse to keep our minds away from him walking away in the morning and us not knowing when we are going to be together again. We will deal with that in the morning; right now, we have to be a couple and do normal couple things.

The heartache we will be going through in less than twelve hours is lingering in the air. "I know you want us to find a place, Spence, but I can't be there when you're not home."

"I'll be there as much as I can, Britt."

"Everyone is going to be suspicious though. You are going to have to say you are dating someone."

Spencer wrapped his arm around me, kissing my head, running his fingers over the scars from the bullets in my back. "I know. What happens when I see a picture of you?"

"Pretend you didn't know I was Brittney, pretend like you are just finding out Cameron is dead." Spencer nodded. This plan sucks. "It's Liz, she will try to comfort you. Max and Theo will automatically love you. Ask her to look at pictures of me. Tell her you feel guilty dating."

"Brittney, this is going to turn into a mess."

"It's the only way we won't blow my cover."

Spencer nodded his head and sighed pulling me in even closer. I really hope him and Lizzy become close, maybe between him and Erik, the blow of my reappearance won't hit her so hard. If she doesn't hate them too.

"I need to tell someone else you're alive." With his words, my entire body tensed. "It will either be Dillon, Liam, or William. They are too caught up with Charlie to even realize that Lizzy is around."

"Do you have too? They are Martin's family."

Spencer kissed my head. "It's hell hiding this, hiding you. We are the family, none of them care about Martin."

Nuzzling myself closer to him, nodding my head in agreement.

Charlie

I woke up the next morning crying out for help. "Help me. Stop!" Someone came charging in, the sound of the door made me jump. I pulled up the blanket over my eyes, shutting them tight, I scooted back on the mattress. "Don't hurt me. Please." I started crying even harder.

"Charlie, it's William. You're safe. You're in Liam's bed."

I reached out to him. "Lay with me, please."

"Okay, I'm coming in."

"Why are you not at school?" I finally tried to open my eyes. "Hey, I can see your ugly face now."

He looked at me, shocked, and I laughed. "Oh, that hurts."

"You are lucky you are already hurt." He laughed. "We all took turns being here with you when you woke up. Three days later, you finally woke up."

"You just had to be here for your best friend?" He put his palm up to his face. "That's right; you are never going to live it down. You became best friends with a girl."

"Oh, shut up. Do you want to try to eat something? I know you need five meals a day, so you're starving."

I nodded and grabbed William's arm. "Please don't tell anyone I'm awake yet. I want to try to eat something with a small audience. Can you pass me my robe?"

I put it on under the blanket, terrified to look down at my body. The robe is fully covering me so I lowered the blanket and stuck my hand out for William to grab it and pull me up. I was expecting him to let go of my hand when I got out of the bed, but he kept holding it down the hallway and into the living room. He wandered away and came back with a glass of water and a cigarette. I found the remote and started looking for something to watch.

I got caught up with the television, and before I knew it, my food is ready. I cut a piece of my chicken and dipped it in BBQ sauce. As soon as I started eating, my stomach started growling. Eating for the first time in eight days is unbearable, I have to fight my body to keep eating. My stomach aches; luckily, that passes and I'm able to eat everything.

"I'm never going for an hour without food again."

William laughed. "I wouldn't put it past you. I need to text everyone now."

I heard the front door of the house open, and five voices piling in. Liam ran up to me. "Charlie, I missed you so much." He bent down and cupped my face with his hands, kissing me.

I reached out for Dillon's hand. "You guys need to stop looking at me like that." I looked down at my shoulder and noticed my robe was sliding down my arm, showing a few of my cuts.

I stood up and raced to my room. I stood with my back in front of the mirror. I pulled down my robe and looked at my reflection. Tears running down my face. The cuts from the whips are covering my back and shoulders.

Flashbacks flashed through my mind, and my anger is stirring up inside of me. I saw red, I started throwing things across the room. I'm not even sure what I'm picking up. Whatever I saw, I threw. My legs gave out from under my body, and I crashed to the ground. I wrapped my arms around my legs.

"I just want my life back. I don't want my scars to remind me." Tears are filling my eyes.

My door started opening. "Scars make us who we are." It's Adam. He sat crossed-legged in front of me on the floor. "You went through it alone." He put his hand on my knee. "You'll never be alone again. I wish we could say something to make this better."

"I made a scene."

"We all have anger issues. This is nothing. Believe me."

"Why did you come in here and not Liam?"

"It's always me destroying shit. I just figured I would be able to relate better."

I studied his face. He is serious and heartbroken. "I heard you used to have a crush on me." I gave him a playful shove backward.

Adam smiled. "Can you blame me? I was just too late to meet you."

"We should get out there." I grabbed his hand and we stood up. "I don't know how I'm going to live every day covering up my back and shoulders. Looking in the mirror and having a constant reminder, everyone looking at me devastated."

I feel tears running down my face. Adam grabbed my arm and pulled me in for a hug; he kept his hands low, trying not hurt me.

He nestled his face in my neck and whispered, "I will talk to everyone and make sure no one treats you differently. We are still in shock you are here with us."

He pulled away from our hug, moving his hand down my arm and reaching down to my hand. I looked at our hands and smiled at him. "None of us realized how much we needed you."

My body jolted me awake; I'm sitting on the bed, panting. My nightmare felt so real, I was reliving everything the McKinnon's put me though. My chest is heaving with my racing heartbeat, sweat is dripping from my face. I frantically pat the bed beside me, looking for Liam, I can't take my eyes away from the closet. I can't feel Liam beside me, I look over, his blankets are in the same position as when he left.

I picked up my phone and started calling him. It rings three times, then voice mail. I need to get hold of him, his phone rings twice and I am at voicemail. Again. I know William and Dillon are in class right now, I can't have them see me like this. Spencer and Josh would be here in an instant, but the only person I want to see is Adam.

I hesitantly picked up my phone to call him.

"Adam, are you in class?" I wiped the sweat from my forehead.

"I just walked out when I saw your call. I'm coming over; what's wrong?"

"I had a bad dream, no one's here. I don't want to be alone."

"I'll be there right away."

I stood up and grabbed my robe. I caught a glance of my reflection in the mirror. I don't see my normal reflection looking back at me. All I see is darkness. My blood is starting to boil. I scream and my fist breaks the glass.

"Fuck!"

I am running to the bathroom with my uninjured hand catching the blood that is dripping. I stick my hand under the water, trying to clean it up. I need to avoid looking in the mirror. I can't see that side of me again. I opened the medicine cabinet and grabbed tweezers to pick out the glass. I grabbed a bandage from the first aid kit and wrapped myself up.

"Why do I do this to myself?" I said as I cleaned the tweezers, throwing them back in the medicine cabinet and staring at the bathroom sink.

I sighed, walking to the living room. I need a distraction, I sat on the couch and flipped through the channels trying to find something to watch. I lit a smoke as soon as the door opened.

"It's just me, Charlie. Where the fuck is Liam?" Adam sat down next to me, reaching for a smoke.

I shrugged. "I don't know. He left last night randomly after his phone went off. I tried calling him but he sent me to voice mail. Is he not at your place?"

Adam is looking at me, unsure of what to say. "We haven't seen him since we left here yesterday." He glanced at my hand. "What did you do?"

"I grabbed my robe and I made the mistake of glancing in the mirror." My voice is shaking. "It was like something inside of me is trying to come out. All I saw was evil. Adam, I'm scared this is going to change me."

William opened the door and stormed in. "Well, I feel left out. Assholes." He stopped and I saw Adam shaking his head.

I passed a cigarette to William, I used my hand that wasn't bandaged up. I wanted to avoid explaining that again. "Have you seen Liam?"

"I talked to him today, he's coming home soon." The door opened. "Speak of the devil."

I shouted from the couch, "Where were you last night?"

Liam walked down the hall. "Out."

I watched Adam stand up and walk towards Liam's room. We heard the door slam behind him and muffled voices down the hall. The muffled turned into them screaming at each other, but I couldn't make out what they were saying. I have a feeling he was with a girl last night. The way he was texting and how he stormed out. I wouldn't put it past him.

William shook his head. "Oh boy."

"What's going on?" My voice is filled with annoyance, I just want someone to tell me the truth.

"If I knew, I would tell you."

Adam came out of Liam's bedroom and gave me a hug over the couch. "Call me later."

I nodded while putting my hand on his arm. "Get back to class. I'll be fine."

William is studying me once the door shut; he shook his head at me. "Why was he here?"

"He's the only one I feel comfortable with seeing me like this. I woke up panicking. Liam left last night, I was alone when I woke up."

"Don't play fire with fire, Charlie." William stood up from the chair and walked over to me, pulling me into his chest. "We both thought Liam was with you last night."

Liam stormed out of his room and slammed the front door behind him.

Later that day, William got called away for work. I insisted that he take Martin's call, but I'm on edge. I know I have to get used to them going back to work, but I don't think I could ever get used to the fear. I don't know what I would do if I lost one of them.

The door to the house opened and Liam paced in front of me. "I want to say sorry about last night."

"Where did you go?"

"With a friend."

"That's all I get?"

"I'm sorry. I won't pull anything like that again. I was being extremely selfish. It's just hard to see you like this."

"It's even harder being like this."

Liam sat beside me and wrapped his arms around me. "I'm sorry." He kissed my head. "Let get dinner ready. I'll be home tonight, I promise. I'll be home every night. I saw your mirror earlier."

"It just kind of happened."

"I'll make a better effort to be here for you."

Lizzy

I have limited myself to only one cup of coffee a day to try and control my caffeine levels. I have so many questions, but we don't have a doctor's appointment for another week. My hormones are going every direction, making me feel crazy. I am so hungry all the time, my energy is completely drained. I really don't understand why they call it morning sickness when it happens all day, every single day.

I'm watching the coffee brew and drip into the coffee pot. My boobs are killing me, wearing a bra feels like torture. I held my hands, pulling the underwire away from my chest and sucking in air.

Erik came behind me, wrapping his arms around my middle, bending over so he can rest his head on my shoulder. He has been staying with me every single night since I told him. "I can take you to buy a more comfortable bra before you go to work. Can you just please move in with me?"

I put my hands over his. "We are already moving fast enough, don't you think?"

"I have been with you every day. Only difference is it will be my place."

"Give me a few weeks, okay?"

Erik nodded and we both sighed when my phone rang for the fiftieth time this morning.

Theo came out of his room, stomping on the floor. "Answer your fucking phone!"

"I don't know who it is!" I pulled it out of my pocket.

Erik is looking over my shoulder, laughing. "Top one is Spencer. One under that is Josh. They both decided you are going to be their new best friend."

I rolled my eyes while adding their number into my phone. I knew Spencer was persistent, but knowing there is another one just like him is a bit scary. Whether I like it or not, they are going to suck me in.

I got ready for work while Erik said bye to Theo and Max and dragged me out of the apartment. I love how close Erik has gotten to my brother and Max.

All three of them are trying hard to have a solid relationship with each other. I appreciate them all trying, it's surprising how good they get along without anything being forced. Somehow, their personalities just mix.

Erik just dropped me off at work and my boobs can finally breathe. These hormones are kicking my ass. I need to put extra concealer on my face to make a better attempt in hiding my acne. I opened the door to *Willie's* and held my breath, slowly letting the smell hit me. Any smell of meat sends my nausea into overload.

Josh walked up to me, wrapping his arm around my shoulder. "I'm not going to say sorry about blowing your phone up."

I smiled, looking straight ahead, I wrapped my arm around his back. I can say it's annoying, but I never really had friends outside of the four of us. We were too close-knit to let anyone else in. It felt amazing having other people care about me.

April looked up from the bar, smiling. "Lizzy, do you know how to make drinks?" I shook my head. "I'm training you today."

April pulled out a thick binder from under the bar. Every page is covered in plastic, pictures of the drinks and pictures to make them step by step. I always thought it was more complicated than this. I think April was just wanting to hang out with me; the entire shift I stayed behind her watching her pour, mix, shake, and garnish the drinks. I'm not complaining, more experience on a resumé is a good thing.

The shift ended and Spencer walked up to the bar, leaning over it. His face is way too close to mine. "I'm giving you a ride home; we are going to take the long way so you can't ignore my calls."

I sighed. "Why the hell is it so important to you that we are close?"

"We need a girl around besides April. The other three have Charlie. We are close with her but Josh, Adam, and me get the shit end of the stick."

"You're using me to fill a void? Fucking smooth, Spencer."

Spencer shot up from the bar, shaking his head. "Not what I meant!"

"Whatever, please don't smoke in the car. I just quit."

Spencer is hard to say no to. His personality lights up rooms. Even though I'm annoyed, he still put his arm over my shoulder, trying to distract me. We are walking out and every girl is staring at him. I think the guys are used to it because they are so oblivious to it. The first time I saw Spencer, he made me stumble over my words.

I sighed as I got in the car. "You annoy me, a lot. I know we are going to be close."

Spencer started grinning as he drove away. I immediately started to regret my words.

Brittney

Rubbing my eyes, raising the phone to my ear, not moving my hand. "Hello?"

"Are you awake? I miss you."

I rolled my eyes. "No, I'm sleeping, that's why I answered."

"I'm coming over, I have a surprise for you."

"I'll unlock the door, crawl into bed with me."

I hung up the phone, getting out of bed and dragging my feet to the door. Checking my phone, it's 3 am. How am I still awake? Falling back on my bed, the springs creaked beside me. I never even heard Spencer open the front door.

"I was already outside your building, I couldn't wait to give you this." He is reaching inside of his pocket and pulling out a ring box, sitting at the end of the bed. "It's not the original one, you wanted to wait for that one. I just feel ridiculous proposing in a stairwell and you still not having a ring."

I pushed myself up my stomach, sitting on my knees. Holding out my hand, he is putting a white gold band with a small diamond on my finger. "I love it."

"Really? It's not your normal flashy style. It's just until you come home."

"I'm getting married to you. The ring doesn't matter. Let's get some sleep."

We stopped to grab us both a coffee, everything has changed so fast but at least we are still predictable with our drinks. I haven't moved my hand from Spencer's; thankfully, he can drive when it's bumper to bumper with one hand. I don't know how I went so long without him at my side, never in my life am I letting that happen again. The band is creating a space between my fingers, finally us getting married feels real.

After what felt like a century in traffic…I'm being over-dramatic, why so many people feel the need to drive in this city is beyond me. Spencer has been taking so many turns I have completely lost all sense of direction. We are in a quiet neighborhood, trees on every lawn, bushes by the sidewalk giving privacy to the yards. Spencer pulled into a driveway and my confusion hit an ultimate high. Looking at the yard out the window, a *For Sale* sign with a sold sticker is at the end of the driveway. I was so distracted looking around, I never even saw the sign.

No way.

He bought a house.

"Is this!" My voice reached a high-pitched noise only dogs can hear.

Spencer is laughing while opening his door. "I could tell from your face this is the one you wanted the most."

I opened the car door, running into the yard and looking at our new home. He is right, this is the one I wanted the most. The price tag had made me change my mind, I knew that wouldn't matter to him. I know he paid for it in cash. The brown house has a two-car garage, with spruce trees standing at the living room window, the deck is wrapped around the front of the house. Standing in awe looking at it, Spencer put his arm around my waist.

"There's a bottle of whiskey inside." Spencer is holding onto my hand, pulling me inside.

Letting out a laugh and shaking my head, I wouldn't expect anything else from him. He opened the door revealing the entryway. Everything looks so much bigger than the pictures. Everything is so open.

"I want to see our room." I'm squeezing his hand.

Spencer is leading me up the stairs; the upstairs is wrapping around the house with the bedroom doors wide open. He is leading me up another small staircase. Walking in, I can see a huge walk-in closet and a large bathroom. This room is big enough to put his king-sized bed, dressers plus extra furniture.

Spencer pulled me into him, wrapping his arms around my shoulders. "We can go online and buy all the furniture we need and I will buy us a new bed so you can stay here as much as you want."

I am blown away, completely speechless that he is doing this for us, for our future. I want to say thank you to him but I don't know how to. The shiny belt buckle on his pants came into my line of sight. Without a second thought, I snapped it open, undoing his suit pants.

"What are you—" I cut him off, putting him inside my mouth. "Jesus."

Stroking him with my hand, I'm feeling him becoming erect. Putting my lips on him and bobbing my head back and forth; his moans and swears are echoing in the empty room. I'm pushing myself to my limits. Hearing and feeling how much he is reacting to me is making me enjoy it. Sucking my lips in creating a vacuum seal, he grabbed my hair, pushing himself deeper into my mouth.

I pulled my mouth away as soon as I gagged and he dropped his hands. "I'm sorry! Lay down, babe."

Shaking my head, pulling him in my mouth again. This is about him. Looking up at him, I can see the pleasure in his face. Spencer has intertwined his fingers in my hair, letting out a moan, his body shook.

Standing up and wiping my face. "Show me the rest of the house now."

Spencer picked me off my feet, planting a kiss on my lips. "You're incredible. Let's go get a drink. I need to talk to you about something."

He set me back on my feet; grabbing his hand, I led him down the first staircase, down the hall then down the second staircase, into the bright modern up-to-date kitchen. On the counter, there are three whiskey cups next to an unopened fourteen-year-old single malt bottle of whisky. Exhaling a breath of air, I remember him wanting to tell one of his friends about me, about everything. Walking up to the counter, turning around, putting my hands on the counter, I jumped up.

"If my bosses find out anyone knows, I'm done for." I'm defeated. I can't blame him for wanting to tell someone else.

"I know. It's just William. I was going to tell Liam, but he's lost too much control. William will keep his head on."

I nodded, watching Spencer open the freezer and reach into the bag of ice. I held out the whiskey bottle, filling my cup to the brim. He passed me my cup, chugging back a quarter of it, feeling my throat burn, letting out a long sigh. Spencer grabbed my head, pulling me in to kiss me on the forehead. His lips are hovering over my skin, neither of us realized how awful it is going to be to bring me back from the dead one by one.

Spencer sat his cup on the counter beside me, giving my leg a squeeze as he ran up the stairs. After a few moments, my cup became emptier and the front door opened.

"Why the fuck did you send me to an empty house? Is this where I die? Are you going to kill me?" William's voice is echoing in the living room. I can hear his shoes walking against the hardwood floors as he gets closer to me. He got into the kitchen, looking at me with his eyes burning with anger.

I closed my eyes tight, remembering he doesn't know I'm dead. Only thing he knows is that I broke Spencer's heart.

He pushed out one laugh, looking at me. "You are stupid to show your face again. Go find someone else's life to destroy, fucking bottom feeder."

Tears are forming in my eyes, the way he is looking at me is making me wish I was dead. Putting the cup to my lips and drinking the remainder of the whiskey in my cup, I can hear Spencer's shoes hitting the floor as he's running down the stairs.

In a fury, Spencer got into William's face. "Talk to my fiancée like that one more time, I dare you."

My mouth dropped open, watching Spencer own me like this, hoping one day I won't be on the bad side of this wrath. "Babe, he doesn't know; come here." Reaching over to the smoke pack, I pulled two out.

I poured a cup for William, holding it out to him. "Take it." He is staring at me. "You just watched me drink it and pour it, it's not poison, just take it."

Spencer came over to me and snatched the smokes out of my hand, lighting both of them. I poured myself another drink, listening to the same story that Davis told him. My body is starting to sway and my mind is light as air. William can say any hateful word to me now and it would be brushed off.

"You aren't an FBI agent. There's no fucking way." William's anger hasn't disappeared.

"Spence, can you go get my purse? It's in the bedroom," I asked Spencer, he is looking at me, reluctant about leaving us alone together. "It's fine." I tried to give my warmest smile, but I'm terrified.

I poured William another drink, passing it to him. Hearing that story feels like I am living someone else's life and I am going to wake up any second and all of this is a dream.

In no time at all, Spencer came rushing back downstairs to us in the kitchen. He set my purse beside me and I dug in it, finding my badge. I tossed it to William, his eyes widening as he looked at it.

I pointed my finger at him. "Keep your mouth shut. What Spencer didn't tell you is that we are ending the Basilisks and we need your help to get everyone on board."

I rolled my eyes, looking down at my ringing phone. Nelson has the worst timing. "Agent Hills."

"Tomorrow at two, we are having a meeting. Spencer and Erik both need to be there in my office, with you."

I hung up the phone, looking up at Spencer. "Call Erik; tomorrow, both of you need to come to work with me."

William cracked his knuckles nervously. "This is really happening? You are going to help us?" I nodded my head and his body came crashing into me for a hug. William pulled away with his hands on my shoulders. "So, does this mean you carry a gun legally?"

I can hear Spencer laughing. I shrugged. "I mean, one of us has to."

"I'm sorry about earlier. I'm so fucking sorry, Brittney."

I jumped off the counter, almost falling over; Spencer caught me before I crashed onto the floor. "You thought you were protecting him; if anything, I should be thanking you."

Spencer stayed the night over. We both woke up in the same position we fell asleep in, I can get used to that. We stayed up late, picking out furniture for our new house, trying to make it perfect. Spencer looks like he hasn't slept all night, I can't blame him though. He is freaking out on the inside about having to go into the bureau. I can tell he is happier having one of his friends know about me. I am terrified William is going to let it slip, I am scared that he is going to have it all backfire on us. I shouldn't have let Spencer tell him, but he needed someone other than Erik to know the truth; if he can trust him with this big of a secret then I have to as well.

Spencer reached over the middle console, grabbing my hand. I sighed, squeezing him. "Don't be nervous."

"I'm not."

"Bullshit! You aren't the bad guy here; do you hear me?"

Looking over at Spencer, I'm expecting him to nod, smile, or anything to tell me he understands but he is made from stone. As well as I know him and as much as I want to read him, I can't. We parked the car and I got out walking to his side of the car, standing on my tippy toes and giving him a kiss. I can already feel people looking at us. An engine turned off beside us.

"Please tell me I'm not the only one who feels fucked up about walking into the FBI." Erik's voice is low.

"Just follow me." I let my fingers travel down Spencer's arm into his hand.

I flashed my badge, waiting for them to sign in. Both of their hands are shaking, they look anything but innocent. Walking to the elevator, Spencer's hand is around my waist, he hasn't stopped touching me since the ride here. I wish I could do something to prove to him that everything is going to be okay.

He should know by now that we don't care about arresting them, it's hard when I don't even know what this meeting is about. The elevator chimed as we got to the floor; as soon as we walked out, all eyes are on us through the glass door. I can feel his grip tightening on me.

Opening the door and looking up the small staircase, I can see a woman wearing a sophisticated black dress, even from afar, I can see her makeup and hair looking perfect. Each step we get closer, I can feel both Erik and Spencer relax.

I opened the door with the agents working the case sitting around the table. Rodriguez looked up and nodded his head. "This is Kinsley. Erik and Spencer, we need you to take these bugs and plant them in Martin's office. Whatever goes on in there, we will know."

Spencer pulled me into his side, exhaling a deep breath of air, every worry vanished. Kinsley is looking at us with all the love in the world. I don't understand how she is still handling Martin when she has turned to us, but I'm happy she has. If it wasn't for her, I wouldn't be able to save my fiancé. Glancing up at him, he is looking down at me with the same look of contentment in his eyes when I had first met him.

For the first time in a very long time, I know everything is going to work out in the end.

Lizzy

Yesterday was our first doctor's appointment. In the past week, my morning sickness has gotten so bad, I need a prescription to help calm my stomach down. I haven't been able to hold much food down, so I have been losing weight. The doctor had to reassure both of us many times that we are still okay. Erik held my hand the entire appointment, the only time he let go of me was when I was getting my weight and blood pressure done. The waiting room was empty and that seemed to make Erik more fidgety. I never thought I would ever see someone so nervous in my life.

Our first ultrasound was hardly noticeable. It was so tiny it was just a little blob. Both Erik and I almost cried when we saw the images on the screen. Erik was trying to say he never cried, but I saw the tear run down his face.

When I had first told Erik about being pregnant two weeks ago, I was terrified. I was terrified it was going to rip us apart. I was scared he was going to leave. It's only been two weeks, but I was crazy to think any of that. He has been so supportive. He has even tried to quit smoking; it isn't going very well. He is still trying.

Max, Theo, myself, and Erik have been sitting outside of my parents' house for over an hour, trying to get enough courage to go inside. I have been watching the time change on the clock, it hit 10 am and I know we have already wasted so much time. They are good people; they both have hearts of gold. It is our fault we have such a broken relationship with them. Just like Max, they thought of Brittney as their child. They helped them pay rent when times were hard, paid for their tutors in college when they started to fail a class. It kills me that we made such shitty decisions to break us apart.

Erik grabbed my hand, kissing each finger. "We can do this another day."

I shook my head and grabbed Theo's shoulder. "No, the three of us got ourselves into this mess; we need to fix it sooner or later."

I took a deep breath, grabbed the handle of the door, and put my foot on the payment, finally exhaling. Erik came up beside me, interlocking our fingers.

To my surprise, Max was the first one who walked up to the door, ringing the doorbell. He has always had a good relationship with his parents, but our house was always the safe house. If he drank too much, he would call my parents and they would grab him without speaking of it ever again.

We stood behind Max, waiting for the door to open; my mother opened the door and her jaw dropped when she saw the four of us standing there. "Hunny! Get down here now. Our kids are finally home."

The three of us plus my mom all instantly started crying. Max walked into the house and my dad grabbed his arm, pulling him in for a bear hug.

Erik kissed my head right before my mom stepped outside to look at me. "Baby."

I wrapped my arms around her and broke down. "Mama. I'm so sorry."

We all sat down in the living room wiping our tears, laughing when we glanced at each other. My dad sat down on the arm of the couch. "You all look so good, how long has it been?"

Theo cleared his throat. "Two months, we all quit cold turkey."

Max laughed once. "Mr. Cop over there gave us a ride home in the back of a cop car, just made our decision to quit clearer."

Both of my parents looked at Erik wide-eyed, probably just realizing he was sitting next to me, holding my hand.

I sank back in the chair, soaking everything up. We were so scared for nothing. I can't say a word, I'm trying, but I can't. Nothing is coming out. Whenever I was about to blurt it out, I squeezed Erik's hand to let him know it was time. I lost count after six. The conversation kept going. I don't know who needed this more: Mom, Dad, Max, or Theo. We never let our parents down, we were all straight A students, minus a few classes we struggled with, but we always got it eventually. College was no different. 3.5 GPAs for all of us, with the help of tutors. No wonder it hit them so hard when Brittney was killed, then we turned into grieving dug users.

My mom let out a sigh. "I'm sorry, but we have to get ready. Max's parents are having a dinner party tonight. They made us feel bad, so now we have to help set up." She turned to look at me. "Elizabeth, what's wrong with you? You haven't said a word since you came in."

Well, it's now or never. "I'm pregnant."

My dad looked like he was going to pass out; he looked at Erik with murder in his eyes. Erik let go of my hand, expecting the worst. My mom put her elbows on her knees with her head in her hands. She is silent, she is only silent when she is disappointed. Theo and Max exchange a paranoid look, they both stand up and start walking to the door.

"Who the hell is the dad? Or do you even know?" Mom slowly raised her head from her hands, her eyes filling with tears.

Theo threw his hands in the air. "Mom, she has never once slept around when she partied."

"How far along are you?" She sounds heart-broken.

I readjusted. "Doctor told me eight weeks. The baby's healthy, mom."

"How are you paying for the doctor's bills?"

I opened my mouth to talk when Erik jumped in for me. "I am paying for everything that she and my child needs."

Dad started walking towards Erik. My heart sank, both Max and Theo flinched. Erik stood up, not making a noise or complaining; he is going to take whatever my dad is going to do to him. Dad wrapped his arms around him and hugged him just like he hugged us at the door. Erik whispered something in his ear, causing my dad to smile.

Dad stood in front of me, grabbing my hand. "Stand up." I did as told and he hugged me. I looked over my dad's shoulder to my mom wiping her face.

"I'm a grandma." Mom sniffled her nose.

I grabbed Erik's arm, standing on my tippy toes as he lowered his face to kiss me. "I love you."

"Are you ready to tell my dad and brother now?"

I buckled up my seatbelt, laughing. "We really should have met each other's parents before we dropped the bomb on them."

Theo hit the dash. "Man, I thought Dad was going to hit you."

Erik smiled. "I was ready for it."

"Liz, why the hell am I driving your car when you're in the backseat?" Max said, confused.

"This is why you are on my insurance." I paused. "Wait, you don't even know where we are going, switch places with Erik."

The car ride is long, I lost where we turned multiple times. Unfamiliar street signs passed us by, the only thing I recognized is us passing Central Park;

other than that, I had no idea where we are. For a born and raised New Yorker, I seriously took advantage of the benefits of living here.

I have never climbed the Statue of Liberty, I have never been to the Empire State Building.

The car came to a stop, Erik started talking pulling me out of my thoughts. "I have my car down the road. I can get her back home."

I shook my head, confused. "Why is your car down the road from your brothers?"

"I live four houses away."

I face-palmed, I don't even know where he lives.

Erik got out of the car and opened my door, I'm standing in front of him, he raised my chin with his hand, planting a small kiss on my lips. "Like I said before, move in with me."

"Erik, that's crazy."

He put his hand on my belly and winked. Seven months from now, we are going to have a screaming newborn, I would have less bills to pay, I can save more and help out, I would be living in a house.

"Are you seriously asking me to move in with you?" He nodded. "Yes."

Erik kissed me again, wrapping his arms around my waist and pulling me in closer to him. My hormones are killing me, whenever he touches me, I need him. I get turned on so much easier now, I let out a moan and he pulled away, laughing.

"That was what got us in our situation in the first place. I'll deal what that later." He bent down, kissing me again, grabbing my ass, and pulling my body closer to him.

He stepped out of my line of sight and I saw the house. I'm so surprised Adam lives in a house with a white picket fence and flowerbeds. I don't know what I was expecting, but this wasn't it. Erik opened the fence and let me up the cement pads to the deck, he opened the door and I can hear Spencer and Josh arguing over which glass was who's. That doesn't surprise me; they are both children.

I started laughing and Erik walked in, tossing a pillow at them and telling them to shut up. Adam walked over to me with a smile, passing me a cup of whiskey; obviously, Erik has somehow kept this to himself.

"I'm fine, thanks." Adam shrugged while drinking it.

Erik grabbed my hand and led me to the kitchen, the house is small but still holds all of us with no problem. The living room has a big open window, letting all the natural light shine in. The living room has a fireplace but no TV.

I got in the kitchen and I tensed. Two of the most intimidating people I have ever seen standing in front of me. I was easily able to pick out Erik's dad; he stood tall, at least 6'5", only a few inches taller than both of his sons. Tattoos covering his neck and arms, there are so many I'm not even able to look at them if I wanted to. He is a monster in muscle, he must have started working out when he was a young teenager and never stopped. The man next to him was just as tall, full of muscles and tattoos, but with brown hair. April stuck her head out from behind him with a big smile on her face and I let out a sigh of relief.

"Dad, Martin, this is my girlfriend Lizzy." I can hear how proud Erik is.

April drank her cup of whiskey while making an awful face of regret. "Dad, this is your best server." Managing to choke out her words.

I shot my eyes wide. I am officially scared of my boss.

Despite how mean they look, they are really nice men, they make fun of Josh and Spencer with us. They instigated their arguments. They had the best manners, that surprises me. I am never one to judge a book by its cover, but I wasn't expecting two men who could pick you up and snap you in half to be gentlemen.

Erik sat down on the couch, pulling me onto his lap with no hesitation. "Are you ready?" I shrugged my shoulders, he kissed my cheek. "Fuckers, get in here."

What I learnt in the last hour: the more they swear at you and the more they insult you, the more they like you.

Everyone stood around us, staring at us. April already knew what was coming, she was trying to do a discrete dance but failing.

I stood up, grabbing Erik's hand and pulling him up. He looked at me with a big smile, he is more excited than I ever thought possible. "We are having a baby."

No one looks disappointed; it took Erik's dad a few minutes to process the news but he instantly called his wife, telling her. He pulled the phone away from his ear, we can hear her shrieking through the phone across the room.

Everyone hugged us, I can feel joy rushing through my body.

Martin hugged me. He pulled away and I saw his neck tattoo.

Basilisk.

Brittney.

Oh my god.

My stomach sank, I can't breathe. I am too stunned to cry.

Erik saw her picture in the apartment and kept it from me. He knew she was killed by this Mafia. The Mafia that he is a part of. I can feel all the blood rushing from my face. Without thinking, I walked up to my purse and grabbed my phone, opening up to Theo's contact.

Erik is standing in front of me with his hands on my shoulders. "What happened? Are you okay?" His voice matches the worry in his face.

"Don't fucking touch me." Erik dropped his hands with his mouth open. I'm trying to keep my voice calm but I started yelling, "You knew what Brittney looked like, you knew a Basilisk killed her."

Erik is looking at me like he was hit by a train. "I swear, Lizzy, I had no idea she was the civilian death. I had no idea what she even looked like or what her name was. It wasn't any of my friends. None of us would do something so stupid. Please believe me."

As much as I didn't want to believe him, I do. He is terrified of losing me and the baby. I looked down at my phone and my heart sank, I forgot I had called Theo. I clicked end on the call..

Erik grabbed my hand, pulling me behind him, I never fought it. The anger in his voice shook the house. "Martin. You need to let me retire. Dad, I can't fucking do this anymore! You stole ten years of my life. I'm going to lose them."

His voice is shaking; he is fighting back tears. I looked up and Spencer, Josh, and Adam had April standing behind them, they are protecting her with their life. It wasn't any of them.

April pulled out her phone and texted me: *I swear, I had no idea.*
I'm so sorry, Lizzy. Don't hold this against Erik.

Martin stood up and I hid my face behind Erik, he has a tighter grip on my arm. "You know the rules. You can't retire, you are nowhere near the age and as long as your dad is under me, you are an acting Basilisk."

I wiped the tears from my face and raised my voice, "Who murdered my best friend?"

"Sammy. It was an honest mistake. He heard gunshots and someone running past a building." Martin controlled his voice when speaking to me.

I can see Adam becoming angrier. "Killing someone like that isn't an honest mistake."

The front door swung open, hitting the wall. I glanced behind my shoulder; Theo and Max are both standing there confused, angry, and hurt. I looked back and Spencer, Josh, and Adam are all hanging their heads with broken hearts. Erik sighed and dropped my arm.

I walked up to Theo and I placed my hand on his arm and he moved it out of the way. "Don't do anything stupid. You need to trust me, okay? It wasn't them."

Max is looking at me with big eyes, shaking his head, he has never looked at me so disappointed before.

I can feel Erik's body against mine, he is standing right behind me. I can see how much that is pissing Theo off. I can tell by his expression he has given up on all the hope he had this morning. Theo's eyes are dark, I have never seen darkness like this in him, it's like his soul is black. Theo raised his arm and met his fist with my jaw.

I heard April gasp. Erik's grip tightened on my arm.

Pain is radiating throughout my face. For once in my life, I am so taken aback that I have nothing to say. I am holding my head to the side, I put my hand up holding my jaw.

Theo opened the door and spoke in a cold tone, "Get the fuck out of the apartment. You and baby basilisk are dead to me."

My body froze expect for a single tear rolling down my face. I can't look at him. I can't look anywhere. My eyes are shut with my face resting against my shoulder.

Max grabbed my face, turning it so I am looking at him. "I love you, Lizzy."

I reached out for his arm. "Keep him off that shit, Max, I'm begging you. Please stay clean."

Max tapped his fingers on the door, thinking of something to say. He sighed and shut the door behind him.

I turned to face Erik. I can't look him in the eyes; I can't see his heart break. "I can't do this, Erik. I can't be with you."

His fingers are intertwined with mine. My eyes shot up to the roof; I can feel them burning with hot tears. "Babe, please don't walk away from me. I need you. I would never let any children of mine become a Basilisk. I wouldn't control them like that. I love you, stay please." His words turned into him begging me.

I'm still holding his hand and staring up at the roof. Tears are falling down my face. No one in the room is saying a word, there's no words in the dictionary to explain what the fuck is happening.

I can hear Erik's breathing becoming scattered and short breaths. He is crying.

What the fuck am I doing? He is getting his heart broken for something that he didn't do.

I started to back up so I am facing Erik. My first instinct is to fix his pain. I need him, I can't do any of this without him. It's only been a few weeks, but I can't imagine my future without him in it.

I put my hand on his face and he froze with my touch. He opened his mouth and shut it, whatever he stopped himself from saying, he swallowed hard and shut his eyes tight. I need to stop acting like this; if one person would understand how love makes you take decisions you wouldn't normally take, it would be Brittney.

I sighed. "Erik, look at me. I need you, I love you. I'm not going anywhere."

He is squeezing my hand. He moved his gaze to look down at me, we are gazing into each other's eyes.

I had almost lost this feeling of peace. Erik lifted my head and kissed me. Everything was fixed in that split second, there was no need to worry anymore.

Erik pulled me into his chest, wrapping his arms around me and kissing my hair. I felt four more bodies against us.

Erik kissed my head again. "I need to take Lizzy home so she can pack before she changes her mind again."

I can feel my heart breaking, I know Erik never meant it in a way to hurt me, but his words cut like a knife. I never want any of us to go through that pain again. I have never been so scared in my life.

The drive to my apartment is quiet. We are sitting hand in hand. Erik squeezed my hand. "You are in danger now that you know. The Basilisks are in a war. I wanted to tell you so many times. I couldn't imagine you going through what Charlie went through."

I looked at Erik, I want to know everything. "What happened?"

"I promise I will tell you when we deal with them. I don't want you to live in that much fear." He parked the car next to the curb. "I will tell you. No more secrets?"

I frantically nodded my head, reaching over the middle console, tugging on his shirt and pulling him closer to me. I am pissed at myself for ever second guessing him. Erik looked at me; without any hesitation, he leaned in and kissed me. I pulled away and opened my door, climbing out.

Erik is holding my hand through the lobby and up the elevator. Every second that passes gets us closer to our forever. I unlocked the apartment door as soon as I opened it. Erik put his hand on my shoulder, pushing me back into the wall. He is kissing me with more passion than I thought was ever possible. He pulled away, resting his head on my forehead. Nothing else in the world matters, as long as we have each other, everything else will work out in the end.

Erik stepped back from me, not saying a word, just gazing into my eyes. I turned around, opening the closet behind me and pulling out the bin with pictures in it.

I ran into my bedroom and started tossing all my clothes into a suitcase; thankfully, I really don't have much. I zippered it up and pulled a blanket from the shelf at the top of my closet, smelling it. Brittney's awful perfume is still on it. She brought this blanket over to my house in the third grade and somehow it ended up in my room seventeen years later. The design of the butterflies are faded, but the outline is still sort of visible. The cotton is completely worn down, I think she only had it here for comfort.

Standing in the apartment right after I lost my brother and best friend is putting the weight of the world on my shoulders. I wish I had never pulled up his contact, I wish I had waited. Theo was out for blood, it wouldn't matter how long I waited to tell him, or how I told him. It was all going to turn out the same way. Waiting would have just made it worse.

Lizzy

The entire ride back to Erik's, he has his hand in mine. He isn't going to let go of me ever again. I keep glancing over at him; the sun is lowering, lighting up his face. His sunglasses are covering his deep blue eyes. I know he isn't innocent, I know he has blood on his hands. The truth is, I don't care. I don't care about any of that. I love him more than I can put into words. I fell in love with him fast and without any warning. Whenever I look at him, he squeezes my hand and starts to smile. He loves me as much as I love him, if not more. In just a few short months, the back seat of his Lexus is going to have a car seat, we are going to be arguing every day. Our lives are changing faster than we can control, but we are both more than okay with that.

Erik pulled over and took off his glasses. "We're home, babe."

I pulled on his shirt, bringing him over the console to kiss him. I let go and opened my door, the lights are on in his living room and voices float outside. Everyone moved here from next door. I open the back door, reaching for my makeup wipes, forgetting I haven't taken off my smudged eyeliner. I sat back down in the car, pulling the visor down.

I started laughing. "How can you kiss me when I look like this?" I turned to look at him while wiping my face; he looked at me with a smile and winked.

My eyes are puffy and red, Erik has his hands on the roof of the car, watching me. Never again am I going to be so stupid.

Getting out of the car, putting all of my weight into his body, resting my head on his arm and listening to the chatter from the inside of his house. He kissed my hair and closed the gate behind us. Erik stayed close behind me, walking up to the house. I turned the door handle and Erik sat the pictures down, touching my hand to tell me to leave everything at the front door.

He grabbed my hips and put his face in my neck. "She's home."

Everyone shot around in their seats with a smile. Being a topic of conversation was definitely not my favorite thing, but they were worried. All six faces look so relieved. I walked to the kitchen to pour Erik a drink.

They know we made up, but seeing me here at his place was probably what they needed to see to know we weren't screwing around.

April came running behind me, hugging me. "My god, if my two best friends were done for, that would have put me in an awful position."

I started to laugh. "You know we both love you too much for that to happen."

She dropped her arms and I walked over to Erik with his whiskey in my hand. The rest of the night, no one spoke about anything that happened today. Erik has his arm over my shoulder the entire night. He hasn't stopped touching me since we made up.

Adam wrapped his arms around me, squeezing me before he left with everyone else out the door. "My brother loves you more than I've ever seen someone love another person. All of our hearts were breaking when you almost walked away from him."

I sighed and whispered back, "I love him."

Adam let go of me and smiled before he shut the front door. Erik looked at me with his eyebrows pulled in with a slightly turned head. I grabbed his hand and smiled as I pulled him up the stairs. We got upstairs and I saw a straight hallway with four doors.

"This one is our bedroom. Across the hall is the bathroom, then the spare room and the other room used to be a storage room. I cleaned it out after you told me you were pregnant; it's waiting to be turned into a nursery," Erik said behind me.

Without thinking, I turned around, jumping on him. Erik has one hand on my legs and the other is under my shirt, touching my bare back. I pulled my shirt over my head and unclipped my bra. His eyes got wide and a devious smile appeared on his face. I put my lips on his, my breathing is becoming heavier. Erik is pulling me closer to his chest while walking to our bed. I can feel every muscle in his arms flexing from him carrying me.

He sat me on the bed, I pulled his shirt over his head, staring at every muscle on his body. I stood up to kiss him, I pulled my lips from him, moving to his neck, kissing down his chest and running my fingertips over his V that I love so much. I started to unsnap his jeans.

Erik tipped my head up to look at me. "Have you been tested?"

I nodded. "Over a year ago. You are the only one I've been with since."

"You're already pregnant, so we have nothing to worry about."

I looked back down, pulling off his pants. I don't know how his jeans were able to contain him. I held onto him while guiding him into my mouth. Erik started cursing and grabbed my hair. I started to gag and he loosened up his grip, pushing me onto the bed and taking off my pants. He put his hand on the most sensitive part of my body and smiled. He put his forearms by my head and I kissed him.

He slid in and moaned loudly. "Lizzy, you feel incredible."

Sweat is dripping off Erik, making his body glisten. He stopped and put my knees over his shoulders. After three thrusts, I screamed his name, holding onto the sheets with every ounce of strength I had. He put my legs back down, leaning in to kiss me; he pulled away and I watched every muscle in his body tense and instantly relax while listening to him moaning.

Erik lay beside me, pulling me into his chest. I don't care how sweaty he is, I nuzzled my face into his chest.

Erik sighed, pulling me in closer. "I love you."

"I'm sorry I hurt you earlier. I have been beating myself up over it."

He squeezed me in closer. "You are here now. Nothing else matters. I don't give a shit about anything else. Tomorrow when I'm at work, I want you to decide on how we decorate the nursery."

"Do you want to find out the gender when we are further along?"

"I don't care if it's a boy or a girl. I kind of want to keep it a surprise."

"Surprise it is."

Erik held me until his breathing evened out and he fell asleep. His grasp on me loosened, but I can't bring myself to pull away from him. He is everything I have always dreamed of.

"I love you too," I whispered before drifting off.

Charlie

It's been two months since I woke up from my three-day slumber. My face is healed; my internal bleeding has fixed itself. Dillon and I have become a lot closer. I am still unsure of my feelings for Liam, he is putting a lot of effort into us. William is back to work, he promises me every day he will be safe. I have missed so much school since the school year started, I ended up dropping out. My days are filled of binge-watching TV series, cooking, and cleaning. As much as I hate to admit it, day drinking has become a new normal for me. I try to resist drinking so much, I just can't get through a day without drinking. Whenever I close my eyes, it replays in my head.

Only a few weeks till Christmas. I never cared about Christmas before, but this year feels different. Dillon and Liam both came home from school early, we made plans for the four of us to finally buy a Christmas tree.

I'm taking deep breaths trying to calm myself down while I'm getting ready. Ever since I snapped and punched my mirror, I have been avoiding looking at my reflection. I took another deep breath and ignored my demons so I can get ready.

"Why can't I find anything to wear!" I threw my clothes on my bed. I heard the door open, Dillon came into my room. "None of these clothes suit me anymore." This is my breaking point, tears are forming in my eyes. "Everything leaves my back so exposed." I crashed onto my knees.

"We can go get you an entirely new wardrobe." He sat beside me on the floor. "An even better one! Just toss something on, that will be the first stop we make tonight."

I kissed his cheek and stood up, checking to see if my makeup is ruined. I froze when I saw my reflection. I know it is not happening. I know it is not real. It is my mind playing tricks on me; my reflection stared back at me frozen. I looked away, reaching for my flask.

I looked in the mirror again, and everything is normal. I opened my flask and took a huge drink; twisting the lid on, I tossed it in my purse. Dillon is still standing behind me, watching me. He wants to say something to make me feel better, but there is nothing he can say. I know he feels guilty for making me a Basilisk. I stopped blaming him. Putting the blame on him wasn't doing me any good.

Dillon took us into a store. Large windows light up the room, mannequins are on display with the designer's latest winter outfits. He is walking backwards with his arms open. "Whatever you need, they will have it! What do you have in mind?"

"I need a jacket. I need everything new. Darker colors." My voice is hollow.

Liam and Dillon walked away from me together, looking at racks. I put on a gorgeous dark purple jacket that hung down to my knees, oversized collar, and buttons. "Dillon, what about this?"

"It makes you look too square." He made a humming noise with his throat. "Stay here!"

I watched Dillon walk away, he came running back with a belt. "Put this on."

I looked at the thick black belt, confused, I remembered Dillon telling me to stay away from them. I shrugged my shoulders, putting it on anyways. It blended together perfectly with the collar. I looked up at Dillon, he has a smile that stretches from ear to ear, clearly proud of himself.

I couldn't just leave my bright colors behind. I want that part of me to come back so bad. I grabbed a yellow blouse, just in case—the rest of my clothes are neutral colors. I made sure they all had sleeves and are not low cut. I ran into the changing room to double check that all the clothes would cover everything.

I took off the tag of my white sweater dress and put my new jacket on over the dress. I'm walking to the cashier and a pair of black stiletto boots caught my attention. I handed Liam my arm full of clothes, I set the tags down on the counter and ran over to the boots. Eagerly looked for my size, tried them on, and ripped off the price tag. I turned around and Liam has his card out ready to pay, patiently waiting for me.

"I have the most beautiful girlfriend in the universe." Liam kissed my lips, wrapping his arm around my waist.

We all grabbed a bag, leaving the store to walk to the closest Starbucks. Dillon put his hand on my shoulder. "William's calling."

I felt my phone buzz. I looked down, it's from Spencer. *Josh and I are alright.*

Everyone made it a habit to let me know when they were in the clear. I might have been overreacting, but I need to know everyone is safe.

I leaned into Liam and looked at him. "Can we go on another date? It's been so long."

I can see a smile appear on his face. "How about we send the guys home after we buy everything. I know what we can do together."

William arrived at the store the same time we did. He ran up to me and wrapped his arm over my shoulder as we walked in. Christmas music was playing from the speakers; tree ornaments took up half the building. I can feel my excitement building up inside me.

I laid my eyes on a tall Christmas tree. I ran up to it, pointing with a big smile on my face. Dillon grabbed my hand and dragged me down an aisle with silver ornaments, the fluorescent lights from the store making all the ornaments shine. The entire aisle is lit up.

I'm staring at the guys as they are placing ornaments in the cart. "Are you guys sure you want to stick with silver? It's so basic."

Liam put his arm around my waist. "We always had silver at Christmas when we were growing up. It's just kind of our thing now."

I smiled and nodded my head. William walked away and came back with an angel tree topper holding a harp. I'm so thrilled that I'm not the only one that is happy about Christmas this year. So many bad things have happened to us, I think we all need the joy.

Liam spoke as he is staring at me, smiling, "Do you guys mind if you bring all this back to the house? I am going to spend time with Charlie."

Dillon and William never said anything to us; they smiled, then walked away.

Liam took me for a walk around Manhattan. We asked strangers to take our pictures. I can't remember the last time I was this happy, not a care in the world. We are standing near the giant Christmas tree at Rockefeller Center. I have never seen anything like this before. There is a large crowd around, the bright lights reflecting off everyone's faces.

"Ever since I was little, I always wanted to see New York at Christmas time. This city has given me so much hope since I was a little girl." I looked up, and his face is lit up from the Christmas lights. "Thank you for bringing me here. We need to go skating in Central Park soon. I've been dreaming about that forever."

Liam looked at me. "You didn't think this was all I had planned, did you? Come with me."

"Where are we going?"

He never answered. I saw a smile come across his face.

"Central Park?" I stopped walking. "You had skating planned this entire time, didn't you?"

We got our rented skates, and we went on the pond. I used to live on the ice, then things changed. Things changed and suddenly it's been eight years, but my old talent slowly came back to me.

Liam skated backward, reaching out his hands. "I would do anything to make you this happy every single day."

The last time I was here, the leaves were changing colors and starting to fall. We haven't had a snowfall this year, so the grass is still green. The trees are bare but covered in frost. I'm so happy Liam never took me skating at Rockefeller. This is perfect. Somehow, he knows what I needed at the perfect time. I can't wrap my head around it. Half the time I was wondering if he was even listening to me. He surprised me in the best possible way. The sun is setting, so I know the park is shutting down.

We brought back our rented skates when Liam reached for my hand. "I'm sorry we weren't here long. Last-minute plans don't normally work out in my favor much."

"Thank you so much for tonight."

I squeeze his hand, I can feel him staring at me. "What's going on? I know something is wrong."

"I don't want to ruin this night." I stopped walking and stood up on my toes so I can kiss him.

"I need to know. Please just talk to me."

I took a deep breath. As much as I want to hide the truth from him, I really wanted him to know. "Something inside of me changed. I don't know how to be my old confident self. When I close my eyes, all I see are the memories. I'm trying to adjust, but it's been hard. I have this constant reminder on my body."

Liam kissed my head, he held his face over my hair, not saying a word. I don't know if he was stuck on what to say or if he was intimidated by everything.

Of course, he was intimidated by everything.

I had to give him the benefit of the doubt. He was trying and that was all that mattered.

I wrapped my arm around his waist and started to walk. "Tonight was the first night in two months that I was thinking about something else."

Charlie

Waking up this morning to Liam kissing me. "Good morning, babe. I need you to wake up." I grunted. "My dad called me. I need to do back-to-back sales today. The other guys are all busy. Dillon and William need to come with me." My eyes shot open. "I will text you when I've done each one. My dad is taking us to *Willie's* tonight."

"Is that a brilliant idea though? A bunch of gangsters gathered in one building?" This is the first time we have been apart since he promised me he would do better.

"It'll just be our regular group of friends. We will be fine. I really have to go though, so kiss me. I will see you in a few hours."

I kissed Liam with everything I have. I got out of bed, throwing on my robe over my long-sleeved shirt. I walked up to Dillon and gave him the biggest hug I can manage. I went up the stairs and found William, it became his routine to be the one to hug me first.

William whispered in my ear, "You know we'll be okay. Go pick out your clothes for tonight."

"Thank you for being my best friend—don't tell Dillon."

He laughed and walked down the stairs.

I keep catching myself continuously glancing up at the clock. I decided the only way to keep me distracted was to go for a run. I got changed, put my hair up, plugged my headphones in, and left. I'm trying to keep my mind clear of everything that can go wrong, but my mind keeps racing. The more I worry, the faster I begin to run. I stopped on the sidewalk, putting my hands on my hips and panting; without even realizing it, I am standing outside of our old condo. A family is moving in. The dad is moving things inside; the mom is trying to help, but the children are causing chaos.

I don't know if this is my attempt to prove to myself that I am a good person, or if I need to prove to myself I haven't changed as much as I think I have. Every instinct I have is telling me to help them.

"Do you need help bringing things up?" I shouted while running to the mom. "You look like you are having a hard time. We just moved out. We got a house down the block."

She smiled and pointed towards a box. "This box is awfully heavy. I am not able to pack it upstairs, do you mind?" She set it down, and I saw she was pregnant.

I grabbed it and brought it upstairs. "Where would you like me to set this?" Her husband looked at me and jumped backward. "Sorry, I didn't mean to scare you! I was running by and saw your wife struggling with the kids."

He pointed to me to put the box in the corner. I ran downstairs and helped him unload the moving truck until every box was upstairs. This is the distraction I needed. Multiple trips up and down the stairs, thinking of every good and bad thing that has happened here. I never got to say goodbye to my first real home.

On the run home, I felt a smile on my face and a good feeling came through my body. Even though I am a Basilisk and I have gone through hell, I am proud of myself for being able to still bring out the good side in me. The killings, the torture…I am still a good person.

By the time I got home, William's car was pulling up in the driveway. I ran as fast as I could and tackled Liam. "I just spent two hours helping a family move into our old place. Their kids were pretty cute."

Liam stepped back. "Remember when you told me to slow down?"

"Yeah, yeah, yeah. I'm going to shower."

Later that night, we arrived at *Willie's*. The server took our drinks and we sat down. Martin hasn't seen me since the day I was rescued, so it is a little tense. It isn't just me sensing it either, every one of my friends has their head down, looking at the table.

"Well, you look a lot better," Martin finally broke the silence.

I smiled and put my cup to my mouth. I look a lot better and I am starting to feel a lot better. I never thought a day would pass again where I was excited to crawl out of bed. I looked around the table at my six friends, I can't stop thinking about how much I appreciate them. After all this time, I still haven't put together who the seventh friend is. Laughter broke out around the table and for the first time in a while, I feel peaceful. I watched Kinsley come in and pull a chair to the table next to Martin.

I felt something hit my arm from across the table, bringing me back into the conversation. Spencer is leaning into his arms on the table. "Charlie, Liam's at the bar. A girl is talking to him."

My stomach started turning. Over the last two months, he has proven to me that he is a good boyfriend. I can't shake the night he disappeared after getting the text message. I can't forgive him for kissing another girl. I don't know why I am even with him.

I do know why.

I'm scared to lose another person out of my life. I'm scared to lose my five best friends along with him.

Liam pulled a seat out next to me and huffed. "I'm getting so tired of girls hitting on me."

Josh pointed at me. "Take her wherever you go and you'll be fine. As soon as any girl sees Charlie, they go the other direction."

I looked at Josh with my mouth open. "Hey! I'm so sweet, though!"

"You don't look like it! Together, you guys look like the most intimating couple I've ever seen."

Liam nodded his head and laughed. "It looks like you're never leaving my side."

I missed who it was at the table that started talking about flash mobs but I don't care. I had to chime in. "I'm actually so sad; I've lived here for three months and I haven't seen a flash mob."

Kinsley moved her head, gesturing for me to follow her. She leaned up against a tall table. She is wearing an elegant long black dress, her hair has loose curls, and every strand is precisely in place. She looks so much better than me in my red cocktail dress and brown leather jacket.

"I am making Christmas dinner at my place. I am just assuming you will come. But I want you to help me cook." The way she speaks is perfect. I can't wrap my head around how she carries herself so well.

"You want me to help you?"

"If Liam loves you as much as he says he does, then I need to get to know you so I can love you too." She tabbed my glass with her acrylic nail. "Your martini is empty. Go get another one."

I turned around and saw a tall waitress set a new martini at my seat. Everyone is talking back and forth intensely, even with her in earshot of the conversation.

I pulled out my chair and sat down. "What's going on? What did I miss?"

Martin looked up at me. "We really need Liam and Dillon to come back. They won't be working much, but something has come up and I need all men on deck."

I took a sip. "Okay."

"No argument?"

"I can't tell them what they can and can't do; have you met them? I'll be fine."

Martin looked up and took a sip of his drink. "Watson."

I looked up in Martin's line of sight, two cops are walking in our direction. My hands are trembling. I grabbed onto Liam's arm.

Liam grabbed my chin and moved my head so I'm looking at him in the eyes. "It's okay."

Liam pulled his arm back to drink his whiskey, he looks way too casual right now. I leaned back in my seat, eyeing them down. The one that Martin addressed is tall and built for a fight. He has more muscle mass than the Basilisks at the table. He has shaggy blonde hair, with deep ocean blue eyes. The more I look at him, the more I can see how much he looks like Adam. The police officer that is standing behind him looks nervous. He is shorter, but still average height, maybe a little bit taller than me. He is average-looking, round face and brown hair that is held back with gel. Whenever I look up, I can feel his eyes burning into my soul.

I kept my glass to my lips, leaving a bright red lipstick stain. I'm listening to Martin and Watson's conversation. I'm the only one that is bothered by the interaction.

Watson put his hands on his belt. "I knew I would find you here, Taylor."

Martin swirled his alcohol in his cup. "May I remind you it's my bar? What's this about?"

"I'm actually thrilled I found you."

I almost spit out my drink, listening to the words coming out of Watson's mouth.

"There's been some shady people in town. I'm assuming they have made contact with you." He placed the pictures on the table.

Martin glanced at the images. "Oh, they're already dead. Case closed."

Watson nodded and picked up the pictures. As he was walking by, he stopped. "Is this her?"

I have no idea what to do. I picked up my glass and chugged the rest of my drink back. He stuck out his hand for me to shake; I stood up and shook his hand.

"I'm so confused right now." I made it clear that neither of them intimidated me.

Everyone at the table started laughing, and I exchanged an intimidating look with the other cop. When our eyes met, he smiled at me. I awkwardly sat down, wishing he would pull his eyes from me.

"Charlie, meet my brother Erik. The reason we found you." Adam is talking through his laughter.

"Don't mind my partner. He has no manners." Erik used emphasis on the word 'manners'. "Brooks, see that guy next to her? Stop undressing her with your eyes."

I shook my head at Adam. "Why didn't you tell me your brother is a cop? Or do you just prefer to scare the shit out of me?"

Adam raised his glass at me. "Your reaction was priceless."

Erik interrupted, "I need to go. If I keep standing here in uniform without arresting one of you, it's going to look suspicious."

Josh ran away and came back with a shot for everyone. I slammed mine back, trying to wash away the disturbed feeling I got from Brooks. I leaned back in my chair and let out a laugh. No wonder I couldn't figure out who the seventh member of our group was; he is a cop, that's why he is never around us.

Liam looked at me and smiled. "We are coming back, but we have to go. Now."

"Where are we going? What are we doing?" Liam pulled me out of my seat and dragged me out of *Willie's* faster than I'm able to start an argument.

We caught a cab and headed to Times Square. I asked so many questions along the way. I started to confuse myself. We got out of the cab and the neon lights are lighting up the sky. Liam grabbed my arm, pulling me in closer, kissing me, and wrapping his arms around my body. I looked at a building screen, I can see the confused look on my face.

"What the hell is going on?" I can't stop looking at myself at the screen.

Before I'm able to ask another question, everyone around us started moving. Music began playing, everyone is in sync. Liam pulled me to the middle of the crowd.

A flash mob. I can't believe that this is happening.

I'm so happy I want to cry.

Liam got sucked into the crowd. Everyone cleared out of the way, and Liam is on one knee in front of me, holding a black velvet ring box.

He's proposing, I don't even know if I love him. I need to run far, far away.

"Charlotte, everything we have been through in this short time has made us closer. I still am unable to think straight when you walk away from me. Everything about this terrifies me. The first time I saw you, I knew I needed you for the rest of my life. Will you marry me?"

Standing frozen. My mind is telling me to run away. I keep repeating 'no' in my head. I can't breathe. He is the wrong guy. Adam's face is flashing through my mind. I can see Liam is getting impatient, nothing about this feels right. I'm about to make a horrible mistake. I started to pull away, but I found myself on my knees in front of him.

"Yes!" He put the ring on my finger, and I looked around. "How did you know about the flash mob? I never brought it up until today."

We stood up and he dipped me, held me there, and kissed me. "Your dream growing up was New York, I just knew."

I can't take my eyes off the ring. It is huge, it is no doubt the biggest rock I ever laid eyes on. "Do I even want to know how much you spent?"

Liam shook his head. "Nope." He waved down a cab.

The entire cab ride, I can't shake this feeling of uncertainty. What the hell did I just get myself into? I'm acting happy, cuddling up to him, even though everything feels so wrong. Before I know it, the cab stopped and we are back at *Willie's*. I have never been so disappointed in myself.

We walked in and everyone from the table was looking at us with suspense. Liam pulled me in and shouted, "She said yes!" I held up my hand with the ring.

Martin flagged the server down and ordered two bottles of Cristal for the table. Liam grabbed my hand and pulled me to the table back to our seats.

A girl with brown hair came over to the table. She looks perfect in every way, just like Kinsley did. She is Kinsley's doppelganger.

"Is that your sister?" I'm trying to be discreet.

"Shit, I forgot you hadn't met her yet." He turned around to face her. "April, come here!"

I watched Dillon walk to up April. He walked away from her angry and sat down next to me. "She's the most deceiving person I've ever met."

April never made her way over to me. The look on Dillon's face is making me feel relief that she is ignoring me.

"I could get going." I kissed him on Liam's lips, and he knew exactly what I wanted.

"We are going to head out." I pushed on the table with my palms, pushing out my chair.

Martin approached me as I was getting my purse. He hugged me and whispered in my ear, "If I could handpick anyone to be my daughter-in-law, I'm proud it's you."

"Thank you." My voice broke.

Kinsley walked up to me and hugged me. "I'm so glad you said yes, the wait was killing me."

I pulled away from her and looked at the table. "All of you guys knew?" A few nodded their heads and others shook back and forth.

Spencer came up and hugged me, I whispered in his ear, "Where's Adam?"

He paused. "He's been drinking all day. He thought it was best to go home."

My heart sank. He still has feelings for me. I should have run away. I should have run to him.

April walked by and muttered, "Someone should have stopped the proposal." Loud enough for everyone to hear.

I stepped forward, stopping in my tracks. I quickly collected myself. I put my hand on Liam's shoulder. "Thank you, everyone." I'm pushing Liam out of the building before he gets the chance to say something he will regret to his sister.

We got outside and I waved down a cab. "That's so exciting. I have never gotten a cab like this before," I shrieked and watched Liam's face light up. "What is your sister's problem? I feel so attacked."

"She's like that with everyone. I went on a few dates with one of her friends, and it never worked out. I also didn't help the problem." Liam inhaled a deep breath of air. "After we got into that big fight at *Willie's*, I called her. I was a mess. I needed advice from a girl."

"And now we are getting married." I forced my words out. It shouldn't be this hard to say.

We were almost home when Liam got a call from Martin to do a job. I'm not happy about it but I'm also not let down. I feel so guilty for saying yes, he deserves so much better than to be engaged to a girl who has been thinking of someone else.

I changed into my pajamas, put my hair up, and poured a strong drink. I sat down on the couch, lighting my cigarette in deep thought.

The front door opened. "Is it safe to come in?"

I laughed. "Yes Dillon. It's just me."

William came running in and saw how I was dressed. "Where is Liam?"

"He got a call from Martin to do a job." Both Dillon and William are silent. "Come on. I know you guys well enough to know you are exchanging looks behind my back."

Dillon muttered in a low voice while walking away, his fist came into contact with the wall down the hallway.

I turned around and looked at William. "What is going on?" I watched him shift. "Just tell me. Sit down."

William jumped over the back of the couch. "I'm only saying this because I love you. Martin never phoned him. Kinsley ended up having to walk him out. After you left, he had five shots back to back."

It feels wrong to be mad, even though it still feels like my heart is getting ripped out of my body. "Drunk Martin. That's something I would have paid to see."

William smiled at me. He turned his head to Dillon, who is standing at the end of the hall. "Anything?"

Dillon walked around, picking up my cup. "They have no idea where he is. I heard Josh cussing him out, so there's that at least."

I walked to the kitchen and grabbed myself a new cup. "I'm sure he will turn up."

Brittney

The headphones in my ears are starting to hurt, my fingers are clicking the keys on the computer faster than I thought I could type. Keeping up with Martin's games is starting to become a little bit easier. He is impossible to get one step ahead of.

Sam slammed her hand against my desk, ripping my headphones out of my ears. "We are going out for drinks tonight, Martin is taking a few Basilisks to *Willie's*."

I can't think of anything worse. I rolled my eyes, typing the last few words of my report. "No way in hell. I need sleep."

"Don't be like that. Your boyfriend gets to drink, why can't you?"

"Because I'm fucking exhausted."

Sam is shouting over her shoulder, making dinner plans with the rest of the crew, like we don't see each other enough. My attention is drawn to my phone shivering on my desk, Spencer's name lights up, causing a smile on my face. *I'm going out tonight. I'll be at my place tonight.*

Your place as in with Adam and Josh?

No, with you, it's my house, remember?

Right. I'll leave my rent money on the counter since it's YOUR house.

Damn it, that's not what I meant.

Whatever.

I toss my phone across the desk, ignoring his next text message, annoyed. I know I'm overreacting, but my lack of sleep from this case is making me crazy.

"Agent Lee and Agent Hills, my office, now!" Rodríguez shouted across the room.

Sam sighed, pulling my office chair against the hardwood floor. Everyone has already left for lunch, our heels are tapping against the floorboards echoing in the room. It sounds like we have gotten ourselves into some trouble, the only issue is I don't know what the hell we did wrong.

Inside the room, I can see agents standing and sitting around the room, I'm leaning against the doorframe listening to Nelson talk to everyone. "Martin doesn't have any plans for tomorrow, so we all have a day off." Every single person in the room sighed. "Screw it. Take two days off, go get changed. Let's all get drunk."

Glancing down at my watch to make sure it was only noon and I never let the afternoon get away from me. "Count me out."

"Nope, you're coming." Sam already sounds annoyed with me.

"I'm supposed to be dead."

"Shut up, you're coming."

"I'm sure Angry Leprechaun would be fine," Jones said, mid-yawn, he's as tired with this conversation as I am.

Sam raised her arms to him, looking at me with a smile on her face. I sighed, tipping my head back.

"So, it's settled. Six o'clock." Rodriguez grabbed his keys from the drawer in his desk, slamming the drawer back in.

There are so many pubs in New York City, I'm hoping everyone that knows I'm dead is at a different one than me. Irish music is blaring from the overhead speakers, Guinness beer is advertised on each table. Sam is sitting beside me picking at her nail beds with Jones across the table staring at her. He is going to blow the cover of their relationship without even trying to.

The server is standing beside me, looking down. "ID."

Rolling my eyes, I flicked the card out of my wallet, watching everyone stuff a laugh. I tried to look different than I do at work; even with my blush, cover-up, bronzer, highlighter, lipstick, ten layers of mascara, and thick eyeliner, I still look underage. Not that I'm complaining.

She slid the ID into my hand. "What do you want to drink? It's on us."

Sighing, I looked around the table, watching everyone laugh. "Old Fashioned and coffee. I need coffee." World's weirdest mixture.

Today is my twenty-fourth birthday. I never wanted to come out tonight, hoping that no one would remember. It's six-thirty, so far I'm good. I always hated my birthday; having it so close to Christmas, normally people forgot about it anyways. This year, it's just a reminder that my friends and family are living a separate life.

My phone is sitting on the table next to me, I still haven't read that message from Spencer. I unlocked it, going to my messages. *I'm stupid.*

My drinks arrived with my cream and sugar; pouring in five creamers, opening three packs of sugar, dumping them in, and stirring, I drank half of the coffee in one big gulp.

"The life of a new agent." Even hearing Jones talk makes me want to climb over the table and strangle him.

We have been picking at each other's appetizers for two hours, talking about everything other than work. No one who thinks I am dead has walked into the pub, my cover is still intact. I don't know why I'm so worried, I would be more likely to run into someone on the subway than here.

Three glasses of Old Fashioned in and I am feeling every ounce of alcohol and every cup of coffee. My head is light from my buzz, but my mind is running a mile a minute from the caffeine. The chime for the entryway rang; moving my head up, Theo and Max are walking in. In a split second, I pushed out my chair and fell onto the floor under the table.

"What the actual fuck are you doing on the floor?" Sam laughed, looking amused.

"Max and Theo," I said in a hushed tone.

I can still see them through the chair legs. Both of them look like hell. Their eyes are dark, they are both thin. Putting my hands to my mouth, fighting back my tears. They are walking up to a sketchy group of people at a table. Max slid a wad of cash across and a man wearing a black hoodie and a flat brim hat passed Theo a bag. They both turned around and walked out in a hurry.

Waiting a few more seconds, letting my sobs escape, Sam put her hands on my shoulders, pulling me out from the table. Digging in my body to find every single bit of strength, I have to get myself off the floor. Sam put her arms under mine, pulling me up from the ground. I never knew what it was like to feel absolutely no emotion, but it is fucking hell.

Storming over to the bar, I slammed my hands down. "Three shots of whiskey."

The bartender nodded his head, pouring the shots in front of me on the bar. He poured the first one; I put the glass to my lips, knocking it back, I picked up the second one, taking a deep breath, putting it to my mouth and tipping that one back. Grabbing the third one, I can already feel my gums turning numb. I walked over to the table and set it in front of me.

Tapping my fingers on my phone screen, pulling up Erik's contact and opening his work email, so Lizzy can't see it. *This seems pretty counter-productive since I'm drinking my sorrows away but we have to get Theo and Max into rehab somehow.*

I knew whatever they touched wouldn't be the last time, but I never thought they would let it get *that* bad. I knew they loved me, I had just underestimated how much.

All of the alcohol has hit me at once, letting me forget about what I witnessed, letting me forget it's my birthday and letting me forget how fucked up everything really is. It isn't just me who is drinking more than they should, but every single person at the table has been consuming more alcohol than our bodies can hold.

Sam grabbed my leg, she is focusing on each word. "I'm going to miss you, Hills."

Holding onto her hand squeezing it. "You can't get rid of me that easy."

Two hands are on my shoulders, squeezing me. "Here, I thought you would be okay drinking with these people. Let's get you home."

I turned around in my seat, looking up at Spencer. "You've been drinking though."

"I have been babysitting Adam. I really can't be in here, I'm sort of breaking a code just picking you up."

"What happens if they find out?" Rodríguez put his elbows on the table with his fingers locked in a fist rested on the table.

Spencer grabbed my arm, pulling me up and pushing out a laugh. "No one has been stupid enough to find out."

I locked eyes with Spencer for a split second before turning around to face my coworkers, smiling. The first real smile tonight. "I'll see you guys Monday."

Walking away from the table, I put my arm around Spencer and he put his arm around my shoulders. I'm forcing all of my weight against him, trying not to fall over and break a heel.

Spencer opened the car door for me, helping me inside. I buckled up, taking my shoes off and resting my head against the seat. "I had a rough night."

Spencer put the car in gear and sighed. "So did I."

"You first."

"First, I pissed my fiancée off, she doesn't seem mad at me though." Spencer glanced over at me, his face lighting up from the passing streetlights. I grabbed his hand and smiled. "Then I had to watch Adam become heartbroken. Liam proposed to Charlie; the most fucked up part is that she seemed more bothered that Adam wasn't at *Willie's* when she got back. Now, I know how everyone felt when you left me." He is squeezing the steering wheel so tight with his one hand; even in the dark, I can see his knuckles turning white.

"How is he?" My voice is quiet, filled with regret and guilt.

"Destroyed. Lizzy is with him now; even she was different today. I really hate to tell you this right now, but she's pregnant."

I turned my head towards the window, my head pressed tight against the seat, closing my eyes as tight as I can. I thought my heart was broken before, but this is a new low. I'm supposed to kick Erik's ass. I'm supposed to be her rock. None of this is okay, the fact I have been trying to justify what I am doing is making it worse. "Theo and Max almost saw me today. If they weren't so fucked up, they would have seen me."

Spencer parked the car in our driveway; he unclipped his seatbelt, bringing me back into reality. He opened his door, running around to my side. He opened my door, leaning in, kissing me, and unclipping my seatbelt.

I got out of the car and Spencer picked me up. I wrapped my legs around his waist giggling. Every time he walks, I can feel his muscles flexing through my jacket. He is fumbling with the keys, trying to unlock the deadbolt.

Spencer placed me back on my feet, bending down to kiss me. "Happy birthday." I looked up at him with wide eyes, checking the time on my watch. 11:30. He let out a laugh. "You really didn't think I forgot, did you? Turn around."

I spun around on my heels, looking at bouquets of colorful daisies scattered in the living room. Even after all this time, he remembered my favorite flower.

I put my head down, looking at the floor. "It's beautiful, but I don't deserve any of this."

He spun me back around so I'm facing him. "Britt, they are adults, they make their own decisions. Trust me, you deserve a hell of a lot more than this, I just had no idea what to get you."

"You bought us a house. You have done enough for me."

Spencer is looking down at me with a sparkle in his eyes; standing here with my future husband in our house is more than I could ever ask for. He slid his arm under my ass, picking me up off my feet, wrapping his other arm behind my back, and carrying me up to our bedroom.

I pulled the headphones out of my ears, running into Rodriguez office. "Sir, Martin has set his drug smuggling meeting to be at the docks on New Year's Eve, 10 pm. Adam, Charlie, and Spencer are going. Noah is going to be transporting it." Working on the next words, my stomach is turning. I don't know what he is bringing in, but I know there's a possibility that Max and Theo could get their hands on it. "It's a ten-million-dollar deal."

Rodriguez' jaw is working under his skin. "One last big move before retiring."

"We need to arrest him sooner than later sir."

"We need to wait."

"For what! With all due respect, we are going to miss our opportunity."

The door behind me shut with Agent Lee, Jones, and Nelson standing behind me. They all have their arms crossed. None of them look impressed. We are all sharing the same expression of disbelief.

"She's right. I know you are a higher rank than me, but we need to rethink this," Nelson said, walking up to the desk.

I am too close to this case, the only thing I want to do is protect Spencer. If it was up to me, we would have ended this months ago.

Rodriguez sat back in his chair. "Damn it. You're right. Agent Lee, see if you can find out who the buyers are. Hills, did anything about the buyers come up when you got the date?"

"No sir." I'm trying to hide my excitement.

"Go back and listen."

I nodded my head, turning around to walk back to my desk.

Half the day passed without a sound in Martin's office. My eyes are getting heavy listening to the silence. My elbows are on the table with my head in my hands. The door opened; any exhaustion I felt has disappeared. Pulling up a blank document on my computer ready to type, I'm listening to two voices I don't recognize.

"Where the fuck is Dad?"

"Liam, this is a bad idea. Last time we tried to talk him out of drugs, we both got shot."

"Like you need to remind me," Liam huffed.

"Why did you propose to Charlie? I can't figure it out."

"When he retires, everyone is going to see me as the next boss, the next one to start a family."

A long silence is filling the room, even though the headphones, I can feel the thick air of tension between the two. "We are already fucking Taylors. You decided to marry her because of money?"

Nothing else needs to be said, I know the other person is Dillon. Footsteps are walking through the room, the door slams behind them and the room is back to silence.

I want to tell Spencer more than anything what I heard, but I can't. I can't tell him anything about the case or what is going on with his friends. I am completely torn between the bureau, my fiancé, and Erik. Tapping my fingers on the table, listening to the calming static in my ears. The answer should be coming to me easily; I should be able to tell Spencer without double-thinking it. Nothing is as easy as it seems anymore, I'm crossed between morals and going against all of my training.

Agents aren't supposed to work if they are too close to a case; this is exactly why.

Damn it. I'm telling him.

Fuck. I can't. The little voice in my head is telling me not to.

I'm sorry, Charlie.

Lizzy

"You remember the code for my gun safe, right?" The same question every day before Erik went to work.

I nodded and he grabbed my arm, holding me as tight as he could. I kissed him and pulled away. "Why does it always feel like goodbye when you say bye to me?"

He sighed, holding my face. "There's bad people after us. I'm scared to walk away from you. I'll tell you everything when we can figure this out."

I nodded and kissed him again. Erik backed away from me, not turning around until he was on the other side of the living room. I heard the door shut and I sighed.

Whatever is going on, he will tell me, I'm not worried about that. Both of us are too worried about the baby and the noise of a gun to do shooting lessons. We both know I don't have good enough aim to be able to protect myself. I spend every minute with someone who will be able to shoot. I'm either with Josh, April, Adam, or Spencer.

I shut the door behind me, locking it and starting to walk towards Adam's place. I got there right as all three of them got out and a car squealed away. They all looked down at me and smiled. Spencer opened the gate and Josh opened the door. I got inside and April was sitting there, staring at the fireplace.

Josh kissed the back of her head, April grabbed his hand. For that split second, they both looked like they were in heaven. Confusion is washing over my body. I have to bite my tongue, but I really don't want to.

Every single day since I have moved in with Erik, I have been wanting to marry him. We have been together for only two and a half months. I'm three months pregnant.

The way doctors calculate pregnancy, no one believes it's really his baby.

I hear Adam in the kitchen, grabbing glasses. Josh, April, and Spencer are having their own conversation. My mind is running a mile a minute. The only thing I am certain of is how much I love him. I know for a fact that I need him.

I stared into the fireplace and blurted out my words, "Is it weird for a girl to propose to a guy?"

Adam dropped a glass on the floor in the kitchen; the other three got wide-eyed. Once the initial shock wore off, they all started smiling at me.

I'm definitely missing something here.

"Well…" I let my voice trail off.

"Do it. If anything, it would raise Erik's self-esteem more." Josh grabbed April's hand.

April flung her head back. "Yeah, because we need our most alpha male to have more of an ego?" Adam cleared his throat. "Fucking Watsons."

Spencer shrugged his shoulders. "Do it. You guys are already doing things backward."

Adam came into the living room and sat down next to me. "Spence wouldn't tell you to do it if he didn't think it wasn't a good idea. When are you doing it?"

I leaned back on the arm of the couch, resting my head in my hand. "If I don't do it tomorrow, I'm not going to do it at all."

Josh punched my leg. "We are going to be at Liam's tomorrow. You can do it then; make sure to call us."

I nodded and looked at April's disgusted face. "Be nice to Charlie when you go on Christmas." She rolled her eyes. "I'm serious."

She looked at me with her mouth open. "K, Mom." She slouched in her chair. "Please tell me you're coming?"

I shook my head. "Probably not. I'm making Erik go if he likes it or not; I just can't be in the same room as him."

I can't even say his name. It feels like I am swallowing acid. Spencer grabbed my knee and turned around. We sat there staring at the fire.

Shit, I'm proposing to Erik tomorrow. What the hell am I doing?

Abort mission.

I can't, everyone looks so excited. My nerves are going to be the death of me. What if he says no?

Oh no, I'm going to be sick.

I put my hand on my mouth and ran upstairs, hoping the entire house was the same setup as Erik's. I took a left turn and ran straight into the bathroom.

I flushed the toilet and stood up, looking in the mirror and lifting up my sweater. Week eleven. I'm built small, so there is a tiny baby bump. I ran my hands over it and started smiling.

I got to the stairs and Spencer and Josh are waiting for me with a bottle of ginger ale. They nodded their head towards the door; I followed and we went to my place. I have to admit, I am impressed by how much attention they actually pay to me. They are with Liam, Dillon, Charlie, and William every day, it would be easy to neglect the small things, but they still figure it out.

I am still one hundred percent positive that the rest of their friends have no idea Erik is having a baby. I am also one hundred percent sure Charlie has no idea who I am, so I feel even creepier by knowing things about her. Having a big group of friends is so damn complicated.

Spencer unlocked the door with his key and I ran upstairs to change into my pajamas. After morning sickness strikes, if I am not at work, I go right home and cuddle up. I went down two flights of stairs to the TV room and had they already set up *Family Guy*.

Max knows every episode by heart. I miss them so much, I don't feel complete not having them with me every day.

Josh and April have been replaying in my head; if there's one couple I am cheering for, it's them. "Josh, what's with you and April?"

He has been expecting my question. "It's complicated. Her family, my friends."

"Why's it complicated?"

"They're assholes."

I glanced over at Spencer. "Where the hell have you been disappearing to?"

I feel like their mother.

Spencer is fighting off a smile. "I met someone. She's pretty incredible. Lizzy, I am most definitely in love."

My face lit up and Josh grunted.

"I swear, you're going to get you heartbroken again," Josh sighed.

Instantly intrigued, I scooted over next to Spencer, resting my head on his shoulder. "What's her name? I'll go find her. Once this baby's out, I mean."

Spencer shook his head, laughing once. "Cameron."

Damn, that's Brittney's middle name.

Lizzy

I have officially lost my fucking mind. We have been together for two and a half months. Neither of us are ready to get married. Girls don't propose if it's not leap day in Ireland.

Guess what?

We aren't in Ireland and it's not leap day.

I am making a huge mistake and I am going to scare him off.

It's freezing outside, and I had the brilliant idea of going for a walk at Central Park. My clothes are all over our bedroom floor. I am having a hard time trying to find the right outfit. I have been acting weird all day and he knows something is up. I saw a black wool dress and my eyes got big when my fleece leggings were hidden under it.

I ran to the bathroom to do my make-up. I am trying to be as careful as I can but my damn hand won't stop shaking. I have never been this nervous. I paused, looking in my make-up bag, and saw my hot pink lipstick. I got my make-up on and put my lipstick on when my hand stopped shaking. I looked up in the mirror and I look absolutely amazing. If he doesn't know something's going on, he will now. My dress is already too tight for me and my leggings are digging into my belly. Even since yesterday, I look more pregnant.

I started to walk down the stairs; the second I was in Erik's line of sight, his eyes lit up. "You are absolutely stunning. We need to go buy you a maternity dress." I smiled and nodded my head. "I know you don't want to come tomorrow, but I have to make an appearance. We don't even need to eat. I just want you to meet my mom. I get it if you don't want to. It's going to be hard."

I stood on the step, shuffling my feet. I really don't want to go, but I am going to have him there and my friends. "I will try to go." Hesitation is thick in my voice, I really don't want to spend Christmas alone. If he says yes today, he's going to be my fiancé. I have to try for him. "I'll go."

He pulled me in and kissed me. He rolled his eyes, pulling out his front camera to see if he was wearing any of my lipstick. He stuffed his phone in his pocket and held my hand out the door. He's walking with his arms out, meaning he has his holster under his suit jacket. I am worried why he is always armed, but that might just be a gangster thing. Plus, the instincts of a cop to always be on the lookout.

We got in the car and I can't stop fidgeting; my nerves are getting the best of me. The voices in my head are telling me this is an awful idea.

"Lizzy, what's wrong? You've been off all day. Don't get me wrong, you're always breathtaking but today you're just…" He paused, trying to find the words. "Wow."

I grabbed his hand and watched the maternity clothing store come in our line of sight. "I'm just excited to go to Central Park and to get an eggnog latte. Can we get one. Please?" One thing is for sure, I have always been a horrible liar.

He looked at me, pulling his eyebrows together and shaking his head as he parked. "Yeah. But, actually, I'm not even going to ask."

Shit. I knew he was going to get suspicious.

Despite me acting off, Erik still raced to my door, reaching for my hand for him to get me out followed by a kiss. I always thought couples who had to be touching each other was absolutely disgusting. Now, it's what I find the most comfort in.

We searched around the store; dress shopping in December was almost impossible. Erik wandered to the back of the store and came back with a gorgeous, black, V-neck, fitted dress. I grabbed the price tag and cringed. $250 for a dress is not something I want to pay. Erik put the dress against my chest, lifting my left arm holding it against me; he held my right hand to the change room and gently pushed me in.

I have a problem with people buying me things. Even birthday presents. It has always made me feel awkward and small. I know that isn't his intention, he just wants me to have the best of everything, I know he can afford it, but it still kills me.

The dress looks amazing. My breasts have filled out so much, the fabric of the dress covers the unattractive bra.

"I want to see it," Erik said from behind the curtain.

"You need to wait until tomorrow."

I quickly got undressed and walked back to the bras, grabbing four more in my size.

Erik walked up to me with his hand behind his neck, reminding me of Theo, and sorrow hit me all at once. I miss him so much.

"Lizzy, you need jeans and everything. I'll get you everything you need."

I was about to hesitate, but he was right.

$800 later, I had enough clothes to last me the six months more I had in pregnancy. We have our Starbucks and we are on our way to the park. My heart is beating out of my chest, I'm trying to breathe but my nervous knots are stirring inside of me. Not to mention April, Adam, Josh, and Spencer have been blowing up my phone, waiting to hear what happened. I shut it off and placed it in my handbag.

The park is still green, leaves are on the grass. Most have been raked, but there are still a few hanging around. Families are walking around, couples holding hands are passing us. This park has always held good memories for me, that's why I wanted to do it here. Hopefully, I can continue to keep them all good. The pound has so many skaters, the only thing that is missing is the snowbanks.

The last hour, I have been hanging onto Erik's arm, smelling his cologne radiating off his body. I downed my latte hoping the caffeine would replace alcohol to give me a confidence boost. Snowflakes are falling from the sky, everything is perfect. I inhaled a breath of air, trying to get enough confidence, ignoring the knots in my stomach. With each step we take, I can feel myself squeezing Erik's hand more; he isn't complaining but I can see him looking down at me.

I stopped, causing Erik to jolt backward. He stopped without looking back. I can see his body tense, with every second he isn't facing me, he is getting more worried. I ran out in front of him, not moving my hand from his. I got down on one knee; I looked around and everyone had wide eyes covering their mouths with their hands.

"Liz, what are you doing?" I looked up at Erik and he was fighting back a smile.

I'm gazing into his eyes, everything feels so right, but it is still terrifying. "I feel fucking crazy. I need you, in every way possible. I don't care that our entire relationship is backward. I don't care we haven't even been together for three months. I need you. I love you. Erik, will you marry me."

He tipped his head back and laughed. He reached in his pocket with his free hand while squeezing my hand and pulled out a velvet box. "Open it."

I pushed myself off the cold concrete with his help. I took the velvet box from him and he had the biggest smile on his face. He let go of my hand and I slowly opened it. I can feel him grabbing my hips, pulling me closer to him. A Marquise-cut engagement ring with a pink-tinged diamond is sparkling back at me.

Erik put his hand under my chin, guiding my eyes to meet his. "Yes, I'll marry you."

He kissed me and the entire park erupted. I pulled away, resting my forehead on his cheek as he took the ring out of the box and slid it onto my finger. The ring looks huge on my tiny fingers. He took the box out of my right hand, sliding it back into his pocket.

Erik is right in front of me, running his fingers through my hair. "I almost asked you to marry me dozens of times, but I was so scared it was too early. After you found out about me, I almost asked you then, but it was horrible timing."

"No wonder everyone was so confident you would say yes."

He pulled me into his side, kissing my hair; we started to walk back to the car with his arm wrapped around my waist. Nothing in the world could replace how good I feel at this very moment.

He pushed out a laugh. "You scared the shit out of me today, I didn't know what to expect."

I held my hand out in front of us. "Soon, we will be Mr. and Mrs. Watson."

Erik stopped me, pulling me into him; he put one hand on the lower part of my belly and started to kiss me with more passion than he ever has. "This is going to be one hell of a Christmas."

Charlie

Christmas Eve. My new favorite day of the year.

The doorbell rang throughout the house. I ran to the door and swung it open. When I looked down, I noticed a package addressed to me.

I ran to the kitchen and grabbed a knife. When I cut through the tape, I saw a plastic bag with our matching pajamas. I held the package to my chest, letting out a sigh of relief.

I got downstairs as fast as I could and grabbed wrapping paper from storage. I tried to remember what sizes I had guessed for everyone as I'm writing the names down on the tags. The entire time I'm wrapping the pajamas, I want to call someone and see if they are okay. I keep glancing at the clock hanging on the wall, it feels like the hands are never moving. I hate not knowing what is going on.

I pulled out my phone and ordered enough food for everyone, doing anything I can to distract myself.

I got upstairs and put all the presents under the tree; it finally doesn't look so bare. I bent down and turned the white lights on. The reflection of the lights lit up the sparkling silver ornaments.

My phone buzzed. I don't recognize the number and my beat is racing not knowing who it is, or what terrible thing has happened.

Have you been drinking?
No, why?
Are you home?
Yes, why?
I'm outside.

I backed up from the tree and made my way to my room, grabbing my gun and sticking it in the back of my pants. I'm standing up on my tippy toes, I let out a sigh. It's only Noah.

I swung the door open, backing up. "What are you doing?" I pulled out my gun, walking to the bedroom. "I was ready to shoot you."

"I'm finally able to do your tattoo today, sorry it's taken so long. You kept getting injured."

I placed my gun down in the closet and ran out to the word tattoo, smiling. "No fucking way!"

I sat down on the couch, pulling up my sleeve to put it on my wrist. Everyone else has it there, I have seen the Basilisk tattoo there so much it doesn't seem proper to have it anywhere else. The gun turned on and I can't take my eyes off it. The instant the needle touches my skin, it is nothing like I imagined. The pain is tolerable; in fact, it doesn't hurt at all. It irritates me more than anything.

I looked down and I saw him working on the outline. I've seen this tattoo on everyone, I never expected to see one on me. In a weird way, it feels good that we are all officially connected. A large snake is slithering up my arm, the top half is straight with its mouth open, showing all of the poisonous fangs. I feel oddly relaxed getting inked. I knew I was a Basilisk before, but now it was just written in stone. I finally belong somewhere. I can see Noah starting to get close to finishing my tattoo.

My anxiety is lowering, my mind is distracted, until my phone starts vibrating on the couch next to me.

We are safe. I know you have been sitting there panicking.

I sighed. I didn't know if I was still getting Josh's texts because I suddenly became weak to everyone. Or if it was out of love. Either way, there is no doubt about it, I appreciate it.

All the guys walked into the house, all the anxiety left my body.

I can hear William's voice. "Is that the tattoo gun?"

I heard Spencer laugh. "No way! She's finally getting it done!"

Noah moved his hands away from my wrist. I'm able to examine it closer. The snake has so much detail. The eyes are red. The scales have perfect lines. He wrapped my wrist up.

Josh came up behind me, shaking my shoulders. "It looks badass."

I heard the doorbell ring, I passed Liam my wallet for him to grab the food. I watched Noah pack up and leave. As soon as I heard him shut the door, I skipped over to the tree, grabbing everyone's wrapped pajamas and passing them out.

They took the pajamas and ripped them open. They all have blue onesies with snowmen plastered all over them. I ran to the bedroom, slipping mine on.

I got the movie ready and I went in the kitchen to get my food, I heard Spencer come out of the bathroom. "Is this what our entire future looks like?"

Dillon laughed. "Yup."

I looked up at Adam who is beside me getting his plate ready. "Should I have thought this through?"

I looked up at him and it feels like the world stopped spinning. The sight of him has taken the air out of my lungs. For a split second, we are the only people on this earth. He was too good of a guy to grab me and kiss me, but I want him to. I wish I had met him sooner.

He looked down at me with a sparkle in his blue eyes. "Spence loves it, believe me."

"I love this!" William came over and hugged me. "I wouldn't expect anything else from you."

We sat down with our dinner and I noticed Liam sitting across the room, putting space between us. It isn't just me who has been putting space between us, he has as well. He is disappearing at nighttime again.

I was the last one to finish eating. "I need a smoke." We pushed pause, and I walked to the front door to grab a new pack from my purse. I looked out the window and snow is falling from the sky. "You guys! Come here! It's snowing!"

I turned around, facing everyone. "We look so adorable. We need to take a picture."

Charlie

I got to Martin's and Kinsley's place at 4.30 am. When I arrived, she had the counters covered in vegetables. As soon as I walked in, she is giving me directions on what to do. I feel overwhelmed with the amount of work that needs to be done.

We are working as hard as we can. I would be getting in the zone cutting veggies and the timer would be going off to baste the turkey. I'm already exhausted. I'm starting to become thankful that Thanksgiving was canceled this year; I don't know how people made two giant meals so close together.

I dropped the potato peeler on the cutting board and started opening and closing my hand. "I really need to step outside, do you mind?"

"That's fine by me!"

I'm walking down the path lighting my cigarette, hoping that the cool breeze will wake me up. The road is empty, minus one black car that has driven by twice since I have been outside. I shrugged my shoulders and headed inside, not thinking much of it. I went outside a few hours late and it was parked on the opposite side of the road.

I put my cigarette butt in the ashtray and called Liam. I should have talked to Martin, but he made me feel so uneasy, he is too intimidating.

Within a half hour, Liam came into the kitchen handing me my gun. Kinsley saw it and sighed. Liam turned to her. "We just have to be on the lookout. There are going to be a lot of people here today that don't know anything about us. It's probably nothing."

Dillon came into the kitchen, grabbing my hand and pulling me into Martin's office. I can feel Dillon's nervous energy, it's making me feel weary.

Dillon dropped my hand and let me walk into the office alone. The door is open a crack, so I pushed it open. "Martin?"

"Come in. I know you are not cleared to work yet, but can you do us a favor? You look the less intimidating out of myself or my sons, and I'm not involving Kinsley." I nodded my head. "I need you to go outside and approach the car. Just ask if they are lost, say you have noticed them there for a while. Go unarmed. Dillon and Liam will be watching for you.”

I left the office and walked out the front doors. I unlocked the gate and walked across the road, inspecting the car; it’s a black Charger with black tint on all the windows. I tried get a look inside, but it’s useless.

I smiled and knocked on the window. It rolled down about an inch. “Hey, I’ve seen you outside parked here for a few hours. I just wanted to know if you were lost.”

The window rolled down all the way. I stepped to the side. Dillon would have a clear view of the driver. “I’ve been hired to find you.”

“What are you talking about?” I stood in front of him, blocking the view of Dillon’s gun.

“Your birth parents wanted to find you.”

I looked him in the eyes, growling between my teeth. “Tell them I don’t care, you never found me, got it?”

I stormed across the street in disbelief. It is too good to be true, so I know it can’t be right.

Liam ran up to me. “What was it?”

I’m eyeing the car driving away. “Nothing, it’s okay.” I looked at him. I know he knows I’m lying. “My birth parents hired a PI to find me. I told him to leave and to tell them he wasn’t successful.”

I stormed past Liam to head back into the kitchen to help Kinsley.

“I was starting to think you wouldn’t come back.” Kinsley looked at the clock on the wall.

April walked into the kitchen and rolled her eyes when she saw me.

Kinsley tossed her knife on the counter and sighed. “April, will it kill you to be nice to Liam’s fiancée?”

“Probably,” she muttered as she walked back out.

“I’m sorry about her. I don’t know what has gotten into her.”

“Kinsley, is there anything else I can do, please?”

“We can set the table.”

I followed Kinsley and loaded a cart that was by the cupboards. I pushed the cart to the table, unloading a plate, wine glasses, water glasses, and cutlery at every seat.

Noah came up to me and grabbed my arm. “How is your tattoo feeling?”

I looked at it. "It is so itchy! I put lotion on it when it becomes too much to handle. It helps."

Adam stood behind me, looking down at my wrist. "It's about damn time you got it."

The smell of Adam's cologne intoxicates me. His body is so close to mine, I can feel his body heat radiating off him. I wanted to turn and face him, then I remembered Liam. Liam, my fiancé.

Noah freed my arm and I walked away in a rush. Adam drives me crazy; if I stayed any longer, I would have done something I regretted, or not regretted. I don't know what scares me more.

Martin came running towards me. "I really need you in the field. Please."

I nodded. "What do I have to do?"

Martin grabbed my forearm, leading me into the kitchen. "Violet is on her way to get you. A woman sent the PI; rather, someone who was pretending to be a PI. The McKinnon's are still after us. They keep targeting you since you are the newest link and potentially the weakest link. It's dangerous."

I can feel my stomach turning. I can hear the begging in Martin's voice. I need to help. "What do I need to do?"

Martin handed me a photo of the woman who has short black hair. The men she is standing next to aren't much taller than her, but she has the biggest frame. The angry scowl that looks like it is permanently part of her face would make me cross the street rather than walk past her on a sidewalk.

"Grenade. I have one here. You guys will be back in less than an hour." The begging in Martin's voice has stopped.

My eyes got wide looking at the grenade sitting in my hand. "I only saw it in movies. I pull the pin and toss?"

Martin nodded, he sped up his talking in case someone walks in. "We need you to go in first and make sure it's the right location. She will be protected. We need to finally defeat them. Hopefully, this will cause them to turn on each other." He stopped and listened for a car. "Violet's here, go through the back door. I'm just going to tell everyone you had to run home, so we don't cause panic."

I ran out the door and down the street to Violet's car. "I was wondering if you were ever going to show up today."

"This better be luckier than your last few times." She stepped on the gas and squealed through the open gate.

The address led us down a bad neighborhood. Being two females in a car is setting a target on our backs. We came across a hideout with cars parked outside.

I moved my head forward. "Shit, Violet, there she is. Park here."

I opened the car door, kicked off my heels, and exhaled hard. Keeping my eyes on the entrance, I run towards the building, no one has walked in or out. I open the door and voices are echoing inside the empty building. My heart is pounding in my chest. I don't know how many people are in here, but I do know when I go to bed tonight, I have a huge number of deaths on my chest. I opened my hand, looking down at the grenade. I pulled the pin and tossed it as far as I can. Before it came into contact with the floor, I ran as fast as my legs would take me. Within seconds, the sound of the explosion filled my head.

Heat is racing up my back, my dress is smoking. I dropped onto my knees in the fresh blanket of snow and fell onto my back, hoping that it would be enough to put out the smoke. I forced myself off the ground and got into the car. Violet handed me a blanket and drove off. Taking my singed dress off and wrapped myself in the blanket. Double-checking Violet is keeping her eyes on the road. Even with a burnt dress, I'm not ready to show my scars to anyone. I look out the back window, the entire block is going up in flames.

I sat back, grabbing two smokes from the pack in the cup holder. "Hollywood sucks. That was nothing like the movies."

I'm positive I never burnt my back, but through my adrenaline rush, it is hard to tell.

We got back home, and Violet ran to the bathroom, wetting a face cloth. I stopped her before she looked at my back. "I can do it."

She looked at me, confused. "It will be easier if I do it for you."

"No."

I shut the door behind her and faced my back to the mirror. My back is a little bit black, but nothing bad. I don't know how I walked away from that scratch-free, but I'm not going to argue. I pulled my black sweater dress out from the closet and slipped into my red heels, grabbing my make-up bag and leaving the room.

I pulled out my phone, dreading having to go back to everyone. "I need to fix my makeup on the way back. Jesus, I have thirty-five missed calls."

We both texted one person back then we ran out the front door. We drove over the speed limit to get back as fast as we can. My makeup looks even better than before. I put my mirror up, and I grab Violet's hand, squeezing her.

We walked through the back door and every single member of our crew who was there is standing at the back door waiting for us. I saw relief wash over my friends faces when they laid their eyes on me. Once everyone saw we were okay, they all disbursed. Liam walked into the back room and I followed him.

"What the fuck, Charlie." His voice is cold. "You never answered, and I thought you died. You just killed dozens of people. You could have killed yourself. You still have a month off." His voice is shaking.

Liam can't even look me in the eyes, he is staring at the floorboards under my feet. I can see his anger in his chest by the deep breaths he is inhaling. Through his silence, I can hear chatter from the kitchen. I understand why Liam is pissed, but this isn't my fault. The longer he is standing in front of me not saying a word, the angrier he is getting. No matter what I do or don't say, it is going to start a huge fight.

"I still have a month where I'm not worried sick about you. I refuse to let you to go back to the field ever again. I need you to have a safer job."

I was about to start arguing with him; as soon as I wanted to finally let words leave my mouth, Liam grabbed my arm and dragged me into the kitchen.

Martin is taste-testing the food. In a harsh voice, Liam spoke to him, "This shit will never happen again! Charlie needs a safer job, Dad." Liam's body is trembling from rage.

Martin looked at Liam and started laughing before he turned back into the dining room.

Liam let go of my arm and charged into the dining room. I stood in the kitchen and the realization of what I did hit me. Glasses are stacked on each other by a bourbon bottle on the counter; I walked over and poured a drink. As I was picking up the bottle, my hands started trembling, I slowly poured while making a mess on the counter.

I pulled my smoke pack out of my purse. I heard the door start to swing open, I picked up my glass and chugged it back. Hoping that the bourbon can make me feel normal again.

At least, somewhat normal.

April's called Dillon over; the next thing I know, he is wrapping his arms around me and pulling me into his chest. The tighter he holds on to me, the more I begin to calm down.

I always heard of pressure points for helping with panic attacks, but until this moment, I never believed it. I am slowly starting to calm down, I'm not shaking anymore. I let out a long breath and get out of Dillon's grasp. He put his hand on my back and we made our way back to reality.

Anyone who never knew we were the Basilisks wouldn't have guessed anything had happened. We hid it from everyone who was a plus one, they never suspected a thing. This was the first time so many people got together, and everyone stayed sober. That was a success in itself.

I can tell Kinsley is disappointed in me. Not only did I hurt Liam, I also managed to hurt his mother. I looked around the table and noticed everyone's plate is cleared except for mine. Without saying a word, I went into the kitchen to grab dessert; Kinsley and April both followed me in.

I got into the kitchen and turned around, trying to apologize. "Kinsley, I'm so sorry about today. Martin kept calling me away, and I just blew you off. I know you probably don't want to now, but I was planning on looking at wedding dresses tomorrow to see if I can catch any sales. I would like you to come, but if you don't want to join, I understand."

Kinsley's eyes shined brightly. "I would love to."

April has a small voice. I can hardly hear her. "Do you mind if I come too?" She kicked the ground. "I'm sorry about earlier." She was still trying to talk, but I interrupted her with a hug.

I am determined to find out why Josh has separate feelings about her than her family does.

Liam walked in with a shocked look. "I see you two made up."

"Let's bring these pies out," I said with a smile, nudging April's arm with my elbow.

"Charlie, come back in here when you're done." Martin's tone is tense, I never noticed he had walked in behind us.

April took the pie I was holding, looking me in the eyes, she exhaled a full breath of air before turning around.

Martin never wasted a moment; as soon as the door shut, he started scolding me and Liam. "Liam, I would have shot you on the spot, but I promised your mother it would be a gun-free day. If either of you ever try to outrank me again, it will be your last day on this earth."

Lizzy

I finally turned my phone on and the text messages wouldn't stop. After I read a text from all of them asking if I was dead, I sent a group text to April, Josh, Adam, and Spencer.

Jesus guys, I'm alive. I'll see you soon.

My phone went back on silent and I tossed into my purse. My dress hugs every part of my body just right and this dress is so tight it makes my baby bump look even bigger.

I can hear Erik on the phone with the bedroom door shut. I slowly swung it open so it wouldn't creak; he saw me come in and his eyes got wide with a smile on his face. He isn't wearing a shirt so my eyes are drawn to his chest. "Violet, no. She's coming with me. You know I'm always armed. If she shoots your brother, that's not on me. I won't stop her from going after my gun." He tossed his phone on the bed and came rushing over to me.

He fell on his knees, wrapping his arms around my waist and kissing my belly. "I love you."

I ran my fingers through his hair and he got up, kissing me. "And I love you."

He hugged me and I saw *What To Expect When You're Expecting*. I kissed him on the cheek and ran towards the books. They were all read. Every page in every book.

I turned around with my mouth open. "How did you get all these read?"

"I have been reading them at work."

I ran up to him, wrapping my arms around his middle. "What was that on the phone?"

"Just Violet trying to do damage control for her brother. No amount of damage control can fix what he did. We won't stay long, I promise. I want to show off my fiancée."

"I love the sound of that. Your Basilisk tattoo. I have been trying to look for it but I can't find it."

Erik turned his arm around, the basilisk snake slithering up his forearm. It didn't look like the others, it was light blue. "My dad always had it planned out that I was going to be a cop. When I was sixteen, they made it look more approachable, to raise less questions."

I nodded. "I don't know how I feel with you being one of them."

He sighed, walking over to his closet and reaching for a dress shirt. "I get it that you're not okay with it. I was absolutely ruthless, even while I was a cop. Nothing scared me. I was Martin's best hitman."

I can feel all the blood rush from my face as I reach for the bed. I feel so sick.

Erik rushed to sit on his knees in front of me. "The night I met you, I went straight to Martin. I pulled out of that, I'm just a double-crossed cop now. I never once killed an innocent person. I was so crazy because my life was stolen from me and we are being controlled."

Erik's eyes are full of pain, reliving this conversation is breaking his heart. I leant in and kissed him, wiping away my red lipstick from his face. "We better getting going."

"I don't know if I can let you leave looking like this." He slowly slid his fingertips up my thigh and into my dress, and I can feel my thighs becoming numb. I tipped my head back, quickly collected myself, and swatted his hand out of the way.

The Taylors' house is huge. We parked on the street, walking up to the gate. Erik told the speaker who we were and the gate opened. The house stood four stories tall made from brick. It is the most beautiful and boastful thing I have ever seen. I knew April grew up rich, but seeing this house, her work ethic amazes me.

Even with the fresh snowfall from last night, it was obvious they hired people to upkeep the lawn; the driveway is freshly shoveled. Trees stand in front of the windows for even more privacy. The fence wraps around the entire property.

Erik pulled me into his side as we walked up the pathway to the door. His dad is standing outside with a woman with long beautiful blonde hair. She has an elegant look that only money can buy, just like Mrs. Taylor. As we got closer, they both started smiling at us.

Erik kissed my head. "I never even introduced you last time. Things got a bit crazy, but this is my father, Nick, and my mother, Trish."

Without hesitation, they both pulled me from Erik's grasp and hugged me. I stepped back and Eric grabbed my left hand, showing them the shimmering silver and pink engagement ring. Their faces went from shocked to tears in their eyes within seconds. I stand out in this family; everyone has blonde hair, I am the only one that is a brunette. I am starting to hope the baby catches the blonde hair gene. I can't deny it; his entire family is attractive.

Trish started to fan her face, fighting the tears. "Your father told me she knows everything?"

I looked up at Erik and he nodded his head with a regretful expression. I hated seeing him like this. "He really had no choice. I was caught in it before I even knew it." I shrugged my shoulders.

The more I told myself it was okay, I started to believe it.

She nodded. "Well, he won't let that baby of yours even know about any of this." She started to tear up again before walking away. "I can't stop crying."

I opened my mouth to respond but she walked away with Nick following close behind her. We walked into a big open room. I tried to look around but so many people are standing in here, laughing. All the men are wearing suits, the women are all dressed up. Erik grabbed my hand while a group of guys rushed up to hug him. They all stood around him with respect I have never seen before, I didn't take April seriously when she called Erik the alpha, but now I know what she meant.

Men started to rush into the kitchen; Erik held onto my hand tighter without letting go. The women all sat at the tables, the volume dropped and all I can hear are my heels clicking on the floor. April looked at me and shrugged her shoulders, I can tell she is worried. We got in the kitchen and the first person I recognize is William and Dillon. Erik kept a tighter grip on my hand, leading us to stand by his friends. I'm standing me in front of him so I'm facing his chest, he is holding me tight, protecting me.

"Should she be in here?" asked William.

Josh came up beside me and touched my shoulder. "She knows."

Spencer and Adam came into my line of view, looking at me with questioning eyes. I flashed them my ring, wiggling my fingers, and they started to smile. I felt Erik laugh once then kiss my head.

"So, you just sent them out to blow up a fucking building?" I wasn't sure who asked but I heard one of the guys near me mumble something under their breath. Then someone else mumbled 'Liam'.

"We need to try to get the McKinnon's off our asses. The boss was in town; what else do you expect me to do?" Martin used the same tone he used with Erik in his living room.

"Like you said, Erik is ruthless, he's a better option." Liam was trying to talk quietly but his voice was raised.

"Fuck you, Liam." Erik held me tighter against him.

The room went silent and we heard a car pull up. The back door opened, I heard a breath come out from everyone who was standing near me. Erik's muscles relaxed and he kissed my head again.

A girl walked past me and in a hushed tone, she spoke, "Sammy, let's go."

I felt my heart stop beating, a tear ran down my face and I remembered Erik saying he was always armed. I'm staring at Spencer; he grabbed Josh's arm and pulled Adam back from my line of view. I pushed myself back from Erik's chest and reached into his jacket. I found the handle of the gun, Erik's body tensed. No one moved around me. I can't take my eyes off his chest.

"Just shoot me, I don't think anyone here would blame you." Sammy stopped beside me.

I put the gun back in Erik's holster and his body relaxed, and he held onto my hips. "No, because unlike you, I don't shoot up random people on the street. My god, she was probably wearing something purple and fuzzy. If my brother finds out who you are, you will be dead. I haven't decided if I will tell him or not."

The room is still silent and I felt five hands on me, apart from Erik's.

Erik leant down and kissed my head. "I'm so unbelievably proud of you. Brittney would be too. Let's go home, watch *Hallmark*, and feed my baby sparkling apple juice."

I looked up and kissed Erik, the room cleared out except for us two, Josh, Spencer, Adam, Dillon, and William. We all walked out of the room and April ran up to us. She was going to wrap her arms around Josh, but stopped when her family trailed behind us.

Dillon and William are whispering, "She's pregnant?"

April grabbed my hand. Looking at my ring, she dropped it, giving Erik the biggest hug ever. This is why I felt so intimidated by her. But I can't complain, Spencer was cuddled up with me on the couch multiple times when Erik got home from work. He has never batted an eye or stopped to question what was happening. It felt so wrong, but all of them have become my best friends.

Dillon playfully shoved Erik. "And you're engaged? Jesus. You never tell us anything, man."

Erik shoved Dillon back, they look like ping bong balls. "You guys have been dealing with your own shit. Do me a favor and don't tell Liam or Charlie? They have enough shit going on."

They nodded and Liam came storming out of the dining room, sitting down at the table, and lighting a smoke. April walked into the kitchen calling Dillon, then stormed back out.

"April, be nice to her." I pointed my finger.

Adam hugged me and kissed me on the head. "I have the world's best sister."

Erik looked around the room protectively. "We need to get you out of here, everyone fucking smokes."

Erik walked beside me with his hand on my belly, smiling, showing off to the entire room he is going to be a daddy. We walked outside and more smokers filled the doorway.

Erik picked me up, making me squeal and laugh. "Jesus, they are everywhere." Loud enough for them to hear.

His mom and dad shouted something as we walked away but neither of us heard; Erik didn't care enough for him to stop.

I have never gone out on Christmas; I shouldn't be surprised New York is the city that doesn't sleep. So many stores are open. We loaded up on way too much food.

We got home, I changed out of my dress and put on pajamas, scrubbing my makeup off. A little piece of me is broken. I never had my family. I got downstairs to the lowest level of the house, sitting on the couch with my feet under my ass and staring at my contact list. I dialed Mom's number, it rang five times and sent me to voice mail. I hung up before the beep. I dialed Dad's number and it rang three times before getting sent to voice mail. I tried Theo, he never ignored my call, but he made voice mail pick it up for him. I felt Erik grab my shoulders from behind me. We both stared at Max's number. He hit the call button for me.

"Lizzy?"

"Max, I missed your voice."

"Yeah, same."

This isn't how I wanted the call to go. "I miss you."

"I really have to go."

Tears started to roll down my face. "What happened to you being there for me?"

"Liz. This has nothing to do with that! I promise! I love you."

"I love you. Say hi to Mom and Dad for me."

He hesitated. "I'm not with them."

The line is silent and I can hear Theo shout. "Max, it's your line."

Max waited another minute. "I'm sorry, Lizzy."

The line got disconnected and more tears fell down my face.

"They are using, aren't they?" I nodded my head, wiping my face. "I can afford to send them to rehab if that's what you want. If they ask for it, I will do it."

I cleared my throat and shook my head. "This is my fault. I got them on it."

"Please let me help, they are my brothers now too."

I nodded my head. Erik pulled the table to the couch, bringing all the food closer to me. Despite all the shitty things that happened today, Erik made this one of the best Christmases I have ever had. Asking him if I can be the future Mrs. Watson was the best decision I ever made.

Charlie

The sun isn't even fully raised yet and April is already blowing my phone up. "I'm outside. Mom will be here any minute," I grunted, hanging up the phone.

I answered the door with my eyes still half shut. "Just give me five minutes to put something on and put my hair up." Walking back into the room, starting to regret boxing day shopping.

Liam's face is smothered in his pillow. "Why the hell do I hear my sister?"

"I'm taking her and your mom dress shopping today."

"You're taking my sister?"

"She's going to be my sister too. I need to learn how to get along with her. She really doesn't seem that bad. Go say hi."

Liam dragged himself out of bed and into the living room.

Right before April called out to me about Kinsley's arrival, I was able to get changed, put my hair in a bun, and a light layer of makeup on to make me look less like a zombie. April is standing at the door, waiting for me, looking straight into the house. Her relationship is awful with her brothers, she must have had to get the address of the house from someone. I don't think she has ever stepped foot in here before. My jaw dropped at the sight of a limo parked on the street outside.

April looked at me as I walked out the house, shutting the door behind me. "Thanks for not telling anyone I know about the Basilisks. My parents like to flaunt their money and this car service is just the start."

I crawled in and smiled at the driver who opened the door for us. "Kinsley, this is the last thing I expected to happen today."

"Sparkling water?" Kinsley passed me the bottle before I could even answer.

I looked around the limo in shock. The limo has a television on the back of the driver's seat. There is an ice bin across from where I'm sitting with bottles of champagne on ice. Colorful lights light up the roof, reflecting on the seats.

April stared at my arm. "Why does every damn person have that tattoo?"

Looking at April, I remember Josh telling me that Kinsley is one of the people that doesn't know April knows. "Your dad started it when he was a teenager. It just kind of caught on. Christmas eve came around, and Noah just randomly showed up with his tattoo gun. Dillon made me do it. He says all the best friends in his family have one, and it just became a thing."

The saleswoman came up to us, smiling, she looked at me. "I'm taking it you are the bride to be?" I nodded my head. "What kind of style are you looking for?"

"I want a train. Ruffles, lace."

"Veil?"

"Yes!"

"Let's get you into a dress and see what size you are."

Sizing has to be the most tedious thing I have ever put myself through. I have never been self-cautious of my body until today. The size ten never fit, so we went to a size twelve, which still never worked. Finally, size fourteen fit me. We all walked around the store looking for one that suited me. I feel so overwhelmed that I can't decide.

I walked around to the back of the store, and I fell in love. It has spaghetti straps, V-neck with purple beads down the neckline. The torso is done up the mannequin's back like a corset. At the hips, it turns puffy, there are so many ruffles. The train is at least two feet long.

"I found it." My eyes are glued to it. "I need this one." I thought about the back of the dress and paused. "Do you have anything to cover up my shoulders and back?"

"Why? It's beautiful," April said while looking at it.

I walked away from the dress, looking at the floor. "I don't know, I just don't like the back."

I have to hold back every bit of rage that is igniting in my body. Kinsley is looking at me with a heartbroken look, making it so much harder to control my anger.

The saleswoman walked up to me, holding two shawls. "This one is heavier so it's not transparent like the other. This one is more for style."

I reached my hand out and grabbed the first option. "This one please."

"This might be your lucky day. That dress is our last one from last year's collection. It is 80% off. Marked down to $800. Let me take it down, and we will get it on you."

Standing at the changing rooms, waiting. She finally came back with the dress. I gently grabbed it and jumped into the change room.

"I love it!" I'm trying to reach behind me to do up the dress, but the way it ties up, it is making that difficult, if not impossible, to do it alone. After struggling, I gave up and wrapped the shawl around my shoulders.

"Come out!" Kinsley is standing with anticipation.

I'm standing in front of three mirrors, admiring my dress. This is my dream dress, but I'm not going to be standing at the end of the aisle with the man of my dreams. Me and Liam are so wrong for each other, but I can't bring myself to end our relationship. The moment I lose him, I will lose everyone else I love all over again.

I'm getting married for all the wrong reasons.

Kinsley is looking at me like a proud mother. "You look amazing."

"My brother is going to love it when he sees you! I picked you a few veils. Do you mind me showing you them?" April is backing up, waiting for my reply so I looked at her in the mirror and nodded my head.

"These were all my options, but I just found this one." April must have run to the veils because she was only gone a few minutes. She held it up, and it had the same shade of purple beads lined up at the bottom.

Even April is taller than I am, but I lowered my head so she could put it on. I turned around, looking in the mirror again; the veil is long. It falls to the bottom of my low neckline.

"That's the one; you're getting it." April is a proud big sister, despite their broken relationship.

Kinsley looked at me, uncomfortable. "I know you don't have anyone to help you with your wedding. Would you let me pay for everything here?"

I took off the veil and held it in my hands. "I can't let you pay for it. I have cash with me." I shifted my body uncomfortably when I noticed how disappointed she looks. "If you want to, you can."

Kinsley paid for the dress, veil, and shawl while I ran to a coffee shop a few doors down; by the time I got to the limo, I was consumed by my thoughts. I have no idea how many people are going to be standing with Liam. We both only have guy friends, the same guy friends. I would ask Violet, so at least that gave me one bridesmaid. I looked up at April and she is picking at the sleeve on her cup.

I can ask her. It will probably end up turning into a fucking nightmare, or a full-out Taylor bloodbath.

I sighed. "April, do you want to be a bridesmaid?"

She looked at me and pulled her eyebrows together, moving her head back. After a few seconds, she opened her mouth and started nodding in excitement.

Kinsley sat back in her seat. I can tell she is nervous. "Have you thought about who is going to walk you down the aisle?"

I sat there looking at my cup. "No one. I am fine with it." I moved my head and looked out the window, watching the house appear. "This is me."

Before I got out, I looked at Kinsley. "Thank you for buying me my dress. It means a lot to me." I wrapped the dress bag around my arm and shut the door behind me.

There is an overabundance of shoes at the door. I walked in and I knew I was walking into a house full of the regular people. "William! Come here for a second."

I heard the couch creak from under him then he appeared in front of me. I passed him my dress. "Do you mind keeping this in your closet from peering eyes?"

He grabbed it and walked away from me. I walked over the fridge, twisted my lid, and tossed it on the counter. I walked past everyone in the living room not paying attention to who was here. As I pulled my eyes away from my beer bottle, I let out a quiet gasp, taken aback at Brooks sitting in a chair across the room, staring at me.

"Well, this is a new blend of people in our living room. What's going on?" I said, looking up at Liam walking in my direction.

Liam picked me up. "Celebrating." He put me down on my feet, kissing me. "When you blew up the McKinnon's yesterday, they fell. The rest in LA ratted each other out to get protection. They are no longer here."

I leaned against the counter and took a drink of my beer, grabbing a cigarette pack sitting in front of me. I zoned out into the smoke leaving my mouth. Things like this don't just happen. I know what Martin said, but it couldn't be that easy. Why is Brooks here and not Erik?

I pushed myself from my thoughts and turned around, facing everyone. "What if our names get brought up? In the past month, they've been in New York a lot—dealing with us."

Brooks still hasn't taken his eyes from me. "I have been tapping into the system, making sure we are clear."

"No offense, but how do we know you aren't going to be going back and repeating everything we say?"

"Charlie, he is one of us," Liam snapped at me.

I glanced down at Adam on the floor and I can tell he is thinking the same thing. I watched him look up to Spencer and Josh, they both look like they are on edge. I traded a look with Adam and he slowly took a deep breath. Nothing about this feels right, I'm not the only one who thinks so.

Brooks stood up and walked out of the house, I quickly followed him out to his car. It's a basic white SUV. "It's okay. It's just a box." He paused, reading my body language. "After Erik told me what you went through, I needed to meet you. I couldn't believe you survived. Even after meeting you, I'm still shocked."

I feel so uncomfortable about him being around, not only me but all of us. Something about him isn't right. Glancing up to the house, Liam is keeping a close eye on us, outside the front door.

I walked up and grabbed Liam's hand. "Your sister's a bridesmaid."

Liam is looking at me with confusion written on his face. I was right, this is going to turn into a Taylor bloodbath.

I sat down in the corner of the room, watching everyone. We are all listening to what Brooks has to say. "Erik and I have been putting our asses out for you guys. Him for obvious reasons." He waved his hand towards Adam. "This box contains passports, and new IDs. Without knowing it, for the past year, you have been citizens of Brazil, here on school visas."

We all exchanged nervous looks. Everyone who wasn't nervous before is now.

"We only ask if you need to move, do everything legally. Work a normal person's job. None of this shit you got going on. Absolutely no breaking the law."

I'm glaring at Brooks, trying to figure out what his game is. The more I look at him, the more my memory is getting pieced together. Not from *Willie's*, but from the McKinnon's. My head is spinning with the pieces finally getting placed together. People's mouths moving back and forth in conversation. I can't make out what they are saying. I'm getting dizzier and dizzier by the second. I drop my head into my hands, closing my eyes tight, taking deep breaths. I pushed my back against the wall to get myself off the floor. I can feel my body swaying from being dizzy. My eyes are still closed; I'm too terrified to open them, there is a hand on my shoulders and the other one on my hip, trying to balance me out.

I placed my hand on the wall behind me and tried talking. I don't know how my words came out. I focused each word carefully. "I'm safe. I'm protected."

My mind was becoming clearer. I slowly opened my eyes and Adam standing in front of me. I took a deep breath and grabbed his arm, I walked over to the couch and grabbed Liam's hand, giving him a tug so he would follow us.

Rage is building up in my body, my breathing has turned into panting. I'm doing everything I can to stay calm. "Adam, call your bother now. He is picking us up." I watched Adam pull out his phone and start dialing.

Liam is hesitantly taking small steps to get closer to me. "Charlie, what the fuck is happening to you?" Adam put his hand on Liam's arm, warning him not to ask.

My rage isn't bothering Adam. If anything, he looks calm. He hangs up the phone and shoves it in his pocket. "Is he coming?" Adam nodded.

"You guys need to trust me. I was out there and after I looked at Brooks enough, I recognized him. He was one of the McKinnon's that tortured me. I remember waking up for a split second and seeing a police uniform." I paused. "I thought I was saved."

Rage is firing up in both of them. Liam is turning around to walk away. I stopped him before he opened the door. "Do not go out there. You will fuck this up. Follow my lead." They both nodded.

"Liam, I need you to stay here." I put on my purple coat and shoved my gun in my pocket.

I stormed out of the bedroom and headed directly for the living room. All my anger is in my voice. "Brooks, I need mine and Adam's papers. We are leaving tonight. I can't stay here another day."

Without hesitation, he passed me the papers and I stormed out of the house with Adam right behind me. We are ignoring everyone yelling at us in protest.

We are both walking away, lighting a cigarette. Anger building up in every step we take.

We stepped outside and Erik pulled his car out front. We got in and the car's mood changed.

I'm talking in a hushed tone. "I need to go to Martin's."

To my amazement, neither one of them argued. Erik put the car in gear and drove off. At this point, nothing is going to calm me down. I looked in the front seat, Erik is still in half of his police uniform.

I covered my mouth with my hand. I feel sick.

Either Erik is double-crossing us and had hidden my location from everyone, or Brooks is.

My mind is starting to turn to a very bad thought.

What if it's Martin?

I let out a groan and hit my head against the headrest. Nothing is making sense. I am only pissing myself off more. The drive is taking forever. My destructive thoughts are interrupted with Erik talking to the speaker at the gate.

We pulled into the driveway; as soon as the engine shut off, I opened the door as fast as I could to get out. Adam grabbed my arm. "I trust you."

That is exactly what I need to hear, because I'm bringing all of us to our graves if I am wrong.

I swung the front door open and marched past Kinsley and April with Adam and Erik close behind. From the corner of my eye, I saw Kinsley shove April through a set of doors. I walked into Martin's office, he is having a meeting with an older version of the Watson brothers, and another man that I never recognized.

I spoke, my voice filling the room, "Get the fuck out now!"

Adam's dad walked by me, glaring at me and shaking his head at his sons.

I waited for the door to shut and I pulled my gun out from my coat pocket, cocking my black-market gun. I held it, pointing at Martin's head. I heard the other two guns cock behind me.

Martin looked at me and huffed, not fazed by the three guns pointed at him. "What are you doing here? I was in the middle of something."

I shook my head slightly. "You have some fucking explaining to do."

"What is it?"

"Tell me why there is a McKinnon in my living room. The same one who was in the room with me when they took me."

"I can assure you I have no idea what you are going on about."

I lowered my gun and uncocking it, shoved it into my pocket. I walked up to Martin's desk. "Brooks." I pulled out mine and Adam's Brazilian papers and slammed them on his desk. "Explain this."

"What is this?"

"Brooks made this entire speech about how our group has citizenship in another country."

I relaxed my tone and had a normal conversation. "The night at *Willie's* when Erik came in with Brooks, Erik made that comment about him undressing me with his eyes. I felt something off about him. It was like he was investigating me. I never recognized him, so they figured it was safe to send him over and go on that entire speech conveniently, at a time when Erik was just getting off work. We have a war coming. He was trying to get your best out of the country either to attack you or to kill us."

Adam sighed, putting it all together. "Who would look in Brazil."

Erik scoffed. "One of the places we have no connections."

Martin stood up from his seat, grabbing the papers. "Stay here. Do not leave."

Erik looked at me with his mouth open. "How did you put that together?"

I lit a smoke and slid the ashtray across the desk, sitting down. "I had a super embarrassing moment in the living room."

Adam tried not to laugh. "Everyone lost it when she told them we were going to Brazil tonight."

Adam put his hand on the back of my chair and I looked up at him. His face is full of amusement. I caught the smell of his cologne and I sank into my chair. I looked away from him and Erik is watching me as I'm soaking up his brother's embrace.

"Where's Liam?" I should have expected that question from Erik.

I felt Adam's hand pull away from the back of my chair at the mention of his name. "He's at the house."

"Why did you leave him there?"

"I kind of figured he would rather stay there. He has been distant, it's like we aren't even together anymore. Besides, I knew it would work better if your brother was here. Did it not?"

"You got me there."

Martin texted me, demanding to get the other five of us in his office. I called Liam and informed him of everything that happened and my heart sank, thinking of his anger that I was soon to deal with.

It feels like the clock on the wall is frozen. I'm sitting sunk into my chair, trying to smoke the bad feeling I have out of my body. Erik and Adam are having their own conversation, I keep hearing the name Lizzy, but I'm not tuning in enough to finally figure out who the hell she is.

I have no idea if I am on the right track, but I am scared that I am wrong and I have screwed something up. If I am right, since I have joined in a short three ,months we have had two Basilisks double-cross us.

I can't shake this feeling I have about pulling a gun on my soon to be father-in-law. Unfortunately, that was the only way I had to be taken seriously. Martin's office door flew open, hitting the wall. I tipped my head back, waiting for Liam to unleash his wrath.

"What the fuck, Charlie, you're pulling guns on my family now! Not to mention my sister is upstairs asking questions!" Liam yelled as he walked in.

My head is still tilted over the chair. I don't feel bad, I'm not going to apologize.

Martin slammed the papers on his desk. "Charlie, you are on a roll, pissing off us Taylors today."

William pulled out a chair to sit next to me. "She still has two more to go."

Martin cracked a smile. I watched him set eight bullets on the table. "These were just delivered. There's one for each of you. Pull up a seat, this is going to take a while."

Dillon picked up the bullets, tossing the ones with our names to us. The door opened and Kinsley brought in nine alcohol cups, five ashtrays, and a full bottle of bourbon. She set them on the table and glared at me. Dillon put my designated bullet in my hand, winking at me.

I grabbed my cup, looking at Martin. "Only a few more to go and I have pissed off your entire family in less than two hours."

I turned around, passing out the cups to everyone. I sat back down, pouring a drink. "I need to ask this before we even start figuring out what the hell is going on. Brooks said the McKinnon's empire burned, everyone was ratting each other out for protection."

Martin took a sip, listening to every word. "They did the opposite. They got a new boss. They are the ones who sent the bullets."

"What do we do now?" Josh asked in a muffled voice.

Spencer looked around. "Just cut off Brooks' head and send it to them."

I giggled. "That would start a war, I know for a fact no one in this room wouldn't survive without each other." I put my lips to my cup. "It's tempting though."

Martin put his elbows on his desk. "I faxed over Charlie's and Adam's paperwork to a connection that I have. They look real, but everything is fake. He has no idea how they look so real. I don't mean to add to this, but think of who you will be voting for. I will be retiring."

"We've known for months. Our dads do nothing but gossip," Spencer said with his voice muffled in his cup.

Martin swirled the alcohol in his cup. "Does anyone know any way we can resolve this issue?"

"You normally kill double-crossers." Dillon sat forward with his elbows on his knees.

"I know but this feels too important."

"Why are they even out to get us?" Dillon asked.

"We start our drug smuggling in a few days, very large drug smuggling."

Liam put his head in his hands. "You just saw the opportunity to make money so you just took it!"

Everyone started arguing back and forth. I looked at Adam and he stood up. "This is not solving anything. We still have to deal with this."

The room is silent. I'm drinking as much of my bourbon as I can to try and convince myself I have a good idea. "Just hear me out. Back in the day, mafias never killed double-crossers. They sent messages. They cut out their tongues and delivered them back alive, they couldn't speak again." I looked around and saw everyone's mouths drop.

Josh looked up from his drink, staring at me. "You are a fucking savage."

Martin leaned back in his seat. "It will work though. They would never mess with a Basilisk again."

The doors flew opened and April came charging in. "Charlie, you sick son of a bitch."

I raised my cup. "Make that four Taylors." Other than Liam, everyone's face lit up.

"My first impression of you was exactly right. Stay the fuck away from my family."

I leaned back in my seat and took a small sip, lighting another smoke. I'm getting so sick of her jumping down my throat. I pulled my cigarette from my lips, noticing Erik, Adam, Josh, and Spencer all hanging their heads in defeat. I knew Josh cared about her, but seeing how the other three react to her is making me wonder what the real story is.

Dillon is standing at his seat. "How did you even know to listen to us?"

She scoffed. "Everyone in New York knows the Basilisks. I'm not stupid."

William walked up to April, putting his hand on her shoulder. "You need to leave now."

She pushed his hand off her shoulder. "Cutting a man's tongue out of his mouth. You disgust me. Suddenly, I'm okay with you being in a marriage with mistresses."

As soon as the words left her mouth, everyone in the room turned to Liam, looking at him with murder in their eyes. I shook it off and turned my head to April.

April looked at Liam. "Notice how he hasn't said one word?" She squeezed William's arm. "I'm sorry about the interruption, little cousin."

The door slammed behind her, I can feel William standing behind me.

Martin looked at all of us, slouching his muscular frame in his chair. "I will make phone calls, we will do this over the next few days. Charlie, I need you at this address." He passed me a picture. "This is your guy. Adam, Spencer, and Charlie, you are in charge of the first sale. Before any of you speak up, from what I saw today, she is capable of doing the job."

I put my head down and sighed. "I'll head out now."

Dillon stood up. "You can't go alone."

I shrugged my shoulders and walked out the door.

I followed the address. It took me to the worst part of Brooklyn. Even though I had a gun, I still found myself locking my car doors. Transients filled the street as they saw me drive by slowly. I glanced down at my phone to get another look. He has red hair and freckles. I stopped and rolled down the window. I could see him on the sidewalk beating someone up.

"Hey, Ivan!" He looked up. "That's not very nice!" I shot him through the passenger window. The bullet pierced through his neck.

I can hear the person he was beating up thanking me for firing on him. I drove away and looked out the back window and I saw people rush up to the man, forcing Ivan's limp lifeless body off him.

Lizzy

Liam, William, Josh, Spencer, and Adam are all sitting on the floor in the living room, studying. The fire is crackling and I am cuddled up with a blanket on the couch. The front door swung open and I turned around smiling, when I saw Erik.

He looks off, something happened. He took off his jacket and his police badge and gun are missing. "Babe, I got suspended. I don't even care if I get into shit." Never taking his eyes off me. I stood up and hugged him.

He let go of me and stepped aside. Theo and Max are standing two feet away from me. Their pupils are dilated. They both look like they haven't eaten in weeks. The three of us are standing silent, staring at each other. We are all trying to find the words to say.

"What are you on? I need to hug you both." My hands are shaking. My emotions are mixed between happiness, anger, and confusion.

Theo rubbed the back of his neck. "We came down on the ride here, but blow."

I ran up to them, wrapping my arms around them both. Both of them holding me tight. We pulled away and Erik grabbed my hand.

Erik is standing behind the arm of the couch with his hands on my shoulders, pulling me into him. "You guys look like fucking hell."

Max tipped his head back, covering his eyes. "We need help, Lizzy."

Erik squeezed my shoulders. He is still willing to get them in rehab, I thought he was bluffing. "I already have spots for you guys in rehab. I'm the only one who knows where it is, if you guys are both serious. They can come now."

Theo never took his eyes off Erik. "Why would you do that?" I flashed my ring. "He fucking proposed?"

I shook my head. "Actually, I did."

Theo, Max, William, Dillon, and Liam all started laughing.

Theo shook his head. "Oh! You're serious." I nodded. "We already missed so much, we need help."

I squeezed Erik's hand. "Don't phone yet. I just need five minutes with them."

I got off the couch and ran upstairs, I haven't taken Brittney's blanket out of the garbage bag, I have been waiting to take it out until the three of us were together. Grabbing the bag out of the bottom of our closet and carried it downstairs.

I dropped it in front of me, smiling. "You are never going to guess what I found in my closet when I moved here." I untied the bag and pulled it out. Both of their faces lit up.

Max grabbed it and started to inhale it. "Why the hell did she think it was a good idea to wear perfume that smells like my grandma when she got drunk?"

Theo started laughing. "That's what it is! I couldn't figure it out."

Spencer's face turned white; he frantically got to his feet and sniffed the blanket. "Show me a picture of Brittney, now!"

Erik scrambled up the stairs, our friends exchanging looks. Spencer is fighting back tears, with the blanket held to his nose.

Erik passed him the only picture I had out with the four of us from my nightstand. Spencer fell to his knees, hugging the picture.

All of us are taken aback. Josh and Adam put their hands on his back. I stood up and snatched the picture away from him, putting my body in his arms instead. He is holding onto me as tight as he can. I looked up at Erik and he sat down with his head in his hands; everyone else did the same, they are all feeling his pain.

"The girl I love is dead." He put his face in my neck, gasping for air. "She never broke my heart, she died. I was at her funeral, I didn't know it was her, we were all standing so far back."

None of this makes sense, but I get it. Brittney had a secret boyfriend for months that she never told us about. I can feel Spencer's breathing even out, he put his arms to his side letting me go. I stood up and ran to Erik, he wrapped his arms around me, kissing my hair.

Spencer looked up at Theo and Max. "She told me her name was Cameron."

Theo closed his eyes. "You met her at a bar?"

Spencer nodded.

Max put his head in his hand. "She told guys her middle name at the bar, so it was easy for her to ignore them. She probably felt awkward telling you her real name after she started liking you."

I sighed. "Spence, you changed her life. She was so in love with you."

Spencer looked at me. "No wonder I became so attached to you, Lizzy."

Spencer shift his weight on the floor, adjusting. "She knew everything about the Basilisks. We kept it a secret to keep you guys safe. She never once told me your names. The last conversation I had with her I walked out of a jewelry store, she called me, she told me she was going to marry me one day. I told her to meet me and she never showed."

A tear landed on Erik's hand. He wrapped his arm around my shoulder while he grabbed Theo, squeezing his shoulder. I remember her walking out of my bedroom. "*My fairy godmother called. My prince charming is waiting.*"

"There's eight million people in New York, how the hell did all of us get so intertwined without even realizing it?" Liam hung his head.

Theo grabbed my hand. "Erik phone, we both need to do this." Theo looked around the room, stopping at me. "I'm sorry for all the shit we caused. I'm proud of you, baby sister."

I cuddled into Theo. "It's a sixty-day program. Save your amends for when you're clean."

Knowing Spencer was the contact named Prince Charming, I understand why she never told us anything. She changed for the better when she met him, she became happy. She got so much more protective over us knowing she had an army behind her for backup. Spencer turned her into the person she wanted to be. For the last eight months of her life, she was the happiest any of us had ever seen her.

There was a knock at the door, Erik answered it and both of the boys took one last smell of the blanket before walking out the door. All of us followed them, me and Erik standing on the sidewalk, hugging them. They were thanking Erik for everything he has done for me and for them. Max and Theo both pulled Spencer out from the back of the crowd and hugged him with every ounce of strength left in their body.

Charlie

I refuse to let our first drug deal get in the way of my very first New Year's with my friends. Even though I know it is going to put a damper on our night. I finished my hair and the entire time, I have been trying to think of the perfect outfit to wear. I decide on my long dark purple cardigan, a black tank top, light blue skinny jeans, and stilettos. I dig through my makeup bag and find dark purple lipstick, just like my cardigan.

I walked into the kitchen and grabbed a cigarette from the pack on top of the fridge, William is doing the same. I can see him looking me up from my feet to my head. "The fact that we live together and I haven't tried to sleep with you is beyond me."

Liam came into my line of sight with a grin. "Man, Dillon and I had a bet going on if you would be stupid enough to try. He said no, I said yes."

Rising my hand to William's shoulder and patting him. "Well, thank you for not trying anything. I don't think I could handle that kind of disappointment in my life."

Dillon's laughter is getting louder with his feet dragging on the floor while walking into the kitchen.

William formed a hard line with his lips. "I fucking hate you guys."

"What are we even doing tonight?" I asked, flicking the ash off my cigarette.

"There's a campus party. I need to make an appearance for a girl. But after that, I have no idea."

"Spencer called me before after I got ready. They want to go out for dinner." I laughed. "I thought we were already doing something tonight with them."

Dillon leaned up against the wall. "How do we manage to have such a big group of Alpha personalities and we don't piss each other off?"

Liam smiled. "None of us would hesitate to shoot each other to make a point."

I muttered, "Getting shot hurts."

William laughed. "You would know."

Driving to the docks, thinking about the short time we had at the party. I am getting used to every girl stopping in their tracks and staring at the guys, but they got extra attention tonight from the co-eds. Not like I was ever with them at school, that probably isn't anything new. I understand why so many girls go crazy at the sight of them.

Sitting in the backseat with my arms crossed, huffing at my thinking, my eyes are darting around the vehicle, I could probably shoot lasers from my eyes. Liam has run off, again. I was starting to think that I am overthinking about him cheating on me, but now I really don't know what to think.

Adam parked his car and I flew out of the backseat, charging towards Noah, I just want this to be over with. I don't feel good about this drug smuggling deal, but my annoyance with Liam is overpowering.

Noah jumped onto the dock from the boat with his eyes wide. "There is $10 million worth of drugs."

I'm in the front with Adam and Spencer close behind me. Why I'm stuck being in charge of this deal is beyond me. I am one of the least intimidating Basilisks. A group of four guys are walking up to me, they can't be any older than I am. The ones in the back look younger than me. All of their bodies tense when they see Adam and Spencer. All of their eyes travel down to me and I can see them starting to relax.

The one in the front nodded at me. "Everything looks good. We will take it from here. This is all the money we owe you."

I held out my hand, being passed envelopes. They are bursting at the seams with cash. As soon as the envelopes are no longer in his hand, they all walk away; apparently, they are just as eager to get this over with as we are.

Spencer put his hand on my back as we walked away. I'm constantly looking over my shoulder, looking for anything to go wrong. Last time, it had seemed to be this easy but it wasn't. They were nervous, I know they weren't going to do anything, but I can never be too safe.

Noah looked at me while he stepped closer. I started stepping back to put space between us. His persona changed. He's turning aggressive. "What is Martin thinking?"

Spencer pulled out his gun and made sure Noah can see it. I feel Adam's body next to mine.

Spencer has a serious tone. One I have never heard before. "Noah, I promise none of us had any idea how much we were dealing with."

Noah pulled himself back and walked away while he exhaled heavily.

We jumped back in the car and I hid the cash under the seat. "I like serious Spencer."

He laughed. "Don't get used to it. What is up Liam's ass?"

"When I know, you'll be the first to know."

I watched Spencer nudge Adam. I saw Adam look up at me in the rear-view mirror. Our eyes locked and I know a smile is creeping up on my face. Neither of us can pull our eyes off each other. Adam does this to me, there is something about him that I can't shake.

Spencer rolled down his window, interrupting our moment. "I forgot to tell you, but you look beautiful tonight."

I looked down at my engagement ring and my heart sank. I should have run away like I wanted to. I'm with the wrong man.

I reached over the seat and grabbed Spencer's shoulder. "Thank you."

Charlie

Martin's house has more than 100 people crammed inside. It's a maze trying to find anyone I know. Liam grabbed onto my arm and gently pushed his way to the front of the room. I glanced behind me, William is with Dillon following me. I can tell they are nervous, we are all terrified of our future of being a basilisk.

Martin came downstairs, scanning the crowd. "Oh, Charlie. There you are. Follow me. Alone; you three stay put."

I followed him up the stairs into a bedroom. Noah is sitting in the corner with his tattoo gun. He looked up at me, fire raging in his eyes.

Martin picked up his glass and chugged back the caramel-colored liquid. "Out of all the ideas, why did you have to come up with that brutal one? It's done now. We delivered him. You fucking did it. We are on a truce." He gestured towards Noah. "Pull your sleeve up. You are getting a tattoo above your snake."

I have a million questions running through my head, I know Martin well enough to know he deflects questions. If I ask the wrong one, he will pull out his gun and fire on me without a second thought. I sat down beside Noah, pulling up my sleeve and listening to his commands. Martin extended his arm out with the caramel liquid splashing in the cup. I know better than to drink while getting a tattoo done but something tells me I am going to need alcohol. Before putting my lips to the brim of the cup, I sniffed the contents. The smell of yeast intoxicated me and I immediately took a gulp, ignoring the burn.

The room is silent other than the buzzing of the tattoo gun. I know I should be feeling a sting or some sort of pain, but I am nothing but relaxed. I have been trying to look at my arm but Noah is blocking the tattoo with his hand.

I glared at Martin. "Why am I getting this? Should I be starting to worry?"

"If you should worry is an open-ended question."

My mind is racing back and forth. I'm starting to think that I'm going to be punished because of Brooks. I took a sip of my whiskey trying to control my thoughts, but I'm too nervous. I need to know what the hell is happening.

Martin stood up and walked across the room, picking up a box. "There were fifteen votes for William, twenty-five for Dillon, twenty-nine for Liam, forty-six for Adam, and thirty-three for Josh." He paused and sighed. "Even fucking Spencer got seven votes, I swear, they just voted for him for the hell of it. Apparently, everyone wants a young boss. I can't blame them though."

He sat back down, leaning forward. "I started pulling out more names from the box, including the text messages that I received. Charlie, you had fifty-eight votes."

My mind is blank. This can't be real. My heart is pounding in my chest so loudly I'm sure they can hear it over the tattoo gun. "No. I can't do this. Do not make me do this."

"Besides passing out the jobs you already have been doing it. Think about it."

Martin looked down at my arm. "Almost done." He took my cup and filled it up. "Look what you just made me do. You look like you need another drink."

I took the glass and drank it all in one shot, asking for more. This isn't happening. I caught a glimpse of my tattoo, and I saw what looks like to be a crown.

Shit.

This is happening. I need to change things. I can be the one to change things for everyone. I can help us.

We are all fucked. I can't even keep a plant alive.

Shit. I'm a Mafia boss.

Illegal gambling. That's how I will save us.

Noah put down the tattoo gun. "Done." He stopped and waited. Growling, he said, "Boss."

There it is, looking up at me. The one point, black and grey crown with a red diamond staring at me. Noah bandaged my arm up, forcing me to stop panicking and to form a game plan.

Martin spoke, "That will be all, Noah. Wipe the anger from your face, walk through the house, so you end up at the front door behind the crowd. You are not to tell anyone."

Martin passed the cup back to me; without thinking, I chugged all the contents in the cup in one giant gulp. "No offence, Martin, but I am going to do things completely different." I paused, regretting my words. "Please don't shoot me."

"I got too tangled up with revenge. It happens."

I watched Noah pack up his things and storm out of the room. I can't blame him for being so angry. I have only been a basilisk for a few months. If he is this pissed, everyone else is going to be furious. I can't handle this pressure. I am going to screw up miserably and it is going to all be my fault when they die.

Martin sat back in the chair. I'm panicking so much, I never even notice him walk away. "I need you to sign these. You officially own all of my family businesses."

I took the papers and signed them. I can't stop looking at the deeds.

Martin poured more whiskey in my cup. "Stay in the kitchen, I'll grab you when I need you."

I walked into the kitchen with my cup, lighting a cigarette. April is leaning against the counter; she looks even madder if that is possible. I leaned up against the counter, waiting for her wrath.

"I was going to apologize to you. But then, my dad cut off his tongue." She shivered.

I took a drag from my smoke and exhaled. "You could have left. No one made you stay. You don't like me, let's leave it at that."

I watched April shiver again from the corner of my eye.

I can hear Martin start talking. "I need to go."

April paused. "Wait." She looked at me with a blank face. "No way."

I'm waiting for Martin to walk into the kitchen, but I can hear Adam and William looking for me on the other side of the door.

Martin topped off my already full cup and led me into the dining room. I looked around the room, and I see a mix of anger and confusion gather on everyone's faces. I looked at Liam, he shook his head and looked at the floor. I found Dillon in the crowd, and I'm not able to read his face, which scares me. I know him better than anyone else.

"Your new boss!" Martin muttered, walking and grabbing Kinsley with suitcases.

I'm standing in front of the crowd, scared. Nothing is coming to my mind, I can't think of anything to say. I'm in shock that this is happening to me. I looked at Liam, and he took a sip of alcohol. I looked at the others, and they all look excited.

I took a deep breath. Six of the seven believe in me. That has to count for something. I looked down at the table and I saw an envelope with everyone's name written on it. I looked for mine; once I found it, I opened it; I saw my money and I know exactly what I need to do.

I took a big drink. "I can see some of you are disappointed and clearly pissed off."

Noah is walking up beside me with a gun pointed at my head. I took another drink and turned around to face him. "Well, that didn't take long." I looked at the clock. "I'd say ten seconds. Are you going to shoot me or can I continue?"

I can see from the corner of my eye that all my friends had their guns pointed at Noah. Relief washing over my body, I'm able to relax a bit more having them with me.

Turning back around, facing everyone who now depended on me. "This was the last thing I expected to happen, so I get the shock. You all heard about what happened today when someone talked. That will happen each time we have someone that double-crosses. With that, I am offering every single one of you a way out. I don't care who you are. If you don't believe in me, come tell me."

I raised my voice a notch. "I have every single one of your last paychecks here. This is your way out, but I may remind you. You are never fully out." I flipped through the envelopes until I got to Noah's name and passed it to him. "Anyone else?"

Looking at my friends with nothing else to say, I'm expecting each of them to run up to me, but they aren't moving. Liam is debating. I can see it in his expression. He doesn't want to be a part of this. I watch him step forward then freeze. I kept handing out envelopes, clearing out more than half the room. As the men came and grabbed the envelopes from me, their faces are mixed with confusion and relief. Whoever was mad moments before, has had their anger washed away with a chance of freedom.

I stood waiting for the last to leave. Hearing the front door slam, I continued, "For those of you who decided to stay, I am changing things around here. Absolutely no drugs. We got that war dealt with and paid severe consequences. We are done with black market gun sales. We are no longer killing for other people's benefits."

I'm trying to believe in my words, but it's so damn hard. "Keep my number on speed dial. I am giving everyone two weeks off. When I was getting my tattoo, I decided we are going to be opening a nightclub, with a secret entrance for illegal gambling. If there are any killings, I need to approve it. I am done with the blood spill. If there are any crazy jobs, I will be doing it. I will not put any lives at risk for a job that will get out of hand."

I have this under control. "Times are changing."

Brittney

"Britt, your alarm is fucking annoying, shut that thing up." Spencer reached over my body, swatting his hand in an attempt to shut the alarm off. "I'll drive you, but only if you Shut. It. Off. Now."

I grunted, running my fingertips over his bare arm. He sure is pissy in the morning, but I can't blame him, today the Basilisks' future changes. Reaching for my phone, the moment of peace I get first thing in the morning vanished. It's a New Year, I spent Christmas and New Year's alone, we still haven't arrested Martin, Max and Theo have both been shipped off to a sixty-day rehab program. The only good thing that has happened is that my friends finally know who Prince Charming is.

Rolling over, I pulled myself into Spencer's chest, feeling the warmth of his body; my heart is pounding, I can still smell the cologne on his skin from yesterday. "Are you ever going to tell me who you voted for?"

"No. I'm not even sure it was a good move."

Spencer kissed my hair, letting his lips hover. Now that I have this kind of love, I'm not sure I can go another day without it. I pushed myself away, getting myself out of bed to walk to the closet. I am so tired of pant suits. I tugged on a light blue blazer and grabbed the matching pants and a black shirt.

I put the blazer on, looking up and seeing a smile on Spencer's face. "I can't wait for you to really come home."

He rushed out of bed, walking to me as fast as he can to pick me up off my feet, planting a kiss on my lips. Our lips meld together perfectly, I will never get tired of this. I pulled away, resting my forehead on his chest. "I can't wait to be your wife."

Everyone at the office is in near panic. We are all sitting in the conference room trying to listen to the speech, but nothing is coming through. They are too far away from the bugs. This moment of truth is going to change everything; either we go after the new boss along with Martin or we put the new boss in protective custody.

Sam walked in with a tray of lattes and placed my cup in front of me. I never even noticed but I have been biting my nails for almost three hours. I hate sitting here waiting, I hate not knowing what the future is going to hold.

Looking up, I can see Spencer rushing through the office into the room. Smiling at the sight of him, I ran up to him. "What the hell is going on, Spence?"

He bent down to kiss me. "It's Charlie. She has called off everything that Martin did." I backed away slowly, making a straight line with my lips; he will never be on our side with one of them as a boss. "We are going to be okay. Babe, it's going to be fine." His voice went from cheerful to scared in a matter of seconds.

"Spence." My voice is showing all of the fear that is overflowing my body.

"If she gets in the way of our plan, we can't protect her. Being a Mafia boss is still illegal," Rodriguez spoke with authority in his voice.

Spencer is looking down at me, betrayed. "What are you going to do?"

"He's right, but I can try to help her. Spencer, if she's anything like Martin—" I tried to keep talking but Spencer cut me off.

"I thought of all people, you would understand having to protect your family." His eyes darted to the wall behind me, unable to look at me. "We are done."

Spencer walked away from me, slamming the door behind him so hard that the glass is rattling. I can feel my heart pounding in my chest, I want to run after him in protest, but I know his vision is clouded. My legs gave out from under me, making me fall onto the ground with my palms holding me up. My arms are shaking, struggling to support my body. Everything I have done to try to save him has vanished.

"Everyone out." Sam is sitting in front of me, trying to tuck the loose hair from my face behind my ear.

The door shut for the final time and the sobs I'm holding in start to escape. I want to scream. Nothing is going to make this better. I have risked everything to be with him, to love him, and he leaves me on the floor with a shattered heart.

This is the heartbreak I knew he was going to put me through. I knew he was going to do this to me and I was still stupid enough to fall in love with him.

Wiping my tears from my face, I'm looking at Sam hoping she can read my mind. She smiles as sweetly as she can manage. "I would love to have you back in my apartment."

I nodded, burying my face in her neck. The band of my engagement ring is creating space between my fingers. This can't be the end of us.

Please don't let this be the end of us.

Charlie

We are with the real estate agent looking at multiple properties. I am distracted by this morning, waking up alone after Liam disappeared in the middle of the night, him ignoring my calls but answering everyone else. Him not being here with me. I never asked to be voted in as the boss, I never asked for any of this. He needs to understand that. Even with me being distracted, I know the last building we looked at is the only one that feels right.

The building used to be an old bar, the original setup is still standing; if we are lucky, we can fix it up and try to use the setup, to save time and money. The windows are smashed, every mirror is broken, the floor is far from good condition, The amount of money I need to spend in repairs to make it up to code is going to clean out my bank account.

I can't think about the stress that this is going to cause. I have way too many people looking up to me. Trusting William, Dillon, and Spencer when they say it's the best spot for us I agreed to meet a lawyer to sign papers and make it mine.

I have the keys in my hand, continuously calling Liam. Josh and Adam showed up instantly to see the new place. I never looked up at them but, I can hear from their voices that they are excited.

I kicked the wall. "I can't fucking get hold of Liam." I dug around my jacket that is hanging off my arm, finding the pocket to drop my phone in.

Dillon pulled out his phone to call him. "Seriously, man. Just fucking get here."

I stood there and kicked the wall again. I unlocked the door so that we can talk in private. "I was watching him when I gave everyone an out. He was going to take it. He started walking up to me. Then I saw all of you. Standing there, believing in me."

Adam looked at me with confidence. "We all voted for you."

I heard the front entrance open, I spun around fast. "It's about fucking time."

"Whatever."

"Seriously, what's your problem?"

Liam walked up to me and kissed me as passionately as he can, but he feels distant. When he pulled away, his eye are locked on mine. "I can't do this anymore. Any chance of us having a family is gone."

"Then leave." I'm trying not to gasp for air. "You have your out."

"No. I never left yesterday because of these guys. I can't have a relationship with my boss."

I nodded my head, fighting back the tears. I grabbed his hands and slipped my engagement ring into his fists. "Well then, this is our new location. We just got the keys. Take a look around."

I pulled my eyes off him and walked towards the bar holding in all of my emotions. "If anyone has any color combinations or theme ideas, let me know. We can go to the paint store and pick them out for the painters. I have to go and call a few people to do inspections. Go enjoy your days off."

Dillon stepped forward. "Charlie, someone needs to be with you at all times now."

I shook my head and put my leather jacket on. "Now they don't see my tattoos. No one knows my position yet. I will be fine. I am going to walk around and make my calls. Then I can lock up."

Waiting for them to all leave, I can see that they are all hesitant about leaving me alone; eventually, the door shut behind them and I'm alone.

I put my hand out in front of me and fall into the wall. I'm gasping for air, tears falling down my face. I can hear the traffic outside. Focusing on that to make me calm down. The sound of car horns, chatter of people walking by, the air from city busses when they stepped on their brakes, all brought me back to reality. I held my head up high and wiped the tears away.

My ringtone for text messages is going off.

Spencer: *Me, Adam, and Josh have an extra bedroom. We are going back to pack your things right now.*

William: *It's his loss; you're incredible.*

I replied to William: *Do you mind making a stop to donate my wedding dress?*

William: *You got it.*

I turned the flashlight on my phone and started looking for the bathroom. After a few doors, I found it. Dust is piling everywhere in this building. The bathroom is no different. I took off my dress and wiped down the mirror with the part of my dress that my jacket will hide. I fanned it off in an attempt to get as much dust off as possible. Looking in the mirror and fixing my makeup. It's hard not to start crying again.

My finger feels lighter, not having my ring on it. I stood staring at it, realizing my life will be no different not having him as my fiancé. I'm not hurt. The fear I had of losing everyone from my life is still inside of me. I know they can't get rid of me that easily, but that isn't helping me with the fear of them walking away.

I snapped out of it and called electricians and plumbers to make appointments for them to come over the next few days and repair everything and bring it up to code.

I started walking out the door to head home. I paused; I have no idea where the guys lived. I have no idea where to go. I pulled out my phone, texting Spencer. Shoving it back into my pocket, I jumped at a loud noise at the door.

Spencer is leaning against the building with his phone up. "Correction. You have no idea where you live. Let's go. I never thought Liam would ever be stupid enough to break up with you."

I locked the door. "I don't know, Spencer. No one can really blame him. How is he supposed to be able to vent when I'm the one he wants to bitch about? I just hope my instincts and April are wrong about him having a mistress." Spencer glared at me. "It's a gangster thing to hide their lives from their wives and vent to mistresses. It might not be you guys specifically. I am never going to be able to be in a relationship where I'm not the only one. The only way I can do that is if I date from outside the group."

"You don't give us enough credit." Wrapping his arm around my waist and waving down a cab.

"I actually feel like a weight has been lifted. No more waking up in the middle of the night looking for him."

"There's my girl."

"Thank you for still being around and not leaving me."

"You're going soft on me, stop it." Spencer opened the door for me to get in the cab.

Seeing their house for the first time. It is tall, two stories, a big yard with trees and a white picket fence. I don't know what I was expecting them to live in, but it was nothing like this. We open the door and everything is lit up with natural light. Pictures of all of us hanging on the wall. A fireplace is in the front room, surrounded by two leather couches and a matching chair.

"Spencer, you've gone soft on me! Our matching pajama picture!"

"That was Josh, not me."

"Josh, you make my heart warm." He walked down the stairs, smiling at me.

I remembered my dress covered in dust; I quickly ran upstairs, glancing down the hallway to find my bedroom. I looked to the left room; boxes are scattered, so I know it is mine. Someone laid out my pillows and spread out my comforter. I smiled, I can guarantee it was Josh. I opened a box and clothes exploded out of it. I picked up my black dress with long sleeves and slipped it over my head.

It feels weird having my things here. I got so accustomed to living with William and Dillon. I know they are going to be with me every day, but it isn't making me feel any better.

I walked downstairs and saw all six guys gathered by the fireplace.

Josh looked at me. "Sit. We have a drink here for you."

I tipped my head back and sighed. "Okay, what's going on?"

"We need to chat."

"Already? About what?"

Adam cracked a smile. "This is going to be fun."

Assholes!

Liam laughed. "In all seriousness, what do you have planned for the nightclub?"

I took a drink. I can't take my focus off the floor, I'm scared to see their reactions. "Tables only. We will have to make it look like it is a storage area when it is not in use, in case of raids. Password protected, which changes every night. We will only open a few times a week. The nightclub, on the other hand, is going to be open only on weekends. We will open the doors more if we find other clubs are busy all week. We need to come up with a name before I apply for a liquor license. Once we get everything figured out, painters hired, building fixed, signs up. I am going to be hiring bartenders, servers, and a few cooks. There will be food, but only appetizers."

I paused, waiting to see if anyone was going to start disagreeing. "I am hiring pro bartenders, servers, and cooks to train everyone. I am relieved so many people walked out on me. I wouldn't even be able to employ all of them."

I took a shaky breath. "What is April going to do when she finds out I'm her new boss?"

Liam sighed. "I phoned her and told her everything that happened. She just said, 'good'. Hopefully, she won't give you too much of a hard time, she also knows you would fire her."

I nodded. "This feeling of power is almost too much. What does everyone think?"

Josh laughed. "We were right to vote you in. If that many people walked out on one of us, we would have snapped."

"You guys all got votes. Even Spencer!"

Spencer almost spit his drink out. "What the fuck where they thinking?"

William put his arm around me. "Times are changing." Mimicking my voice.

I wouldn't have been able to do any of this if it wasn't for them supporting me. The feeling of happiness I felt this morning was starting to creep back up on me. So much has changed in less than twenty-four hours, this was the first time in years I feel completely peaceful.

A knock on the door, Spencer started to stand.

"No, sit down." I got up and opened the door.

One man is standing in front of me. "Charlotte?"

"Depends on who's asking."

Erik came out from behind and winked at me, the two of them flashed me their badges. "Do you mind if we come in?"

"Come in." I turned around and stood behind the couches. "Guys, move so they can sit together." Adam and Josh came and stood beside me behind the sofa.

"We heard there was a new boss of the Basilisks. I need to say that you are nothing that I imagined." Erik is walking behind the other police officer, fighting the smile that is trying to break through.

The second cop looked at all of us, I can tell he is uncomfortable. "We couldn't make this with Martin. He scared the shit out of us."

I'm nervous, but I trust Erik. "He tends to do that. I will be running things differently."

Erik leaned back in his seat and discreetly started smiling and shaking his head. "We know, that's why we are coming to you. We know you bought the rundown old pub on 5th."

I stood there, not fazed at what they were saying. I walked around the couch and sat on the arm. "I'm listening."

The second cop is starting to relax. "We are willing to keep other cops away from the nightclub. In exchange, we need your men to keep other organized crime groups away."

"You want to be on my payroll?"

Erik winked. "Exactly."

"That can be arranged."

"When we catch wind of someone on our side of town, we will contact you." They stood up and walked out the door.

From the expression on everyone's faces, I can tell that deals like this were not cut with the basilisks before. All of us are shocked beyond repair. Dillon poured us all a shot and without saying a word, every single one of us slammed it back.

Dillon passed me a smoke, I could tell he is picking his words carefully. "It's going to take a while for us to get used to you and Liam not being together anymore."

I smiled. "I don't think it will be very hard. We were just convincing ourselves we needed to be together. I think both of our hearts have been with someone else." I saw Josh punch Adam's arm.

The mood in the house lifted, there is no awkwardness. We are all eager to start the new chapter. Dillon and Josh came rushing back in the house after hours of being gone and dumped an entire bag full of paint samples on the table. We all needed this change. All of us started to inspect the paint samples, trying to find the perfect pairs.

William looked at the strips. "Yellow makes people happy, red makes people want to drink." We all raised our heads, slowly looking at him. "What? I know things."

I sat back and listened to everyone's ideas on the nightclub. I have a plan to make us fully legal. I can't wait to change all seven of their lives. I don't know what I'm going to do with the rest of the Basilisks.

The guys decided on a probation theme. They called Erik to get him involved. We are awful for picking names. The best we could come up with was Speakeasy. I'm disappointed in us, but we are not creative people.

Everyone started pitching ideas so fast I couldn't keep up with who said what. They all settled on yellow wooden walls, burgundy wooden chairs, probation era photos, flapper girl outfits for the females.

Josh poured us all a shot in celebration of our new plan.

Liam stood up. "Can I talk to you, Charlie?" I stood up and followed him outside to sit on the front step. "You really have this under control so far, hey?"

"If it weren't for any of you guys, I wouldn't know what I was doing."

"I wanted to let you know before I went, but I have a date."

"Already? With who?" I don't know how to react; we broke up not even six hours ago.

He paused and passed me a smoke. "Anna."

"Who's that?"

He waited to answer. "Halloween."

As much as I didn't want to be right about him going off with another girl, I knew my instincts were telling me the truth. I wanted to believe he was a changed man. Looking at him now, I feel nothing. I don't know how long I actually felt this way about him, or if I ever had feelings for him. It was shitty of me to stay with him for so long. It was also shitty of him to be with me when he had another girl. I never questioned why he haven't had sex since before Halloween, but now I know I should have been wondering.

"I was right to vote for you." Liam passed me a lit smoke.

"Why did you get so upset when I won then?"

"I knew I was going to have to end it. This vote just gave me the push I needed."

As I watched him walk away, a feeling of unfamiliar calmness rushes through me. For the first time in my life, I know everything is going to work out in my favor.

Lizzy

Spencer is standing in my line of sight, distracting me from my *Wizards of Waverly Place* reruns. I'm twenty-four, why I still watch the family channel is beyond me. He is standing there with his hands on his hips, looking down at the floor and tapping and shaking his right leg. Spencer is hurting, I have been scared to check up on him. My grieving is done, but to him Brittney just died.

Spencer let a hum out of his throat. "Ever since I have met the three of you, all the things she said in the eight months we were dating is getting pieced together and it is making me love you more. You were my best friend before but now I feel so much closer to you I can't explain it." His eyes are still glued to the floor.

I pushed the power button on the remote, shutting the television off and stood up. Before I was off the couch, Spencer grabbed my hand, helping me. "Follow me, the box is heavy; I need you to carry it."

I opened the closet door downstairs and sat back down on the couch. I am leant forward with my arms on my legs. Spencer came and sat down on the floor with the tub in the middle of us. One thing I learnt watching on the sidelines of these eight Basilisks is that they hide their pain until they hit their breaking point.

Spencer is taking deep breaths, trying to get enough confidence to open the box. He moved his head up and a tear ran down his face, hitting the lid. I can't stand watching him so upset. I stood up and sat on the floor next to him, putting my hand on the lid and opening the bin. I feel so guilty packing her away, but opening this box feels so refreshing.

I placed the lid beside me, watching Spencer start digging into the life the four of us had together.

Spencer pushed out a laugh. "She was such a bitch when I first met her. It just pulled me in more, I fell in love with her within seconds."

Watching a good man talk about my best friend with a sparkle in his eyes made me feel proud, happy, and calm. She was so loved. I hope she knew it.

I tried to hold back a laugh but couldn't. "She was kind of a bitch, but she was what we needed. The first day I met her in grade three, she threw my Barbie across the room and handed me a Snow White doll."

Spencer tipped his head back laughing and wiping a tear from his eyes; whatever I said brought back some sort of memory for him.

We sat there for two hours while I explained every picture, Spencer is tuned in with every word that I say. For the first time in a long time, I'm not crying when I look down at her. I'm not an emotional wreck when I see her perfect picture.

I elbowed Spencer. "Suck it up, Princess."

"I miss her." His voice is low, like the heartbreak is fresh.

I placed my head on Spencer's shoulder. We stared at the bin, breathing hard. The room is getting darker and darker from the sun setting. We are all holding onto hope that isn't really there.

I sighed. "Spence, I hate asking one of Erik's best friends this. How is he for money? He spent $120,000 on Max and Theo's treatments, plus he's covering their bills and rent while they are gone. I just hate his dirty money. I don't want anything to do with it."

I moved my head and Spencer started to pack the pictures away. "You have nothing to worry about, believe me. You guys are better than fine, plus his money from being a cop."

"I've never looked at his paystubs or anything."

"He is a lot richer than any of us. He's now twenty-six, Erik has been doing this for ten years. I'm surprised he has any humanity left in him." He looked at me. "You brought a lot of it back. You are his perfect storm. Sometimes I think Brittney had you two in mind the entire time."

Spencer stood up and packed the bin back in the closet, grabbing my hands to pick me up off the floor. "I know it's dirty money, we all know it. We try to level it out by donating a lot to charities. It doesn't make it better, but it sort of makes us feel better about it."

I wrapped my arms around him. "Thank you for disturbing my pre-teen shows." Spencer's laugh is shaking my body. I pushed away, looking at him. "I wish she felt safe enough to introduce me to you when she was alive. I would give anything to see how much you love her."

He reached in his pocket and pulled out a ring box. He opened it and a blue emerald-cut ring is placed inside. It suited her in every way. "The last time I spoke to her, I just walked out of the store with this. I was going to propose to her, but she never came."

I took the box, smiling. "She would have been a crying hyperventilating mess, lying on the sidewalk and trying to say yes."

As soon as I said yes, Erik came rushing down the stairs.

Shit, this looks really, really bad.

"What the fuck, man?" Erik is standing at the bottom of the stairs with his mouth open, not sure if he should be crying or beating the shit out of Spencer.

Spencer looked at me with his mouth open, turning towards Erik and frantically moving his hands around in the air. "Jesus, this is not what it looks like. I bought that for Brittney. We spent all afternoon reminiscing."

Erik put his hands on his knees, breathing hard. Spencer took the box back from me winking, so I smacked his arm.

I grabbed his sleeve. "Don't ever get rid of that ring. Part of the reason she would love it so much is because it's something a princess would wear."

Spencer walked up the stairs, patting Erik's back. "That's why I bought it. I wanted to toss it out the car window, but I always had this feeling like she was coming back." He turned around. "I am turning fucking psychotic."

Charlie

Dillon flew through my bedroom door and in one swift motion, I put on my jacket. "Why the hell is my sister downstairs, asking for you?"

"I need her help."

I followed Dillon down the stairs. Josh, Adam, and Spencer are in the kitchen avoiding the comments that our friends are going to be making.

April handed me a file. "I figured you needed these. Everything is in there; food supplier, alcohol supplier. With the nightclub you have planned, I would order triple the amount of alcohol we do in one month. See how much you use and judge from there."

"Thanks for bringing these over." I tried to smile, making it easier on half the room.

"Well, you are my boss. I had no choice." April is talking to me like she was on Boxing Day. None of her words are being forced out.

"If you need anything over there, let me know. I will handle it and help in any way possible. I will go there tonight and make my rounds, meeting everyone."

April smiled at me and walked out of the house.

William lit a smoke. "How are you so nice to the cockroach?"

I laughed while sitting on the couch. "It's easier now that she won't be my sister-in-law, she almost seems nice now."

Adam walked behind me and put his hands on my shoulders, whispering in my ear, "I want to talk to you."

His touch is sending a vibration through my body I never felt before. Him breathing on my skin is making the hair on the back of my neck rise. I have never wanted to kiss someone so bad before. I closed my eyes tight, enjoying his body so close to me.

Adam's mouth got closer to my ear when I didn't pull away. "Meet me in the downstairs living room in 10 minutes."

Without thinking, I ran my hand over his, smiling. "Who wants to go with me to *Willie's* tonight?"

Josh poured me a drink, pretending everyone never witnessed our show. "Why don't we all go and have a few drinks?"

I have been staring at the clock, waiting to see Adam. I started tapping my foot every time the second hand moved, I'm becoming more excited. When ten minutes passed, I made my way downstairs.

He is leaning up against the couch, waiting for me. He is focused on me. He is walking closer and my body is tingling. He looks so confident like he always did. If he is nervous, I never would have known.

"I know you are my boss now, but I've wanted to do this since the first time I saw you."

I walked closer to him and put my hands on his hips. "Adam, kiss me."

He moved my blonde hair from the front of my chest behind my shoulders, looking down at me.

He inhaled a deep breath, he is nervous. He put his hands on my hips, pulling me in close. Our lips touched, and sparks flew. The tingling in my body became more intense. I could feel every nerve screaming for him. I never want to pull away from him. His tongue slid into my mouth, and I gently bit his bottom lip. Kissing him again. He pulled away, resting his forehead against mine. I kissed him one last time.

I never want to let go of him.

I'm out of breath. I want to rip his clothes off. "That was something, wasn't it?" I'm lost in his blue eyes.

"I've been thinking about that for months."

"You better go get ready, I think they are about to leave soon."

Dillon is upstairs. "Charlie, where the fuck did you go?"

"I'm down here, Dilly."

Adam kissed me one last time and slid his fingers up my arm as he walked away, smiling.

"What's happening down here?"

Adam walked past Dillon. "Just what I've been dreaming of."

Dillon looked at me and smiled. "See, I told you he was waiting for Liam to screw up."

I sat down on the couch, trying to catch my breath. "No, Dillon, you don't understand. Kissing Liam, I felt nothing like that. I kissed Adam, and it was like our bodies collided."

We got to *Willie's*; as usual, there is a group of smokers standing outside with a cloud of smoke over their heads. It never mattered what day it was, or what time it is; *Willie's* is packed from opening to closing.

Josh ran up and tackled Liam. "I heard you had a date. How did it go?" He punched him in the arm.

Liam opened the door for all of us. "Amazing, she's meeting us here. Is that alright?"

I shrugged. "Doesn't bother me."

"Good, she doesn't know we were engaged or that we dated, so everyone shut the fuck up about it."

I raised my arm in the air to signal that I heard him. I looked around and saw April talking to a girl at the bar. "Hey, April. I'm ready to meet everyone."

As soon as I walked in, the familiar smell of hot wings and citrus garnishes filled the air. It was different this time, it was all mine.

"First things first. This is Anna." April looked at me with a smug smile.

It was her, the girl Liam had kissed on Halloween. She wasn't dressed as Catwoman, but I remembered her olive skin and short black hair.

I stuck my hand out to shake Anna's. "I swear I'm not as bad as she makes me seem. The guys are in the corner at the big booth. Liam's waiting for you."

I turned and looked at April. "Could you print me up a sheet that says the expenses, daily profit, and employee pay for the last few months?"

April rolled her eyes. "We make money every day."

"That's fine. I just want to see where we are sitting, so there are no surprises. I'm going to walk around; just bring it to the table. Thank you."

Introducing myself to everyone is extremely intimidating. I'm the youngest person in the building, and I'm the owner. Anna has been sitting across the table, staring at me and asking questions about how I got to be in charge. Thankfully, Dillon came up with a lie that Martin only trusted me with his bar.

April came up to the table, dropping the file on the table, with a server behind her carrying a tray with our drinks. Opening the file and looking at the numbers on the paper, my eyes got wide. The numbers said *Willie's* made $40,000 a week in profit. I guess that's what happens when you have enough money to start a business with no debt weighing you down. I glanced around the table and started smiling. I knew from the start I wasn't going to be able to keep all the money to myself. I'm not going to set myself up for life and screw everyone else out of their chance. *Willie's* is the start of making us legal.

I pulled out my phone and opened my calendar to set a reminder.

I zoned out on the conversation; by the time I started listening, Dillon is laughing and winking at me.

I looked over at Adam, I had to fight all my urges not to jump over the table to get to him.

Josh is tapping my shoulder. "Charlie, can you let me out?" He got in close and whispered, "I'll move our drinks around so you can sit next to Adam."

I got out of the booth, then scooted in next to Adam. I sat a little closer to him than I needed, I can't stay away from him, I'm craving him. I can feel his body against mine. I can't stop thinking about that kiss. I grabbed his hand, and my body became electric. I looked up at him, his shaggy blonde hair, defined cheekbones, blue eyes. He is beautiful.

He looked down at me and caught me staring. He unlinked our fingers, put his hand on my shoulder, turning me, so I'm facing him. His hand moved from my shoulder, into my hair. His eyes are locked onto mine. We are both aware everyone is watching, but we don't care. He slouched down, pulled my hair lightly to tell me to move my head up, and he put his lips on mine. The world stopped turning. We are frozen in time. I slowly moved my mouth from his and pulled away, not breaking eye contact.

Josh sat in the booth next to me. "It's about fucking time."

Adam wrapped his arm around my shoulder, whispering in my ear, "You are blushing."

I got in as close as I can and sank into him. He tightened his arm around my shoulder, holding me in as tight as he can. He needs me as much as I need him.

Josh is eyeing Anna up. I know him well enough he is about to get protective. "How long have you been seeing each other?"

Liam chugged back the rest of his drink. Anna looked proud. "Four months."

I noticed every guy at the table flinch towards Liam. I put my hand on Adam's chest, feeling his heart speed up. The server walked by, and I ordered a shot for all of us.

I quickly did the math in my head. The entire time Liam was with me, he was dating Anna at the same time. When I had caught them kissing, he wasn't kissing a random girl, she was his girlfriend.

Everyone at the table all look ashamed of themselves for not catching on. I managed to wiggle out of Adam's arm and put my hand on Josh's hand to let him know everything is okay. I looked up and saw fire in Spencer's eyes; I reached out my other arm and grabbed his hand, giving him a squeeze.

April came racing back with the shots at the perfect time. Without any hesitation, we all slammed it back.

April walked away but came racing back to us. "Charlie, two cops just came in."

I never even had to ask Josh to move; he was out of the booth before April finished talking. As I got closer, I recognized one from the house.

"Ahh, Charlotte. Just the girl I was looking for." I leant in and read his name tag.

"Alexander. What seems to be the problem?"

He flashed up a picture. "Have you seen this man?" I shook my head no. "Watson saw him and called me."

I took the picture and saw the lion tattoo on his neck. "Damn it. I will handle it. Thank you."

I walked outside, lighting a smoke and walking around the building. I pulled up a contact that read McKinnon.

The man on the phone snapped, "What do you want, Basilisk!"

I inhaled my smoke with my game face on. He can't see me, but that won't stop me. "I wanted to remind you of our truce."

"You're not Martin."

"Martin retired. He told you about me. I am the dangerous one. I got word that your man was caught in my jurisdiction."

"My men are not there."

"He had a lion tattoo similar to your men's."

He growled. "Freddy. Stand down, Basilisk."

"Just get him out of my territory," I growled and hung up the phone.

I walked by Alexander and nodded. He got into his cruiser and drove away. I'm not ready to go back inside. I need to finish my smoke and take pride in something that Martin was never able to do.

With my ban on weapon and drug smuggling, I have no idea how we are going to make money. Everyone has so much guilt on their shoulders, I can't be the one to add to that pain. I know they all had enough money in their bank accounts that they would be good for two, if not three, lifetimes.

I hate feeling so responsible for everyone.

I got back to the table. Anna is nowhere to be found. William whispered to me, "What happened?"

Sliding into the booth, explaining the phone call, feeling proud of myself. Watching all of them relax, I know I need to be the one to save them. I need to be the one to end the Basilisks.

Brittney

My head is pounding, I have to take deep breaths to get through my hangover. The only way I can sleep is if I get drunk. The only thing powerful enough for me to numb my pain is tequila. I have been hung over for the last week and a half.

I have been trying to convince Rodriguez and Nelson that them sending Charlie into protective custody would be a huge mistake. These group of people would move hell and earth to be together. For any of them, it is safer to keep them together than to separate them. After my days of convincing, I have finally gotten through to them.

Going through the pictures that Agent Jones has taken over the last few days has makes me feel like the craziest ex-girlfriend in history. This file is pictures from them looking at real estate. According to Erik, Charlie is planning illegal gambling.

All the other files are just Dillon, Liam, Adam, Spencer, and Josh at school. Someone from the group is always missing, because they are with Charlie as her protection. The images of Charlie no longer have her draped around Liam. In fact, it seems Adam has taken his spot.

Good, she got rid of the scumbag.

What bothers me most about pictures of Spencer is that he looks fine. Better than fine. He isn't hurt at all. Losing me hasn't affected him in anyway.

"Agent Hills."

I twisted around in my chair, grabbing my purse; I don't even know if it's time to leave yet, but I'm not staying. "Don't fucking talk to me, Jones, I can't deal with you."

"I was just going to ask if you wanted a ride home. Jesus."

I pointed my finger, looking up at him. "You don't talk to me on the way, and we are stopping at a liquor store."

Slamming the car door behind me, letting out a puff of air, I'm pissed off. I was assuming Jones was leaving me at the apartment alone, but it was probably an excuse to see Sam outside of the office walls. My heels are tapping against the sidewalk, sounding as eager as I am to mend my broken heart. I want to take a hammer to my phone to stop myself from calling Spencer, but I can't, it's a work phone. It wouldn't matter anyways; I know his number by heart.

I'm pissed at myself for remembering his number in this modern day and age.

Jones reached beside me, pushing the elevators button. "Why do you hate me so much?"

"You're a douchebag."

"I haven't even talked to you much."

"Let me rephrase that, you look like a douchebag."

The elevator door opened and I stepped in while opening my new tequila bottle and pressing it against my lips. "Want some?"

"If I have to deal with your bitchy ass, I'm going to need it."

I passed him the bottle, watching him press it up to his lips, his entire face is crumpling. "How did you do that straight-faced? It's awful."

"Used to it." I kicked the ground, walking out of the elevator.

The apartment door is unlocked, meaning Sam is home from her appointment. I dropped my bag in the entryway, falling down onto the couch and taking another big drink. I have never been this person to use a substance to hide from my feelings. My feelings are too much to handle sober.

"I am not drinking again." Sam fell on the couch, putting her legs over Jones.

"I don't need you to drink, your boyfriend volunteered."

"You don't like him."

"If you drink with me, I like you."

I slouched in the seat, not recognizing myself, this isn't who I am. I don't do this. I don't even drink tequila.

Another episode in, I still have no idea what we are watching, something about vampires. I have killed half of the bottle and all of my common sense has evaporated with the alcohol. My teeth are numb. I don't even know how it's possible to have numb teeth.

Does everything think about this when they are drunk? They must.

I need to see him. I'm going to see Spencer.

Taking another big drink, I screwed the cap back on the bottle. Standing up, trying not to fall over. I need to change, I'm still in my awful pants suit. I sighed, trying to walk a straight line to the bedroom. All of my clothes are still in bags, I haven't unpacked anything hoping that he is going to show up, begging for me back.

I slipped on a pair of skinny jeans, put on my black knee-high boots, and a light purple fleece sweater over my black t-shirt. Rushing out of the apartment as fast as I can in the condition I am is challenging. Sam is asking where I am going, but I have to ignore her. I shut the door behind me, coming to the realization I don't have my phone, purse, wallet, or keys.

I open the door, nearly falling over, grabbing onto the door handle to pull myself up. Ignoring the looks from the couch, grabbing my purse from the floor, and shutting the door behind me.

"Just park here for a second." I can hear my words being slurred; the longer time passes, I can feel the tequila creeping up on me more.

Dillon, Adam, Josh, Charlie, and Liam all piled out of the house, getting in two separate cars.

"Just wait for them to drive away and park where they were." I told the cab driver. I can see him looking back at me in the rear-view mirror.

I tossed up a bill with President Grant's face on it. I shut the door behind me.

Looking at the house, it looks the same, but it looks so different now. I shouldn't be standing here, it's off limits and foreign. This was a very, very, very bad idea.

"Brittney, what the fuck are you doing here?"

Turning around and looking up, William is standing in front of me. He doesn't look mad, but he looks concerned. "I needed to see him. I'm going crazy."

Right as soon as I opened my mouth, his eyes became wide. "How much have you been drinking?"

"Not enough."

"Jesus, woman. Lizzy is at work, you're coming with me to Erik's."

Before I could protest, he grabbed my elbow, dragging me down the street. I have no idea where Erik lives, but I'm hoping it isn't far.

William swung open the white gate, giving me another tug so I would follow him. He opened the front door and Lizzy's perfume is the first scent I can smell. On the back of the couch, my old faded purple blanket is draped over the back, I can't even remember what design was on it, but she still has it.

I held it up to my face, sniffing it. *My god, I did smell like a drunk grandma.*

"Spencer and Erik are downstairs, don't fucking move." William stormed away. I can't blame him for being pissed off.

Knowing he's in the same house I am, I can feel my body being drawn to him. Taking a few more steps following where William had walked away, I'm standing in the entryway of the kitchen listening to their conversation.

"Spencer, push pause." William has annoyance in his voice.

"I was dying anyways, what's up?" Spencer sounds perfectly okay; I was right, he isn't bothered about losing me.

"You need to call Brittney."

"No man, you were right. She is a bottom feeder, sorry I got so pissed at you."

The words left his mouth and tears are falling down my face. I do everything I can to be a good person, I don't deserve someone thinking of me that way. Footsteps are coming up the stairs, it's probably just William to kick me out. Wiping the tears from my cheeks, Spencer is standing on the steps, looking like a deer in the headlights.

"Brittney." Spencer reached out his hand to me, but I backed away. "Don't go."

Backing up, I can see the staircase from the corner of my tear-filled eyes. I grabbed onto the staircase, trying to stop my head from spinning. "I'm just a bottom feeder, right? By the way, we were going to put Charlie into protective custody, but I knew none of you guys could live without each other. So, you're welcome."

I closed my eyes tight, trying to stop my wave of overwhelming emotion and the tequila make my decisions. A pair of familiar hands are on my hips, my body is screaming at me to give in to him and kiss him. Slowly opening my eyes, he is staring at me, he looks like he is in pain. I don't know if it's from me hearing what he called me, or him needing to see me so he can feel the same heartbreak I am feeling.

"I'm sorry." The begging in Spencer's voice cut my breath off.

"For what? Me hearing what you said, or you breaking my heart?"

"For breaking your heart and me saying that about you."

I pushed his hands off my hips. "I guess it was just my turn to have my heart broken. Don't worry; when you are finally free and I'm off the case, I promise I'll leave the city. It'll be like I never existed."

Walking away, I can hear Spencer swearing and trying to stop me. I opened the door, walking away faster than I ever thought I could. I am never that dramatic. That is another promise to add to the handful I have made in my life. I intend to keep it.

Charlie

I have spent all day at Speakeasy getting my licenses framed and hung on the wall. I have uniforms stacked up by sizes on the bar. Counting sheets are ready for the end of the night—drink menus scattered throughout the bar. Advertisements have been posted around the city. We have been waiting for this night.

I stood in one spot, admiring our work. Yellow wooden walls, burgundy wooden furniture. Pictures from the probation era hung on the walls. Colorful lights lit up the alcohol bottles. Drapery hung on the windows, pulled together in the middle. Black tint on the windows. In the 1920s, Gin was favored the most, so we made sure to advertise that throughout the building. I took a deep breath, proud of what we had all created.

The door swung open and Violet came charging in. "What the fuck, Charlie! You leave Liam, and now you are on to Adam? Why would you do that to him? God, April was right about you. I should have left with the others."

I watched Adam, Liam, and William walk in with their guns drawn. They would only do that if someone is standing behind me armed.

"He's my family and you left him for another guy in the group! I could shoot you right now!"

I rolled my eyes and stood up straight. "This is ridiculous. Who I date has nothing to do with anyone else. Who's going to pull the trigger first, you or Sammy?" I saw a confused look spread across her face. "Can you just get ready for opening night?"

I watched the guns behind Violet lower. I turned around and walked outside and lit a smoke. "I keep having guns pulled on me."

Liam laughed. "At least you stopped getting shot."

William and Adam burst out in laughter.

I turned to face Adam and reached for his hand. "You know you are not my rebound, right?"

Adam nudged his head to Liam and William to give us space. He took a breath. "I have been trying to keep a bit of space between us; I am worried that I am."

"I would never do that to you." I looked at him directly in the eyes. "I only want you."

"I spent the last few months wanting to punch Liam every time he kissed you. No one is keeping me away from you a minute longer."

I wrapped my arms around his neck and kissed him. "No one is going to keep us apart."

"The instant I pull my lips away, you're my girlfriend. Do you have a problem with that?" I shook my head, rubbing our lips together.

"It's safe now. Come back." I can hear the excitement in my new boyfriend's voice.

I sighed. "Can we just take a moment to appreciate this bar? I can't get over how wonderful it is."

Liam nudged his head forward. "You guys, look at that line-up."

Adam looked over his shoulder. "We are at overfull capacity."

I shrieked and danced on one spot. "Let's go in!"

We got inside, and the bartenders are getting ready. The servers are dressed in uniform. I gave everyone two options on their clothes: burgundy or yellow flapper outfits. I can't take my eyes off the uniforms, the building, everything. I have never been this excited before.

The doors opened and it took no time for us to be at full capacity. I have been losing track of time between keeping everyone safe, helping the bartenders, refilling the liquor. I never ran around so much in my life. Every time I made my way back to the bar, the tip jars had to be emptied. The bartenders worked fast, getting every drink out.

Alexander approached me. "Whatever you did the other night, he's out of town. I just wanted to thank you." I smiled and shook his hand. "We have more cops from other precincts wanting to be on your payroll now. It looks like you Basilisks are going to run Manhattan after all."

I watched Erik approach. "I need to check all your licenses. Make sure they are valid."

"Yes, follow me." I brought them up to the bar where I had them displayed.

"Do you mind?"

"Go ahead."

I turned back to my conversation. "Alexander, I just want these people protected from the other bad guys."

Alexander looked around. "You don't look like the bad guys to any of us." He paused. "Maybe I spoke too soon, I don't want to know what you did to make them scared of you."

"I can assure you. The Basilisks are no threat to New York."

The night came to an end and we all walked into the house, exhausted. Josh and Spencer walked up the stairs like a couple of zombies.

Adam wrapped his arms around me. "First night, we share a room?" I nodded my head in agreement and he held my hand up the stairs into my room.

"I'm just going to go change." I grabbed a long-sleeved shirt and pajama shorts from my bed.

"You can do it in here." He watched me shift my body uncomfortably. "I'll be waiting."

I got in the bathroom, and I took my dress off. I exposed my back and cringed. It's been months, and I haven't shown my back to anyone. I ran my fingers over my scars, terrified that no one is going to be able to look at me the same ever again if I ever show them. Putting my clothes back on and remembering Adam is in bed waiting for me, I shut the lights off, running into the bedroom.

"I'm back." I crawled into bed.

Adam ran his hand up my arm. "I just want you to know. You don't need to feel ashamed or embarrassed around me. Nothing can change how I've always felt."

I didn't respond. I only kissed him and curled up on his chest, running the tips of my fingers over his abs.

The sunrise filled the room with light. Adam is already awake, stroking my back.

"Hmm, Adam. I smell bacon." I'm still cuddled up into his chest from the night before.

His chest started rising from his laughter. "William warned me about your constant need to be eating."

"Let's go down." I looked at him and smiled.

I looked down on his chest, I can finally see the rest of the tattoo that would always peek out from his suit's collar. On the right side of his chest, there is a blue dragon blowing fire from its mouth. The dragon's head went over his collarbone, the wing was extended onto his neck. The detail in it amazes me, each scale is carefully done. It would have taken multiple sessions to complete it. Everything about it screamed power and strength.

I kissed him, I can't bring myself to pull away from his lips. I slid my tongue in his mouth, and I felt his in mine. I got up on my knees and pushed him on his back. Without moving my lips, I got on top of him and straddled my legs around his waist.

He pulled away. "Oh, you are a hard one to say no to."

"Then don't."

"I'm not just going to have sex with you. I've been waiting for this to happen. I'm making it special."

He moved fast and flipped me onto my back. I squealed and started laughing. He made it look so easy.

"Let's go get food." He grabbed my hand and led me downstairs.

Half the day went by, it ended up starting normal, until we heard the door upstairs burst open. We all ran up the stairs in panic. It is still in the guys' instinct to guard me behind them but when I pushed past them, I saw Dillon and Liam holding up Violet.

"What the fuck happened?" I looked at Violet, blood is dripping from her face.

Liam sat her on the couch. "We were walking by a back alley, and three guys were attacking her."

Dillon looked at me, and I know exactly what he meant. Her dress is torn and her tights are ripped.

"Get her cleaned up. Where did this happen?"

"Behind *Willie's*."

"Dillon, you saw them. I need you to come with me. Josh and Spencer, I need you to come too. Someone call and get Sammy there with a van."

I ran upstairs and changed into yoga pants and put on a coat with big enough pockets to hold all the weapons I think I will need. It has been weeks since I felt any kind of anger flow through my body. The anger is firing in my body even faster since it happened at my bar. I can feel my adrenaline kicking in faster than I remember, my stomach twisting into knots. I went into Adam's room and unlocked his gun safe, scanning everything. I shoved a revolver in my pocket.

I was about to walk away and I paused, looking outside and seeing the sun shining. It's mid-day, and people are going to be around, a gun is going to cause attention. I laid eyes on a knife with a long blade. I pulled off the cover, quickly sharpening it. Once I thought it was good enough, I slipped the cover back on and ran downstairs.

Like I expected, the outside of *Willie's* was busy. People are rushing around, trying to make it back to work. Large groups of bodies swarmed the sidewalks. We walked in and the darkness inside shocked my eyes. It wasn't until a few seconds later, I only noticed a few people sitting at the bar and two groups sitting at tables.

I raised my voice so I could grab everyone's attention. "Which three of you bastards attacked my girl less than an hour ago!"

I saw fear rushing over faces. No-one stopped me or spoke up. "That's okay. You don't need to confess. My guy here, he saw your faces."

Dillon whispered in my ear what table they were at, and I walked with anger, slamming my hands on the table. "Why do you three think it is okay to attack and sexually assault a woman walking down the street?"

Dillon and Spencer cleared out the bar, paying everyone off so they wouldn't talk. I could feel Josh standing behind me.

"Let's go outside, why don't we?" I pushed myself off the table, glaring at them.

I walked in front; my men are bigger than all of them, they walked behind the guys, shoving them and making sure they were following me.

"Call for a body pick-up."

The men fell on their knees in fear. "No, please don't. We didn't realize it."

I scoffed in disgust. "So, if wasn't protected, you would have done it anyways?"

Josh walked up beside me and hung up his phone. They all pinned the men down, so they can't move. I pulled the knife out of my pocket and I slit their throats one by one.

A black van came down the alley and Sammy jumped out. "Jesus, Charlie."

Spencer ran to the vehicle and grabbed every napkin he could find, soaking half of them with a water bottle. He wiped the blood off my face the best he could.

We got back home and I ran up the stairs into the shower. I stripped off my clothes and the realization of the brutal attack hit me all at once.

I'm scared that I never hesitated. There wasn't a voice in my head telling me I was doing something wrong. I was right, the darkness I saw turned me into a monster.

I stepped into the shower, the water running red from under me. Blood is in my hair, on my face, my hands. I shampooed four times, scrubbed myself with soap three times, and I still feel disgusting. A sob came out of my throat.

I shut the water off, wrapped myself up with a towel, ran into my room, and pulled the blankets over my shoulders, sitting on my bed.

I'm staring at my comforter. I forgot to breathe. I gasped deeply the same time my bed squeaked. I looked beside me and Adam lit a smoke, holding it out in front of me. He put his arm over my shoulder and pulled me into his chest. I can't cry, I can't do anything. I feel nothing. All I know is that my body is numb.

I'm afraid of myself.

Brittney

"The video is pretty awful, but this is what happened at *Willie's*." Nelson hit play on his phone that is connected to the television.

Charlie is walking in the back door followed by Spencer, Adam, and Josh pushing three men out of the door. Charlie is furious, I wish we can hear what she is saying. The men look terrified. At the same time, the basilisks hold down one man, each pushing on their shoulders, easily controlling them. A shiny blade is being pulled out from her coat pocket. The Basilisks that are pinning them down are looking to the side with their eyes shut.

Blood is soaking Charlie. I moved my head, looking away from the TV and covering my hand with my mouth. What the hell caused her to slit three men's throats? My stomach is twisting in knots. Sam elbowed me, so I looked back at the TV. A man with fire red hair has pulled up in the alley, Adam and Josh are helping him haul the bodies into the van. Spencer is wiping Charlie's face.

Nelson unplugged his phone and the television went black.

"Who pulled up?" I asked.

Rodriguez's chair squeaked as he leaned back. "That would be Sammy, the same getaway driver who saw you, shot you, and almost killed you."

"Can I kill him?" I mumbled.

Sam muffled a laugh.

"This has been the only criminal act since Charlie has been the boss. I have been stopping by her nightclub and nothing is popping up. There are no signs that there is any criminal activity."

"What you are saying is that we have no work until Martin comes back into the States?" Jones asked, letting out a puff of air.

Rodriguez nodded.

"How do you even know he left?" Sam tipped her head back.

"Kinsley," Nelson said, already bored.

"What do we do when we arrest him?" Not knowing how we are going to go about it has been driving me insane.

"Excited to get your boyfriend back?" Jones looked at me, already regretting his question.

"He's gone. I've accepted it." Jones looked down at my engagement ring. "Fine, maybe not completely."

Nelson slid a burner phone across the table; I caught it, creating a net with my palms. "When we get word from Kinsley, send everyone including Max, Theo, Lizzy, and April a group text. Your friends are going to be there so you don't have to explain it twice. There will be three cars, each one will have three basilisks, one will have two plus April."

"We need a Taylor to phone Kinsley when we get there so she can open the gates of the house. We go in and arrest Martin. He is taught to fire when he gets cornered, so we need to be ready in case someone gets shot. Davis will have squad cars with us, and there will be a few ambulances."

"This is a bit excessive for one man."

Nelson laughed once. "Just wait until the reporters get hold of the story."

Charlie

The next few days, no one was walking on eggshells around me, I couldn't have been more thankful. The terror has been slowly slipping away. I'm starting to feel like myself again. Whenever the memories came back, I went for a run or worked out at the Basilisks' gym. I always kept myself busy; if I didn't, that's when the memories came back.

I'm not a monster. I'm a Mafia boss.

Eight words I kept repeating to myself day in and day out.

I'm starting to think that I became a Mafia boss because I'm a monster.

If it meant saving everyone else the pain, I would do it again and again.

Sitting on the couch, sipping my whiskey, staring at the fireplace. I smelt Adam's cologne as he wrapped his arms around my shoulders. "I'm taking you on a date. Stand up."

I never hesitated. I jumped off the couch and grabbed his hand. We walked outside and a cab is waiting for us.

He opened the door for me. "It seems pretty useless for us to catch a cab to go for a walk."

I laughed. "What are we doing?"

"You'll see."

The sunset colored the sky yellow and orange. Building lights and streetlights had all turned on, lighting up the horizon. I can hear the sound of cars humming as they raced past below us. Other couples walked hand in hand just as we are. Everything I have been dreaming about in New York is right here in front of us. Taking a walk at sunset on the Brooklyn Bridge has always been a dream date of mine after watching romance movies.

"I remember you telling me you thought life in New York would always be a movie." He bent down and kissed my head. "Ever since then, I have been planning this."

Adam gives me a feeling I never felt before; I love him.

We kept walking; we both were soaking up every second that we had this moment of peace together. Every step we take, I fall more in love with him. He is the one I want to spend the next seventy years with.

I stopped walking and tugged on his arm so he would face me. I jumped up and wrapped my legs around his waist, kissing him. I pulled away, gazing into his eyes. I moved my head down so my mouth is against his neck and I kissed it. I ran my tongue along his neck then I kissed it again.

Before I was able to register what Adam is doing, he placed my feet back on the ground and started dragging me back home.

We walked into a living room full of people, but we don't care. We ran upstairs as fast as possible. I opened the door to his bedroom and slammed my mouth against his, pulling away just enough so I can take off his shirt. Adam dimmed the lights to fit the mood and so we can still see each other.

I took off my dress, standing exposed. My body started shaking. I put my head down, shutting my eyes tight; I feel awful about myself. I immediately regret my decision. I'm expecting him to put his shirt back on and slam the door behind him.

I never hear the door slam. Instead, I feel Adam's hands on my shoulders as he walks behind me.

His fingers running over my back, his breath on my neck. "You are the most breathtakingly beautiful woman I have ever laid eyes on. Are you sure you want to do this?"

I turned around to face him, reaching behind my back and unsnapped my bra, letting it fall. I took a step up to Adam, kissing him and unbuckling his pants. I let my panties fall to the ground. He picked me up and backed me into a wall. He is kissing me harder. He pulled away; I'm panting. He is smiling at me, showing how much he enjoys teasing me. He placed me on the bed and kept kissing me. I heard the condom wrapper rip open. He pulled away and put it on as fast as he could.

He climbed over me and I felt him go in. The feeling of him inside me makes every hair on my neck stand up. He put his head next to mine and moaned. Hearing what I'm doing to him is driving me crazy. I can see every detail of his body in the dim light. I can see every drop of sweat running down his muscles. I looked up at his face, and he's looking into my eyes. With every thrust, we became more and more in sync.

"Adam." We locked eyes, my legs are shaking and becoming weak, rolling my eyes to the back of my head.

"Charlie." Adam's body shook. His arms are holding up all his weight.

I kissed him one last time. "Holy shit." I saw a pack of smokes on his nightstand, so I grabbed us both one.

He is staring at me. "I've had sex, but never like that." He grabbed my head and pulled me in for a kiss.

I rolled onto my belly and lit our smokes, passing him one. "Me either. I think we cleared the house."

He laughed. "I don't even care."

I watched him bite his bottom lip. He kissed me, pulling away slowly. "I love you. Don't say it back. I know you got burned by those words. I just needed to tell you. You taught us never to hold things back."

I kissed him passionately. "Adam, I love you. It's always been you."

Lizzy

No offence to Doctor Miller, I love her and I'm thankful for her, but I just want this baby out of me. I wish I could sleep more than four hours a night; at this point, it is impossible. No matter what I do, I am uncomfortable. Being pregnant is the hardest thing I have ever had to do.

I still have another six weeks.

Erik is pacing back and forth; even though the baby moves, he is still in panic mode every single time we go to an appointment. He isn't the only one who panics; all of his friends sit around waiting for Erik to text one of them an ultrasound picture. I think they panic so much because they have seen so much evil. All of them, other than Charlie, were bred to become soldiers of the Basilisk Mafia. This is the one good thing that has happened in a long time. I'm not sure if Erik is being honest about keeping the baby away from the Mafia, but after seeing how they are all acting when we are at appointments and when I get Braxton-Hicks, something tells me they would die before this child has to endure the same life that they have had to live.

"Elizabeth," the receptionist called.

Erik grabbed my hand and pulled me out of my chair. I held his hand with him following right behind me into the room. He slid my handbag off my shoulder and I stepped on the scale. Even this far in my pregnancy, I have gained thirty pounds and I am in no rush to work it off. I have been trying to gain weight my entire life, but I have never been able to.

I sat down in the chair next to Erik waiting for the doctor to come in. I hate the smell of doctor's offices, I normally couldn't smell it before, but the smell of sanitizer is overwhelming now.

Dr. Miller came into the room and as usual, she is in a great mood. Her crooked smile, curly dark auburn hair falling around her face. Her short round body is covered by a light purple lab coat. "Lay on the bed!" I stood up, pulling the band on my jeans below my belly and my shirt up to my bra and lying down. "You look good, your tests are normal, your weight gain is perfect."

She put the gel on my belly and started the ultrasound. Our little baby is running out of room and she looks so squished. Erik bends down and kisses my hair.

He does it twenty times a day and it still give me butterflies.

Erik is choking back tears. "That's our son in there."

I grabbed his hand. "Or daughter."

"Oh, no. If it's a girl, I'm going to jail when boys start to notice her."

The doctor looked at me, unsure if he was kidding, and the room filled with her laughter. "Everything looks good. The baby is facing the right way."

She pushed a button and the ultrasound turned into 3D. It isn't just black with white lines, but we can see every detail of the baby's face. I can feel Erik squeezing my hand with his arm trembling. He or she has my full lips, chubby cheeks, Erik's perfect nose. This is so surreal. I looked up at Erik with happy tears filling my eyes right as a tear ran down his face.

If anyone is made to be a father, it's him.

Dr. Miller started to wipe off my belly, printing off the pictures; she knows our normal routine so she handed the 3D picture to Erik. He let go of my hand, pulling his phone out of his jeans pocket and took a picture, sending it to everyone. They must have been waiting for the group text; instantly, his phone was going off. I counted seven dings and I knew everyone is either taking a deep breath or sitting there staring at the picture.

Dr. Miller looked at me, smiling. "I think your friends are more scared then he was."

I nodded my head, smiling. "You have no idea."

"Stay down here, okay?" Erik led me down to the basement, he is trying to hold back a smile.

He ran back upstairs, I can hear the front door open and shut behind him. I have no idea what is happening.

I can hear footsteps shuffling along the floor above me. I'm staring at the stop of the stairs, Theo ran down the stairs, wrapping his arms around me.

I can't see from the tears filling my eyes, but I can feel my arms struggling to wrap around him. He has more muscle mass than ever before. His body is shaking against mine; we are both uncontrollably crying.

He pushed me back and we both wiped the tears covering my face. Theo pushed out a laugh. "It's about time you invested in waterproof mascara. I know you are going to not listen to me, but I need you to shut up and not interrupt me when I talk, okay?"

I nodded and led him to the couch; we both sat down. I can't take my eyes off my big brother. He looks better than he ever has before. His buzz cut has grown out, he has been eating a lot better, he's been working out. I am so proud of him.

"What I did to you has been haunting me. I lost sleep knowing that I hit you. I don't know how you didn't go crazy and smack me into my place. I can't change any of that and I'm sorry. I have changed and I'm going to be proving to you every single day that I am the brother you deserve."

"I love you, Theo."

Theo stood up, giving me another hug. "I can't even give you a proper hug. When is this baby coming out?"

"Not for another six weeks. I am so bloody uncomfortable. Have you seen Mom and Dad?"

Theo paused and put his hand on his neck. "Yeah. You and Erik were our last spot. Worst for last. They accepted both of our amends. But don't expect them to come to your wedding."

I nodded and sat on the couch. Theo grabbed my shoulder as he walked behind me. I was hoping my dad was going to walk me down the aisle. I was hoping my mom would help me pick out a dress. None of that is going to happen. I honestly can't blame them though.

"Lizzy."

I got up as fast as I could off the couch as soon as I heard Max. He ran up to me to help support me. I'm standing in front of him and my face is once again soaked in tears. A part of me thought I was going to lose them forever. I wasn't sure if I was ever going to see them again. I thought for sure they would be the next funeral I go to.

"My god, I forgot how beautiful you are." Max pulled me into a hug.

Just like with Theo, I can feel his body trembling, but Max was different. He is crying harder than I have ever seen him crying before. I pulled away from him and grabbed his hand as we both sat down on the couch.

We are sitting silently; I am wiping my tears away and he is trying to catch his breath. Max is double the size as when he left. He was so skinny from not eating and now he is at a healthy weight with muscles. I swear the both of them worked out to burn off all their frustrations. They weren't even at the same rehab center but they both had the same intuitions.

"Don't interrupt me." Max glanced at me.

I rolled my eyes, why on earth does everyone assume I'm going to interrupt them?

"I am shocked you helped us. I wouldn't have blamed you if you had just kicked us out. Lizzy, you and Erik saved our lives. I am never going to be able to repay you, but I promise, I don't care how long it takes, you guys are going to see every cent from me. If you don't let me in the baby's life, I understand, but either way, I am going to show you that the old me is still in here."

I'm staring at Max with my mouth open, I don't know why he is saying any of this. I don't know how many times he has run this through his head and it's turning out to be a disaster.

I grabbed his hand. "Erik wouldn't have spent the money if he didn't want you in the baby's life. He didn't just do it for me. He did it for the three of us."

Max put his head on my shoulder and his hand on my baby bump, waiting for a kick. "That's what he said too."

"I love you, Max."

I heard running down the stairs and Theo came rushing over to me, cuddling up on the other side of me. Theo reached for the remote under him and turned the television on. We don't care what is on; all we want is a little bit of normal. After two months of missing quarters of myself, here we are cuddled up on the couch together. They came back and I can finally catch my breath.

I inhaled a shaky breath. "I am so proud of you guys. Max, how did it go with your parents?"

He held me a little bit tighter. "We can do this without parents."

Theo sat up. "It's weird how close we are. Like, it's really fucking weird. I couldn't be more thankful for our relationship."

Max started laughing. "I called you beautiful, no wonder everyone thought we were dating."

I started to stand up off the couch. "What's the plan now?"

Theo leaned forward. "Take it day by day, try for the third time to get into the fire department."

Max crossed his arms. "I'm going to take an entrance exam to the NYPD."

I feel like a proud mother. I reached out my arms, pulling them up. "Come on, I have sparkling apple juice. Let's celebrate."

They followed me upstairs. Erik is waiting for us in the kitchen dressed in his police uniform. He wrapped his arms around me, bringing me in as close as he can. "Don't even ask me to help Max, I'm already on it."

I smiled, squeezing him. I don't know how I got so lucky to find a guy that will not only work to make my life better, but also my family's.

Erik gave me a passionate kiss before walking out of the house and shutting the door behind him. I pulled out the ultrasound pictures from earlier in the day and passed them to the boys.

Theo is looking at it with wide eyes. "I knew it had a face, but this is crazy."

Max set the picture down on the island and hugged my belly. "You have a lot of uncles but I'm going to love you the most."

My heart is so full. I never thought I would feel this way again. For the first time in fourteen months, I know I'm going to be okay.

Charlie

I opened the safe at the bottom of my bedroom closet and opened a file that I had hidden in the back from peering eyes. I sat on the floor and flipped through the papers, paper-clipping a check to the right deeds. I can't wait to break it to the guys that they are all owners of the Basilisks' companies. I have more good news that I have been holding in for weeks. I had to make sure we were in the clear before I said anything to them. This was going to be the best day of our lives.

I stuffed the folder in my dresser and ran downstairs and saw Dillon on the couch. I threw my legs on him. "Oh, you guys are going to love me."

Spencer looked at me. "We actually have something to talk to you about."

William took over. "We haven't worked in months. What the fuck is going on? You have never even talked about your casino."

I light my cigarette. "That's exactly when I wanted to talk to you about."

Liam opened the door. "That's going to have to wait. Everyone come here."

We all piled through the door. A driver is standing with the door of the limousine wide open for us to get in.

I looked at Liam. "What the hell is going on?"

He winked at me. "You'll see."

"Has anyone seen Adam?"

"He's coming along."

Erik raced up to us on the sidewalk on the other side of the white picket fence. "I'm here! I'm here!"

"Just get in the damn limo, Charlie." Before I was going to argue, everyone plowed past me.

I sighed and got into the limo. They are hiding something from me. I'm trying to read their body language, but for once, I can't. We are taking a lot of turns. No one is saying a word, just looking at each other and smiling.

I looked out the window. "I have never seen this neighborhood before. Where are we going?"

William wrapped his arm around me. "Do you trust us?"

"Obviously."

"Then stop talking."

I watched Josh hit Spencer's shoulder. "We're here."

Before we piled out of the limo, William and Dillon both hugged me.

"What's going on, you guys, I'm getting kind of worried." I'm begging for an answer, I don't want my good day turned into another nightmare.

They both grabbed my hand.

William laughed. "Don't be worried."

Dillon smiled. "I love you."

I ignored all the bad feelings that have risen out of my body, and I saw a path of roses leading up to a house. I got out of the limo and looked at everyone's smug smiles.

Liam tossed me a set of keys. "Go in."

I caught the keys, looking at Josh and Spencer, dangling the key ring on my finger and remembering the last time keys were tossed at me. They both smiled at me, waving their hands towards the house silently telling me to go in.

I followed the rose trail and tried to open the door; it's locked, so I used the key Liam gave me. It opened. I turned my head and looked behind me. The guys are still standing there, smiling.

What the hell.

I walk in, and the trail continues up the stairs. The roses leading me down a hallway. I know nothing bad is going to happen, but I'm suddenly really nervous. I pushed open the door, and there is Adam. Wearing a tuxedo, at the end of the rose trail, on one knee.

"Charlie, since the first day I met you, I fell in love with you. The way your blonde hair falls against your light skin and the sparkle you get in your eyes when you laugh. I thought about it every single night before I went to bed. A weight has been lifted off my shoulders now that you are the last thing I see every night. Will you do me the honor of being my wife?"

"Yes." I never even thought about it. I yelled my answer and ran over to him. Tears are running down my face.

Adam stood up; he put the ring on my finger and kissed me. He held my hand out in front of me, the ring sparkling. It has one large oval diamond with small diamonds around the band.

No matter how hard I'm trying to stop crying, I can't stop. I'm too happy to be able to keep myself collected. Adam is wiping my tears away with his hands. I looked in his eyes and all I see is calmness.

I pulled myself into his chest and looked around. "This room is huge, Adam, where are we?"

"I may have bought you a house. So, we can have a family down the road. If that's what you want." I nodded my head and squeezed him tighter. "If you would have said no, I needed to sell it, I couldn't live here without the one person I bought it for." He kissed my head. "This is our bedroom. Central Park is only a few blocks away."

"I would never have said no to you." I pulled away, sniffling my nose. "It's beautiful. Everything, my ring, this house. Adam Watson, you are the love of my life."

I pulled his arm and led him downstairs. I wanted to stop and look around, but that needed to wait. I don't care what we lived in. I don't care the size of my ring. The only things in life I need I already have.

We got outside, Adam picked me up and twirled me into the air, kissing me. I heard the guys cheering from excitement.

William and Dillon both ran up to me. "I need both of you guys standing with me. I need my two best friends with me." I started crying harder and they both wrapped their arms around me.

Erik walked up to me and hugged me. "I always wanted a sister." I watched him hug Adam. "I knew you would get the girl."

Spencer and Josh both picked me up, squeezing me as tight as they can. Watching everyone walk back to the limo, I'm shocked that I'm engaged to the man that I love.

I turned and faced Adam. I don't think I have seen him this happy. "I can't wait to spend the rest of our lives together."

I got up on my tippy toes to kiss him. He took my hand and walked me back to the limo. I looked behind my shoulder and saw a tall house made from brick, trees in the front lawn, flower beds, a deck. This is the perfect place to start our new lives and start a family.

The entire drive home, I'm soaking up the energy, the laughs, and the smiles from my family. Life is going to get even more perfect; they just had no idea. Liam put his hand on my knee and squeezed it. I know Adam got him to help pick out the house, no one other than him and William knew Central Park is important to me.

We finally got back to the house and I ran upstairs as fast as I could. I can't keep my secret any longer. I opened my dresser and grabbed the file. I'm about to head back downstairs, pausing and looking at myself in my long-sleeved shirt.

I'm tired of overheating constantly from covering up. I'm tired of hiding.

I pulled my shirt over my head and reached for a tank top. "Well Charlotte, it's time to stop hiding."

For the first time in months, I didn't cringe when I saw my reflection.

I walked downstairs, ignoring the looks of admiration.

I stood in front of everyone, staring at the file with a smile on my face. "We no longer have cops on our payroll."

Erik stomped his feet in excitement. "I'm no longer a cop!"

I know they were all exchanging looks but I couldn't stop looking at the brown file in my hands. "A few days after I explained how the casino was going to work, I dropped the idea. When we were planning the nightclub, I decided right then that the seven people who had my back were going to be put on the deeds to everything."

I paused and looked up. Everyone's jaws dropped. "I spent a lot of money on Speakeasy. I'm still in the hole, but I still put your names on the deed. I cleaned out my bank account completely with that place."

William shook his head, confused. "Why would you put us on the deeds to Basilisk companies?"

"Everyone has retired. The only Basilisk Mafia members left are in this room." I looked back down, trying to control my smile, I know I'm failing. "After I cut all our ties, we have been ghosts. I have officially resigned all of our positions, from this moment forward. We are now nothing but legal business owners."

Everyone paused. No words could ever be able to describe this moment.

"I have everyone's deeds and checks here from the last few months from the companies that you own one eighth of." I tossed the file on the table.

Josh is hesitant on what I'm saying, he passed out all the papers to everyone.

Liam was shaking his head in disbelief. "I thought we would never retire having one of us as a boss. I thought we were going to be stuck in the Mafia forever."

Dillon pulled his face from the papers, all the color in his face disappeared from shock. "You fucking saved us."

I looked around the room, doing everything in my power to remember this day, while pushing all of the bad memories from my mind.

A tear ran down my cheek. "Thank you, for being the family I never had."

Brittney

Days started to pass, then it turned into weeks, then weeks turned into months.

"Where do you think would be better to live, California or Florida?" I asked Sam.

Sam rolled on her chair, reaching her arms out and pulling herself closer to the desk. "Google Florida, man."

"You're right. Cali."

"Why are you doing this? You are *still* wearing your engagement ring."

"I promised him."

I started to pull up the job search for the entire state of California, hoping something would catch my eye along the beach.

"You could stay with the Bureau."

"I don't have a bachelor's degree, princess. It's a qualification."

Rodriguez is standing at my desk frowning while looking at my screen. "Use the burner. Tomorrow morning at 9 am, you come back from the dead."

I'm frozen.

My lungs have been struggling for air. I let in a long gasp of air before reaching my hand into the drawer beside me, looking for the phone. Creating a text message to send to all of my preprogrammed contacts.

Attention Basilisks, April, Max, Theo, Lizzy. Tomorrow morning, be at Erik and Lizzy's house at 9 am.

I hit send, taking the battery out and setting it on the desk. My heart is beating in my ribs, it's hard to breathe. After all of my work and dedication, I finally get to come back from the dead. I finally get my life back.

Well, I get my life back in another city.

"Come with me, Sam." She is staring at the desk with her eyes watering.

"I can't. Add me on Facebook."

I leaned forward, hitting my head against the desk. I never even thought about my social media exploding after the reporters get hold of this story.

I grabbed her hand, squeezing it. "I love you. Thank you for dealing with me. Let's go pack my shit, order food, and watch movies."

I'm staring at my desk, I couldn't sleep last night; having the case come to an end after a few slow months feels bittersweet. I'm so happy to be moving on with my life, but I am so upset that I will no longer be an agent after today. Tossing all of my pants suits is probably the best feeling in the world. I have been saving my favorite pants suit for my one and only run as an FBI agent. It's classic Brittney, so it's purple.

Taking a deep breath, blinking dozens of times fast, trying to fight the tears without destroying my makeup. The car ride to work was a lot shorter than the both of us remembered it being, probably because we were singing at the top of our lungs. We tried not to notice everyone staring at us at the many red lights. As hard as today is, this is going to be a good day.

A paper cup is placed in front of me. I didn't even bother to look up. "Oh, I love you."

"It's about damn time." Jones laughed.

"I was talking to the coffee." I looked up, winking at him taking a sip.

"Let's go vest up."

This is the day I have been waiting for, I should be happier. There is a lingering sadness in my chest, I just don't know if it's from it being my last day, leaving New York, or getting my friends back, then taking off again. It's probably all of the above.

I'm watching everyone put their vest on. "I can't go in there wearing a vest, or with a gun."

"Sam, you'll be driving with her. Bring her vest and gun to her when we need to leave." Rodriguez holstered his gun.

"Got it, sir." Sam grabbed my vest, shoving it to me.

Sitting outside of Erik's house, all I can feel is humiliation. Showing up here wasted, William and Erik watching the show that Spencer and I put on. That is the only night I have ever experienced drinker's remorse. But now, I have to face all three of them for the last time, begging for help. I need to show my friends I'm alive.

Looking in the side mirror, I can see the two other black SUVs parked behind us. Like promised, they are here waiting. Looking at the clock, it's 9 am exactly. My nervous are running at an all-time high. Despite my shitty feeling, I open the door and hop out.

Opening the gate and bracing myself for the hate, the words, blame, and doubt.

In front of me, the door flew open with Max and Theo both standing there, they look so much better than the last time I saw them. I am going to owe Erik my life for paying for the rehab.

"What the fuck!" Max rushed up to me, pushing me on the shoulders.

I fell back, but caught my footing. "I'm sorry."

"You're fucking sorry?" Theo is disgusted, I have never heard him use this tone.

"I'm sorry I destroyed you guys, I'm sorry I almost killed you two." Tears are filling my eyes.

To my surprise, Theo pulled me in hugging me. He is holding me so tight that I can't breathe. I don't care, being in my best friend's arms again is more than I could ever ask for. He dropped his arms and Max grabbed my hand. Using every bit of strength, I pulled him in. His body is trembling, that's only making me hold on to him tighter.

I loosened my grip. "We don't have much time. I need to go in and explain everything."

They both looked up at each other worried, but they never hesitated. They both grabbed my hand, pulling me inside behind them.

The room is full of tension. Spencer hasn't turned to look at me and Lizzy is standing with her back facing Erik, his arms around her. She looks so confused and hurt. Looking down at her pregnant belly, I feel a smile on my face.

Being in the same room as her is all I have wanted. "Lizzy." I can hear the begging in my voice.

She turned around, facing Erik. "I can never forgive her."

I shut my eyes, I was trying to prepare myself, I knew she would be the hardest but it doesn't make it easier.

"Babe, let her explain." Erik looked at me, exhaling a breath.

"You knew! You knew she was alive!" She pushed him away from her.

"What the fuck is going on?" April is moving her head back and forth between me and Erik.

"Everyone, sit down." There is a single chair by the front window, I sat down, looking at everyone. Confused looks are being exchanged from everyone. I'm trying to find the words, but it seems impossible. "When I was shot, the FBI was already on Martin's trail. They used me to their advantage, because of what Spencer and I had."

Saying what Spencer and I had feels like acid to my mouth.

I put my elbows on my knees holding my head, I don't know why I thought I was able to do this. I can't do this.

"You still wear your engagement ring." Spencer's voice caught me off guard.

I moved my hands from my head, looking down at it. I couldn't bring myself to take it off. I can smell his cologne getting closer to me. I took a deep breath, shaking my head, pulling it off my left ring finger. "Oh yeah…take it, burn it, bury it. Whatever, I don't care." Looking at it before tossing it on the table in front of me is one of the hardest things I've ever had to do.

Anyone who knows me, knows that was the biggest lie I ever told.

I began talking, telling my story to everyone. The hospital, the training, the work I put in, the conversations I heard, the pictures, the files. The further I get into my speech, the more I can see their faces crumble; everything that Erik and Spencer didn't know, they know now.

"I was the most recent boss though." Charlie is scared. Adam pulled her into his chest, kissing her hair.

"You let three people die on your watch. You know how hard it was to convince my supervisors not to put you in protective custody?" Charlie turned her head to me with a smile on her face. "I knew all of you were safer together."

The front door opened, bringing everyone's attention to Sam. "Sorry Agent Hills, but it's time."

I nodded, pushing myself up off the chair to grab my vest and gun. I holstered the gun to my hip, while slipping the vest over my head. "I'll explain everything, Agent Lee, go wait in the car." Sam nodded before walking out.

"Who knew she was alive?" Lizzy asked through her teeth. I turned around to see Spencer, William, and Erik drop their heads, waiting. "Jesus, Brittney." Her voice filled the house.

"I'll be out of your hair by the end of the day, I promise, Liz." Velcroing my vest and looking at everyone in the room. "Lizzy, Max, Theo, stay here. There are three FBI vans outside, three in the backseat per van. I need one Taylor to call Kinsley when we get there, she will open the gate for us. Paramedics will be outside, Martin will be cornered, so he might try to shoot his way out. Are the Basilisks ready for one more run?"

Josh stood up, winking at me. "You fucking know it."

"Let's go."

I opened the door, walking down to the gate, opening it, looking behind me; all I see is a chance of real freedom and payback on their old boss. They are all dressed up, Charlie's hair is done perfectly, her beauty wasn't justified in her files.

I got in the car, pulling out my phone, glancing behind me to see who is taking up the backseat, Dillon is behind Sam, Liam is in the middle, and William is behind me. Thankfully, the backseats are roomy, or they wouldn't fit.

"Is Carpinteria nice?" I asked Sam without looking up.

"Where the fuck is that?"

"Apparently, it's not far from Santa Barbara. Very small."

Sam couldn't hide her laughter even if she wanted to. "You're kidding, right? Go from New York to a small town?"

"You're right. I just bought a one-way ticket to San Clemente."

"I was thinking more like LA. When do you go?"

"Tonight. I have enough time to see my parents."

The radio between cars turned on. "Fuck, this traffic is brutal, use your sirens. The reporters are going to give us away," Nelson huffed.

I leaned forward, flicking the switch for the lights and sirens. Leaning back in my seat, watching New York fly past.

We got closer and I shut the lights off. "You guys must be feeling pretty uneasy."

I looked back when I heard laughter, Dillon is looking at me amused. "You're hilarious. This is the easiest thing we have ever had to do."

"I just wanna see his face." Liam smiled.

The SUV came to a stop and we all got out. Liam picked up his phone and held it to his ear. Just like Nelson had suspected, reporters were already covering the story.

Spencer grabbed my wrist, pulling me to the side. "You're leaving tonight?"

"I can't do this right now. But, yes. I promised. Just like I promised I would finish this case."

"You also promised you would marry me!" His voice is louder than he intended, I can feel the eyes of his friends on us.

"You broke up with me, remember?"

"Agent Hills!" Rodriguez called for me.

"Sorry sir!" I shouted as I ran up to him.

The gate opened, all the agents who have been killing themselves to end this are ready. "Let's end him." Nelson cracked his neck before turning around.

Months of training and months of hard work have been leading us to this moment. This is the moment that changes everything.

Kinsley opened the door, looking behind us to her children. "He's not alone. All of their dads are in there too."

"Agents, weapons ready." Rodriguez turned to look at all of us. "If you are not FBI, do not fire your gun. I need you nine to go in first though, just be casual."

A hand is on my shoulder; I looked up and Josh is smiling at me with his mouth open. Spencer glances back at me as he's walking away, with a sadness in his eyes.

"I wish I had this much money," Sam murmured. "I got into the wrong line of work."

The voices in the room are light, laugher is bursting out.

Rodriguez looked at Nelson, they both nodded their head and started walking towards the large doors. Rodriguez put his gun in his holster as he walked in; the rest of us have them in front of us ready to shoot.

Martin doesn't look fazed, until he looked at me and his expression changed. "Brittney? What the hell?"

"To you, it's Agent Hills."

"Basilisks, move to the side." Rodriguez's hand is hovering over his holster.

"What is going on here?" Martin asked in a stern voice.

"You are under arrest for 50 charges of arms trafficking, drugs trafficking, and 700 charges on contract killing."

Watching the eyes of everyone in the room grow big, Martin reached to his desk, pulling out a gun.

"Gun!" I yelled.

My body is being forced back, landing hard on the ground. The wind is knocked out of me and flashbacks are running through my mind. My ears are ringing. Opening my eyes, I can see Spencer trying to run up to me but he is being held back by Dillon and William. I raised my hand to tell him to stop. Bringing my attention back to the room, my hearing has come back.

"Shoot one of my agents again and I won't miss your heart next time. Bastard." Nelson stormed over to me, holding his hands out for me to get up.

Looking down at my vest, I can see the hole from the bullet; the only thing I can do is laugh.

"Come on, Britt. Our job's done."

We are all walking away with a sense of completion; paramedics are rushing past us to get to Martin. Reporters are standing outside at the door, asking so many questions my head is spinning.

Nelson looked down at me, smiling. "If it wasn't for Agent Brittney Hills, we would have been working on this case for another three years."

All of us are standing side by side, getting a photo taken. I walked away with Rodriguez following me. I took off my vest, dug in my pocket for my phone, flipped open my badge one last time looking at it before handing it over. "Thank you, sir." In exchange, he passed me my old phone that Davis had.

Without another word, I turned around, walking to the vehicle. I stopped mid-step, wanting to run to Spencer, but it's too late. If he never took me back when I randomly showed up, he never will. I hung my head, taking a deep breath, walking faster to the car before I break down. I opened the SUV's door, unable to hold back my tears.

"Brittney, wait." Spencer put his hand on my hip.

"I have to go." I sniffled my nose.

He spun me around, picking me up like he used to, I slammed my lips against his, he opened his mouth, letting my tongue slide into his mouth, we have both been starving for each other. A tear slid down my face.

"Don't go." The begging in his voice is breaking my heart all over again.

"Spence."

He set me on my feet, extending his arms to touch the top of the vehicle, looking down at me. "I'm sorry I said that, I'm sorry you heard me say that. I was trying to convince myself you were a terrible person. I put the house up for sale, then I had to take it off the market, no one deserves to live in there other than you. I saw you with the ring on today, and it broke me. I can't do any of this without you."

"I couldn't take it off." Spencer grabbed my left hand, kissing where the ring used to be. "Do you still see me as the future Mrs. Spencer Cohen?"

He shut his eyes tight, kissing my hand again. "There will be no one ever again."

"No more us being dramatic, no more one-way plane tickets. Just us forever."

"Did you just propose to me?"

"I don't think our engagement really ever ended."

I thought I was feeling nervous showing up in front of my friends, this is a thousand times worse. I know for a fact that my parents have their friends inside, watching the news with them. Reaching across the middle console and grabbing Spencer's hand, the blue sapphire emerald cut ring is shining from the light of the sun. He was right; this ring is perfect for me.

Pulling my hand back and opening the door, I stepped outside. Immediately, Spencer is at my side; reaching for his hand, we are walking to the house. Without knocking, I opened the door, walking in.

Max's parents, Theo and Lizzy's parents, and my parents are standing there in disbelief.

"I'm sorry." I'm getting so tired of apologizing.

"You're sorry for almost killing your friends? You're sorry for destroying our marriage?" My mom is looking at me with her eyes glossing over. "Who is that?"

Looking up at Spencer, he put his arm around me, pulling me into him. "My fiancé, Spencer."

The second the words left my mouth, my dad shot daggers at him. "He's a Basilisk, saw him on the news."

Spencer cleared his throat; his arm is tensing. "Retired Basilisk."

Lizzy's mom huffed. "Our daughters have lost their minds."

I grabbed Spencer's hand, turning around. "That's enough for one day."

"Brittney, wait." My mom called out.

"I'm not going to stand here and let you badmouth him. I have been living the last year in hell. It was an easy decision to save him, I get it, you can't understand, but just try."

The room is so quiet crickets could be heard. It wouldn't surprise me if they never forgave me, the fact I am still standing in the living room is a sign that one day they might. I can feel his grip tighten, I know he is biting his tongue. At this point, I wish he would just say it. I put my hand on his chest and took a step backwards, heading for the door.

Spencer is taking a deep breath, working on his confidence. "The last boss ended it all, but Brittney gave us a peace of mind locking Martin up. Lizzy is my best friend, she is acting like she doesn't care that you guys hate her, but it's killing her. Max and Theo got sent to rehab, Erik paid their way. I know this is a lot to take, but before you judge us, maybe look at how you are acting. The five of them all have a family, with or without you."

Pride is all I can feel. Tugging on Spencer's hand, walking to the door. I knew this was going to be hard, I thought I was at least going to get a hug. The way they are all looking at me is imprinted in my mind. I will never forget the look of disappointment on their faces.

Spencer opened the car door for me, he has no emotion on his face. He is probably expecting a fight, but that's the last thing on my mind. Not only did he defend me, he defended all of his friends, my friends, and the unborn baby. He is driving faster than the speed limit, in and out of traffic, running yellow lights. He is bracing himself for me to yell, cry, and, with our record, break up. I can feel his nerves on the other side of the car.

We are parked outside of his house. His knuckles are white from gripping the steering wheel. "I know what you are going to say. I'm sorry, I just got caught up."

"How do you think I'm mad right now? Let's go in and have a drink."

He is turning his head, looking at me, laughing. I pulled him in, letting our lips melt together. Nothing can compare to the way he kisses me. My body is becoming weak, my thighs are becoming numb.

I pulled away before I am unable to stop myself. I opened the door and stepped out. Spencer is in front of me, bent over and telling me to hop on his back. Giggling, I jump up, wrapping my arms around his neck; he is opening the gate and walking to the door. I can see everyone in the window sitting around the fireplace, waiting for us. Being outside of this house doesn't feel foreign anymore, it feels like I am exactly where I need to be.

Lizzy

All morning I have been having pain shooting through my belly and my back. I'm only thirty-seven weeks pregnant. It's not real labor. It can't be. It's the stress from Brittney coming back.

It has to be. I'm not ready to be a mom yet.

I haven't seen her since she showed up, dropping the bomb on everyone. Spencer, Max, and Theo have been splitting their time with us. It is hard on all five of us. I know she wants to see me. God, I want to see her too, but I haven't forgiven her. I'm pissed at Erik and William for keeping it from me. I'm furious at Spencer for pretending he didn't know Cameron was Brittney.

I'm sure I am acting childish. I know I am, but I can't stop myself. She caused way too much pain to everyone. If Spencer can't hate her for breaking his heart, I sure as hell can.

Even when you think you know someone, like really know them, they still manage to surprise you. The worst part is, I know she never second-guessed her actions, she doesn't need to tell me. I now understand why my parents are still pissed off about me having a baby with a retired Basilisk.

"Fuck!" I put my hand on my belly, tipping my head over the back of the couch trying to breathe.

Erik is on his knees in front of me, sitting on the floor. "I am calling everyone, we are leaving now."

The pain is becoming worse and worse. The contractions are only eight minutes apart, we probably should have left a while ago. Erik is holding my hand and pulling me up from the couch, he has been waiting for this. Me, on the other hand, I don't know if I can or want to put my body through this again.

Who am I kidding? We can't keep our hands off each other; there is going to be another baby Watson soon enough.

Thankfully, I had packed my hospital bag last week. Erik tossed it over his shoulder, running back to me. The smile on his face is contagious, even through my screaming womb.

Waddling outside, Liam, Max, and Theo are standing on the other side of the gate with their mouths open. The three of them have been attached to the hip for weeks. Weirdest friendship, but everyone has noticed Liam transforming into a better person.

"We will meet you there!" Theo shouted, running to Liam's car.

Lying in the bed, my body is in pain that I could never explain. As much as I wanted to have drugs, I couldn't. I needed to do it naturally. Our baby girl is fed, but still nameless. Erik is holding her with his eyes red and puffy.

"Lizzy, you did it. I fell in love with you all over again."

"I know what I want to name her."

"If it's what I think it is, I love it."

Erik stood up, walking over to me and kissing me as soft as he can. Sliding our baby into my arms, standing at my bedside, admiring his little family.

Listening to his shoes on the ground, my gaze is fixated on her face. She already has a head full of blonde hair, she has my full lips, perfect chubby cheeks. She is a fifty-fifty split of us.

I can feel Erik next to my bedside; without looking up, I know that the ten other friends have followed him in. Looking around the room, everyone has their eyes fixated on us. Charlie and April are fighting back tears, but failing. Theo bends down to kiss my head, followed my Max.

"Spencer." Looking up at him, I can tell how proud he is.

"Lizzy," he said with a smirk.

"Is Brittney here?"

"What kind of question is that? You know she is. She was so worried on the way here, I thought she was going to be sick."

"Go get her."

Spencer's shoes are squeaking on the freshly waxed ground as he is in a panic to go get his fiancée.

Brittney runs into the room, standing at the side of my bed; I have to muffle a laugh. Other than the first day she came back, I never saw her around everyone. She is a foot shorter than almost everyone in the room. Brittney is looking at me with tears filling her eyes; being away from her has been as hard on her as it was on me.

Looking her in the eyes, trying not to cry, I said, "Meet Cameron."